A LIFE-CHANGING...

Several years ago I received a letter that changed my life. Sadly, I don't remember who wrote it, only what she said. In essence, this was her plea:

> Dear Dr. Wheeler,
>
> I have a big favor to ask you. First of all, though, I want you to know how much I enjoy your story collections; they have greatly enriched my life. Now for the favor: I was wondering if you have any interest in doing with books what you are doing with stories.
>
> You see, while I love to read, I haven't the slightest idea of where to start. There are millions of books out there, and most of them—authors too—are just one big blur to me. I want to use my time wisely, to choose books which will not only take me somewhere but also make me a better and kinder person.
>
> I envy you because you know which books are worth reading and which are not. Do you possibly have a list of worthy books that you wouldn't mind sending to me?

I responded to this letter, but most inadequately, for at that time I had no such list. I tried to put the plea behind me, but it dug in its heels and kept me awake at night. Eventually, I concluded that a Higher Power was at work here and that I needed to do something about it. I put together a proposal for a broad reading plan based on books I knew and loved—books that had powerfully affected me, that had opened other worlds and cultures to me, and that had made me a kinder, more empathetic person.

But that letter, writer had asked for more than just a list of titles. She wanted me to introduce her to the authors of these books, to their lives and their times. To that end, I've included in the introduction to each story in this series a biographical sketch of the author to help the reader appreciate the historical, geographical, and cultural contexts in which a story was written. Also, as a longtime teacher, I've always found study-guide questions to be indispensable in helping readers to understand more fully the material they're reading, hence my decision to incorporate discussion questions for each chapter in an afterword at the end of the book. Finally, since I love turn-of-the-century woodcut illustrations, I've tried to incorporate as many of these into the text as possible.

There is another reason for this series—perhaps the most important. Our hope is that it will encourage thousands of people to fall in love with reading, as well as help them to discover that a life devoid of emotional, spiritual, and intellectual growth is not worth living.

Welcome to our expanding family of wordsmiths, of people of all ages who wish to grow daily, to develop to the fullest the talents God lends to each of us—people who believe as does Robert Browning's persona in *Andrea del Sarto:*

Ah, but a man's reach should exceed his grasp,
Or what's a heaven for?

Joe Wheeler

Note: The books in this series have been selected because they are among the finest literary works in history. However, you should be aware that some content might not be suitable for all ages, so we recommend you review the material before sharing it with your family.

It was the heart of the house, so close at hand that even a stranger could catch a glimpse of it by chance.

FOCUS ON THE FAMILY®
Great Stories

The Twenty-fourth of June
MIDSUMMER'S DAY

by
Grace S. Richmond

Introduction and Afterword by
Joe Wheeler, Ph.D.

TYNDALE

Tyndale House Publishers, Wheaton, Illinois

THE TWENTY-FOURTH OF JUNE
Copyright © 1999 by Joseph L. Wheeler and Focus on the Family
All rights reserved. International copyright secured.

Library of Congress Cataloging-in-Publication Data
Richmond, Grace S. (Grace Smith), 1866–1959.
    The twenty-fourth of June: midsummer's day / Grace S. Richmond; with an introduction
and afterword by Joe Wheeler.
        p. cm. — (Focus on the Family great stories)
    Includes bibliographical references.
    ISBN 1-56179-763-4
    I. Wheeler, Joe L., 1936–   . II. Title. III. Series.
PS3535.I4224T94   1999
813'.52—dc21   99-10191
                                                                               CIP

A Focus on the Family book published by Tyndale House Publishers, Wheaton, Illinois.

The illustrations featured in this book are from Joe Wheeler's 1914 Doubleday, Page & Co.
edition of *The Twenty-fourth of June*.

Joe Wheeler is represented by the literary agency of Alive Communications, 1465 Kelly Johnson
Blvd., Suite 320, Colorado Springs, CO 80920.

Cover Design: Candi Park D'Agnese/Charles Hubbard
Cover Photograph of the Flower Background: Tim O'Hara Photography, Inc.

Printed in the United States of America

99 00 01 02 03 04 05/10 9 8 7 6 5 4 3 2 1

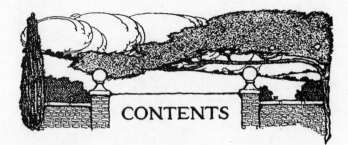

CONTENTS

Introduction

GRACE S. RICHMOND
AND *THE TWENTY-FOURTH OF JUNE*

I have found this true time after time: An author becomes one of the most popular of his or her age—is a household name—yet no one chronicles that life (neither while living nor afterward). So what happens, then, many years later, when someone like me becomes interested in one of these once well-known but now almost forgotten writers? When a trail has grown cold—not much!

A very cold trail indeed was Grace Richmond's. There was *nothing*. I had almost concluded that we'd have to do this one without a biography when my wife stumbled on the faintest of trails: At the back of one of Richmond's books was a one-page life sketch, in which the statement was made that she lived in Fredonia, New York. At last, a lead!

First of all, we looked Fredonia up on the map and found that it is a small town on Lake Erie in western New York. After a number of phone calls, I finally struck pay dirt: I got on the phone with Jack Ericson, chief archivist and curator of the Daniel A. Reed Library at the Fredonia campus of State University of New York.

My wife and I went to Fredonia, registered at the venerable White Inn, and then found our way to the Reed Library. Jack Ericson was incredibly helpful, not only in welcoming us to the library and archives but also in showing us some of the countryside, including the famed Chautauqua Institution. Carole Somerfeldt, Ericson's able associate, was also extremely helpful. Julia Fairbanks, then director of the McClurg Museum and associate director of the D. R. Barker Museum, assisted us as well, making available the Grace Richmond Collection housed in the Barker Library.

Professor James S. Cummings, one of the foremost authorities on the life and times of Richmond (and author of *Grace S. Richmond: A Reassessment*, unpublished manuscript, Reed Library), met with us several times, offering us every assistance in his power.

And, one evening during a torrential rainstorm, the current owners and restorers of the Richmond home, Frederick and Bonnie Liener, opened up their house to me, gave me a tour, and shared memories and insights.

Altogether, the good folks of Fredonia and Chautauqua County were ever so gracious, hospitable, and helpful in assisting us to make a success of our research there in western New York.

Rising Like Cream to the Top

The home. It all starts there, the action happens there, and it all ends there. Because of this, Grace Richmond is known as the "Novelist of the Home." Of the thousands of writers who have written about the home, only Richmond earned that title. Only in her fictional world is the home the all-in-all, the core, the bedrock. Thus, there was no question about whether or not we would include Richmond's books in Focus on the Family's *Great Stories* series; the only question had to do with which one. But only one rose like cream to the top— *The Twenty-fourth of June.*

Winging backward in time to my first reading of this book, I remember how limp I was at the end—and yet how joy and tears struggled for supremacy. I was totally drained. Yet the proof of a powerful book cannot be limited to the initial reading, for many books that once overpowered our defenses when we were young, read again years later leave us cold. So, it was with some trepidation that I returned to *The Twenty-fourth of June.* I needn't have worried: I was gripped with the same fascination as before, even though I knew how it all came out.

I was further encouraged by the feedback from Fredonia, New York, Richmond's hometown. One Fredonian declared, *"The Twenty-fourth of June?* Great! That's my favorite of Richmond's books!" And others who knew and love her books concurred.

Why this is so, when she wrote so many splendid books, is hard for me to say. It's just that the first time I read the book, it commandeered my heart. Something there was about the plot, the characters, the challenge, the quest—the deadline—that, in today's vernacular, blew me away!

Of course the title itself has had a lot to do with it. That was an inspired choice, for there is a symbiotic relationship between the plot and the title—each enhances the other. How many book titles can you think of which are limited to month and day? Richmond's genius is this: If you can remember the title, you can remember the plot.

But it's more than that, because the date represents far more than the cutting of the proverbial Gordian knot, the denouement; it is the source of all the suspense. All through the last part of the book, the reader reels back and forth between two questions: Will he make it? and, If he does make it, will it be enough? I know of no other book that incorporates quite the same structure, the same crescendo, of suspense.

About the Introduction

For decades, one of the few absolutes in my literature classes has been this: Never read the introduction before reading the book! Those who ignored my thundering admonition lived to regret their disobedience. Downcast, they would come to me and say, "Dr. Wheeler, I confess that I read the introduction first, and it wrecked the book for me. I couldn't enjoy the story, because all the way trough I saw it through someone else's eyes. I didn't agree with the editor on certain points, but those conclusions are in my head, and now I don't know what I think!"

Given that God never created a human clone, no two of us will ever perceive reality in exactly the same way—and no two of us ever should! Therefore, no matter how educated, polished, brilliant, insightful, or eloquent the teacher might be, don't ever permit that person to tell you how to think or respond, for that is a violation of the most sacred thing God gives us—our individuality.

My solution to the introduction problem was to split it in two: an introduction, to whet the appetite for, and enrich the reading of, the book; and an afterword, to generate discussion and debate after the reader has arrived at his or her own conclusions about the book and is ready to challenge my (the teacher's) perceptions.

About the Author
Grace S. Richmond
(1866–1959)

Once upon a time love came first. Then marriage. And then sex and children. It was true in most books, in most magazines, in most dramas, in most stories. Purity and virginity were ideals in that world, not the butt of ridicule, humor, and sarcasm as is sadly the media norm today. The undisputed patron saint of that world was "Mother," the stay-at-home rock upon which that civilization was built.

In that world, the sexual roles were clearly defined, and any deviance was severely punished by an unforgiving society. The usual price for such deviance was ostracism from the community. The male in that society was trained to believe that career achievement was a male preserve, as was earning a living. The male was virtually guaranteed a lifelong support system: a stay-at-home mother in childhood, complete with supporting cast of sisters, aunts, and grandmothers. In adulthood, wife and daughters continued in that role. Girls were trained to excel in homemaking arts and were expected to lead out in church life, education, and the arts (usually as patronesses rather than as artists). It was accepted that girls would be educated and could even dabble with careers for a brief time. But society never let them forget for a moment that such "playtime" must be brief: By her mid- to late twenties, "play" was over; now, if she wished to continue in society's good graces, she must accept a marriage proposal, enjoy her engagement period to the fullest, marry, and let the honeymoon length be determined by the affluence—or lack of it—of the groom.

After the honeymoon was over, the man would bring his wife home to a house he had either inherited or prepared for her. From this moment on, their paths diverged. He would earn a living for wife and future children; she was expected to abandon career goals and concentrate on domesticity. Large families were the norm. Since housework was both unending and brutally hard, and married life was a long succession of pregnancies, the average woman aged at a far more rapid rate than is true today.

It was into that now-vanished world that Grace Richmond was born, had her childhood and youth, and wrote her stories. These stories would both reflect her childhood world and set the stage with a new cast of women, women who were neither subservient to men nor independent, but rather were somewhere in between.

For 40 years, she was never out of print. Of the dominant family authors of the first half of the twentieth century, only Zane Grey, Gene Stratton Porter, and Harold Bell Wright were better known than she; and her name ranked up there with Frances Hodgson Burnett, Kate Douglas Wiggin, Lucy Maud Montgomery, Pearl S. Buck, Bess Streeter Aldrich, and Temple Bailey. It was illustrious company indeed.

But in the days in which Richmond wrote, book sales represented only part of the picture, for magazine was king. Early popular magazines tended to underemphasize authorship and overemphasize title and illustrations. That began to change, however, as the nineteenth century drew to a close: The author became important. Fierce battles were fought by magazine editors over those few gilt-edged authors whose name on the cover would dramatically increase newsstand sales. Especially sought after were those authors whose stories lent themselves to serialization, for serialization was the soap opera, sitcom, or miniseries of the age. Writers with that kind of name recognition could virtually name their price, receiving offers of vast sums from magazine editors, far higher advances than book editors or cinema producers were offering in those days. Among these writers was Grace Richmond, at the height of her popularity being paid upward of $30,000 for magazine serialization rights for a book-length manuscript (a princely sum at that time).

In those far-off days, the names of dominant family magazine editors were as well known to contemporary Americans as are Oscar-winning Hollywood producers today, for *everyone* read those magazines—read them both alone and out loud, as families. In the annals of literature, it is unlikely that very many authors could successfully challenge Richmond's serialization record: Between her first known published work, "The Flowing Shoe-string" (*Ladies' Home Journal*, November 1891), when she was 25, and "Bachelor's Bounty" (*McCall's*, 1932–33), when she was 66, she published 39 book-length serials, as well as stories, essays, and plays. Meanwhile, Doubleday would sell more than 2.5 million copies of her 32 books. A span of more than 41 years is a long time to stay in vogue!

A Minister's Daughter

On March 3, 1866,–less than 11 months after the close of the Civil War, Grace Louise Smith was born in Pawtucket, Rhode Island. In fact, she was a direct descendant of the state's founder, Roger Williams. Her father, the Reverend Dr. Charles E. Smith, and her mother, Catherine "Kitty" Kimball Smith, were firm believers in education. Dr. Smith, Phi Beta Kappa and a distinguished scholar with an earned doctorate, was a force to be reckoned with. In 1866 the average American had little formal education, perhaps three to six years if lucky; a bachelor's degree in those days was a mark of distinction, a master's degree carried far more status than today's doctorate, and a doctorate then placed that person among the elite of the age. Baptist clergymen, in those days, were expected to periodically change parishes. In 1885, after having pastored churches in Mt. Auburn, Ohio; New Haven, Connecticut; and Syracuse, New York, Dr. Smith was called to Fredonia, New York, and there he would remain for the rest of his career and life.

Grace was an only child, an anomaly in that age of large families (six to 12 children being the norm). This fact too would be of major significance in her life, for had there been sons it is extremely unlikely that Dr. Smith would have mentored and tutored his daughter to the extent that he did.

Hers was a happy childhood, as she felt loved, cherished, and respected. The Baptist church represented the core of her childhood world, and its values were hammered into her soul by her father's weekly sermons and by mealtime discussions of ideas at home. Yet both mother and father encouraged her to enjoy and revel in each day as it came.

Were it not for Grace's later correspondence, we would know little about her growing-up years. And for the glimpses we do have, we can thank two granddaughters, Mary Sickels and Ann Sickels, for it was only in letters to *them* that Grace reached back into her childhood for memories.

Funny, isn't it, how difficult it is to envision our parents, grandparents, and other ancestors as ever having been young like us. Writing to her granddaughters, Richmond described an incident that occurred during the Syracuse years:

> When I was ten years old and my mother sent me down town to do an errand for her, I always used to take some other girl with me. We had a beautiful idea that we could go up into office buildings, rap on doors, and run away. So we did it, in a certain building we had picked out. Nobody was ever heard coming after us, and finally we learned that it wasn't occupied at all, and that we had had all our trouble for nothing at all. (Grace Richmond to Ann and Mary Sickels, May 12, 1935, Reed Library)

Toys were few and precious in those days, so children made up their own games and created their own imagery, developing their imaginations far more than is true today. Early on, Grace began plotting out story settings visually: "I loved to take a big sheet of wrapping paper and mark out the floor plan of a hotel on it. Then I would use spools for people, have a clerk at the desk in the office, make the people ask for rooms and make the clerk send them to the room with a bell boy. You see I used my imagination in this way, and that is always a good thing" (Grace Richmond to Mary Sickels, Dec. 3, 1934, Reed Library). Snow of just the right texture and consistency could be put to good use: "When the snow was just wet enough so that it could be made into something I used to plaster a lot of it on the brick wall of our Fayette Street house in Syracuse, and then with a knife carve out figures. Sometimes quite interesting pictures could be made that way" (Grace Richmond to Ann Sickels, Dec. 25, 1934, Reed Library).

In those long-ago days, pretty much all long-range communication took place by mail, hence the fascination with post offices:

When I was a little girl my cousin Julia and I had a post-office! It was in Fulton where Grandmother Kimball lived. Both her house and that where Julia lived were in a park, and in the middle of the park was a band stand. In the lattice walk at the foot of this was a small hole. We found this and used to write little notes to each other and put them in this hole. I liked to make little drawings, mostly of myself and Julia, to illustrate the letters. Some of them were quite funny, I think. Anyhow she laughed over them. I did that, in letters, until I was quite grown up. They used to amuse my mother very much, and as she was quite an invalid I was always glad when I had made her laugh. (Grace Richmond to Ann and Mary Sickels, April 13, 1935, Reed Library).

Like most little girls, Grace loved to play with dolls—especially those made of paper:

I was very fond of making "houses" for my paper dolls, out of blank books. . . . I would name the pages—"Hall"—"Living room," "Bed-room" and so on, and then hunted in the magazines for pictures of furniture for them. I drew the doors and windows, and put tissue paper curtains at them. This used to keep me busy for days. I pasted in the furniture. . . .

I really liked paper dolls better than other dolls. I cut them out of fashion magazines and made dresses for them. I had mothers and daughters, fathers and sons. Sometimes I married a particularly pretty girl to a man cut from a clothing store advertisement, making ever so many clothes and hats for her. The man had to come as he was dressed in the picture. I couldn't make clothes for him. (Grace Richmond to Mary Sickels, Dec. 3, 1934, Reed Library)

And of course she had her favorite books. In a letter to Mary, she asked:

I wonder if you . . . ever read Susan Coulidge's *What Katy Did* and *What Katy Did at School?* I used to love those when I was Ann's age. I think you both would like them. I don't know if they can be found in libraries now, but they were so popular and so really true to life that they may have kept alive all these years, as Louisa Alcott's stories and books have.

I suppose you have read *Gulliver's Travels* . . . and *Robinson Crusoe,* and *The Swiss Family Robinson.* (Grace Richmond to Mary Sickels, June 4, 1935, Reed Library)

Poetry too she had always loved:

Do you happen to know this little poem by Robert Louis Stevenson, from *A Child's Garden of Verses?* I am going to write it out for you so that you can learn it if you want to. There is music for it, which I think Mother knows.

> In winter I get up at night and dress by yellow
>   candlelight,
> In summer, quite the other way, I have to go to
>   bed by day.
> I have to go to bed and see the birds still hopping
>   on the tree
> And hear the grown-up people's feet still going
>   past me in the street;
> Now does it not seem hard to you, when all
>   the skies are clear and blue,
> And I should like so much to play, I have to go
>   to bed by day!! (Grace Richmond to Ann
> Sickels, undated 1933, Reed Library)

Other memories had to do with music—all the music was live, in her early experience. How the children used to love singing rounds. One of their favorites was a tongue-twister:

> My dame had a lame tame crane,
> My dame had a crane that was lame,
> Oh, pray, gentle Jane, let your dame's lame tame crane
>   drink and come home again.

And another:

> Come follow, follow, follow, follow, follow, follow me.
> Whither shall I follow, follow, follow, whither shall
>
>   I follow, follow thee?

> Down by the willow, willow, willow, down by the
> willow, willow tree.

Others were rounds still sung today, such as "Scotland's Burning" and "Three Blind Mice." Of them all, Richmond concluded that 'Gentle Jane' is the funniest to do for the music is the prettiest, and somebody's tongue is sure to get tangled up with the dame's tame lame crane when the words are sung fast, as they should be" (Grace Richmond to Mary Sickels, June 4, 1935, Reed Library).

Special days stood out above others. Such as the time when, at the seashore, her mother made her wear rubber boots to wade in.

> Of course I got them full of water first thing, so they didn't even keep my feet dry. Afterwards, when I was older she let me have a bathing suit, but I shall always remember the rubber boots. My cousin and I waded quite far out in them when the tide was out, and then the tide turned and we had a hard time getting in to shore again with those miserable boots on. I never thought of taking them off, as I should have done, for then I could have waded more easily. (Grace Richmond to Mary Sickels, undated ca. 1934–35, Reed Library)

Always, Grace would revel in live drama—the roots of this love of the stage reaching all the way back to her childhood games:

> When I was a little girl I used to have plays in an empty room upstairs at the back of the house. Lottie, the girl who played with me oftenist, and I used to string up clothes-lines and hang sheets from them, to make a stage, with curtains, and with "boxes" on either side. Then we would spend a lot of time making ourselves clothes out of paper. . . . We didn't think very much about the play we were going to give. We had an idea that once we were dressed for it and had our audience we should know what to do!
>
> So we would invite the family to come in and sit on the boxes. We would raise the curtain and come out in our paper clothes. The very minute we were in sight of the people we would begin to laugh, and we laughed so hard we couldn't say a word. Naturally, the audience laughed too. Sometimes we would manage to speak a few words

and get in a little action, but mostly it was just giggling. We never tired of giving these performances, because getting ready for them was such fun! (Grace Richmond to Mary Sickels, Dec. 3, 1934, Reed Library)

As for studying, Richmond rued the time she wasted as a child. In a letter to Ann, she asked:

What do you think I did when I went to school? I idled! I just didn't study. Years afterwards I was very sorry that I hadn't studied, for it made it much harder for me than if I had. I don't know how I stayed in school at all. It was the same with my music lessons. I had lessons on the piano from a very expensive teacher, and I ought to have worked hard, but I did my practicing with one eye on the clock, and when I went to take my lessons, played so badly that my teacher's left eyebrow was almost all the time cocked up in the air. It was a shame. It wasn't until I began to write stories and books that I really learned how to work hard, and I know I could have written much better stories and books if I had worked hard all the way along at whatever I had to learn. (Grace Richmond to Ann Sickels, undated 1935, Reed Library)

Chautauqua, Love, and Marriage

On a bitterly cold and stormy day, the 16th of January in the year of our Lord 1885, the new pastor of the Baptist church, the Rev. Dr. Charles Smith, arrived with his family at the Park House. Their coming was big news both in the city of Fredonia and in Chautauqua County. Perhaps even bigger news, to the young bachelors of the area, had to do with the preacher's lovely daughter, just on the verge of turning 19.

Most significant in Grace Richmond's life, Fredonia was the seat of lyceum education in America. The lyceum concept originated in ancient Greece and had to do with the education and development of the whole person, not just the mind. In 1826 Josiah Holbrook of Derby, Connecticut, outlined a visionary plan for worldwide learning and called it a *lyceum,* for the place where Aristotle once lectured Athenian youth. Alas, the global dream was never fully realized, but a national lyceum exploded across America: Within two years, more than 100 branches had been established, and within six years there were nearly 3,000 branches, in practically every state in the Union. Of primary importance to those who attended lyceums was the establishment of a strong system of public education for everyone.

But the lyceum was way ahead of the time in its recognition that education ought to be lifelong rather than being restricted to the young. Thus local lyceum chapter meetings were, according to *Encyclopedia Britannica* editors, "voluntary associations for self-culture, community instruction and discussion of public questions." Essays, debates, discussions, and lectures, all home-talent productions, were presented at weekly meetings. After about a decade, the custom of inviting outside lecturers to whom fees were paid became established. James Russell Lowell, Henry David Thoreau, Bronson Alcott, Ralph Waldo Emerson, Henry Ward Beecher, Oliver Wendell Holmes, Horace Greeley, Daniel Webster, Nathaniel Hawthorne, and Susan B. Anthony were among those who frequently addressed lyceums.

For some unexplainable reason, the largest and most electric national lyceum convention, held in 1839, was destined to be the last. The collapse of the national organization was not reflected on the local level, for individual chapters continued to thrive across America until the Civil War brought such meetings to a halt.

But the torch was to be passed. Just a short horse and buggy ride from Fredonia is beautiful Chautauqua Lake. In the summer of 1874, on the shores of the lake, the Methodist-Episcopal camp meeting was held as usual. But this time, the Reverend (later Bishop) John H. Vincent and Lewis Miller launched a training program for Sunday school teachers and church workers. Gradually, the curriculum expanded and broadened to include general education and popular entertainment. Summer lectures, in turn, spawned home programs of directed reading and correspondence study. After William Raney Harper (later, president of the University of Chicago) took over as educational director in 1883, the Chautauqua movement entered into its greatest years. By 1900, the Chautauqua Institution featured a school of theology, a correspondence school, and a publishing house. (This section is documented by Encyclopedia Britannica [Chicago: Encyclopedia Britannica, 1946], 14:512; 1984 edition of Micropaedia, 2, 6:410.)

As for Richmond, it would be difficult to overestimate the difference Chautauqua would make in her life. It would provide lifelong intellectual ferment: She would grow as a result of attending its lectures, and she would help others to grow by giving lectures and reading from her own writings there.

But all that was in the future that bitterly cold January of 1885. There are two versions of the first meeting of Grace and Dr. Nelson G. Richmond. One version has it that he saw her first on the trolley the very day the family arrived in Fredonia—and fell in love with her at first sight. The other version has them meeting at an ice-skating rink and that the popular physician was quite taken with the "new pretty face in town" (Cummings, 6).

While Nelson most likely had little idea that the young woman he was dating would turn out to be a professional writer, he was certainly conditioned to the possibility. His mother, Euphemia Johnson Richmond, was a prolific writer of temperance novels, publishing more than 25. Her five brothers were doctors, and there were doctors on her husband's side as well, so it was not surprising that her son would follow this profession.

Nine years Grace's senior, Nelson was ready for marriage, having taught school, attended Cazenovia Seminary, Syracuse University, New York University, and Belleview Medical School. He was now in practice in Fredonia as an obstetrician, pediatrician, and country doctor and was already widely respected. He was viewed by the fair sex as "quite a catch." Grace herself was viewed as quite a catch by the young men of Fredonia. Years later, during the longest separation of their married life, Grace wrote Nelson a poignant love letter. In it she brought up both some of his competition and his wonderful gift to her.

> Do you remember, long, long, ago, when you got into the "Panacea" (!) and sat down beside me, and then Fred Keller got in and attempted to sit down between us, and you pulled me up tight to you, with your hand inside my arm and never took it away for the whole drive? I, being eighteen, and not a bit used to contact of even that ordinary sort with a man, was so thrilled I can recall it yet! You told me long afterwards you *thought* I didn't mind that closeness. I guess I didn't.
>
> Funny, what little things persist in one's mind. Your always saying "All right," to Billy [his horse] when you wanted him to go along. Your having the phaeton built for me. But that wasn't a little one—it was very, very big—much the greatest material gift I ever had. I was so proud of it. It was much the most beautiful vehicle in town, and I enjoyed every mile I ever went in it. I learned not to mind Billy's running in his customary running places—he just *had* to. Other people thought I was going to be dashed to pieces, being only a woman!

(Grace Richmond to Nelson Richmond, Dec. 10, 1934, Reed Library)

The romance blossomed, and tongues really began to wag when the young doctor purchased the house next door to the manse. One wing was dedicated to his medical practice. Before long, the bride-to-be was joyously shuttling back and forth between the two buildings, setting her imprint on what would soon be "their" nest. On October 29, 1887, a little over two years after they met, Dr. Smith took the long journey next door to where he married his daughter to his new neighbor. That house would be home to Grace for the next 72 years!

In those days, *home* meant stability and embodied all the lasting qualities that were associated with marriage and family. In the nineteenth century, with no welfare state to take care of the elderly, families took care of their own. Only five years after their wedding, the Richmond house was enlarged to provide an apartment for Dr. and Mrs. Smith after his retirement from the ministry.

Dr. and Mrs. Richmond were very happy in that house on the tree-shaded, dusty street. The bride and groom had a snuggling winter to remember, for the winter of 1888—known as the "Year of the Great Blizzard"—remains a reference point even today, the winter with which all other winters are compared. It was so cold that trains stuck to the tracks. The storm's vast shadow spanned thousands of miles. Ice and snow cut telegraph communications, and in New York, drifts piled up 15 feet high—and hundreds died in that city alone, from exposure, pneumonia, and the flu. But Nelson and Grace had another reason to remember 1888, for wee Joyce Kimball Richmond cried her way into that bitterly cold world on December 12. When Grace discovered she would be a mother at 22, she had mixed feelings: On one hand she welcomed their first child, on the other hand she rued this end to her extended honeymoon, their doing things together as a couple, and the opportunity to spread her own wings.

The year 1889 brought widespread celebrations during the centennial of America's national government. It also brought the other side of blizzards: floods such as the one at Johnstown, Pennsylvania, which left 2,000 dead in its wake and stunned the nation. Washington, Montana, North Dakota, and South Dakota became states. Bessemer Steel's development of the I-beam would make modern skyscrapers possible, and the Wizard of Menlo Park, Thomas Edison, invented the kinetoscope, which would launch the age of motion pictures.

During the Richmonds' second year of marriage, the census people told them they were now a nation of 63 million people, a mind-boggling 25 percent increase in but 10 years, with immigrants flooding in faster than the nation could integrate them. Alas for the serenity of the old way of life, the new catch-word was *speed:* The Atchison, Topeka & Santa Fe Railroad set a new world speed record of 78.1 mph; George Francis Train completed an around-the-world balloon trip in 67 days, 13 hours, 3 minutes, and 3 seconds (Nelly Bly took 5 days longer, circling the globe by train and steamship). Oklahoma and Wyoming became states, and Yosemite was established as a national park. Emily Dickinson's poems were published posthumously, and Elizabeth Cady Stanton and Susan B. Anthony launched the women's suffrage movement. The year ended on a somber note with the December 29th slaughter of Native Americans at Wounded Knee.

During the Richmonds' third year of marriage, the International Copyright Law was at last signed, basketball was played for the first time, there was a gold rush at Cripple Creek in Colorado, Whitcomb L. Judson invented the zipper, and William Burroughs the adding machine.

Only a couple of weeks after Abraham Lincoln's birthday was declared a national holiday, on March 3, 1892, the Richmonds' second child, Marjorie Guernsey Richmond, was born. The joy of her safe delivery was soon changed to heartbreak as little Joyce, the sunshine of the house, weakened and died two weeks after her sister's birth. Childhood diseases were like that then: In those pre-antibiotics days, most any disease would result in yet another small coffin in the town cemetery. Joyce's passing almost tore out her mother's heart by the roots. Only the solace of the new baby and the need to nurture and care for her kept the grief-stricken and weakened mother from following her firstborn to that cemetery.

But life must go on. In Baltimore, William Painter invented the first bottle-capping machine. Only six years before, in Atlanta, William Styth Pemberton had come up with a recipe for Coca Cola. A nation of primarily European immigrants celebrated the 400th anniversary of Columbus's landing in the New World with great gusto: The U.S. Postal Service issued the Columbian Exposition stamps, and millions thronged the Chicago World's Fair to see all the marvels of the then-known world—not least of which was the towering Ferris wheel and naughty "Little Egypt." At the very moment when Thomas Edison and George Westinghouse were battling for control of the Age of Electricity, quiet John Muir was founding the Sierra Club.

During little Marjorie's second year, Charles and Frank Duryea invented the gas-powered motorcar, Edison established "Black Maria" (the first motion picture studio), New York Central and Hudson's Locomotive 999 became the fastest vehicle on earth, and the first long-distance telephone call was placed (between Boston and New York). But what would hurt most was a decision made in far-off India to switch its currency base from silver to gold, sending tidal waves of fear around the world. On June 27, Wall Street crashed—600 banks closed their doors, 74 railroads collapsed, and 15,000 businesses failed. The days, weeks, months, and years that followed constituted the worst depression in the nation's history.

Only five days before the birth of Edward "Ted" Guernsey Richmond, on January 8, 1894, a terrible fire burned down almost all of architect Louis Sullivan's splendid Columbian White City in Chicago. During Ted's second year of life, after a 16-year legal battle, George Selden was awarded the patent for a clutch-operated vehicle; and Sears & Roebuck joined forces to start a mail-order business in Chicago. Thanks to the new pneumatic bicycle tire, a bicycle craze swept the nation. These "silent steeds" were so popular that hems rose several inches so proper young ladies could safely pedal their bicycles. There were now more than 300 motorcars on the road, and battling for gate position were White Sewing Machine, the Studebaker brothers, George Pierce (a manufacturer of bird cages), and Ransom E. Olds.

During Marjorie's fourth year, Utah became a state, gold was discovered in the Klondike, Diamond Matches came up with pocket-sized 20-match books, and audiences flocked to see Edison and the Lummiere Brothers's "flickers" (so named because the movie imagery did just that).

By the time Marjorie was seven, Barnum & Bailey's "Greatest Show on Earth" was thrilling millions, the battleship *Maine* blew up in Havana's harbor, and the Spanish-American War was fought, costing around 4,289 lives—4,000 due to typhoid fever or yellow fever. President McKinley took a ride in an auto car (a Stanley Steamer; of the 4,000 auto cars on the road, three-quarters were powered by steam or electricity).

Marjorie turned eight in 1900, now part of a nation of almost 76 million people. More than 100 immigrants an hour passed through Ellis Island. As for foreign-born population, percentage-wise they were in this order: Germans, Irish, Canadian, British, and Swedish—but now came huge waves of Slavs, Poles, and Italians. George Eastman came out with a $1 Brownie camera, and America's roads were shared by 8,000 auto cars, 10 million bicycles, and 18 million horses and mules. On September 8, fourteen-foot waves swept over Galveston, Texas, drowning more than 8,000 people.

During Marjorie's ninth year, a new auto speed record was set: a mile in 52 seconds. While the average American earned but a few hundred dollars a year, J. P. Morgan bought out Andrew Carnegie for $250 million to create U.S. Steel (the largest corporation in the world), Andrew Carnegie stating that during the second part of his life it was his duty to give his fortune away. On May 8, Wall Street panicked as robber barons fought for railroad control. In the crash, U.S. Steel alone lost more than $100 million. On September 6, McKinley was shot by an anarchist, and Teddy Roosevelt was sworn in as the new president.

During 1902, Marjorie turned 10; Helen Keller's *The Story of My Life* was published; "The Good Old Summertime" sold a million copies; a new gelatin dessert, Jell-O, came on the market; Twentieth Century United set a new speed record by making the New York–to–Chicago run in 16 hours; and on June 18, Jean Kimball Richmond was born. With her, Grace and Nelson's family was complete, ready to face a new, exciting, and a bit terrifying world—a far different world from the one they had faced at the altar in 1887, only 15 years before. (This section is documented by Clifton Daniel's *Chronicles of America* [Mount Kisco, N.Y.: Chronicle Publications, 1989], 425–537.)

But for Nelson and Grace Richmond, living in peaceful Fredonia, it was a much quieter world than that larger one. The life of a country doctor was an extremely demanding one, as every day and every night, he wrestled with death, sometimes winning and sometimes losing. During these early years, Grace would occasionally assist her husband during night operations by holding high a kerosene lamp: According to their daughter Marjorie, once when her husband and other town doctors were unavailable, Grace herself answered an emergency call—and delivered the baby herself! (Cummings, 10). The good doctor made his rounds by horse and buggy, in winter by sleigh. Should someone bring an urgent summons to the office while he was on the road, Grace would hang a towel from a front upstairs window; if he saw it there when he looked up, he knew that he was not to stable the horse, as there was another call to make.

Church continued to be the rock upon which their marriage and family were built. After marriage, Grace joined her husband in attending the Fredonia Presbyterian Church, where he was an elder. She led Sunday school and continued in that role for many years.

This Old House

Home

It takes a heap o' livin' in a house t' make it home,
A heap o' sun an' shadder, an' ye sometimes have t' roam
Afore ye really 'preciate the things ye lef' behind,
An' hunger fer 'em somehow, with 'em allus on yer mind.
It don't make any differunce how rich ye get t' be,
How much yer chairs an' tables cost, how great yer luxury;
It ain't home t' ye, though it be the palace of a king,
Until somehow yer soul is sort o' wrapped round everything.

Home ain't a place that gold can buy or get up in a
minute;
Afore it's home there's got t' be a heap o' livin' in it;
Within the walls there's got t' be some babies born, and
then
Right there ye've got t' bring 'em up t' women good, an'
men;
And gradjerly as time goes on, ye find ye wouldn't part
With anything they ever used—they've grown into yer
heart;
The old high chairs, the playthings, too, the little shoes
they wore
Ye hoard; an' if ye could ye'd keep the thumb-marks on
the door.

Ye've got t' weep t' make it home, ye've got t' sit an' sigh
An' watch beside a loved one's bed, an' know that Death
is nigh;
An' in the stillness o' the night t' see Death's angel come,
An' close the eyes o' her that smiled, an' leave her sweet
voice dumb.
Fer these are scenes that grip the heart, an' when yer tears
are dried,
Ye find the home is dearer than it was, an' sanctified;
An' tuggin' at ye always are the pleasant memories
O' her that was an' is no more—ye can't escape from these.

Ye've got t' sing an' dance fer years, ye've got t' romp an'
play,
An' learn t' love the things ye have by usin' 'em each day;
Even the roses 'round the porch must blossom year by year

Afore they 'come a part o' ye, suggestin' someone dear
Who used t' love 'em long ago, an' trained 'em jest t' run
The way they do, so's they would get the early mornin' sun;
Ye've got t' love each brick an' stone from cellar up t'
dome:
It takes a heap o' livin' in a house t' make it home.

> Edgar A. Guest, *A Heap O' Livin'!*
> (Chicago: Reilly & Lee Co., 1916)

Willson Whitman, in his landmark interview with Richmond, observed that:

At Fredonia, New York, anyone will direct you. . . . But suppose no one could? You would be safe enough in looking for a house that was obviously a home, that seemed to welcome you before you got there, with warm red walls and a white doorway, with a front yard shaded with trees and fragrant with lilacs, a house with rambling, hospitable porches and—

—Yes, it ought to have two entrances: one of them for the doctor, with his office hours in gold letters on the door. And it has.

Mrs. Richmond herself will meet you at the other door. You get a quick impression of a welcoming smile, of friendly gray—or are they blue?—eyes beneath soft waves of hair; and then, before you know it, you are comfortably seated in a living room that greets you as an old friend.

An open fire behind the brass andirons has sparked at you for a beginning.

"Not that we need it," Mrs. Richmond admits. "But this morning's cold for June, and we like the fire so much—"

It requires no explanation. There *had* to be an open fire.

Above, on a white mantel shelf, are June flowers—bridal wreath and bachelor buttons, with widespread tulips to repeat the colors of the flames.

And on each side, literally on every side of the room, are bookshelves. Not books, glassed away for safe-keeping, but books ready to hand—begging to be looked at—

After a walk—Mrs. Richmond took vigorous walks every day—they return the back way.

> On the back-yard hillside there are trees, and from it there is a view. Stand knee deep in June flowers, and look around. Here beneath the trees are seats—half the summer is spent in this outdoor living-room, and a better place would be hard to find. At the foot of the hill is the garden, with trim rows of vegetables—(we'll have some at dinner). At one side there is another garden of old-fashioned flowers, with brick walks, and a rambler-arched gate; this is the special pride of Dr. Smith, Mrs. Richmond's father. The gardens spread fanwise to reach the hill, and a row of young poplars make for the privacy of an English estate, because Mrs. Richmond is so fond of working out of doors.

Later on, Whitman returns to the house and sees everywhere the atmosphere and objects he recognizes from the Richmond stories and books.

> Rooms like these are filled with a gracious charm which reflects their owner, and in turn impresses itself upon the visitor. It would be difficult to be disagreeable in such a room. But what good times there have been in it!
>
> Christmas greens have decked that mantel year after year. Stockings have been hung at it, and may be hung again, you know—for this is a home they'll always come back to at Christmas! It wouldn't, it couldn't, be a "forgetting" family. On Mother's day the tall vases were filled with flowers. The conventional thing? No! Snapdragons!
>
> There have been enthusiastic arguments and delightfully inconsequential discussions in this room. There has been music around the big piano—one daughter plays the violin, and the other, the cello. In *The Twenty-fourth of June* you remember that Roberta has this none too common accomplishment, and in the Gray family there was such a family orchestra as this must have been. That piano is loved; come early in the morning and you may find Mrs. Richmond herself dusting its keys.
>
> And there have been impromptu theatricals, with lively guests taking thrilling parts, amidst much applause.

Later on, everyone gravitates to the dining room with its cheery English-hunting-scene wallpaper. Outside the windows is a dogwood tree.

Dr. Richmond carves, and well, too! But first there is grace before meat, and the rankest heretic would not deny that grace belongs in this room.

Not that it isn't a room, like the rest, for gaiety. There has been many a spontaneous give-and-take across the table. Today there are family jokes, conversation about Fredonia improvements, and the trip to Florida in the car. . . .

And now—halfway through the meal—occurs something you might have known would happen. The maid appears with a message—there's a man who would like to see the Doctor.

And Dr. Richmond puts down his napkin, as you know he has done a thousand times before, times which have furnished the inspiration for Red Pepper Burns' performance of that same act!

You would not have it otherwise, in spite of your loss. This is an American home, as clear and perfect a picture of the ideal type as you are likely to see in your life. Much has been said of late about the disappearance of such homes, the substitution of some other state of society in which institutions shall replace that selfish and inefficient system called family life. To which the apologist for the family is apt to reply that there is nothing better for the *community* than the right sort of *family*. For our lives do touch, and peace and contentment flow out in ever-widening circles.

Here, at least, you can believe it true. The Doctor is at the service of the community; the writer at the service of countless readers who, if they cannot come into this quiet dining-room, have enjoyed its spirit when brought to them. (Willson Whitman, *Grace Richmond: Builder of Homes* [Garden City, N.Y.: Doubleday, Doran & Company, 1928], 3–17)

Editorial Power Plays

Editors! Richmond knew full well she lived and wrote in a male-dominated editorial world. Had she any doubts on the subject, they would have been put to rest by pontificational letter intros such as the following: "There comes a time in the affairs of men about this season of the year, particularly if a man is a publisher, when he wishes to talk of many things with an author" (Frank Doubleday to Grace Richmond, Nov. 18, 1915, Barker Library, Fredonia, N.Y.).

In that letter, Doubleday outlined a course of action and "suggested" that Grace come to Olympus (Doubleday editorial office) and discuss her responses. Contrary to all accepted editorial practices of the day, it was *they* who took the long trips and waited at *her* door, took long walks with her, and tried to break down her resistance on her home turf. Who were they? Luminaries such as Frank Doubleday and his brother Russell Doubleday, Dan Longwell (a close friend of Henry Luce; he later left Doubleday to become editor of Life magazine), Philip S. Rose and H. L. Paxton of Country Gentleman, Hayden Carruth and Gertrude Lane (who also served as editor for Edna Ferber and Willa Cather) of Woman's Home Companion, as well as Franklin B. Wiley and his legendary boss, Edward William Bok, of Ladies' Home Journal.

So important is Edward William Bok to the story of Grace Richmond, that it behooves us to step backward in time and study the man and his impact upon the American psyche. How did he, a Dutch immigrant, come to be editor of the most prestigious and most widely circulated women's magazine in America? Sometime in 1914 Bok was interviewed in depth by Marvin Ferree, of the *Independent* (later reprinted in the September 7, 1915, *Youth's Instructor*).

Bok's father, born to great wealth in Holland, lost his fortune and emigrated to America when his son was six years old. Unfortunately, the stress of trying to rebuild his fortunes proved too much for him: He died, leaving his widow and two boys to fend for themselves. Bok pointed out that his mother, who once had servants to do her work, now had to do her own housework. "My brother and I tried to help her. Every afternoon when we came home from school, we helped her in every way we could. We used to scrub the floors. . . . I washed the dishes for her. I learned to cook, and used to relieve her of that as much as I could. In this way I learned what I have never forgotten— the fearful, interminable routine of a housewife's life." At 13 he dropped out of school and entered the workaday world full-time. His first job was as an office boy for Western Union Telegraph Company, where he learned how to take dictation. While doing this, he still found time to edit and publish the *Brooklyn Magazine,* publishing in it the sermons of Dr. T. DeWitt Talmage and Henry Ward Beecher: "I got some of the most notable men in the country to write for us for nothing. It was cheek. . . . We ran the magazine for two years and sold it for a profit."

Then, still 16, he became acquainted with publisher Henry Holt and became his stenographer. A year later, in the same role, he moved to Scribners; he remained with them for seven years, most of that time writing advertising copy. During those same years, he and his brother founded Bok Syndicate Press. He conceived the idea of getting 40 celebrated women to write a letter apiece for the Syndicate, then wrote editors around the country, suggesting that if they would publish these letters in their newspapers, women would read their paper and read their advertisements—and thus was born the Women's Page.

About this time, Cyrus Curtis, publisher of *Ladies' Home Journal* (and other magazines), was intrigued enough to track Bok down:

> Mr. Curtis called upon me, and said that his magazine was being edited by his wife; but that, as they had a little daughter who was growing up and needed her mother's care, she had no longer the time necessary to be given to the magazine. He asked me if I knew of any young man whom I could get for the position.
> I said I did not. He smiled.
> "How about you?" he said.
> . . . I decided to go. That was 24 years ago.

Bok, vice president of Curtis Publishing Company for 39 years, would remain chief editor at *Ladies' Home Journal* for almost 30 years.

Ferree then asked if he edited the magazine with any particular type of reader in mind. Bok answered,

> Yes. For 21 years I have edited the magazine with one woman in view. . . . A year or two after I became editor Mr. Curtis and I made a tour of the smaller cities to study the needs of the American people. In one city, a small city . . . , I saw a woman who seemed to me by her dress and manners, and in every way, to be typical of the best American womanhood. I saw her at church and at a concert with her husband and children. I passed her home and saw about it the same air of typical "homeness" and refinement I had noted in her. *That woman,* I said to myself, *is the woman I shall have in view in editing the magazine.*

I made inquiries and found she did not read the magazine. Two years later I saw her name on the subscription list. A few years later I received a letter from her telling me how the magazine had helped her in her home and with her family. That woman will never know how gratifying was her letter.

But Ferree had one last question: It had to do with Bok's family. In answer, Bok admitted that he had fallen in love with the Curtises' little girl and had waited for her to grow up. During the Boks' 17 years of marriage, two sons had been born to them.

This remarkable portrait is so important to this life sketch, for, in a very special sense, Grace Richmond was Bok's discovery; she was a writer who wrote (without knowing it) for that prototype reader Bok edited for. A frequent visitor at the Richmond home, Bok saw in her a woman who communicated values, patriotism, and all that was best in American life. That is why he published 14 of her stories and serialized 16 of her books in his great magazine. Interestingly enough, after he retired, *Ladies' Home Journal* serialized but one more. (The information in this section is found in "Mr. Bok," by Marvin Ferree, *The Youth's Instructor*, Sept. 7, 1915. Text was used by permission of Review and Herald Publishing Association, Hagerstown, MD 21740.)

Early in her relationship with what insiders hubristically referred to as *The Journal*, Senior Editor Edward Bok attempted to show this fledgling housewife author who was boss. Characteristically, he had one of his associates relay his directives secondhand, obviously hoping the imperial "we" would awe Mrs. Richmond into submission. That such an expectation was a slight miscalculation can be seen from the following letter, returned with Richmond's handwritten commentary between the typewritten lines:

Dear Mrs. Richmond:
Dear Mr. Wiley:
 It was naturally a disappoint-
 Of all the cut and
ment to us to learn that you were not favorably
dried "official letters" I ever
inclined toward our suggestion about a series of
had from you, this is the thinnest.
"girl studies" for next year. Mr. Bok hoped that

"Favorably inclined" indeed!
on reflection you would be attracted by the idea
"Attracted by the idea!" You know
and give us half-a-dozen short articles at least
perfectly well that "the idea"
along the lines indicated in his memorandum. Of
does not *"appeal to me for treatment*
course we do not wish to urge you against your
in any other form." The next sug-
own judgment, but still, even if you cannot do
gestion will be for me to do a
the articles, does not the idea appeal to you
series of articles on embroidery
for treatment in any other form—in story form,
or table decoration!
for instance?
     You won't "be glad to
     If this suggestion also is out
know" it—you think yourself
of the question, we would be glad to know: if you
that the Journal can get along
have any plans in mind or any work under way
without me perfectly well for a
that we might be privileged to hear about and to
fairly long period of time.
consider later. . . . (Franklin B. Wiley to Grace Richmond,
June 28, 1907, edited letter returned to Wiley by
Richmond, Barker Library)

It is both to Mr. Wiley and Mr. Bok's credit that neither of them cut
off their noses to spite their faces when this sassy response got back to
Ladies' Home Journal headquarters in Philadelphia; rather, both of them
respected her the more for it and became, over time, two of her most
cherished friends.

The Finest of Frenzies

Grace Richmond once wrote, "I can't write stories when I'm not in the 'finest of frenzies' " (Cummings, 1). Considering her impressive output of stories and books, she must have had the "frenzies" often.

The Richmond story is unusual in literature in that here was a nineteenth-century husband who was so secure in his gifts, in his profession, and in his sense of self-worth that he was the prime motivating force behind his wife's writing career: encouraging her to be all that was in her to become. The first encouragement must have come during her pregnancy with Marjorie. Once having written her first story, she mailed it to the *Ladies' Home Journal.* Many years later one of the editors remembered that first submission this way:

> One morning in 1891 the mail brought to the office of this magazine a short story signed by the then unknown name of Grace S. Richmond—a story of the reform, through love, of a charmingly untidy little literary genius.
>
> It was so bright and well done that the first reader promptly passed it on to the editor, who as promptly accepted it, and it appeared under the title of "The Flowing Shoe-string" in the Thanksgiving issue of *THE JOURNAL* for that year. . . . She was encouraged to try again. But she was modest and very, very busy with family and household cares, and seven years slipped by before she once more appeared in *THE JOURNAL* in 1898, with "A Silk-lined Girl," again in the Thanksgiving issue. ("The Novelist of the Home," *Ladies' Home Journal,* June 1915)

Why the seven-year hiatus in her writing, after having hit the big time with her very first story submission? Undoubtedly the pregnancy and birth of Marjorie, the devastation resulting from the untimely death of Joyce, and the birth of Ted two years later—all overwhelmed her with the constant attentions small children require. That they were always her first priority is clear in Whitman's interview:

> "No, the children certainly weren't neglected," Mrs. Richmond agrees, with a reminiscent smile. "I was fortunate in having people I could trust around me, but the children never called for *Mother* without her being right there. I had a work room at the back of the house then, and when they came in from playing outdoors, or

when school was over, later, it was always the first place
they made for."

Next time you read *Red Pepper Burns* will you please
try to imagine its writing interrupted by demands for
the author to look at a new butterfly, or soothe a five-
year-old's "hurted feelings"?

"Perhaps it was due to reading about Mrs. Jellaby at
an early age," Mrs. Richmond suggests. "I resolved then
never to be that sort of a mother!" (Whitman, 6)

Grace and her husband must have talked about her reentry into the
writing world as the children grew older. By 1900, when she was 34,
with Marjorie now eight and Ted six, she must have decided to get serious about writing. Three of her stories were published in *Young People*
and a skit in *Truth* during the year. The year 1901 was her biggest year
yet: five stories in *Young People*, and one story in each of the following:
The Ledger Monthly, Munsey's, and *Woman's Home Companion.*

Clearly, she and Nelson concluded by this time that she had the stuff
to become a professional writer. In those days, a man was viewed as a failure who could not provide for his wife and family, and this Nelson had
no trouble accomplishing. Rather, it was decided that Grace's writing
income would be for extras, for improving the quality of their lives.

That first check so excited her that she ran out and bought a new
bedroom set—well, *partially* bought: Since she didn't sell any more
stories for some time, the good doctor, with a wry grin, ended up paying
for it. (Janet H. Richmond to Jim Cummings, Aug. 31, 1977, Reed
Library.)

The year 1902 was a tough year for Grace writing-wise, for on June 18,
Jean Kimball Richmond was born. In spite of this, Grace still managed
to get four stories and a serial published. From that time on, more and
more of her stories and serialized books began to appear in the pages of
the best known magazines in the country. Grace was 39 when her first
book, *The Indifference of Juliet,* was published. It was successful enough
that the family (she, Nelson, their three children, her father, and bicycles)
decided to take an eight-month trip to England and Scotland the following year. Quite a 40th birthday present! Well, it was a *working* vacation,
as she would be researching the setting and outlining the plot for the
sequel to her first book, *With Juliet in England,* and Dr. Richmond
would be studying in Edinburgh.

Starting about this time, not only did she continue writing in magazines, but she incorporated the completion of a book a year into her schedule as well. She stayed organized and tried to write each day.

And what kind of stories did she write? According to Cummings, her heroines tended to be from "good families in straitened circumstances" who are pluckily "attempting to make good as writers, proprietors of bookshops, editors, interior decorators with architectural firms, photographers in hamlets," and so on. Each, of course, needs a deserving husband, and these individuals Grace dishes up as "young ministers, physicians, and spoiled young men of independent means who are either in poor health, seem to lack backbone enough to protest family arrangements for their futures, or—most heinous of all character traits—are selfish. . . . The heroines, after choosing the most likely suitor and tantalizing him a bit by twirling a scarf about, will then, rather unfeelingly, arrange goals the young man must accomplish since he isn't quite up to scratch, and may even set deadlines for their accomplishment as in *Twenty-fourth of June*" (Cummings, 4).

One thing is certain: Grace's women are *strong* and are thus perfect bridges connecting the world Richmond grew up in to the world of her children and grandchildren. Cummings points out that Grace's books portray "America in a transition period: a time of moving away from the horse and buggy for transportation to the automobile, even the airplane; a time when the kerosene lamp was being superseded by the electric light; and a time, too, when America's women were wanting suffrage, and after achieving it, were wanting careers and lives equal to those of men" (Cummings, 13).

Writers' lives are littered with publishing house mismatches—many writers' careers have been darkened by association with the wrong publisher. Not so with Richmond and Doubleday, Page, and Company (later, Doubleday, Doran, and Company; and even later, Bantam, Doubleday, Dell). Of course, there were occasional bumps in the road, but they were all minor: Mutual respect and admiration characterized the relationship on both sides.

Comparatively few of Grace Richmond's books were in the nature of sequels, as she preferred to plow new ground with each book. Her first book (a *Ladies' Home Journal* story composite), *The Indifference of Juliet* (1905), was one of those exceptions, as two years later, mirroring the family's trip to the British Isles, *With Juliet in England* was published. The Juliet books proved that a series of books with common characters could catch popular interest. (The information in this section is found in Ronald A. Norris, "Grace Richmond: A Descriptive Bibliography,"

Master's Thesis, State University of New York at Fredonia, 1979, 6.)

The Second Violin (born in *The Youth's Companion)* was first published in 1906. The plot has to do with what happens when the busy mother of five children is laid low by illness and forced to leave for a warmer climate with her husband, hoping this rest cure will save her life. Deprived of the father's income, the five children are left to cope. Initially, the oldest daughter, Celia, takes charge of the household, but after she is disabled in an accident, the house is left temporarily rudderless. Finally, Charlotte, the second oldest—"second violin"—steps into the breach.

Christmas was always a special time of year for the Richmond family. Her first Christmas story, *On Christmas Day in the Morning,* came out first in *Everybody's Magazine* before publication in book form in 1908. It has to do with what happens when the grown children of an aging couple belatedly discover how lonely their parents are at Christmas without them—and what they do about it. Two years later, the sequel, *On Christmas Day in the Evening* (a much longer novelette), was also published in *Everybody's* before being published as a book. It would not be until 1925 that the two related stories would come together in one book: *On Christmas Day in the Morning and the Evening.*

Also published in 1908 was *Round the Corner in Gay Street* (first published a year earlier in *The Youth's Companion).* The plot has to do with what happens when a family in rather straitened financial circumstances moves in "round the corner" from the wealthy and discontented Townsend family. Forces are set in motion that suddenly move into high gear as the result of a fire in the Townsend house. Altogether, the book is an idyllic picture of family life. The sequel to this saga of the Bells and Townsends, "Worthington Square," was also published in *The Youth's Companion* but was never published in book form.

Richmond's book in 1909, *A Court of Inquiry,* consisted of a collection of her magazine stories. Yet, they were not merely unrelated short stories; rather, the first batch of stories features a half-dozen girl characters; the second batch of stories revisits them later in life. The "court" consists of a group of friends who compare the women they have become to the girls they once were. Consequently, the book is neither a novel nor a collection of short stories, but rather something in between. The third part of the book stirs in some unrelated short stories. The book ends up being a one-of-a-kind in Richmond's canon.

Her sixth book, *Red Pepper Burns* (first appearing in *Ladies' Home Journal),* marked in 1910 the launching of Richmond's single most beloved and enduring character, Dr. Red Pepper Burns. Readers gathered the fiery doctor to heart and filled its author's mailbox with tributes. Helping keep Red Burns alive was an unexpected serendipity: Contrary to the norm with books that spawn sequels, some of the sequels proved to have more power and poignancy than the original. Each new book added layers, and hence multidimensionality, to his personality.

In 1911, *Strawberry Acres* was published by Doubleday after first being serialized by *The Youth's Companion*. In some ways, it is similar to *The Second Violin* in that absentee parents force the coming-of-age children to assume adult roles early, only in this case, the parents are deceased and there are four children instead of five. The catalyst—as often is the case in Richmond—is an old, deserted house, a once splendid country mansion that the Lane children inherit. In this book, however, the surrounding acreage is as significant to the plot as is the house itself. A cast of fascinating characters makes the plot-line crackle: Max, the self-acknowledged head of the family, is portrayed as the invariable pessimistic wet blanket; Alec, as the follower of his elder brother; Sally, as the most lovable and enchanting person in the book; and Robert, as the natural protector of his sister. Uncle Timothy is the live-in surrogate parent. Sally has two men apparently in love with her: Jarvis Burnside, who's almost blind because of excessive studying; and Donald Ferry, a young minister. Jarvis's sister Josephine is a constant presence (almost a sister to Sally). Both the Lanes and Burnsides move out of town to the mansion, and there begin to develop a strawberry business. These acres of strawberries become the setting for character change—and love.

In 1912, *Brotherly House* (Richmond's third Christmas book) was published; it was followed a year later by *Under the Christmas Stars,* and her last, a moving hybrid of love, war, and Christmas, *The Bells of St. John's,* in 1920.

The Brown Study, first published in 1915 by *Woman's Home Companion,* was yoked together with "The Real Thing," first published by *Ladies' Home Journal* in 1913 to form a book. In the title story, Donald Brown (a runaway cleric) sets up shop in a humble city apartment, seeking to help people who don't know who he is. The suspense is tied to Helena, the beauty who earlier rejected him. The second story is also a romance, but the two stories don't really mesh—they remain separate.

It took a blitz of sinking American ships to belatedly bring America into the Great War, which had already been raging for three years. By then, Germany had England on the ropes and was not at all afraid of isolationist America. President Wilson declared war on April 6, 1917. Almost immediately, the nation began to mobilize all its forces, civilian as well as military. America had stayed out of the conflagration so long that even now, perhaps, it might be too late. Editor Bok knew from his relatives in occupied Holland how devastating the war was, and how high the stakes. Somehow, someway, he and his staff had to help alter the average American's attitude toward involvement in the war—and do it *fast!* There was not a moment to lose. Only one writer they knew could pull it off. Almost certainly, Bok, Wiley, or both, got on the train for western New York. What they were asking was for Richmond to pull off one of the greatest propaganda feats in American history: change ardent pacifists into equally ardent militants. There was, initially, not even a plot to build upon. No one knew how long the story might need to last. Could Grace, in a matter of days, construct a plot that could be expanded or shrunk, as the fortunes of war dictated? On their end, the challenges were equally daunting. Normally, editors had the luxury of six months to two years of lead time after receiving a given story or serial (in its complete form), the artwork alone taking a lot of time. The project would require two battle stations: one in Philadelphia, one in Fredonia. Copy would need to be rushed back and forth by train.

Miraculously, they pulled it off! In Richmond's fertile mind was born the concept of a woman named Mrs. Redding who would somehow help to "see America through," along with a cast of key characters, including a combative minister. By mid-August, they were ready for the September issue—but only that issue; the novel would have to be written simultaneously to its serialized printing, an act of hubris almost unprecedented in the annals of American publishing. No one, from Bok on down, even knew if the novel would work.

On September 8, Bok's associate, Franklin B. Wiley, wrote to Grace, telling her how anxious everyone was to see the next installment. In it, he told her that he loved the one that featured the "recruiting sermon." Just before mailing the letter, her next installment arrived, and he added a rave postscript: "It is fine, *fine,* exactly what is needed on the subject" (Franklin B. Wiley to Grace Richmond, Sept. 7, 1917, Reed Library).

Richmond did indeed see to it that Mrs. Redding saw America *through* the war. Even as the serial's devoted readers read the last issue in August 1918, Marshals Foch and Pershing were preparing for the great final offensive. On November 8, 1918, a demoralized and shaken German delegation sued for surrender terms. On the 11th, bells rang around the world—the long bloody war was finally over.

But the battering ram of a year's worth of monthly deadlines, and the stress-induced awareness that failure anywhere along the line would jeopardize the entire propaganda venture, had taken a terrible toll on Richmond's health. However, the longest book of her lifetime was destined never to see book covers—its work was already done. So was Bok's: One year later, he surrendered the reins of *Ladies' Home Journal* to another.

Richmond somehow had found time to dream up and write two short stories during this same time, also geared to generating war support. *The Journal* published them both, and Doubleday dutifully followed suit (in book form): *The Whistling Mother* in 1917 and *The Enlisting Wife* in 1918. In fact, so exhausted was Richmond at the end of the war that she significantly cut back on her short-story writing. From the early twenties on, she would—with few exceptions—limit her writing output to one book a year.

Red and Black, next to the last of her books to be serialized by *Ladies' Home Journal,* was her first postwar book, released in 1919. Within its covers is the memorable story of two men—a preacher and a doctor—whose deep friendship greatly enriches both their lives. It also includes another ingredient: romance—unexpected because the woman involved had determined to never let herself fall in love with a preacher. It is one of the most powerful and moving of the Red Pepper Burns books.

She wrote even less the following year, only the short Christmas book *The Bells of St. John's,* and she published no book at all in 1921. But in 1922, *Ladies' Home Journal* and Doubleday published *Foursquare,* one of her most significant books. *Foursquare* is perhaps the finest fictional tribute to the small college (and to those who lead and teach in such an environment) ever penned. Willson Whitman pointed out, "You remember the dedication of *Foursquare*—'To the small college with the big ideals.' No particular college was meant; but Colby, up in Maine, was grateful for the words. So Colby gave Mrs. Richmond the degree of doctor of literature. . . . The same book so stirred the wrath of a professor at a great Western university that he said he'd burn it, if he could! And it is these *two* events, taken together, which delight Mrs. Richmond's heart. Not merely [the] honor, but the joy of having an antagonist to her principles show he had received a palpable hit" (Whitman, 20–21).

The year 1923 brought *Rufus* (first serialized in *Woman's Home Companion),* one of Richmond's most memorable achievements. The protagonist, Dr. Lynn Bruce, like so many others of his generation, is severely crippled during the war. Because of this disability, he loses all interest in life. The catalyst is little Rufus, an unloved and debilitated waif off the streets who is brought into Dr. Bruce's home. Enter pretty, rich Nancy Bruce Ramsey, Dr. Bruce's niece by marriage, who nurses both her uncle and Rufus. In the process, the lovely widow sets powerful forces in motion.

The fifth Red Pepper Burns book, *Red of the Redfields,* was serialized by *Country Gentleman* before the book was published in 1924. It was followed, a year later, by *Cherry Square,* first serialized by *Woman's Home Companion.* All those who believe houses have souls will love this book about Cherry House, fronting on Cherry Square, in the eastern town of Cherry Hills. Cherry House had been lonely for several years—aloof and deserted by all human life. Suddenly, "a young Irishman, whistling blithely, set about mowing the lawns, trimming the hedges, grubbing the weeds out of the paths and driveways; and then presently, when everything was in readiness, life came again into Cherry House—rushed into it" (*Cherry Square* prologue). The multi-tiered love story that follows—woven into a fabric of self-sacrifice and service for others—takes second place to none.

Both *Lights Up* and *At the South Gate* were serialized in 1927: the former by *Country Gentleman,* the latter by *Woman's Home Companion.* *Lights Up* reflects, better perhaps than any other book she ever wrote, Richmond's lifelong love affair with the stage. Joan Dare, one of Richmond's more-liberated female leads, is a tomboyish, free-spirited daughter of well-to-do vagabonding parents. The plot has to do with her personal journey through the transitory world of stage players, casts, and sets to knowledge of herself and her values at the end. Two very different men provide the human textbooks on what love can mean. Which of them represents *true* love, she doesn't find out until the third act.

At the South Gate is another tour de force. Actually, the manuscript had been a work-in-progress for a long time. Richmond had a tough time getting the lead characters going. Back in 1923, she wrote Marjorie about it: "It is so much more fun to write you than to struggle with Michael and Ann, whose charms have long since palled on me" (Grace Richmond to Marjorie Sickels, Dec. 18, 1923, Reed Library). She wouldn't finish it until late in 1924. Eventually, as she always did, she regained interest in her characters and ended on a surge of enthusiasm. The story is a riveting one: a triple love story. Ann and Michael Paige (he a struggling young author and she his wife); Ann's brother, Dr. Dan Gaysworthy, and Julia Heath (he a doctor on leave from a hospital in Korea and she a social secretary); and Charlton and Beatrice Braithwaite (he a puffy, idle, dilettante millionaire and she a terrible mother, a drug addict, an unfaithful wife, and old before her time). The book is about the only values that really matter in life—all based on selfless service for others. Money without a cause to live for is shown as a sure pathway to loss of self-respect and disintegration.

The Listening Post (1929) was published by Doubleday without being first serialized in a magazine. As is true of most of Richmond's books, it is a love story—but a most different one. Beautiful society belle Judith Kent sends her husband, Rawley, away for a year. Married five years, passionately in love for three of them, the last two had brought estrangement. She remains in the East and he goes to Montana, buys a ranch, and begins to rebuild his life. The glue that holds the book together is gossip, hence the title. All around Judith and Rawley are listeners and watchers, some wishing them well, some not. At the core of the story is one of Richmond's most convincing premises: Without goals, without hard work, without serving those less fortunate, neither long-term love, nor long-term respect are possible, no matter how much money there may be to lubricate a given relationship. The young Grace Richmond could never have written such a book!

High Fences (1930) was the last of her books to be serialized by *Woman's Home Companion*. She remained on the cutting edge between the old and the new. In this book, she tackles self-centered flapperism as opposed to traditional marriage and family; career goals and dreams of women as opposed to marriages based on two paychecks and separate living accommodations; the religion of excitement, speed, and constant change as opposed to a deep and abiding belief in God; virginity until marriage as opposed to sex divorced from long-term commitment.

Along the way, she explores the difference children make, the lure of cities that never sleep, the mesmerizing world of drama and concert hall, the role motorcars had in catapulting society into change before it could possibly know whether such change would result in good or evil. *High Fences* introduces Rosamond "Ross" Collins, the most sophisticated, urban, streetwise, witty, clever, irresistible liberated woman Richmond ever unleashed in print. On the opposite end of the spectrum, Richmond introduces David McRoss. Both romantic leads are writers; one writing in depth about country life, and the other writing about the froth of city life and dazzling by wit, turns of phrasing, and biting irony—two totally different worlds. So advanced for its time is this remarkable book that even today, two-thirds of a century later, we are *still* grappling with these very same issues.

Sequels often lack vitality. Not so the sixth Red Pepper Burns book, *Red Pepper Returns* (1931), which was not serialized. There are many subplots in the book, many love stories, many deep insights into life. If one had to come up with one theme out of all these interrelated stories, it would be this: Life without work or growth is a dead-end, leading to dissolution, divorce, death. And life without God is hollow, meaningless, and not worth living. It is also a great book about love especially mature married love that has stood the test of time. With it there are heart-breaking stories of unrequited love: love that will not, or cannot, be returned. There is much of the Richmonds' own love story here, along with Grace's need for other friendships (of both sexes) of the soul and mind. There is also a great deal about transitory love—love that lasts not at all—a reflection of societal instability that tears Richmond apart. All in all, it is a fitting coda to the Red Pepper series and deeply moving. Did Richmond have a sixth sense that it would be her last? It almost seems so, for she brings back the Reverend Robert Black of *Red and Black*, Ellen Pepper of *Mrs. Red Pepper*, James Macauley of *Red Pepper's Patients,* and so many others, in this remarkable swan song.

Bachelor's Bounty (1933) was serialized by *McCall's* (Curtis Publishing paying $31,000 for it) before book publication. Other than the 1936 anthology, *The Mammoth Book of Red Pepper Stories,* it was fated to be the last of Richmond's books. Here she was with her highest advance ever, and one of her more memorable books, at the pinnacle of her fame. The protagonist, Scott Farrington, is a recovering alcoholic and dilet-tante, who is told by his doctor that his only salvation is to leave New York and find a quiet place in which he can go on the wagon for at least a year. He finds a wreck of a house in a quiet New England community, and on a whim, he buys it. He is tracked down and intruded upon by his affluent friends, most suffocatingly by the beautiful widow Caroline Lenhart, who leaves her little son with him while she roams the world seeking thrills. Scott's salvation comes from next door, from the remark-able Jeremiah Keane (greatly weakened physically but strong inside) and his faithful daughter Barbara. For these two, but especially for Jeremiah, Scott begins to change from a playboy to a self-sufficient newspaper publisher. Both father and daughter serve as life-changing mentors. Again the theme has to do with Richmond's contention that a life without a serious purpose can lead to no good; certainly it cannot lead to lasting happiness or fulfillment.

The Many Worlds of the Richmonds

From all indications, the Richmond marriage appears to have been one of those rare ones: nearly perfect balance between the two, with clear divisions of responsibility and roles. Nelson reigned supreme over his medical practice, finances, farming, and trip planning; Grace reigned supreme over the home (including servants), writing career, and public engagements. Where family relations were concerned, the lead was hers. His income paid for all the necessities, and her income was all discretionary. As an added bond, Nelson and Grace shared the same birthday: March 31.

Through the years, many people would attempt to describe Grace Richmond. James Cummings feels there is a pattern in these descriptions, with these adjectives used most often: "lovely, charming, kind, generous, poised, graceful, gracious, and feminine—and a daughter when asked for a descriptive word, supplied 'ebullient' " (Cummings, 7).

According to her daughter-in-law, "She was rather quick in her motions and her walk was brisk. She was medium height, not quite so tall as Dr. Richmond, and her eyes were brown, light brown hair and light complexioned. She wore very little jewelry—a wedding band and a simple engagement ring" (Janet Richmond to Jim Cummings, Aug. 31, 1977, Reed Library).

Her publishing years were better than good years for the Richmond clan. Dr. Richmond's practice was among the largest in the city, and his wife had become a household name all across the English-speaking world. The money poured in, in an ever-increasing stream. At the center of the family hive was the queen bee herself, delightedly distributing the wealth. First came their many investments in the stock market; these would guarantee the good life for all of them, even after her writing years would come to an end. Next came Nelson's hobby, his farm at Moon Station, called Grasslands. Nelson loved to shed the cares of his practice there, sink his hands into the rich earth, and regenerate. Grace often joined him there. Supposedly, it was a business; in reality, it was a fiscal bottomless pit, money going into the hole continuously, sometimes more than $10,000 a year! Next came the extras at home, followed by travel (including extensive sojourns in Florida, on the seacoast, and in New York City). There was always plenty left over for subsidizing the lifestyles of their three children, as well as generous gifts to friends, relatives, and those in need.

Grace Richmond was first and foremost wife, mother, and daughter; no other priority ever came close to those three, not even writing. Nelson remained her all in all, and her he openly adored. Although they each lived part of the time in other worlds—she with her writing, publishing, speaking engagements, civic responsibilities, and membership in the Shakespeare Club; he with church and civic responsibilities and member-ship in the popular men's organization the Monday Club—they were a team in most everything else. Undoubtedly, the stress involved in having her folks live with them so long (her mother for almost 30 years and her father for 37) took a considerable toll. It was perhaps because of this long ordeal that the Nelsons rarely, if ever, spent a night under the roof of any of their children, with or without her parents.

The relationship between family members was extraordinarily close, with endearing nicknames being the norm. Marjorie, for instance, was known variously as "Wogs," "Woggy," "Woggity," or "The Oracle"; Jean was called "Jakey," "Jinks," or "The Child"; and Edward was either "Ted" or "Teddy."

That she actually had a philosophy about the mother-daughter rela-tionship is revealed in a letter to Marjorie: "Your darling Mother's Day letter came yesterday, and adds one more to the lovely succession of them, most of which I have put away as priceless. And Jakey sent me a big box of sweet peas today, which rejoiced my eyes as your letter had rejoiced my heart. How splendid to have a daughter who knows how to say things like that—in either way."

Going on to discuss mother-daughter relationships, she declared that "the biggest trouble . . . is that the relationship is made too much of at the expense of the personalities. Scott Fitzgerald says that mothers don't often enough think of their daughters as persons—real persons—not just daughters, to be everlastingly 'brought up.' I believe he's absolutely right. Long ago I formulated the thesis that mothers should do their best to be charming to their children, as they are to other people" (Grace Richmond to Marjorie Sickels, May 11, 1925, Reed Library).

Pets were always underfoot, especially dogs. Once, one of their dogs failed to come home. In a letter to Marjorie, her mother retold the story, complete with her father's stoic acceptance of the loss, declaring, " 'He was a very nice little dog,' and I shouted, 'Oh, don't say *was!* He isn't dead and buried yet!' Found him—took him to Sunday morning prayers in Grandfather's room" (Grace Richmond to Marjorie Sickels, Oct. 9, 1921, Reed Library). And the dogs almost always accompanied her on her daily walks, rain or shine: "Blizzardy weather—even so walk the doggums" (Grace Richmond to Marjorie Sickels, Jan. 22, 1922, Reed Library).

While Nelson was exceedingly proud of his wife's publishing success, he did not often enter into the fictional worlds she created; in fact, he did not even proof her works, nor were they read aloud to the family. For such soul kinship, she would have to turn elsewhere. As we know, no one person can possibly answer all our needs, hence the special dimension friends occupy in our lives. Fortunately, Grace had such friends, male as well as female. She had two very special ones in Ben and Charlotte Larrabee of Fredonia. He, a brilliant ex-minister and ex-English teacher, loved to proof Richmond's manuscripts and suggest ways to make them even stronger. Charlotte, too, delightedly entered into this process of creation. For many years, Richmond's fiction was enriched by this literary couple. Unfortunately, Charlotte's untimely death in 1928 terminated the relationship, for what had been proper with two women and a man was no longer so with just a man and a woman alone together, day after day.

After he retired, however, Nelson took the time to read her completed works. Late in 1933, after finishing *Bachelor's Bounty*, he wrote his wife how much he appreciated the skillful work: "I could hardly believe it, even of you my life companion. It is the best you've ever done. . . . I am prouder of you than ever—and love you better" (Nelson Richmond to Grace Richmond, undated 1933 letter, Reed Library).

Many were the friendships of the Richmonds. They were one of the couples in what they called "the gang." This group entertained themselves by playing charades; making up bands by using pots and pans as musical instruments; and once the ladies made rather stylish dresses—of newspapers—that they modeled (Cummings, 10). Few people outside the region know that Mark Twain had exceedingly strong ties to the Fredonia-Dunkirk area, for his mother, Jane Clemens, lived there, as did Pamela Clemens Moffett (Twain's sister) and Alice Jean Webster (Twain's niece and author of the best-selling book *Daddy-Long-Legs*). All of these members of Twain's family were among Grace Richmond's closest friends. Nevertheless, while they had many friends, other than their "gang" they did comparatively little entertaining, for most formal gatherings bored Grace; she was always happiest with just the family and their closest friends.

Often, she presented papers, gave readings of poetry, or read from her novels at Chautauqua Institution—usually to large or overflow audiences. On one such occasion, in 1919, she spoke out on women's rights to an audience of young women: "I have made up my mind that a woman needs all her feminine qualities, and one great big one that comes almost purely from the man's side of the world. A woman, if she is going to see things thru from beginning to end, must not make too much of little things; she must have the masculine faculty of seeing the broader, larger aspects of things. . . . A girl should be able to do some job and do it as well as any man can" ("Young Women's Club: Mrs. Richmond Spoke on Essentials of Womanhood," *The Chautauquan Daily*, Aug. 19, 1919, in Cummings, 11).

Richmond was a voracious and eclectic reader, devouring the best of classical and contemporary writers, whether it be biography, drama, novel, religion, short story, poetry, essay, history, philosophy, adventure, or travel. Among those she read were William Shakespeare, Lytton Strachey, Harry Emerson Fosdick, John Galsworthy, Faith Baldwin, William Allen White, Mark Twain, Philip Gibbs, Pearl Buck, Edith Wharton, Temple Bailey, Ellen Glasgow, Charles Dickens, Robert and Elizabeth Browning, Don Marquis, Eugene O'Neill, Woodrow Wilson, Gene Stratton Porter, Charles Kingsley, Ring Lardner, Stuart Sherman, Thomas DeQuincey, F. Dostoyevsky, Robert Burns, L. N. Tolstoy, Francis Thompson, Dorothy Canfield, A. A. Milne, Walter Lippman, James Joyce, H. G. Wells, David Grayson, Louisa May Alcott, and Ogden Nash.

All her life, Richmond remained an avid devotee of the theater. As a result of attending multiple productions of a given play, she privately ranked them in terms of emotive power: "The N.Y. Theater list makes me sigh for January. . . . I saw David Marfield's *Merchant of Venice*—a magnificent thing. He was far more restrained than most of the Shylocks, and by that he was much more effective, since it's restraint that marks the master these days" (Grace Richmond to Marjorie Sickels, Dec. 7, 1923, Reed Library). Not only was she an avid playgoer, but she also frequently participated in area dramatic productions herself, as did Nelson.

Of the three children, unquestionably she was closest to Marjorie, who was not only lovely outside but also lovely inside; she was a singer with a heart-stopping voice and possessed only virtues and apparently no vices. After serving overseas in France with the YMCA (the ground along the way littered with rejected suitors), she returned, graduated from Wellesley, and married a descendant of two of New York's most eminent families, John Stuyvesant Sickels. Apparently, the marriage was a happy one. They had three children.

Ted was early on a playboy, but later he settled down and married Janet DeLong; they too were happy but were destined to never have children of their own. Ted and Janet moved in the highest circles of New York society; professionally, he gradually moved up into top management at Doubleday. In fact, he often proofread his mother's galley.

Jean was the difficult one, manifesting to the fullest the youngest child syndrome. Though musical like her sister, she lacked Marjorie's drive and perseverance. Very much a child of the Flapper Age, she sought constant excitement and change. She married Donald McWhinney, a veteran who lost an arm in the Great War. They had one child, and then she opted for a divorce, bringing into the lives of her parents great anguish. Maturity came to her late in life.

The Best of Times, the Worst of Times

Richmond's heyday was the teens and twenties. The war years spawned idealism, patriotism, and all the family values that were so central to her books and stories. The United States belatedly entered the Great War "to make the world safe for democracy." But with the long war over at last, and millions of surviving veterans back home looking for jobs that tended not to be there, the nation entered into a depression. Thousands of veterans—many of them maimed, mangled, or incapacitated by poison gas—roamed the streets, seeking a way to make a living.

As time passed, however, prosperity came back. But the old values, at least among the veterans and the young women who during the war took the jobs vacated by men in the armed forces, often did not. As it became increasingly clear that the terrible bloodbath had not made the world safe for democracy, as the robber baron tycoons tightened the screws and slowly but inexorably created an ever-wider chasm between the haves and the have-nots, as a new rootless generation refused to go back home to dull small towns (choosing instead the bright lights and speakeasies of the cities), the collapse of the family began. F. Scott Fitzgerald and Ernest Hemingway were the hedonistic voices of this "Lost Generation."

By 1928, the economy was roaring, and everyone, it seemed, was convinced that things would only get better. It became easier to buy stocks on ever smaller margins, thus millions of people—from millionaires to stenographers— invested as if there were no tomorrow. The Wall Street Stock Exchange ticker got so stoked with this unprecedented flood of investor money that it would sometimes take up to 16 minutes to catch up after trading stopped.

Herbert Hoover was elected president in a euphoria of optimism, having chortled all through the campaign that, if elected, he would ensure "a chicken in every pot and a car in every garage," and he went on to trumpet the gladsome news that America was close to "triumph over poverty." Life was good indeed: The average American worker (most of them men) earned almost $2,000 a year (about $39 a week), and 78 percent (or 20 million) of all the automobiles in the world ran on American roads. But serious economists were worried: There were far too many "inexperienced suckers" buying every stock or security in sight, regardless of whether or not they could afford them or could stay in if the stocks reversed direction.

The end came suddenly and without warning. It began on October 24, 1929—known as "Black Thursday"—and continued its downward plunge through October 29—thereafter remembered in chilling horror as "Black Tuesday." Frantic efforts to stabilize things and stop the free fall were met by equally frantic efforts to "*sell—must sell—at any price!*" The pandemonium was only increased by despairing but insistent brokers calling for more cash to back the loans behind the falling stocks.

In Washington, the Federal Reserve Board went into continuous session, not even stopping to eat, but its members could come up with no solution. On Black Tuesday alone, $9 billion was lost—within two weeks, $30 billion! Nationwide panic was the result. In New York, because visitors were not permitted to enter galleries overlooking the chaos of the trading floor, desperate investors mobbed the brokers' offices—each with its glass-domed ticker unit that typed out the dizzying descent of their fortunes. They could not help but hear the sirens of ambulances speeding to the site of yet another suicide. A number were millionaires overnight turned paupers—now totally unable to come up with the money demanded by their brokers. Many of the investors were poor to begin with, and now they were not only broke, but they were in debt for more than they could ever earn. To declare bankruptcy, in that age, was to proclaim oneself unprincipled: a stigma to many worse than death itself.

Unfortunately, Hoover managed to address everything that needed to be done—too late, bull-headedly resisting pressures to increase government spending to offset the devastation in the private sector. Keep in mind that there were no credit cards in those days, no unemployment benefits, no food stamps, no Social Security retirement income—either people had money or they didn't.

Things started out horrific, and as day after day, week after week, month after month, and year after year passed—things only got worse! There were wry signs of the times: "Hoover flags" (pockets emptied and turned inside-out), "Hoover blankets" (newspapers covering park bench indigents), and "Hoovervilles" (makeshift shantytowns where the down-and-outers struggled to stay alive). Poor Hoover learned a sad truth: Presidents are unfairly credited with good times as well as being blamed for bad ones. By December 1930, there were 4.5 million unemployed.

On the 11th of that month, 400,000 depositors of the Bank of the United States found the bank's doors closed to them and mounted police barring access.

The year 1931 proved even worse. Now almost 5 million were unemployed. By early October, 400 banks had failed. Jobless rates in some cities climbed to 50 percent. More than 2 million people (out of a total population of 122 million) wandered across the country as vagrants. Everywhere one looked, once proud, self-sufficient men and women were now reduced to begging for enough food so their families could survive another day. Not without reason were six words then seared into American consciousness for all time: *Brother, can you spare a dime?*

By the following January, more than 2,000 banks had failed, and 13 million workers were without jobs. Just as terrible, for those who still had jobs, hourly wages had been slashed 60 percent since 1929. State governments were hard-pressed to do much, relieving destitute families, at the most, by $5 a week. Foreclosures were now up to 25,000 a week.

That November, desperate Americans tossed Hoover out of the White House and elected Franklin Delano Roosevelt, who announced in ringing words, in his first inaugural address, that "the only thing to fear is fear itself!" It was a sober nation that sat glued to the radios that day, for now fully 25 percent of the entire nation's workforce was unemployed—the national income was less than half of what it had been three years before, more than 5,000 banks had now collapsed and— without federal insurance on any of that money—9 million family savings and checking accounts disappeared into the maelstrom. Even in 1937, in his second inaugural address, President Roosevelt mourned that, in looking out across the nation, he saw "one-third of a nation ill-housed, ill-clad, ill-nourished."

For Grace Richmond, the Depression dealt her a double blow. First, she had to realize that the times were changing. The world she had tried to mirror in her fiction was no more. But she was already making the transition. It might be a difficult one at her age, but it *was* possible.

Second, all the money she had been able to save over the years— monies that, safely invested in the right securities and stocks, were intended to make the rest of her family's lives comfortable, even affluent—should have been more than enough to enable the good life to continue, even if she laid down her pen tomorrow, never to pick it up again. Alas! The crash was no respecter of persons: She was no more able to get out in time than were so many thousands of others. They were not destitute by any means. The doctor had brought in an adequate income over the years, but an awful lot of their money went to keep that bottomless pit, their farm, solvent. And much money was faithfully and regularly distributed among the three children. How could the children be faced, with their now high level of expectation, and told that there would henceforth be no more discretionary money coming to them?

And with that money would also go the control that such money always gives its possessor. More than most people, Grace truly loved to give—she *lived to give.* Thus the turning off of her income and investment faucets represented a terrible blow.

It happened suddenly, but ominous cracks had been showing up in her protective wall in recent months and years. It had all started 30 years before with the tragic death of three-year-old Joyce, an anguish from which Grace's heart had never completely recovered. Through the years, she suffered the death of so many she knew and loved, including her mother and father. The death of Charlotte Larrabee dealt her a double blow, for with her passing went the closest male friend she had, for Charlotte's husband, Ben—like herself a lover of ideas, and the wall upon which she had bounced her story ideas for many years—could no longer be her editor and confidant.

And we mustn't forget the hammer blows represented by an almost fatal accident in Florida (one she never completely recovered from), the toll taken by the wartime serial, "Mrs. Redding Sees It Through," and 32 years of publishing deadlines that further drained the shrinking pool of emotional reserves. But her father had taught her—all too well—never to leave a job partly done. By September 1932, it had all become too much for Grace's overburdened, overworked, overstressed body and nervous system.

Having a nervous breakdown in 1932 was far more terrible than would be true today. We have learned so much about the mind and the effects of extreme stress since that time. And today we have far more remedies than was true then. Furthermore, there was the stigma that was then attached to anything having to do with the mind: To experience a nervous breakdown was akin to coming down with leprosy in the eyes of contemporaries. It seems probable that were Grace living today and experiencing such a breakdown, proper therapy would have been provided; and in due time, with medication and rest, she would have been able to resume her writing career. But sadly, that was not so back then.

When the breakdown occurred, 75-year-old Nelson was too old and fragile himself to cope with the disaster. In spite of a lifetime of medical service, this crippling of his beloved wife was more than he could face alone—so he turned to the oldest daughter; so did his wife, who urged her daughter to hurry to her side. *What are we going to do with Mother?* Marjorie—now 40 years old—must have thought, as the passing land-scape out the train window blurred through her tear-filled eyes; the Woggity years were now over. Arriving in Fredonia, Marjorie took stock of the situation, and her worst fears were confirmed. Neither her father nor she could remedy her mother's condition—it would require profes-sional help. After extensive debate, they decided to place her in the hands of "Dr. John A. P. Millet, an internationally recognized psychiatrist who has his own private sanitarium, Silver Hills Foundation, New Canaan, Connecticut" (Cummings, 12)—and there Marjorie took her, and then left her, hoping they had made the right decision.

In retrospect, it appears probable that they did not—but this is only Monday morning quarterbacking; most certainly they acted upon what appeared to be the best of the alternatives open to them. In a letter to her father on her return to New York, Marjorie noted that "Dr. Millet can do the slow, quiet, careful job of building her up again. You and I know that she was about at the end of her rope, and the hysteria of years can't be sloughed off in a few days." Dr. Millet felt confident that, as a result of his treatment, Mrs. Richmond would eventually become calmer and happier than she had ever been before, but he had cautioned Marjorie, "Above all, nothing of finances in letters to her," for Millet "knows that you have lost largely in the stock market, and that Mother has not been earning for a year. But that is a very common situation now. Expense must not be considered at this time. Mother's health is beyond price. . . . Don't talk particulars with anyone. People might think she is insane, or some-thing. That is not true and never will be true" (Marjorie Sickels to Nelson Richmond, Sept. 10, 1932, Reed Library).

Later in the day, she wrote her father again, comforting him with the knowledge that she had secured the services of an experienced psychiatric nurse who promised to take good care of her mother. Furthermore, she had been able to secure for her the best room in the facility (windows on three sides, a fireplace, a sleeping porch). Remembering back, Marjorie wrote, "When Mother summoned me to Fredonia, she was like a person on the edge of a precipice, hanging on with fingers and toes." At times she seemed completely natural and her old self, but when she was alone with her, "she was terribly excited and terribly afraid." Between times, whether on sedatives or restlessly "pacing up and down like an animal," she kept pushing her limits—but when she arrived at Silver Hills, "she just let go." Marjorie closed by urging her father to just have patience:

"The way back may take a while" (Marjorie Sickels to Nelson Richmond, Sept. 10, 1932, Reed Library).

Sadly, Grace remained in literal incarceration in several different facilities for three and a half long years—years of humiliation, mistreatment, and adversarial treatment by doctors and nurses; years during which all her teeth were removed, against her will, and not replaced until almost too late. She viewed that violent act as a nightmarish violation of her will. One indignity after another filled and overfilled her cup of anguish.

She heard and experienced things that would have crushed the spirit of a lesser woman. Fourteen years later, Mary Jane Ward would shock the nation with her fictional exposé of psychiatric treatment in America: The Snake Pit (1946). Richmond's case was far worse because she, a sane person, was treated as if she had lost her mind.

Belatedly, Marjorie realized that unless she acted quickly, her mother would be lost to her and her family, for it finally became clear to her that the system would never admit enough improvement so that they would be deprived of the monthly income she represented. So, with the collusion of an understanding doctor, she abducted her mother and brought her home to a house full of flowers.

But the damage had been done: The woman who was brought home was not the woman who went away. Never again would she complete another story or another book. Never again would she be completely in control of her body. More and more, she would live in the simple present, rocking on her porch, and in the dazzling past.

During their long separation, she and Nelson often reassured each other of their love through letters. One of his notes to her is most poignant:

> My Darling:
> Remember Oct. 29. It was some years ago that I fell in love with the sweetest girl I ever met. . . . She has been the most helpful and stimulating of companions. I owe her a great debt which I can never pay.
> She watches me from the corner of the front living room—also from the table beside the big chair where I always read; I kiss her every night before going up to bed; and I pray as often, and many more times, for her peace of mind and vigor of body.
> And my prayers are being answered. (Nelson Richmond to Grace Richmond, Nov. 29, 1935, Reed Library)

Sometime later, after receiving flowers from him, Grace wrote, thanking him for being "so sweet" to send her tulips "on no birthday or special occasion, just out of a clear sky. How did you come to do it? They are on a table here in the hall, and every few minutes I look up from my writing to feast my eyes on their rich hues" (Grace Richmond to Nelson Richmond, May 23, 1935, Reed Library).

In 1937, Nelson and Grace celebrated their Golden Wedding Anniversary, with family, friends, flowers, and much happiness.

In 1944, after a protracted illness, Nelson died in Florida Hospital in Orlando. With Nelson gone, life became even lonelier for Grace. It was now that Jean proved her devotion and love: She moved in with her mother and dedicated herself to the task of making her last years happy ones. Grace continued to correspond with friends and family. At 90, she wrote a friend, "It is no joke, being 90 years old, and [I] advise you to be a long time getting there" (Grace Richmond to Ruth Lambert Miller, undated, Reed Library).

As she rocked on the porch, automobiles and trucks sped by in a never-ceasing stream. Overhead, transatlantic airliners carried passengers west at speeds that seemed almost unbelievable. So much had changed—but not inside the old house; there remained so many memories in each room! Through the magic of memory, there was little Joyce playing in the hall, her ever-present smile lighting up her mother's still-aching heart. There was Teddy sliding down the banister—that boy was *always* getting into mischief! She peered under the staircase, chuckling, remembering Marjorie's hiding there. And there was Jean, never still, always flying somewhere—she had a hard time identifying her with that much older Jean who now flitted through the house. But more than any of these, Grace saw Nelson, in his many roles of sweetheart, father, physician, farmer, golfer, elder, actor—she felt his presence everywhere and knew that love like theirs could never really die. She saw friends and family, knocking on her door again, just as they had long years ago, and those dear editors who were here in this house so often and walked with her down the tree-shaded street. Intersticed in all these memories were other characters just as real: the ones she had conceived and given birth to in her stories and books. How impossible, with all these swirling memories, to tell which was real and which was not. For that matter, who was to say that those characters—such as Red Pepper—weren't just as real as those who had once lived, but lived no more. With such company, how could she possibly be lonely?

So she lived on, through all the passing seasons, the years seeming now a seamless garment rather than separate things. *Love.* That was all that really mattered in life. Love and Nelson—more and more, she yearned for him, and *Home.*

On Thanksgiving Day, 1959, she finally departed to that other home.

— — —

Ye've got t' weep t' make it home, ye've got t' sit an' sigh
An' watch beside a loved one's bed, an' know that Death is
nigh;
An' in the stillness o' the night t' see Death's angel come,
An' close the eyes o' her that smiled,
an' leave her sweet voice dumb.
Fer these are scenes that grip the heart,
an' when yer tears are dried,
Ye find the home is dearer than it was, an' sanctified;
An' tuggin' at ye always are the pleasant memories
O' her that was an' is no more—ye can't escape from these.
Ye've got t' sing an' dance fer years, ye've got t' romp an'
play,
An' learn t' love the things ye have by usin' em each day;
Even the roses 'round the porch must blossom year by year
Afore they 'come a part o' ye, suggestin' someone dear
Who used t' love 'em long ago, an' trained 'em jest t' run
The way they do, so's they get the early mornin' sun;
Ye've got t' love each brick an' stone from cellar up t' dome:
It takes a heap o' livin' in a house t' make it home.

Joseph Leininger Wheeler
The Grey House
Conifer, Colorado

The Works of Grace Richmond

Magazines

1898   "The Silk-lined Girl," *Ladies' Home Journal*, November

1900   "The Campaign of the Lieutenant's Furlough," *Young People*, July

"The Difference," *Truth*, June

"His Little Chum," *Young People*, May

"His Vacation Athletics," *Young People*, December 1, 8

1901   "Comradeship of Virginia," *Munsey's Magazine*, July

"Her Post-Graduate Course," *Young People*, June, July, August

"How Gerry Came to Apologize," *Young People*, April

"Kent and Company, Limited," *Young People*, May 11, 18

"The Men Who Nancy Refused," *The Ledger Monthly*, July

"The Stimulus of a Hope," *Woman's Home Companion*

"When He Became a Man," *Young People*, June

"While the Orchestra Played," *Young People*, April

1902   "The Essay Bob Did Not Write," *The Christian Endeavor World*, February

"His Most Unusual Case," *The Youth's Companion*, September

"The Indifference of Juliet," *Ladies' Home Journal*, May, June

"Love's Fool," *Young People*, April

"Their Christmas Eve," *Ladies' Home Journal*, December

1903   "The Argument for the Defense," *McClure's Magazine*, May

"From Off His Pedestal," *Young People*, April

"Her Right Guard," *Young People*, May

"Honor—and the Girl," *Ladies' Home Journal*, February

"The Quick-Decision Board," *McClure's Magazine*, April

"Roses and Raphael," *The Youth's Companion*, May

"A Summer Constellation," *Young People*, May

"The Supreme Test," *McClure's Magazine*, November

"The Wedding of Juliet," *Ladies' Home Journal*, March

1904 "By Virtue of the MacPherson-MacDonald Cookery," *Woman's Home Companion*, June

"Entertaining the Chamberlains," *The Youth's Companion*, June

"The Home-making of Juliet," *Ladies' Home Journal*, April, May, June, July

"Kilbreth of Ballyraggan," *McClure's Magazine*, November

1905 "Billy's Orgy," *McClure's Magazine*, January

"His Handicap," *The Youth's Companion*, January

"Jimmy's Christmas Gift," *Ladies' Home Journal*, December

"On Christmas Day in the Morning," *Everybody's Magazine*, December

"Ruth Endicott, Schoolmistress," *Ladies' Home Journal*, January, February, March, April

"The Top Bureau Drawer," *The Youth's Companion*, August

"Unwelcome Feminine Touch," *Ladies' Home Journal*, August

"The Second Violin," *The Youth's Companion*, February, March, April (9 issues?)

1906 "The Dixons," *Ladies' Home Journal*, May, June, July, August, September

"Girl Sketches," *Ladies' Home Journal*, May, June, July, August, September

"The Man Milliner," *Success Magazine*, March

"The Churchills' Latch String," *The Youth's Companion*, January, February (8 issues?)

1907 "Brother in Arms," *McClure's Magazine*, April

"Half a League Onward," *The Youth's Companion*, May

"With Juliet in England," *Ladies' Home Journal*, June, July, August, September, October, November

"Round the Corner in Gay Street," *The Youth's Companion (8 issues?)*

"Worthington Square," *The Youth's Companion* (series begins in December)

1908 "Worthington Square," *The Youth's Companion* (series ends in February)

"The Armistice," *Woman's Home Companion*, December

1909 "Husband and Wife Sketches," *Ladies' Home Journal*, January, February, March, April, May, June

"Mix-up at the Christmas Party," *Ladies' Home Journal*, December

"Sixteen Miles to Boswell's," *Everybody's Magazine*, October

1910 "Brothers Four," *Woman's Home Companion*, June, July, August, September, October, November

"On Christmas Day in the Evening," *Everybody's Magazine*, December

"Red Pepper Burns," *Ladies' Home Journal*, March, April, May, June, July, August

"Five Minutes Out," *The Youth's Companion* (series begins in November)

1911 "Five Minutes Out," *The Youth's Companion* (series ends in February)

"Mr. John," *Woman's Home Companion*, July

"Strawberry Acres," *The Youth's Companion*, April, May, June (9 issues)

"The Twenty-fourth of June," *Ladies' Home Journal* (series begins in November)

1912   "The Twenty-fourth of June," *Ladies' Home Journal* (series ends in May)

"In Partnership with Pluck," *The Youth's Companion* (series of unknown length)

"Under the Christmas Stars," *Woman's Home Companion*, December

"Country Doctor," *Ladies' Home Journal* (series begins in November)

1913   "Country Doctor," *Ladies' Home Journal* (series ends in May)

"Red Head," *Woman's Home Companion*, June

"Time of His Life," *Ladies' Home Journal*, June, July, August

1914   "Reasonable Woman," *Good Housekeeping*, October, November, December

"The Brown Study," *Woman's Home Companion* (series begins in October)

1915   "The Brown Study," *Woman's Home Companion* (series ends in February)

"Any Port in a Storm," *Woman's Home Companion*, July

"Robin Hood and His Barn," *Woman's Home Companion*, November

"Star in the Country Sky," *Ladies' Home Journal*, April, May, June, July, August, September, October, November

1916   "Her Father's Daughter," *Ladies' Home Journal*, March, April, May, June

"Red Pepper's Patients," *Ladies' Home Journal* (series begins in September)

1917   "Red Pepper's Patients," *Ladies' Home Journal* (series ends in May)

"Flaming Knight," *Woman's Home Companion*, October, November

"The Whistling Mother," *Ladies' Home Journal*, August

"Mrs. Redding Sees It Through," *Ladies' Home Journal* (series begins in September)

1918   "Mrs. Redding Sees It Through," *Ladies' Home Journal* (series ends in August)

"The Enlisted Wife," *Ladies' Home Journal*, March

"When the Boys Came Home: A Play in One Act," *Ladies' Home Journal*

"Anne Exeter," *The Youth's Companion* (series begins in December)

1919   "Anne Exeter," *The Youth's Companion* (series ends in February)

"Back from Over There," *Ladies' Home Journal*, February

"Red and Black," *Ladies' Home Journal*, March, April, May, June, July, August, September, October, November

"When Our Boys Come Back," *Ladies' Home Journal*, February

1920   "The Bells of St. John's," *Good Housekeeping*, December

1921   "The Perfect Church," *Ladies' Home Journal*, June

1922   "For Value Received," *Woman's Home Companion*, October

"Foursquare," *Ladies' Home Journal*, March, April, May, June, July, August

"That Last Hour," *Ladies' Home Journal*, October

"The Visits of Mrs. Trelawny," *Ladies' Home Journal*, December

1923   "Rufus," *Woman's Home Companion*, June, July, August

1924   "The Redfields," *Country Gentleman*, February, March, April

1926   "Cherry Square," *Woman's Home Companion*, October, November, December

1927   "At the South Gate," *Woman's Home Companion*, June, July, August

"Lights Up," *Country Gentleman*, May, June, July, August, September

1928   "Must Great Women Be Ruthless?" *Ladies' Home Journal*, February

"My House Means Home to Me," *American Home*, December

1930   "High Fences," *Woman's Home Companion*, February, March, April, May

1932   "Housewife Remembers," *American Home*, June

"Bachelor's Bounty," *McCall's Magazine* (series begins in September)

1933   "Bachelor's Bounty," *McCall's Magazine* (series ends in January)

1934   "His Word of Honor," *The Youth's Instructor*, June 12

Books
1905   *The Indifference of Juliet* (Garden City, N.Y.: Doubleday, Page, and Company), Juliet Book #1

1906   *The Second Violin* (Garden City, N.Y.: Doubleday, Page, and Company)

1907   *With Juliet in England* (Garden City, N.Y.: Doubleday, Page, and Company), Juliet Book #2

1908   *On Christmas Day in the Morning* (Garden City, N.Y.: Doubleday, Page, and Company), Christmas Book #1

1909   *A Court of Inquiry* (Garden City, N.Y.: Doubleday, Page, and Company)

1910   *Red Pepper Burns* (Garden City, N.Y.: Doubleday, Page, and Company), Red Pepper Book #1

         On Christmas Day in the Evening (Garden City, N.Y.: Doubleday, Page, and Company), Christmas Book #2

1911   *Strawberry Acres* (Garden City, N.Y.: Doubleday, Page, and Company)

1912   *Brotherly House* (Garden City, N.Y.: Doubleday, Page, and Company), Christmas Book #3

1913   *Mrs. Red Pepper* (Garden City, N.Y.: Doubleday, Page, and Company), Red Pepper Book #2

         Under the Christmas Stars (Garden City, N.Y.: Doubleday, Page, and Company), Christmas Book #4

1914   *The Twenty-fourth of June* (Garden City, N.Y.: Doubleday, Page, and Company)

1916   *Under the Country Sky* (Garden City, N.Y.: Doubleday, Page, and Company)

1917   *Red Pepper's Patients* (Garden City, N.Y.: Doubleday, Page, and Company), Red Pepper Book #3

         The Brown Study (Garden City, N.Y.: Doubleday, Page, and Company)

         The Whistling Mother (Garden City, N.Y.: Doubleday, Page, and Company), World War I Book #1

1918   *The Enlisting Wife* (Garden City, N.Y.: Doubleday, Page, and Company), World War I Book #2

1919   *Red and Black* (Garden City, N.Y.: Doubleday, Page, and Company), Red Pepper Book #4

1920   *The Bells of St. John's* (Garden City, N.Y.: Doubleday, Page, and Company), Christmas Book #5

1922   *Foursquare* (Garden City, N.Y.: Doubleday, Page, and Company)

1923   *Rufus* (Garden City, N.Y.: Doubleday, Page, and Company)

1924   *Red of the Redfields* (Garden City, N.Y.: Doubleday, Page, and Company), Red Pepper Book #5

1925   *On Christmas Day in the Morning and the Evening* (Garden City, N.Y.: Doubleday, Page, and Company), Christmas Book #6

1926   *Cherry Square* (Garden City, N.Y.: Doubleday, Page, and Company)

1927   *Lights Up* (Garden City, N.Y.: Doubleday, Page, and Company)

1928   *At the South Gate* (Garden City, N.Y.: Doubleday, Doran, and Company)

1929   *The Listening Post* (Garden City, N.Y.: Doubleday, Doran, and Company)

1930   *High Fences* (Garden City, N.Y.: Doubleday, Doran, and Company)

1931   *Red Pepper Returns* (Garden City, N.Y.: Doubleday, Doran, and Company), Red Pepper Book #6

1932   *Bachelor's Bounty* (Garden City, N.Y.: Doubleday, Doran, and Company)

1936   *The Mammoth Book of Red Pepper Stories* (New York: A. L. Burt), Red Pepper Book #7

Note: Sources used in compiling this bibliography include the David A. Reed Library of the State University of New York at Fredonia; the D. R. Barker Library, Fredonia, New York; Ronald A. Norris's *Grace S. Richmond: A Descriptive Bibliography*; James S. Cummings' *Grace S. Richmond: A Reassessment;* Frederick and Bonnie Liener's Richmond Collection; the Library of Congress; and Joe Wheeler's library.

If any of our readers find errors or items missing from this listing, please send them to me care of the publisher.

Chapter 1

THE CURTAIN RISES ON A HOME

None of it might ever have happened if Richard Kendrick had gone into the house of Mr. Robert Gray, on that first night, by the front door. For if he had made his first entrance by that front door, if he had been admitted by the maidservant in proper fashion and conducted into Judge Calvin Gray's presence in the library, if he had delivered his message from old Matthew Kendrick, his grandfather, and had come away again, ushered out of that same front door, the chances are that he never would have gone again. In which case there would have been no story to tell.

It all came about—or so it seems—from its being a very rainy night in late October, and from young Kendrick's wearing an all-concealing motoring raincoat and cap. He had been for a long drive into the country, and had just returned mud-splashed, when his grandfather, having taken it into his head that a message must be delivered at once, requested his grandson to act as his messenger.

So the young man had impatiently bolted out with the message, had sent his car rushing through the city streets, and had become a still muddier and wetter figure than before when he stood upon the porch of the old Gray homestead, well out on the edge of the city, and put thumb to the bell.

His hand was stayed by the shrill call of a small boy who dashed up on the porch out of the dusk. "You can't get in that way," young Ted Gray cried. "Something's happened to the lock—they've sent for a man to fix it. Come around to the back with me—I'll show you."

So this was why Richard Kendrick came to be conducted by way of the tall-pillared rear porch into the house through the rear door of the wide

1

central hall. There was no light at this end of the hall, and the old-fashioned, high-backed settee that stood there was in shadow.

With a glance at the caller's muddy condition, the young son of the house decided it the part of prudence to assign him this waiting place, while he himself should go in search of his uncle. The lad had seen the big motor-car at the gate; quite naturally he took its driver for a chauffeur.

Ted looked in at the library door; his uncle was not there. He raced off upstairs, not noting the change that had already taken place in the visitor's appearance with the removal of the muddy coat and cap.

Richard Kendrick now looked a particularly personable young man, well built, well dressed, of the brown-haired, gray-eyed, clear-skinned type. The eyes were very fine; the nose and mouth had the lines of distinction; the chin was positive. Altogether the young man did not look the part he had that day been playing—that of the rich young idler who drives a hundred and fifty miles in a powerful car, over the worst kind of roads, merely for the sake of diversion and a good luncheon.

While he waited, Richard considered the hall, at one end of which he sat in the shadow. There was something very homelike about this hall. The quaint landscape paper on the walls, the perceptibly worn and faded crimson Turkey carpeting on the floors, the wide spindle-balustrade stair-case with the old clock on its landing; more than all, perhaps, on an October night like this, the warm glow from a lamp with crystal pendants that stood on the table of polished mahogany near the front door—all these things combined to give the place a quite distinctive look of home.

There were one or two other touches in the picture worth mentioning, the touches that spoke of human life. An old-fashioned hat tree just opposite the rear door was hung full with hats. A heavy ulster[1] lay over a chair close by, and two umbrellas stood in the corner. And over hat rack, hats, ulster, and chair, with one end of silken fringe caught upon one of the umbrella ribs, had been flung by some careless hand, presumably feminine, a long silken scarf of the most intense rose color, a hue so vivid, as the light caught it from the landing above, that it seemed almost to be alive.

From various parts of the house came sounds—of voices and of foot-steps, more than once of distant laughter. Somewhere far above, a child's high call rang out. Nearer at hand someone touched the keys of a piano, playing snatches of Schumann—*Der Nussbaum, Mondnacht, Die Lotosblume*. Richard recognized the airs that thus reached his ears and was sorry when they ceased.

---

[1] Overcoat.

Now there might be nothing in all this worth describing if the effect upon the observer had not been one to him so unaccustomed. Though he had lived to the age of twenty-eight years, he had never set foot in a place that seemed so curiously like a vague dream he had somewhere at the back of his head. For the last two years he had lived with his grandfather in the great pile of stone that they called home. If this were no real home, the young man had never had one. He had spent periods of his life in various sorts of dwelling places: in private rooms at schools and college—always the finest of their kind—in clubs, on ships, in railway trains; but no time at all in any place remotely resembling the house in which he now waited, a stranger in every sense of the word, more strange to the everyday, fine type of home known to the American of good birth and breeding than may seem credible as it is set down.

"Hold on there!" suddenly shouted a determined male voice from somewhere above Richard. A door banged, there was a rush of lightly running feet along the upper hall, closely followed by the tread of heavier ones. A burst of the gayest laughter was succeeded by certain deep grunts, punctuated by little noises as of panting breath and half-stifled merriment. It was easy to determine that a playful scuffle of some sort was going on overhead, which seemed to end only after considerable inarticulate but easily translatable protest on the part of the weaker person involved.

Then came an instant's silence, a man's ringing laugh of triumph; next, in a girl's voice, a little breathless but of a quality to make the listener prick up ears already alert, these most unexpected words:

> O it is *excellent*
> To have a giant's strength; but is *tyrannous*
> To use it like a giant!

"Is it, indeed, Miss Arrogance?" mocked the deeper voice. "Well, if you had given it back at once, as all laws of justice, not to mention propriety, demanded, I should not have had to force it away from you. Oh, I say, did I really hurt that wrist, or are you shamming?"

"Shamming! You big boys have no idea how brutally violent you are when you want some little thing you ought not to have. It aches like anything," retorted the other voice, its very complaints uttered in such melodious tones of contralto music that the listener found himself wishing with all his might to know if the face of its owner could by any possibility match the loveliness of her voice. Dark, he fancied she must be, and young and strong—of education, of a lighthearted wit, yet of a temper—

all this the listener thought he could read in the voice.

"Poor little willful girl! Did she get hurt, then, trying to have her own way? Come in here, jade, and I'll fix it up for you," the deeper tones declared.

Footsteps again; a door closed. Silence succeeded for a minute; then the Schumann music began again, a violin accompanying. And suddenly, directly opposite the settee, a door swung slowly open, the hand upon the knob invisible. A picture was presented to the stranger's eyes as if somebody had meant to show it to him. He could but look. Anybody, seeing the picture, would have looked and found it hard to turn his eyes away.

For it was the heart of the house, right here, so close at hand that even a stranger could catch a glimpse of it by chance. A great, wide-throated fireplace held a splendid fire of burning logs, the light from it illumining the whole room, otherwise dark in the October twilight. Before it on the hearth rug were silhouetted, in distinct lines against its rich background, two figures. One was that of a woman in warm middle life, sitting in a big chair, her face full of both brightness and peace; at her feet knelt a young girl, her arm upon her mother's knees, her face uplifted. The two faces were smiling into each other.

Somebody—it looked to be a tall young man against the fire-glow—came and abruptly closed the door from within, and the picture was gone. The fitful music ceased again; the house was quiet.

Thereupon Richard Kendrick grew impatient. Fully ten minutes must have elapsed since his youthful conductor had disappeared. He looked about him for some means of summoning attention but discovered none.

Suddenly, a latchkey rattled uselessly in the lock of the front door; then came lusty knocks upon its stout panels, accompanied by the whirring of a bell somewhere in the distance.

A maidservant came hurriedly into the hall through a door near Richard, and at the same moment a boy of ten or eleven came tearing down the front stairs. As the lad shouted through the door, Richard recognized his late conductor.

"You can't get in, Daddy; the lock's messed up. Come around to the back. I'll see to him, Mary," the boy called to the maid, who, nodding, disappeared.

At this moment the door opposite Richard opened again, and the mother of the household came out, her comely waist closely clasped by the arm of the young girl. The two were followed by the tall young man.

Richard stood up and was, of course, instantly upon the road to the delivery of his message.

Ted, ushering in his father and spying the waiting messenger, cried repentantly, "Oh, I forgot!" and the tall young man responded gravely, "You usually do, don't you, Cub?" This elder son of the house, waving the small boy aside, attended to taking Richard to the library and to summoning Judge Calvin Gray.

In five minutes, the business had been dispatched, Judge Gray had made friendly inquiry into the condition of his old friend's health, and Richard was ready to take his departure. Curiously enough, he did not now want to go. As he stood for a moment near the open library door while Judge Gray returned to his desk for a newspaper clipping, the caller was listening to the eager greetings taking place in the hall just out of his sight. The father of the family appeared to have returned from an absence of some length, and the entire household had come rushing to meet and welcome him. Richard listened for the contralto notes he had heard above and presently detected them declaring with vivid emphasis: "Mother has been a dear, splendid martyr. Nobody would have guessed she was lonely, but we knew!"

"She couldn't possibly have been more lonely than I. Next time I'll take her with me!" was the emphatic response.

Then the whole group swept by the library door, down the hall, and into the room of the great fireplace. Nobody looked his way, and Richard Kendrick had one swift view of them all. Vigorous young men, graceful young women, a child or two, the mother of them all on the arm of her husband—there were plenty to choose from, but he could not find the one he looked for. Then, quite by itself, another figure flashed past him. He had a glimpse of a dusky mass of hair, of a piquant profile, of a round arm bared to the elbow. As the figure passed the hat tree, he saw the arm reach out and catch the rose-colored scarf, flinging it over one shoulder. Then the whole vision had vanished, and he stood alone in the library doorway with Judge Gray saying behind him: "I cannot find the clipping. I will mail it to your grandfather when I come upon it."

I knew that scarf was hers, Richard was thinking as he went out into the night by way of the rear door, Judge Gray having accompanied him to the threshold and given him a cordial hand of farewell. What a voice! She could make a fortune with it on the stage if she couldn't sing a note. The stage! What had the stage to do with people who lived together in a place like that?

He looked curiously back at the house as he went down the box-bordered path that led, curving, from it to the street. It was obviously one of the old-time mansions of the big city, preserved in the midst of its grounds in a neighborhood now rampant with new growth. It was outside, on this chill October night, as hospitable in appearance as it was inside; there was hardly a window that did not glow with a mellow light. As Richard drove down the street, he was recalling vividly the picture of the friendly looking hall with its faded Turkey carpet worn with the tread of many rushing feet, its atmosphere of welcoming warmth—and the rose-hued scarf flung over the dull masculine belongings as if typifying the fashion in which the women of the household cast their bright influence over the men.

It suddenly occurred to Richard Kendrick that if he had lived in such a home even until he went away to school, if he had come back to such a home from college and from the wanderings over the face of the earth with which he had filled in his idle days since college was over, he should be perhaps a better, surely a different, man than he was now.

Louis Gray, coming into the hall precisely as Richard Kendrick, again enveloped in his muddy motoring coat, was releasing Judge Gray's hand and disappearing into the night, looked curiously after the departing figure. His sister Roberta, following him into the hall a moment after, rose-colored scarf still drifting across white-clad shoulder, was in time to receive his comment:

"Seems rather odd to see that chap departing humbly by any door but the front one."

"You knew him, then. Who was he?" inquired his sister.

"Didn't you? He's a familiar enough figure about town. Why, he's Rich Kendrick. Grandson of Matthew Kendrick, of Kendrick & Company, you know. Only Rich doesn't take much interest in the business. You'll find his doings carefully noticed in certain columns in certain society journals."

"I don't read them, thank you. Do you?"

"Don't need to. Kendrick's a familiar figure wherever the merry and youthful rich disport themselves—when he's in the country at all. He's doing his best to spend with the money his father left him. Fortunately, the bulk of the family fortune is still in the hands of his grandfather, who seems an uncommonly healthy and vigorous old man." Louis laughed. "Can't think what Rich Kendrick can be doing here with Uncle Cal. I believe, though, he and old Matthew Kendrick are good friends. Probably grandson Richard came on an errand. It certainly behooves him to do his grandfather's errands with as good a grace as he can muster."

"He was sitting in the hall quite a while before Uncle Cal saw him," volunteered Ted, who had tagged at Roberta's heels and was listening with interest.

"Sitting in the hall, eh? Like any district messenger?" Louis was clearly delighted with this news. "How did it happen, Cub? Mary take him for an everyday, common person?"

"I let him in. I thought he was a chauffeur," admitted Ted. "He was awfully wet and muddy. Steve took him in to Uncle Cal."

An explosion of laughter from his interested elder brother interrupted him. "I wish I'd come along and seen him. So he had the bad manners to sit in our hall in a wet and muddy motoring coat and go in to see Uncle Cal—"

"The young man had on no muddy coat when Stephen brought him in to see me," declared Judge Calvin Gray, coming out and catching the last sentence. "He put it on in the hall before going out. What are you saying? That was the grandson of my good friend Matthew Kendrick and so had claim upon my goodwill from the start, though I haven't laid eyes upon the boy since his school days. He was rather a restless and obstreperous youngster then, I'll admit. What he is now seems pleasing enough to the eye, certainly, though of course that may not be sufficient. A fine, mannerly young fellow he appeared to me, and I was glad to see that he seemed willing enough to run upon his grandfather's errands, though they took him out upon a raw night like this."

But Louis Gray, though he did not pursue the subject further, was still smiling to himself as he obeyed a summons to dinner.

At opposite ends of the long table sat Mr. and Mrs. Robert Gray. The head of the house looked his part: fine of face, crisp of speech, authoritative yet kindly of manner. His wife may be described best by saying that one had but to look upon her to know that here sat the queen of the little realm, the one whose gentle rule covered them all as with the brooding wing of wise motherhood. Down the sides of the board sat the three sons: Stephen, tall and slender, grave-faced, quiet but observant; Louis, of a somewhat lesser height but broad of shoulder and deep of chest, his bright face alert, every motion suggesting vigor of body and mind; Ted—Edgar—the youngest, a slim, long-limbed lad with eyes eager as a collie's for all that might concern him—this was the tale of the sons of the house. There were the two daughters: Roberta, she of the rose-colored scarf—it was still about her shoulders, seeming to draw all the light in the room to its vivid hue, reflecting itself in her cheeks—Roberta, the elder daughter, dusky of hair, adorable of face, her round, white throat that of a strong and healthy girl, her laugh a song to listen to; the other daughter, Ruth, a fair-haired, sober-eyed creature of sixteen, as different as if of other blood. One would not have said the two were sisters. There was one more girl at the table; no, not a girl, yet she looked younger than Roberta—a little person with a wild-rose, charming face and the sweetest smile of them all—Rosamund, Stephen's wife, quite incredibly mother of two children of nursery age, at this moment already properly asleep upstairs.

Last but far from least, loved and honored of them all, above the lot of average man to command such tribute, was the elder brother of the master of the house, his handsome white head and genial face drawing toward him all eyes whenever he might choose to speak—Judge Calvin Gray. All in all, they were a goodly family, just such a family as is to be found beneath many a fortunate roof; yet a family with an individuality all its own and a richness of life such as is less common than it ought to be.

Chapter 2

RICHARD CHANGES
HIS PLANS

The next time Richard Kendrick went to the Gray home was a fortnight later, when old Matthew Kendrick was sending some material for which Judge Gray had written to ask him—books and pamphlets and a set of maps. This time he would have sent a servant, but his grandson Richard heard him giving directions and came into the affair with a careless suggestion that he was driving that way and might as well take the stuff if Mr. Kendrick wished it. The old man glanced curiously at him across the table where the two sat at luncheon.

"Glad to have you, of course," he commented, "but you made so many objections when I asked you before, I thought I wouldn't interfere with your time again. Did you meet any of the family when you went?"

"Only Judge Gray and two of his nephews," responded Richard truthfully enough.

So he went with the big package. This time, it being a fine, sunny, summerlike day almost as warm as September, he went clad in careful dress with only a light motoring coat on to preserve the integrity of his attire. He left this in the car when he leaped out of it, and he appeared upon the doorstep looking not at all like his own chauffeur, but quite his comely self.

The door lock was in full working order now, and he was admitted by the same little maid whom he remembered seeing before. Upon his inquiry for Judge Gray he was told that that gentleman was receiving another caller and had asked to be undisturbed for a short time, but if he could wait . . .

Now, there was no reason in the world for his waiting, since the

9

package of books, pamphlets, and maps was under his arm and he had only to bestow it upon the maid and give her the accompanying directions. But at this precise moment, Richard caught sight of a figure running down the staircase; concluded in one glance, as he had concluded in one glance before, that if a personality could be expressed by a speaking voice, a laugh, and a rose-hued scarf, this must be the one they expressed; and decided in the twinkling of an eye to wait. The maid conducted him toward the room on the right of the hall, and he followed her, passing as he did so the person who had reached the foot of the stairs and who went by him in such haste that he had only time to give her one short but—it must be described as—concentrated look straight in the eyes. She in turn bestowed upon him the one glance necessary to inform her whether she knew him and so must stay long enough in her rapid progress to greet him. Their eyes therefore met at rather close range, lingered for the space of two running seconds, and parted.

Richard Kendrick accepted the chair offered him and sat upon it for the space of some eighteen-odd minutes; they might have been hours or seconds, he could not have told which. He could hardly have described the room to which he had been shown, unless to say that it was a square, old-fashioned reception room, a little formal, decidedly quaint and dignified, and clearly not used by the family as other rooms were used. Certainly, the piano, from which he had heard the Schumann music on his former visit, was not here, and certainly there were no rose-hued scarves flung carelessly about. It was undoubtedly a place kept for the use of strange callers like himself and had small part in the life of the household.

At length he was summoned to Judge Gray's library. He was met with the same pleasant courtesy as before, delivered his parcel, and lingered as long as he might, listening politely to his host's remarks and looking for a chance to make a reason to come again. Quite unexpectedly, it was offered him by the judge himself.

"I wonder if you could recommend to me," said Judge Gray as Richard was about to take his leave, "a capable young man—college-bred, of course—to come here daily or weekly as I might need him, to assist me in the work of preparing my book. My eyes, as you see, will not allow me to use them for much more than the reading of a paragraph, and while my family are very ready to help whenever they have the time, mine is so serious a task, likely to continue for so long a period, that I shall need continuous and prolonged assistance. Do you happen to know . . . ?"

Well, it can hardly be explained. This was a rich man's heir and the grandson of millions more, in need—according to his own point of view—of no further education along the lines of work, and he had a voyage to the Far East in prospect. Certainly, a fortnight earlier the thing furthest from his thoughts would have been the engaging of himself as amanuensis and general literary assistant to an ex-judge upon so prosaic a task as the history of the Supreme Court of the state. To say that a rose-hued scarf, a laugh, and an alluring speaking voice explain it seems absurd, even when you add to these that which the young man saw during that moment of time when he looked into the face of their owner. Rather would I declare that it was the subtle atmosphere of that which in all his travels he had never really seen before—a home. At all events, a new force of some sort had taken hold upon him and was leading him whither he had never thought to go.

If Judge Gray was surprised that the grandson of his old friend Matthew Kendrick should thus offer himself for the obscure and comparatively unremunerative post of secretary, he gave no evidence of it. Possibly, it did not seem strange to him that this young man should show interest in the work the judge himself had laid out with an absorbing enthusiasm. Therefore, a trial arrangement was soon made, and Richard Kendrick agreed to present himself in Judge Gray's library on the following morning at ten o'clock. The only stipulation he made was that if for any reason he should decide suddenly to go upon a journey he had had some time in contemplation, he should be allowed to provide a substitute. He had not yet so completely surrendered to his impulse that he was not careful to leave himself a loophole of escape.

The young man laughed to himself all the way down the avenue. What would his grandfather say? What would his friends say? His friends should not know—confound them!—it was none of their business. He would have his evenings; he would appear at his clubs as usual. If comments were made upon his absence at other hours, he would quietly inform the observing ones that he had gone to work but would refuse to say where. It certainly was a joke, his going to work; not that his grandfather had not often and strenuously recommended it, saying that the boy would never know happiness until he shook hands with labor; not that he himself had not fully intended someday to go into the training necessary to the assuming of the cares incident to the handling of a great fortune. But thus far—well, he had never been ready to begin. One journey more, one more long voyage . . .

Her eyes—had they been blue or black? Blue, he was quite sure, although the masses of her hair had been like night for dusky splendor,

and her cheeks of that rich bloom which denotes young vigor and radiant health. He could hear her voice now, quoting a serious poet to fit a
madcap mood—and quoting him in such a voice! What were the words?
He remembered her mockingly exaggerated inflection:

> O, it is *excellent*
> To have a giant's strength; but it is *tyrannous*
> To use it like a giant!

Well, from his flash-fire observation of her, he should say that a man
might need a giant's strength to overcome her if she chose to oppose him
in any situation whatever. What a glorious task—to overcome her—to
teach that lovely, teasing voice gentler words . . .

He laughed again. Since he had left college, he had not been so interested in what was coming next, not even on the day he met Amelie
Penstoff in St. Petersburg. Nor on the day, in Japan, when his friend
Rogers made an appointment with him to meet that . . . girl, half-
Japanese, half-French . . . —he could not even recall her name at this
moment. . . . And now, here was a girl—a very different sort of girl—
who interested him more than any of them. He wondered what her
name was. Whatever it was, he would know it soon, call her by it soon.

He went home. He did not tell his grandfather that night. There was
not much use in putting it off, but somehow he preferred to wait till
morning. Business sounds more like business in the morning.

The first result of his telling his grandfather in the morning was a note
from old Matthew Kendrick to old Judge Gray. The note, which almost
chuckled aloud, was as follows:

> MY DEAR CALVIN GRAY:
>
> Work him—work the rascal hard! He's a lazy chap
> with a way with him that plays the deuce with my fool-
> ish old heart. I could make my own son work, and did;
> but this son of his—that seems to be another matter.
> Yet I know well enough the dangers of idleness—know
> them so well that I'm tickled to death at the mere
> thought of his putting in his time at any useful task. He
> did well enough in college; there are brains there
> unquestionably. I didn't object seriously to his traveling
> for a time after his graduation; but that sort of life has
> gone on long enough, and when I talk to him of
> settling down at some steady job, it's always "after one
> more voyage." I don't yet understand what has given

him the impulse (whim, caprice—I don't venture to give it any stronger name) to accept this literary task from you. He vows he's not met the women of your household, or I should think that might explain it. I hope he will meet them, all of them; they'll be good for him — and so will you, Cal. Do your best by the boy for my sake, and believe me, now as always,

Gratefully your old friend,
MATTHEW

"Eleanor, have you five minutes to spare for me?" Judge Gray, his old friend's note in hand, hailed his brother's wife as she passed the open door of his library. She came in at once, and though she was in the midst of household affairs, sat down with that delightful air of having all the time in the world to spare for one who needed her, which was one of her endearing characteristics.

When she had heard the note, she nodded her head thoughtfully. "I think the grandfather may well congratulate himself that the grandson has fallen into your hands, Calvin," said she. "The work you give him may not be to him the interesting task it would be to some men, but it will undoubtedly do him good to be harnessed to any labor that means a bit of drudgery. By all means do as Mr. Kendrick bids you: 'Work him hard.' " She smiled. "I wonder what the boy would think of Louis's work."

"He would take to his heels probably, if it were offered him. It's plain that Matthew's pleased enough at having him tackle a gentleman's task like this and hopes to make it a stepping-stone to something more muscular. I shall do my best by Richard, as he asks. You note that he wants the young man to meet us all. Are you willing to invite him to dinner sometime—perhaps next week—as a special favor to me?"

"Certainly, Calvin, if you consider young Mr. Kendrick in every way fit to know our young people."

Her fine eyes met his penetratingly, and he smiled in his turn. "That's like you, Eleanor," said he, "to think first of the boy's character and last of his wealth."

"A fig for his wealth!" she retorted with spirit. "I have two daughters."

"I have made inquiries," said he with dignity, "of Louis, who knows young Kendrick as one young man knows another, which is to the full. He considers him to be more or less of an idler and as much of a spendthrift as a fellow in possession of a large income is likely to be in spite of the cautions of a prudent grandfather. He has a passion for travel and is correspondingly restless at home. But Louis thinks him to be a young man of sufficiently worthy tastes and standards to have escaped the worst contaminations, and he says he has never heard anything to his discredit. That is considerable to say of a young man in his position, Eleanor, and I hope it may constitute enough of a passport to your favor to permit of your at least inviting him to dinner. Besides, let me remind you, your daughters have standards of their own that you have given them. Ruth is a girl yet, of course, but a mighty discerning one for sixteen. As for Roberta, I'll wager no young millionaire is any more likely to get past her defenses than any young mechanic—unless he proves himself fit."

"I am confident of that," she agreed, and with her charming gray head held high, she went on about her household affairs.

Chapter 3

WHILE IT RAINS

The advanced age of the Honorable Calvin Gray, and the precarious state of his eyesight, made it possible for him to work at his beloved self-appointed task for only a scant number of hours daily. His new assistant, therefore, found his own working hours not only limited but variable. Beginning at ten in the morning, by four in the afternoon Judge Gray was usually too weary to proceed further; sometimes by the luncheon hour he was ready to lay aside his papers and dismiss his assistant. On other days, he would waken with a severe headache, the result of the overstrain he was constantly tempted to give his eyes, in spite of all the aid that was offered him. On such days Richard could not always find enough to do to occupy his time and would be obliged to leave the house so early that many hours were on his hands. When this happened, he would take the opportunity to drop in at one or two of his clubs and so convey the impression that only caprice kept him away on other days. Curiously enough, this still seemed to him an object; he might have found it difficult to explain just why, for he assuredly was not ashamed of his new occupation.

Rather unexplainably to Richard, nearly the first fortnight of his new experience went by without his meeting any members of the family except the heads thereof and the younger son, Edgar, familiarly called by everyone "Ted". With this youthful scion of the house, he was destined to form the first real acquaintance. It came about upon a particularly rainy November day. Richard had found Judge Gray suffering from one of his frequent headaches, as a result of the overwork he had not been able wholly to avoid. Therefore, a long day's work of research in various ancient volumes had been turned over to his assistant by an employer who left him to return to a seclusion he should not have forsaken.

Richard was accustomed to run down to an excellent hotel for his luncheon and was preparing to leave the house for this purpose when Ted leaped at him from the stairs, tumbling down them in great haste.

"Mr. Kendrick, won't you stay and have lunch with me? It's pouring 'great horn spoons,' and I'm all alone."

"Alone, Ted? Nobody here at all?"

"Not a soul. Uncle Cal's going to have his upstairs, and he says I may ask you. Please stay. I don't go to school in the afternoon, and maybe I can help you, if you'll show me how."

Richard smiled at the notion but accepted the eager invitation, and presently he found himself sitting alone with the lad at a big, old-fashioned mahogany table, being served with a particularly tempting meal.

"You see," Ted explained, spooning out grapefruit with an energetic hand, "Father and Mother and Steve and Rosy have gone to the country to a funeral—a cousin of ours. Louis and Rob aren't home till night except Saturdays and Sundays, and Ruth is at school till Friday nights. It makes it sort of lonesome for me. Wednesdays, though, every other week, Rob's home all day. When she's here, I don't mind who else is away."

"I was just going to ask if you had three brothers," observed Richard. "Do I understand 'Rob' is a girl?"

"Sure, Rob's a girl all right, and I'm mighty glad of it. I wouldn't be a girl myself, not much; but I wouldn't have Rob anything else—I should say not. Name's Roberta, you know, after Father. She's a peach of a sister, I tell you. Ruth's all right, too, of course, but she's different. She's a girl all through. But Rob's half-boy, or—I should say there's just enough boy about her to make her exactly right, if you know what I mean."

He looked inquiringly at Richard, who nodded gravely. "I think I get something of your idea," he agreed. "It makes a fine combination, does it?"

"I should say it did. You know a girl that's all girl is too much girl. But one that likes some of the things boys like—well, it helps out a lot. Through with the grapefruit, Mary," he added over his shoulder to the maid. "Have you any brothers or sisters, Mr. Kendrick?" he inquired interestedly when he had assured himself that the clam broth with which he was now served was unquestionably good to eat.

"Not one—living. I had a brother, but he died when I was a little chap."

"That was too bad," said Ted with ready sympathy. He looked straight across the table at Richard out of sea-blue eyes shaded by very heavy black lashes, which, it struck Richard quite suddenly, were much like another pair that he had had one very limited opportunity of observing. The boy also possessed a heavy thatch of coal-black hair, a lock of which was continually falling over his forehead and having to be thrust back. "Because Father says," Ted went on, "it's a whole lot better for children to be brought up together, so they will learn to be polite to each other. I'm the youngest, so I'm most like an only child. But, you see," he added hurriedly, "the older ones weren't allowed to give up to me, and I had to be polite to them, so perhaps"—he looked so in earnest about it that Richard could not possibly laugh at him—"I won't turn out as badly as some youngest ones do."

There was really nothing priggish about this statement, however it might sound. And the next minute the boy had turned to a subject less suggestive of parental counsels. He launched into an account of his elder brother Louis's prowess on the football fields of past years, where, it seemed, that young man had been a remarkable right tackle. He gave rather a vivid account of a game he had witnessed last year, talking, as Richard recognized, less because he was eager to talk than from a sense of responsibility as to the entertainment of his guest.

"But he won't play anymore," he added mournfully. "He took his degree last year and he's in Father's office now, learning everything from the beginning. He's just a common clerk, but he won't be long," he asserted confidently.

"No, not long," agreed Richard. "The son of the chief won't be a common clerk long, of course."

"I mean," explained Ted, buttering a hot roll with hurried fingers, "he'll work his way up. He won't be promoted until he earns it; he doesn't want to be."

Richard smiled. The boy's ideals had evidently been given a start by some person or persons of high moral character. He was considering the subject in some further detail with the lad when the dining room door suddenly opened and the owner of the black-lashed blue eyes, which in a way matched Ted's, came most unexpectedly in upon them. She was in a street dress of dark blue, and her eyes looked out at them from under the wide gray brim of a sombrero-shaped hat with a long quill in it, the whole effect of which was to give her the breezy look of having literally blown in on the November wind that was shaking the trees outside. Her cheeks had been stung into a brilliant rose color. Two books were tucked under her arm.

"Why, Rob!" cried her younger brother. "What luck! What brought you home?"

Rising from his chair, Richard observed that Ted had risen also, and he now heard Ted's voice presenting him to his sister with the ease of the well-bred youngster.

From this moment Richard owed the boy a debt of gratitude. He had been waiting impatiently for a fortnight for this presentation and had begun to think it would never come.

Roberta Gray came forward to give the guest her hand with a ready courtesy that Richard met with the explanation of his presence.

"I was asked to keep your brother company in the absence of the family. I can't help being glad that you didn't come in time to forestall me."

"I'm sure Ted's hospitality might have covered us both," she said, pulling off her gloves. He recognized the voice. At close range it was even more delightful than he had remembered.

"I doubt it, since he tells me that when you're here, he doesn't mind who else is away."

"Did you say that, Teddy?" she asked, smiling at the boy. "Then you'll surely give me lunch, though it isn't my day at home. I'm so hungry, walking in this wind. But the air is glorious."

She went away to remove her hat and coat and came back quickly, her masses of black hair suggesting but not confirming the impression that the wind had lately had its way with them. Her eyes scanned the table eagerly like those of a hungry boy.

"Some of your scholars sick?" inquired Ted.

"Two—and one away. So I'm to have a whole beautiful afternoon, though I may have to see them Wednesday to make up. I am a teacher in Miss Copeland's private school," she explained to Richard as simply as one of the young women he knew would have explained. "I take singing lessons from Servensky."

This gave the young man food for thought, in which he indulged while Miss Roberta Gray told Ted of an encounter she had had that morning with a special friend of his. This daughter of a distinguished man—of a family not so rich as his own but still of considerable wealth and unquestionably high social position—was a teacher in a school for girls, a most exclusive school, of course—he knew the one very well—but still in a school and for a salary. To Richard, the thing was strange enough. She must surely do it from choice, not from necessity; but why from choice? With her face and her charm—he felt the charm already; it radiated from her—why should she want to tie herself down to a dull round of duty like that instead of giving her thoughts to the things girls of her position usually cared for? Taking into consideration the statement Ted had lately made about his elder brother, it struck Richard Kendrick that this must be a family of rather eccentric notions. Somewhat to his surprise, he discovered that the idea interested him. He had found people of his own acquaintance tiresomely alike; he congratulated himself on having met somebody who seemed likely to prove different.

"So you rejoice in your half-holiday, Miss Gray," Richard observed when he had the chance. "I suppose you know exactly what you are going to do with it?"

"Why do you think I do?" she asked with an odd little twist of the lip. "Do you always plan even unexpected holidays so carefully?"

It occurred to Richard that up to the last fortnight his days since he left college had been all holidays, and there had been plenty of them throughout college life itself. But he answered seriously: "I don't believe I do. But I had the idea that teachers were so in the habit of living on schedules scientifically made out that even their holidays were conscientiously lived up to, with the purpose of getting the full value out of them."

Even as he said it he could have laughed aloud at the thought of these straitlaced principles being applicable to the young person who sat at the table with himself and Ted. She a teacher? Never! He had known no women teachers since his first governess had been exchanged for a tutor, the sturdy youngster having rebelled, at an extraordinarily early age, against petticoat government. His acquaintance included but one woman of that profession, and she was a college president. He and she had not got on well together, either, during the brief period in which they had been thrown together on an ocean voyage. But he had seen plenty of teachers, crossing the Atlantic in large parties, surveying cathedrals, taking coach drives, inspecting art galleries—all with that conscientious air of making the most of it. Miss Roberta Gray one of that serious company? It was incredible!

"Dear me," laughed Roberta, "what a keen observer you are! I am almost afraid to admit that I have no conscientiously thought-out plan— but one. I am going to put myself in Ted's hands and let him personally conduct my afternoon."

Blue eyes met blue eyes at that and flashed happy fire. Lucky Ted!

"Oh, jolly!" exclaimed that delighted youth. "Will you play basketball in the attic?"

"Of course I will. Just the thing for a rainy day."

"Bowls?"

"Yes, indeed."

"Take a cross-country tramp?" His eyes were sparkling.

Roberta glanced out of the window. The rain was dashing hard against the pane. "If you won't go through the West Wood marshes," she stipulated.

"Sure I won't. They'd be pretty wet even for me on a day like this. Is there anything you'd specially like to do yourself?" he bethought himself at this stage to inquire.

Roberta shrugged her shoulders. "Of course it seems tame to propose settling down by the living room fire and popping corn after we get back and have got into our dry clothes," said she, "but . . . "

Ted grinned. "That's the stuff," he acknowledged. "I knew you'd think of the right thing to end up the lark with." He looked across at Richard with a proud and happy face. "Didn't I tell you she was a peach of a sister?" he challenged his guest.

Richard nodded. "You certainly did," he said. "And I see no occasion to question the statement."

His eyes met Roberta's. Never in his life had the thought of a cross-country walk in the rain so appealed to him. At the moment he would have given up his eagerly planned trip to the Far East for the chance to march by her side today, even should the course lie through the marshes of West Wood, unquestionably the wettest place in the country on that particular wet afternoon. But nobody would think of inviting him to go—of course not. And while Roberta and Ted were dashing along country lanes—he could imagine how her cheeks would look, stung with rain, drops clinging to those bewildering lashes of hers—he himself would be looking up references in dry and dusty State Supreme Court records and making notes with a fountain pen. A fountain pen—symbol of the student. What abominable luck!

Roberta was laughing as his eyes met hers. The merry curve of her lips recalled to him one of the things Ted had said about her concerning a certain boyish quality in her makeup, and he was strongly tempted to tell her of it. But he resisted.

"I can see you two are great chums," said he. "I envy you both your afternoon, clear through to the corn-popping."

"If you are still at work when we reach that stage, we will . . . send you in some of it," she promised and laughed again at the way his face fell.

"I thought perhaps you were going to invite me in to help pop," he suggested boldly.

"I understand you are engaged in the serious labor of collecting material for a book on a most serious subject," she replied. "We shouldn't dare to divert your mind; and besides I am told that Uncle Calvin intends to introduce you formally to the family by inviting you to dinner some evening next week. Do you think you ought to steal in by coming to a corn-popping beforehand? You see now I can quite truthfully say to Uncle Calvin that I don't yet know you, but after I had popped corn with you . . . "

She paused, and he eagerly filled out the sentence: "You would know me? I hope you would! Because, to tell the honest truth, literary research is a bit new and difficult to me as yet, and any diversion . . . "

But she would not ask him to the corn-popping. And he was obliged to finish his luncheon in short order because Roberta and Ted, plainly anxious to begin the afternoon's program, made such short work of it themselves. They bade him farewell at the door of the dining room like a pair of lads who could hardly wait to be ceremonious in their eagerness to be off, and the last he saw of them they were running up the staircase hand in hand like the comrades they were.

During his intensely stupid researches, Richard Kendrick could hear faintly in the distance the thud of the basketball and the rumble of the bowls. But within the hour these tantalizing sounds ceased, and in the midst of the fiercest dash of rain against the library windowpanes that had yet occurred that day, he suddenly heard the bang of the back hall entrance door. He jumped to his feet and ran to reconnoiter, for the library looked out through big French windows upon the lawn behind the house, and he knew that the pair of holidaymakers would pass.

There they were! What could the rain matter to them? Clad in high hunting boots and gleaming yellow oilskin coats, and with hunters' caps on their heads, they defied the weather. Anything prettier than Roberta's face under that cap, with the rich yellow beneath her chin, her face alight with laughter and good fellowship, Richard vowed to himself he had never seen. He wanted to wave a farewell to them, but they did not look up at his window, and he would not knock upon the pane like a sick schoolboy shut up in the nursery enviously watching his playmates go forth to valiant games.

When they had disappeared at a fast walk down the graveled path to the gate at the back of the grounds, taking by this route a straight course toward the open country, which lay in that direction not more than a mile away, the grandson of old Matthew Kendrick went reluctantly back to his work. He hated it, yet he was tremendously glad he had taken the job. If only there might be many oases in the dull desert such as this had been!

"How do you like him, Rob?" inquired the young brother, splashing along at his sister's side down the country road.

"Like whom?" Roberta answered absently, clearing her eyes of raindrops by the application of a moist handkerchief.

"Mr. Kendrick."

"I think Uncle Cal might have looked a long way and not picked out a less suitable secretary," said she with spirit.

"Is that what he is? What is a secretary anyway?" demanded Ted.

"Several things Mr. Kendrick is not."

"Oh, I say, Rob! I can't understand . . . "

"It is a person who has learned how to be eyes, ears, hands, and brain for another," defined Roberta.

"Gee! Hasn't Uncle Cal got all those things himself—except eyes?"

"Yes, but anybody who serves him needs them all, too. I don't believe Mr. Kendrick ever helped anybody before in his life."

"Maybe he has. He's got loads of money, Louis says."

"Oh, money! Anybody can give away money."

"They don't all, I guess," declared Ted with boyish shrewdness. "Say, Rob, why wouldn't you ask him to the corn-pop frolic?"

Roberta looked around at him. Drenched violets would have been dull and colorless beside the living tint of her eyes, the raindrops clinging to her lashes. "Because he was too busy," she replied and looked away again.

"I didn't think he seemed so very much in a hurry to get back to the library," observed Ted. "When I went down to the kitchen after the corn, I looked in the door and he was sitting at the desk looking out of the window. But then I look out of the window myself at school," he admitted.

"Ted, shall we take this path or the other?" asked his sister, halting where three trails across the meadow diverged.

"This one will be the wettest," said he promptly. "But I like it best."

"Then we'll take it." And she plunged ahead.

"I say, Rob, but you're a true sport!" acknowledged her young brother with admiration. "Any other girl I know would have wanted the dry path."

"Dry?" Roberta showed him a laughing profile over her shoulder. "Where all paths are soaking, why be fastidious? The wetter we are the more credit for keeping jolly, as Mark Tapley[1] would say. Lead on, MacDuff!"

---

[1] A character in Charles Dicken's Martin Chuzzlewit known for remaining "jolly" no matter what happened to him.

"You seem to be leading yourself," shouted Ted as she unexpectedly broke into a run.

"It's only seeming, Ted," she called back. "Whenever a woman seems to be leading, you may take my word for it she's only following the course pointed out by some man. But when she seems to be following, look out for her!"

But of this oracular statement Ted could make nothing and wisely did not try. He was quite content to splash along in Rob's wake, thinking complacently how hot and buttery the popped corn would be an hour hence.

Chapter 4

PICTURES

Richard Kendrick had been a guest at a good many dinners in the course of his experience, dinners of all sorts and of varying degrees of formality. Club dinners, college class dinners, stag dinners at imposing hotels and cafés, impromptu dinners hurriedly arranged by three or four fellows in for a good time, dinners at which women were present, more at which they were not—these were everyday affairs with him. But, strange to say, the one sort of dinner with which he was not familiar was that of the family type: the quiet gathering in the home of the members of the household, plus one or two fortunate guests. He had never sat at such a table under his own roof, and when he was entertained in the homes of his friends, the occasion was invariably made one for summoning many other guests and for elaborate feasting and diversion of all kinds.

It will be seen, therefore, that Richard looked forward to a totally new experience without in the least realizing that he did so. His principal thought concerning the invitation to the Grays' was that he should at last have the chance to meet again the niece of his employer, in a way that would show him considerably more of her as a woman than he had been able to observe on the occasion when they had so hurriedly finished a luncheon together and she had escaped from him as fast as possible in order to set forth on a madcap adventure with her small brother.

On the day of which he expected to spend the evening with the Grays, he found it not a little difficult to keep his mind upon his work with the judge, and that gentleman seemed to him extraordinarily particular, even fussy, about having every fact brought to him painstakingly verified down to the smallest detail. When at last he was released, and he rushed home in his car to dress, he discovered that his spirits were dancing as he could not remember having felt them dance for a year. And all over a simple invitation to a family dinner!

As he dressed, it might have been said of him that he also could be particular, even fussy. When, at length, he was ready, he was as carefully attired as ever he had been in his life—and this not only in body but in mind. It was curious, to his own observation of himself, how differently he felt, in what different mood he was, than had ever been the case when he had left his room for the scene of some accustomed pleasure-making. He just could not define this difference to himself, though he was conscious of it; but there was in it a sense of wishing the people he was to meet to think well of him, according to their own standards, and he was somehow rather acutely aware that their standards were not likely to be those with which he was most intimate.

When he entered the now familiar door of the Gray homestead, he was surprised to hear sounds that seemed to indicate that the affair was, after all, much larger and more formal than he had been led to suppose. Strains of music fell upon his ears—music from a number of stringed instruments remarkably well played—and this continued as he made his entrance into the long drawing room at the left of the hall, of whose interior he had as yet caught only tempting glimpses.

As he greeted his hosts, Mr. and Mrs. Robert Gray, Judge Calvin Gray, Mr. and Mrs. Stephen Gray, wondering a little where the rest of the family could be, his eye fell upon the musicians, and the problem was solved. Ruth, the sixteen-year-old, sat before a harp; Louis, the elder son, cherished a violin under his chin; Roberta—ah, there she was! wearing a dull-blue evening frock above which gleamed her white neck, her half-uncovered arms showing exquisite curves as she handled the bow that was drawing long, rich notes from the cello at her knee.

Not one of the trio looked up until the nocturne they were playing was done. Then they rose together, laying aside their instruments, and made the guest welcome. He had a vivid impression of being done peculiar honor by their recognition of him as a new friend, for so they received him. As he looked from one to another of their faces he experienced another of those curious sensations that had from time to time assailed him ever since he had first put his head inside the door of this house, the sensation of looking in upon a new world of which he had known nothing and of being strangely drawn by all he saw there. It was not alone the effect of meeting a more than ordinarily alluring girl, for each member of the family had for him something of this drawing quality. As he studied them, it was clear to him that they belonged together, that they loved each other, that the very walls of this old home were eloquent of the life lived here.

He had of course seen and noted families before, noted them carelessly enough: rich families, poor families, big families, and little, newly begun families. But of a certain sort of family—the interesting and inviting type—he knew as little as the foreigner newly landed on American shores knows of the depths of the great country's interior. And as he studied these people, the desire grew and grew within him to know as much of them as they would let him know. The very grouping of them against the effective background of the fine old drawing room made, it seemed to him, a remarkable picture, full of a certain richness of color and harmony such as he had never observed anywhere.

The evening did not contain as much of lively encounter with Roberta as he had anticipated, but—somehow, as he afterward looked back upon it, he could not feel that there had been any lack. He had fancied himself, in prospect, sitting beside her at the table, exchanging that pleasant, half-foolish badinage with which young men are wont to entertain girls who are their companions at dinners, both nearly oblivious of the rest of the company. But it turned out that his seat was between his hostess and her younger daughter, Ruth, and though Roberta was nearly opposite him at the table and he could look at her to his full content—conservatively speaking—he was obliged to give himself to playing the part of the deferential younger man where older and more distinguished men are present.

Yet—to his surprise, it must be admitted—he found himself not bored by that table talk. It was such table talk, by the way, as is not to be had under ordinary roofs. He now recognized that he had only partially appreciated the qualities of mind possessed by Judge Gray,— certainly not his capacity for brilliant conversation. Mr. Robert Gray was quite his elder brother's match, however, and more than once Kendrick caught Louis Gray's eye meeting his own with the glance that means delighted pride in the contest of wits that is taking place. All three young men enjoyed it to the full, and even Ted listened with eyes full of eager desire to comprehend that which he understood to be worth trying hard for.

"They enjoy these encounters keenly," said Mrs. Gray, beside Richard, as a telling story by Mr. Robert Gray, in illustration of a point he had made, came to a conclusion amid a burst of appreciative laughter. "They relish them quite as much, we think, as if they often succeeded in convincing each other, which they seldom do."

"Are they always in such form?" asked Richard, looking into the fresh, attractive face of the lady who was the mistress of this home and continuing to watch her with eyes as deferential as they were admiring. She, too, represented a type of woman and mother with which he was unfamiliar. Grace and charm in women who presided at dinner tables he had often met, but he could not remember when before he had sat at the right hand of a woman who had made him begin, for almost the first time in his life, to wonder what his own mother had been like.

"Nearly always at night, I think," said she, her eyes resting upon her husband's face. Richard, observing, saw her smile and guessed without looking that there had been an exchange of glances. He knew because he had twice before noted the exchange, as if there existed a peculiarly strong sympathy between husband and wife. This inference, too, possessed a curious new interest for the young man—he had not been accustomed to see anything of that sort between married people of long-standing—not in the world he knew so well. He seemed to be learning strange new possibilities of existence at every step, since he had discovered the Grays—he who at twenty-eight had not thought there was very much left in human experience to be discovered.

"Is it different in the morning?" Richard inquired.

"Quite different. They are rather apt to take things more seriously in the morning. The day's work is just before them and they are inclined to discuss grave questions and dispose of them. But at night, when the lights are burning and everyone comes home with a sense of duty done, it is natural to throw off the weights and be merry over the same matters that perhaps it seemed must be argued over in the morning. We all look forward to the dinner table."

"I should think you might," agreed Richard, looking about him once more at the faces that surrounded him. He caught Roberta's eye as he did so—much to his satisfaction—and she gave him a straightforward, steady look, as if she were taking his measure for the first time. Then, quite suddenly, she smiled at him and turned away to speak to Ted, who sat by her side.

Richard continued to watch and saw that immediately Ted looked his way and also smiled. He wanted so much to know what this meant that, as soon as dinner was over and they were all leaving the room, he fell in with the boy and, putting his hand through Ted's arm, whispered with artful intent: "Was my tie under my left ear?"

Ted stared up at him. "Your tie's all right, Mr. Kendrick."

"Then it wasn't that. Perhaps my coat collar was turned up?"

"Why, no," the boy laughed. "You look as right as anything. What made you think . . . "

"I saw you and your sister laughing at me and it worried me. I thought I must be looking the guy[1] some way."

---

[1] A grotesquely dressed person.

Ted considered. "Oh, no!" he said. "She asked me if I thought you were enjoying the dinner as well as you would have liked the corn-popping."

"And what did you decide?"

"I said I couldn't tell, because I never saw you at a corn-popping. I asked her that day we went to walk why she wouldn't ask you to it, but she just said you were too busy to come. I didn't think you acted too busy to come," he said naïvely, glancing up into Richard's down-bent face.

"Didn't I? Haven't I looked very busy whenever you have seen me in your uncle's library?"

Ted shook his head. "I don't think you have—not the way Louis looks busy in Father's office, nor the way Father does."

Richard laughed, but somehow the frank comment stung him a little, as he would not have imagined the comment of an eleven-year-old boy could have done. "See here, Ted," he urged, "tell me why you say that. I think myself I've done a lot of work since I've been here, and I can't see why I haven't looked it."

But Ted shook his head. "I don't think it would be polite to tell you," he said, which naturally did not help matters much.

Still holding the lad's arm, Richard walked over to Roberta, who had gone to the piano and was arranging some sheets of music there.

"Miss Gray," he said, "have you accomplished a great deal today?"

She looked up, puzzled. "A great deal of what?" she asked.

"Work, endeavor, strenuous endeavor."

"The usual amount. Lessons, and lessons, and one more lesson. I have really more pupils than I can do justice to, but I am promised an assistant if the work grows too heavy," she answered. "Why, please?"

"I've been wondering if the motto of the Gray family might be 'Let us, then, be up and doing.' Ted gives me that notion."

Roberta glanced at Ted, whose face had grown quite grave. "Can you tell him what the motto is, Ted?"

"Of course I can," responded Ted proudly. "It's *Hoc age.*"

Richard hastily summoned his Latin, but the verb bothered him for a minute. " 'This do,' " he presently evolved. "Well, I should say I came pretty near it."

"What's yours?" the boy now inquired.

"My family motto? I believe it is *Crux mihi ancora*; but that doesn't just suit me, so I've adopted one of my own." He looked straight at Roberta. "*Dum vivimus, vivamus.* Isn't that a pleasanter one in this workaday world?"

Ted was struggling hard, but his two months' experience with the rudi-
ments of Latin would not serve him. "What do they mean?" he asked
eagerly.

"The second one means," said Roberta, with her arm about the slim
young shoulders, " 'While we live, let us live—well.' " Her eyes met
Richard's with a shade of defiance in them.

"Thank you," said he. "Do you expect me to adopt the amendment?"

"Why not?"

"Even you take cross-country runs."

She nodded. "And am all the better teacher for them next day."

He laughed. "I should like to take one with you sometime," said he.
He saw Judge Gray coming toward them. "I wonder if I'm likely ever to
have the chance," he added hurriedly.

"*You* take a cross-country run when you could have a sixty-mile spin
in that motorcar of yours instead?"

"I couldn't go cross-country in that. You see I've been by the beaten
track so much, I should like to try exploring something new."

He was eager to say more, but Judge Gray, coming up to them, laid an
affectionate hand on his niece's shoulder.

"She doesn't look the part she plays by day, does she?" he said to
Richard. "Curious how times have changed. In my day a teacher looked
a teacher every minute of her time. One stood in awe of her—or him—
particularly of her. A prim, stuff[2] gown, hair parted in the middle and
drawn smoothly away." His glance wandered from Roberta's ivory neck
to the dusky masses of her hair. "Spectacles, more than likely, with steel
bows. And a manner—ye gods!—the manner! How we were impressed
by it! Well, well! Fine women they were and true to their profession.
These modern girls who look younger than their pupils . . . " He shook
his head with an air of being quite in despair about them.

"Uncle Calvin," said Roberta demurely with her hand upon his arm,
"do tell Mr. Kendrick about your teaching school 'across the river' when
you were only sixteen years old."

And, of course, that settled the chance of Richard's hearing anything
about Roberta's teaching, for though Judge Gray was called out of the room
in the midst of his story, Stephen and Louis came up and joined the group
and switched the talk a thousand miles away from schools and teaching.

Presently, there was music again, and this time Richard found himself
sitting beside young Mrs. Stephen Gray. Between numbers he found

---

2 Woven material or fabric.

questions to ask, which she answered with evident pleasure.

"These three must have been playing together a good many years?"

"Dear me, yes. Ever since they were born, I think. They do make real harmony, don't they?"

"They do—in more ways than one. Is that color scheme intentional, do you think?"

Mrs. Stephen's glance followed his as it dwelt upon the group. "I hadn't noticed," she admitted, "but I see it now; it's perfect. And I've no doubt Ruth thought it out. She's quite a wonderful eye for color, and she worships Rob and likes to dress so as to offset her—always giving Rob the advantage—though of course she would have that, anyway, by virtue of her own coloring."

"Blue and corn color—should you call it?—and gold. Dull tints in the background, and the candlelight on Miss Ruth's hair and her sister's cheek. It makes the prettiest picture yet in my new collection of family groups."

Mrs. Stephen looked at him curiously. "Are you making a collection of family groups?" she inquired. "Beginning way back with your first memories?"

"My first memories are not of family groups, only of nurses and tutors, with occasional portraits of my grandfather making inquiries as to how I was getting on. And my later memories are all of school and college, then of travel. Not a home scene among them."

"You poor boy!" There was something maternal in Mrs. Stephen's tone, though she looked considerably younger than the object of her pity. "But you must have looked at plenty of other family groups, if you had none of your own."

"That's exactly what I haven't done."

"But you've lived in the world," she cried under her breath, puzzled.

A curious expression came into the young man's face. "That's exactly what I have done," he said quietly. "In the world, not in the home. I've not even *seen* homes like this one. The sight of brother and sisters playing violin and harp and cello together, with the father and mother and brother and uncle looking on, is absolutely so new to me that it has a fascination I can't explain. I find myself continually watching you all— if you'll forgive me—in your relations to each other. It's a new interest," he admitted, smiling, "and I can't tell you what it means to me."

She shook her head. "It sounds like a strange tale to me," said she, "but I suppose it must be true. How much you have missed!"

"I'm just beginning to realize it. I never knew it till I began to come here. I thought I was well enough off. It seems I'm pretty poor."

It was rather a strange speech for a young man of his class to make. Possibly it indicated the existence of those "brains" with which his grandfather had credited him.

"Well, Rob, do you think he had as dull a time as you said he would have?"

The inquirer was Ruth. She stood, still in the corn-colored frock, in the doorway of her sister's room, from which her own opened. "Please unhook me," she requested, approaching Roberta and turning her back invitingly.

Roberta, already out of the blue silk gown, released her young sister from the imprisonment of her hooks and eyes.

"His manners are naturally too good to make it clear whether he had a dull time or not," was Roberta's noncommittal reply.

"I don't believe his manners are too good to cover up his being bored, if he was bored," Ruth went on. "He certainly wasn't bored *all* the time, anybody could tell that. He's very good-looking, isn't he?"

"If you care for that sort of good looks, yes."

"What sort?"

"The kind that doesn't express anything except having had a good time every minute of one's life."

"Why, Rob, what's the matter with you? Anybody would think you had something against poor Mr. Kendrick."

"If he were 'poor Mr. Kendrick,' there might be a chance of liking him, for he would have had to *do* something."

Roberta was pulling out hairpins with energy and now let the whole dark mass tumble about her shoulders. The half-curling locks were very thick and soft, and as she shook them away from her face, she reminded Ruth of a certain wild little Arabian pony of her own.

"You throw back your head just like Sheik when he's going to bolt," Ruth cried, laughing. "I wish my hair were like that. It looks perfectly dear whatever you do with it, and mine's only pretty when it's been put just right."

"It certainly was put just right tonight then," said a third voice, and Rosamond, Stephen's wife, appeared in Roberta's half-open door. "May I come in? Steve hasn't come up yet, and I'm so comfortable in this loose thing I want to sit up a while and enjoy it."

Rosamond looked hardly older than Roberta; there were times when she looked younger, being small and fair. Ruth considered her quite as much of a girl as either herself or Roberta and welcomed her eagerly to the discussion in which she herself was so much interested.

"Rosy, did *you* think our guest was bored tonight?" was her first question.

"Bored?" exclaimed Mrs. Stephen in surprise. "Why should he be? He didn't look it whenever I observed him. And if you had seen him when the trio was playing you wouldn't have thought so. By the way, he has an eye for color. He noticed how your frock and Rob's went together in the candlelight, with the harp to give a touch of gold."

"Did he say so?" cried Ruth in delight.

"He asked if the color scheme was intentional. I said I thought it probably was—on your part. Rob never thinks of color schemes."

"Neither does any *man,*" murmured Roberta from the depths of the hair she was brushing with an energetic arm. "Unless it happens to be his business," she amended.

"Rob doesn't like him," declared Ruth, "just because he has money and good looks and doesn't work for his living and likes pretty color schemes. He probably gets that from having seen so much wonderful art in his travels. Aren't painters just as good as bridge-builders? Rob doesn't think so. She wants every man to get his hands grubby."

Roberta turned about, laughing. "This one isn't even a painter. Go to bed, you foolish, analytical child. And don't dream of the beautiful guest who admired your corn-colored frock."

"He only liked it because it set off your blue one," Ruth shot back.

"He said nothing whatever about my lovely new white gown," Rosamond called after her.

Roberta came up to her sister-in-law from behind and put both arms about her. "Stephen came and whispered in my ear tonight," said she, "and wanted to know if I had ever seen Rosy look sweeter. I said I had, an hour before. He asked what you had on, and I said, 'A gray kimono— and the baby on her arm.' He smiled and nodded, and I saw the look in his eyes."

"Rob, you're the dearest sister a girl ever had given to her," Rosamond answered, returning the embrace.

"And yet you two say I don't care for color schemes," Roberta reminded her as she returned to her hair-brushing. "I care enough for them to want them made up of colors that will wash—warranted not to fade—that will stand sun and rain and only grow the more beautiful!"

"What *are* you talking about now, dear?" laughed Rosamond happily, still thinking of what Stephen had said to Roberta.

Chapter 5

RICHARD PRICKS HIS FINGERS

Hoofbeats on the driveway outside the window! Beside the window stood the desk at which Richard was accustomed to work at Judge Gray's dictation. And at the desk on this most alluring of all alluring Indian summer days in middle November sat a young man with every drop of blood in his vigorous body shouting to him to drop his work and rush out, demanding, "Take me with you!"

For there, walking their horses along the driveway from the distant stables, were three figures on horseback. There was one with sunny hair— Ruth, her brown habit the color of the pretty mare she rode; one with russet-gaitered legs astride of the little Arabian pony called Sheik—Ted; one, all in dark, beautifully tailored green, with a soft gray hat pulled over masses of dusky hair, her face—Richard could see her face now as the horses drew nearer, all happy and eager for the ride—Roberta.

Judge Gray, his glance following his companion's, looked out also. He rose and came and stood behind Richard at the window and tapped upon the pane, waving his hand as the riders looked up. Instantly, all three faces lighted with happy recognition and acknowledgment. Ruth waved and nodded. Ted pulled off his cap and swung it. Roberta gave a quick military salute, her gray-gauntleted hand at her hat brim.

Richard smiled with the judge at the charming sight and sighed with the next breath. What a fool he had been to tie himself down to this desk when other people were riding into the country! Yet, if he hadn't been tied to that desk he would neither have known nor cared who rode out from the old Gray stables, or where they went.

The judge caught the slight escaping breath and smiled again as the riders passed out of sight. "It makes you wish for the open country, doesn't it?" said he. "I don't blame you. I should have gone with the young folks myself if I had been ten years younger. It *is* a fine day, isn't it? I've been so absorbed I hadn't observed. Suppose we stop work at three and let ourselves out into God's outdoors? Not a bad idea, eh?"

"Not bad," agreed Richard with a leap of spirits, "if it pleases you, sir. I'm ready to work till the usual time if you prefer."

"Well spoken. But I don't prefer. I shall enjoy a stroll down the avenue myself in this sunshine. What sunshine for November!"

It was barely three when the judge released his assistant, two hours after the riding party had left. As he opened the front door and ran to his waiting car, Richard was wondering how many miles away they were and in what direction they had gone. He wanted nothing so much as to meet them somewhere on the road—better yet, to overtake and come upon them unawares.

A powerful car driven by a determined and quick-witted young man may scour considerable country while three horses, trotting in company, are covering but a few short miles. Richard was sure of one thing: Whichever road appealed to the young Grays as most picturesque and secluded on this wonderful Indian summer afternoon would be their choice. Not the main highways of travel, but some enticing byway. Where would that be? He decided on a certain course with a curious feeling that he could follow wherever Roberta led, by the invisible trail of her radiant personality. He would see! Mile after mile—he took them swiftly, speeding out past the West Wood marshes with assurance of the fact that this was certainly one of the favorite ways.

Twelve miles out he came to a fork in the road. Which trail? One led up a steep hill, the other down into the river valley, soft-veiled in the late sunshine. Which trail? He could seem to see Roberta choosing the hill and putting her horse up it while Ruth called out that the valley road was better. With a sense of exhilaration he sent the car up the hill, remembering that from the top was a broad view sure to be worthwhile on a day like this. Besides, up here he might be able to see far ahead and discern the party somewhere in the distance.

Just over the brow he came upon them where they had camped by the roadside. It was a road quite off the line of travel, and they were a hundred feet back among a clump of pine trees, their horses tied to the fence rail. A bonfire sent up a pungent smoke half-veiling the figures. But the car had come roaring up the hill, and they were all looking his way. Two of the horses had plunged a little at the sudden noise, and Ted ran forward. Richard stopped his engine, triumphant, his pulses quickening with a bound.

"Oh, hullo!" cried Ted in joyful excitement. "Where'd you come from, Mr. Kendrick? Isn't this luck!"

"This is certainly luck," responded Richard, doffing his hat as the figures by the fire moved his way, the one in brown coming quickly, the one in green rather more slowly. "Your uncle released me at three, and I rushed for the open. What a day!"

"Isn't it wonderful?" Ruth came up to the brown mare, which was eyeing the big car with some resentment. She patted the velvet nose as she spoke. "Don't you mind, Bess," she reproached the mare. "It's nothing but a puffing, noisy car. It's not half so nice as you."

She smiled up at Richard, and he smiled back. "I rather think you're right," he admitted. "I used to think myself there was nothing like a good horse. I'd like to exchange the car for one just now; I'm sure of that."

"It wouldn't buy any one of ours." Roberta, coming up, glanced from the big machine to the trio of interested animals, all of which were keeping watchful eyes on the intruder. "Nonsense, Colonel. Stand still!"

"I don't want to buy one of yours; I want one of my own, to ride back with you—if you'd let me."

"Anyhow, you can stop and have a bite with us," said Ted with a sudden thought. "Can't he, Rob?"

Roberta smiled. "If he is as hungry as he looks."

"Do I look hungry?"

"Starving. So do we, no doubt. Come and have some sandwiches."

"We're going to toast them," explained Ruth, walking back to the fire with Richard when he had leaped with alacrity over the fence, his hat left behind, his brown head shining in the sun, his face happier than any of his fellow clubmen had seen it in a year, as they would have been quick to notice if any of them had come upon him now. "We have ginger ale, too. Do you like ginger ale?"

"Immensely!" Richard eyed the preparations with interest. "How do you toast your sandwiches?"

"On forks of wood. Ted's going to cut them."

"Please let me." And the guest fell to work. He found a keen enjoyment in preparing these implements and afterward in the process of toasting, which was done everyone-for-himself, with varying degrees of success. The sandwiches were filled with a rich cheese mixture, and the result of toasting them was a toothsome morsel most gratifying to the hungry palate.

"One more?" urged Ruth, offering Richard the nearly empty box that had contained a good supply.

"Thank you, no. I've had seven," he refused, laughing. "Nothing ever tasted quite so good. And I'm an interloper."

"Here's to the interloper!" Ruth raised her glass and drank the last of her ginger ale. "We always provide for one. Usually, it's a small boy."

"More often a pair of them. And always there are Bess, Colonel, and Sheik." Roberta rose to her feet, the last three sandwiches in hand, and walked away to the horses tied to the fence rail.

Richard's eyes followed her. In the austere lines of her riding habit he could see more clearly than he had yet what a superb young image of health and energy she was.

"Rob adores horses," Ruth remarked, looking after her sister also. "You ought to see her ride cross-country. My Bess can't jump, but her Colonel can. I don't believe there's anything in sight Rob and Colonel couldn't jump. But I can never get used to seeing her; I have to shut my eyes when Colonel rises, and I don't open them till I hear him land. But he's never fallen with her, and she says he never will."

"He won't."

"Why not? Any horse might, you know, if he slipped on wet ground or something."

"He never will with her on his back. He's more likely to jump so high he'll never come down."

Ruth laughed. "Look at Colonel rub his nose against her, now he's had the sandwich. Don't you wish you had a picture of them?"

"Indeed I do!" The tone was fervent. Then a thought struck him, and he jumped to his feet. "By all luck, I believe there's a little camera in the car. If there is, we'll have it."

He ran to the fence, took a flying leap over, and fell to searching. In a moment he produced something that he waved at Ruth. She and Ted went to meet him as he returned. Roberta, busy with the horses, had not seen.

"There are only two exposures left on the film, but they'll do, if she'll be good. Will she mind if I snap her, or must I ask her permission?"

"I think you'd better ask it," counseled Ruth doubtfully. "If it were one of us, she wouldn't mind."

"I see." He set the little instrument rapidly with a skilled touch, then walked toward Roberta and the horses. He aimed it with care, then he called: "You won't mind if I take a picture of the horses, will you?"

Roberta turned quickly, her hand on Colonel's snuggling nose. "Not at all," she answered and took a quick step to one side. But before she had taken it, the sharp-eyed little lens of the camera had caught her, her attitude at the instant one of action, the expression of her face that of vivacious response. She flew out of range and before she could speak the camera clicked again, this time the lens so obviously pointed at the animals and not at herself that the intent of the operator could not be called into question. She looked at him with indignant suspicion, but his glance in return was innocent, though his eyes sparkled.

"They'll make the prettiest kind of a picture, won't they?" he observed, sliding the small black box back into its case. "I wish I had another film[1]; I'd take a lot of pictures about this place. I mean always to be loaded, but November isn't usually the time for photographs, and I'd forgotten all about it."

"If you find you have a picture of me on one of those shots I can trust you not to keep it?"

"I may have caught you on that first shot. I'll bring it to you to see. If your hat is tilted too much or you don't like your own expression . . ."

"I shall not like it, whatever it is. You stole it. That wasn't fair—and when you had just been treated to sandwiches and ginger ale!"

He looked into her brilliant face and could not tell what he saw there. He opened the camera box again and took out the instrument. He removed the roll of film carefully from its position, sealed it, and held it out to her. His manner was the perfection of[2] courtesy.

"There are other pictures on the roll, I suppose?" she said doubtfully, without accepting it.

"Certainly. I forget what they are. But it doesn't matter."

"Of course it matters. Have them developed and give me back my own."

"If I develop them, I shall be obliged to see yours—if you are on it. If I once see it, I may not have the force of character to give it back. Your only safe course is to take it now."

Ted burst into the affair with a derisive shout. "Oh, Rob! What a silly to care about that little bit of a picture! Let him have it. It was only the horses he wanted anyway!"

The two pairs of eyes met. His were full of deference, yet compelling. Hers brimmed with restrained laughter. With a gesture, she waved back the roll and walked away toward the fire.

"Thank you," said he behind her. "I'll try to prove myself worthy of

---

[1] Roll of film.
[2] Ultimate in.

the trust."

"Rufus! Dare you to run down the hill to that big tree with me!" Ted, no longer interested in this tame conclusion of what had promised to be an exciting encounter, challenged his sister. Ruth accepted, and the pair were off down a long, inviting slope none too smooth, with a stiff stubble, but not the less attractive for that.

Richard and Roberta were left standing at the top of the hill near the place where the fire was smoldering into dullness. Before them stretched the valley, brown and yellow and dark green in the November sunlight, with a gray-blue river winding its still length along. In the far distance, a blue-and-purple haze enveloped the hills; above all stretched a sky upon whose fairness wisps of clouds were beginning to show here and there, while in the south the outlines of a rising bank of gray gave warning that those who gazed might look their fill today—tomorrow there would be neither sunlight nor purple haze. The two looked in silence for a minute, not at the boy and girl shouting below, but at the beauty in the peaceful landscape.

"An Indian summer day," said Roberta gravely, as if her mood had changed with the moment, "is like the last look at something one is not sure one shall ever see again."

At the words, Richard's gaze shifted from the hill to the face of the girl beside him. The sunshine was full upon the rich bloom of her cheek, upon the exquisite line of her dark eyebrow. What was the beauty of an Indian summer landscape compared with the beauty of budding summer in that face? But he answered her in the same quiet way in which she had spoken: "Yes, it's hard to have faith that winter can sweep over all this and not blot it out forever. But it won't."

"No, it won't. And after all, I like the storms. I should like to stand just here, someday when Nature was simply raging, and watch. I wish I could build a stout little cabin right on this spot and come up here and spend the worst night of the winter in it. I'd love it."

"I believe you would. But not alone? You'd want company?"

"I don't think I'd even mind being alone if I had a good fire for company. And a dog; I should be glad of a dog," she owned.

"But not one good comrade, one who liked the same sort of thing?"

"So few people really do. It would have to be somebody who wouldn't talk when I wanted to listen to the wind, or wouldn't mind my not talking—and yet who wouldn't mind my talking either, if I took a sudden notion." She began to laugh at her own fancy, with the low, rich note that delighted his ear afresh every time he heard it. "Comrades who are tolerant of one's every mood are not common, are they? Mr. Kendrick, what do you suppose those dots of bright scarlet are, halfway down the hill? They must be rose haws,[3] mustn't they? Nothing else could have that color in November."

"I don't know what 'rose haws' are. Do you want them, whatever they are? I'll go and get them for you."

"I'll go, too, to see if they're worth picking. They're thorny things; you won't like them, but I do."

"You think I don't like thorny things?" he asked her as they went down the hillside, up which Ted and Ruth were now struggling. It was steep, and he held out his hand to her, but she ignored it and went on with sure, light feet.

"No, I think you like them soft and rounded."

"And you prefer them prickly?"

"Prickly enough to be interesting."

They reached the scraggly rosebush, bare except for the bright red haws, their smooth, hard surfaces shining in the sun. Richard got out his knife, and by dint of scratching his hands in a dozen places, succeeded in gathering quite a cluster. Then he went to work at getting rid of the thorns.

"You may like things prickly, but you'll be willing to spare a few of these," he observed.

He succeeded in time in pruning the cluster into subordination, bound them with a tough bit of dried weed that he found at his feet, and held out the bunch. "Will you do me the honor of wearing them?"

She thrust the smooth stems into the breast of her riding coat, where they gave the last picturesque touch to her attire. "Thank you," she acknowledged somewhat tardily. "I can do no less after seeing you scarify yourself in my service. You might have put on your gloves."

"I might—and suffered your scarifying mirth, which would have been much worse. 'He jests at scars that never felt a wound,'[4] but he who jests at them after he has felt them is the hero. Observe that I just jest." He put his lips to a bleeding tear on his wrist as he spoke. "My only regret is that the rose haws were not where they are now when I photographed the horses. Only, mine is not a color camera. I must get one and have it with me when I drive, in case of emergencies like this one."

A whimsical expression touching his lips, he gazed off over the landscape as he spoke, and she glanced at his profile. She was obliged to

---

3 Hawthorn berries (hawthorn is a member of the rose family).

4 From Shakespeare's Romeo and Juliet.

admit to herself that she had seldom noted one of better lines. Curiously enough, to her observation there did not lack a suggestion of ruggedness about his face, in spite of the soft and easy life she understood him to have led.

Ted and Ruth now came panting up to them, and the four climbed together to the hilltop.

Roberta turned and scanned the sun. Immediately, she decreed that it was time to be off, reminding her protesting young brother that the November dusk falls early and that it would be dark before they were at home.

Richard put both sisters into their saddles with the ease of an old horseman. "I've often regretted selling a certain black beauty named Desperado," he remarked as he did so, "but never more than at this minute. My motorcar here strikes me as disgustingly overadequate today. I can't keep you company by any speed adjustment in my control, and if I could, your steeds wouldn't stand it. I'll let you start down before me and stay here for a bit. It's too pleasant a place to leave. And even then I shall be at home before you—worse luck!"

"We're sorry, too," said Ruth, and Ted agreed vociferously. As for Roberta, she let her eyes meet his for a moment in a way so rare with her, whose heavy lashes were forever interfering with any man's direct gaze, that Richard made the most of his opportunity. He saw clearly at last that those eyes were of the deepest sea blue, darkened almost to black by the shadowing lashes. If by some hard chance he should never see them again, he knew he could not forget them.

With beat of impatient hooves upon the hard road the three were off, their chorusing farewells coming back to him over their shoulders. When they were out of sight, he went back to the place on the hilltop where he had stood beside Roberta and thought it all over. In that way only could he make shift to prolong the happiness of the hour.

The happiness of the hour! What had there been about it to make it the happiest hour he could recall? Such a simple outdoor encounter! He had spent many an hour that had lingered in his memory—hours in places made enchanting to the eye by every device of cunning, in the society of women chosen for their beauty, their wit, their power to allure, to fascinate, to intoxicate. He had had his senses appealed to by every form of attraction a clever woman can fabricate, herself a miracle of art in dress, in smile, in speech. He had gone from more than one door with his head swimming, the vivid recollection of the hour just past a drug more potent than the wine that had touched his lips.

His head was not swimming now, thank heaven, though his pulses were unquestionably alive. It was the exhilaration of healthy, powerful attraction, of which his every capacity for judgment approved. He had not been drugged by the enchantment that is like wine; he had been stimulated by the charm that is like the feel of the fresh wind upon the brow. Here was a girl who did not need the background of artificiality, one who could stand the sunlight on her clear cheek and the sunlight on her soul. He knew that, without knowing how he knew. It was written in her sweet, strong, spirited face, and it was there for men to read. No man is so blind but he can read a face like that.

The darkness had almost fallen when he forced himself to leave the spot. But—reward for going while yet a trace of dusky light remained— he had not reached the bottom of the hill road, up which his car had roared an hour before, when he saw something fallen there that made him pull the motor up upon its throbbing cylinders. He jumped out and ran to rescue what had fallen. It was the bunch of rose haws that he had so carefully denuded of thorns and that she had worn upon her breast for at least a short time before she lost it. She had not thrown it away intentionally, he was sure of that. If she had, she would not have flung it contemptuously into the middle of the road for him to see.

He put it into the pocket of his coat, where it made a strange bulge, but he could not risk losing it by trusting it to the seat beside him. Until he had won something that had been longer hers, it was a treasure not to be lost.

Four miles toward town, he passed the riding party and exchanged a fire of gay salutations with them. When he had left them behind, he could not reach home too soon. He hurried to his rooms, hunted out a receptacle of silver and crystal and filled it with water, placed the bunch of rose haws in it, and set the whole on his reading table under the electric droplight, where it made a spot of brilliant color.

He had an invitation for the evening. He had cared little to accept it when it had been given him; he was sorry now that he had not refused it. As the hour drew near, his distaste grew upon him, but there was no way in which he could withdraw without giving disappointment and even offense. He went forth, therefore, with reluctance, to join precisely such a party as he had many times made with pleasure and elation. Tonight, however, he found the greatest difficulty in concealing his boredom, and he more than once caught himself upon the verge of actual discourtesy because of his tendency to become absentminded and let the merrymaking flow by him without taking part in it.

Altogether, it was with a strong sense of relief and freedom that he at last escaped from what had seemed to him an interminable period of captivity to the uncongenial moods and manners of other people. He opened the door of his rooms with a sense of having returned to a place where he could be himself—his new self—that strange new self who singularly failed to enjoy the companionship of those who had once seemed the most satisfying of comrades.

The first thing upon which his eager glance fell was the bunch of scarlet rose haws under the softly illumining radiance of the droplight. His eyes lighted, his lips broke into a smile—the lips that had found it, all evening, so hard to smile with anything resembling spontaneity.

Hat in hand, he addressed his treasure: "I've come back to stay with you!" he said.

Chapter 6

UNSTAINED APPLICATION

"M r. Kendrick, do you understand typewriting?"
Judge Gray's assistant looked up, slight surprise on his face. "No, sir, I do not," he said.

"I am sorry. These sheets I am sending to the capitol to be looked over and criticized ought to be typewritten. I could send them downtown, but I want the typist here at my elbow."

He sat frowning a little with perplexity, and presently he reached for the telephone. Then he put it down, his brow clearing. "This is Saturday," he murmured. "If Roberta is at home . . ."

He left the room. In five minutes he was back, his niece beside him. Richard Kendrick had not set eyes upon her for a fortnight; he rose at her appearance and stood awaiting her recognition. She gave it, stopping to offer him her hand as she passed him, smiling. But, this little ceremony over, she became on the instant the businesswoman. Richard saw it all, though he did his best to settle down to his work again and pursue it with an air of absorption.

Roberta went to a cupboard that opened from under bookshelves and drew therefrom a small portable typewriter. This she set upon a table beside a window at right angles from Richard and all of twenty feet away from him; she could hardly have put a greater distance between them. The judge drew up a chair for her; she removed the cover from the compact little machine and nodded at him. He placed his own chair beside her table and sat down, copy in hand.

"This is going to be a rather difficult business," said he. "There are many points where I wish to indicate slight changes as we go along. I can't attempt to read the copy to you, but should like to have you give

43

me the opening words of each paragraph as you come to it. I think I can recall those that contain the points for revision."

The work began. That is to say, work at the typewriter side of the room began, and in earnest. From the first stroke of the keys it was evident that the judge had called to his aid a skilled worker. The steady, smooth clicking of the machine was interrupted only at the ends of paragraphs, when the judge listened to the key words of the succeeding lines. Roberta sat before that "typer" as if she were accustomed to do nothing else for her living, her eyes upon the keys, her profile silhouetted against the window beside her.

As far as the mechanical part of the labor was concerned, Richard had never seen a task get under way more promptly nor proceed with greater or smoother dispatch. As he sat beside his own window, he nearly faced the pair at the other window. Try as he would, he could not keep his mind upon his work. It was a situation unique in his experience. That he, Richard Kendrick, should be employed in serious work in the same room with the niece of a prosperous and distinguished gentleman, a girl who had not hesitated to learn a trade in which she had become proficient, and that the three of them should spend the morning in this room together, taking no notice of each other beyond that made necessary by the task in hand—it was enough to make him burst out laughing. At the same time he felt a genuine satisfaction in the situation. If he could but work in the same room with her every day, though she should vouchsafe him no word, how far from drudgery would the labor be then removed!

He managed to keep up at least the appearance of being closely engaged, turning the leaves of books, making notes, arising to consult other books upon the shelves. But he could not resist frequent furtive glances at the profile outlined against the window. It was a distracting outline, it must be freely admitted. Even upon the hill, seen against the blue-and-purple haze, it had hardly been more so. What indeed could a young man do but steal a look at it as often as he might? There was no knowing when he should have such another chance.

Things proceeded in this course without interruption until eleven o'clock. The judge, finding it possible to get ahead so satisfactorily by this new method, decided to send on considerably more material to be passed upon by his critical coadjutor at the capitol than he had originally intended to do at this time. But as the clock struck the hour, a caller's card was sent in to him; with a word to Roberta, he left the room to see his visitor elsewhere.

Roberta finished her paragraph, then sat studying the next one. She did not look up, nor did Richard. The moments passed, and the judge did not return. Roberta rose and threw open the window beside her, letting in a great sweep of December air.

Richard seized his opportunity. "Good for you!" he applauded. "Shall I open mine?"

"Please. It will warm up again very quickly. It began to seem stifling."

"Not much like the place where you want to build a cabin and stay alone in a storm. Or, not alone. You are willing to have a dog with you. What sort of a dog?"

"A Great Dane, I think. I have a friend who owns one. They are inseparable."

By the worst of luck, the judge chose this moment to return, and the windows went down with a rush.

The judge shivered, smiling at the pair. "You young things, all warmth and vitality! You are never so happy as when the wind is lifting your hair. Now I think I'm pretty vigorous for my years, but I wouldn't sit and talk in a room with two open windows in December."

Neither can we—hang it! thought Richard. *Why couldn't that chap have stayed a few minutes longer? We'd just got started!*

At lunchtime Roberta's part in the work was not completed. Her uncle asked for two hours more of her time, and she cheerfully promised it. So at two o'clock the stage was again set as a business office, the actors again engaged in their parts. But at three the situation was abruptly changed.

"I believe there are no more revisions to be made," declared Judge Gray with a sigh of weariness. "I have taxed you heavily, my dear, but if you are equal to finishing these eleven sheets for me by yourself, I shall be grateful. My eyes have reached the limit of endurance, even with all the help you have given me. I must go to my room."

He paused by Richard's desk on his way out. "Have you finished the abstract of the chapter on Judge Cahill?" he asked. "No? I thought you would perhaps have covered that this morning. But I do not mean to exact too much. It will be quite satisfactory if you can complete it this afternoon."

"I am sorry," said his assistant, flushing in a quite unaccustomed manner. "I have been working more slowly than I realized. I will finish it as rapidly as I can, sir."

"Don't apologize, Mr. Kendrick. We all have our slow days. I undoubtedly underestimated the amount of time the chapter would require. Good afternoon to you."

Richard sat down and plunged into the task he now saw he had merely played with during the morning. By a tremendous effort he kept his eyes from lifting to the figure at the typewriter, whose steady clicking never ceased but for a moment at a time, putting him to shame. Yet, try as he would, he could not apply himself with any real concentration; and the task called for concentration, all he could command.

"You are probably not used to working in the same room with a typewriter," said his companion, quite unexpectedly, after a full half hour of silence. She had stopped work to oil a bearing in her machine. There was an odd note in her voice; it sounded to Richard as if she meant, *You are not used to doing anything worthwhile.*

"I don't mind it in the least," he protested.

"I'm sorry not to take[1] my work to another room," Roberta went on, tipping up her machine and manipulating levers with skill as she applied the oil. "But I shall soon be through."

"Please don't hurry. I ought to be able to work under any conditions. And I certainly enjoy having you at work in the same room," he ventured to add. It was odd how he found himself merely venturing to say to this girl things that he would have said without hesitation—putting them much more strongly withal—to any other girl he knew.

"One needs to be able to forget there's anybody in the same room." There was a little curl of scorn about her lips.

"That might be easier to do under some conditions than others." He did not mean to be trampled upon.

But Roberta finished her oiling in silence and again applied herself to her typing with redoubled energy.

He went at his abstract, suddenly furious with himself. He would show her that he could work as persistently as she. He could not pretend to himself that she was not absorbed. Only entire absorption could enable her to reel off those pages without more than an infrequent stop for the correction of an error.

Turning a page in the big volume of records of speeches in the state legislature that he was consulting, Richard came upon a sheet of paper on which was written something in verse. His eye went to the bottom of the sheet to see there the source of the quotation—Browning—with reference to title and page. No harm to read a quoted poem, certainly; his eyes sought it eagerly as a relief from the sonorous phrasing of the speech he was attempting to read. He had never seen the words before; the first line—and he must read to the end. What a thing to find in a dusty volume of forgotten speeches of a date long past!

---

[1] Not to be able to take.

Such a starved bank of moss
Till, that May-morn,
Blue ran the flash across:
Violets were born!

Sky—what a scowl of cloud
Till, near and far,
Ray on ray split the shroud:
Splendid, a star!

World—how it walled about
Life with disgrace
Till God's own smile came out:
That was thy face!

Speeches were forgotten; he devoured the words over and over again. They seemed to him to have been made expressly for him. A starved bank of moss—that was exactly what he had been, only he had not known it but had fancied himself a garden of rich resource. He knew better now; starved he was, and starved he would remain unless he could make the violets his own. No doubt but he had found them!

He followed an impulse. Rising, the sheet of yellowed paper in his hand, he walked over to the typewriter. Without apology, he laid the sheet upon the pile of typed ones at her side.

"See what I've found in an old volume of state speeches."

Roberta's busy hand stopped. Her eyes scanned the yellow page upon which the stiff, fine handwriting, clearly that of a man, stood out legibly as print. Businesswoman she might be, but she could not so far abstract herself as not to be touched by the hint of romance involved in finding such words in such a place.

"How strange!" she owned. "And they've been there a long time, by the look of the paper and ink. I never saw the handwriting before. Perhaps Uncle Calvin lent the book to somebody long ago and the 'somebody' left this in it."

"Shall I put it back or show it to Judge Gray?"

He remained beside her, though she had handed back the paper.

"Put it back, don't you think? If you wrote out such words and left them in a book, you would want them to stay there, not to be looked at curiously by other eyes fifty years after."

"That's somebody's heart there on that sheet of old paper," said he. Apparently, he was looking at the paper; in reality, he was stealing a glance past it at her down-bent face.

"Not necessarily. Somebody may merely have been attracted by the music of the lines. Put it back, Mr. Secretary, and concern yourself with Judge Cahill. It's to be hoped that you won't find any more distracting verse between his pages."

"Why not? Oughtn't one to get all the poetry one can out of life?"

"Not in business hours."

He laughed in spite of himself at the failure of his effort to make her self-conscious by any reading of such lines in his presence. Clearly, she meant to allow no personal relation to arise between them while they were thrown together by Judge Gray's need of them. She fell to typing again with even more energy than before, if that were possible, while he—it must be confessed that before he laid the verses away between the pages for another fifty years' sleep he had made note of their identity, that he might look them up again in a seldom-opened copy of the English poet on his shelves at home. They belonged to him now!

In half an hour more, Roberta's machine stopped clicking. Swiftly she covered it, set it away in the book cupboard, and put her table in order. She laid the typewritten sheets together upon Judge Gray's desk in a straight-edged pile, a paperweight on top. In her simple dress of dark blue, trim as any office woman's attire, she might have been a hired stenographer—of a very high class—putting her affairs in order for the day.

Richard waited till she approached his desk, which she had to pass on her way out. Then he rose to his feet.

"Allow me to congratulate you," said he, "on having accomplished a long task in the minimum length of time possible. I am lost in wonder that a hand that can play the cello with such art can play the typewriter with such skill."

"Thank you." There was a flash of mirth in her eyes. "There's music in both if you have ears to hear."

"I have recognized that today."

"You never heard it before? Music in the hammer on the anvil, in the throb of the engine, in the hum of the dynamo."

"And in the scratch of the pen, the pounding of the boiler shop, and the . . . the . . . slide and grind of the trolley car, I suppose?"

"Indeed, yes, even in those. And there'll surely be melody in the closing of the door that shuts you into solitude after this distracting day. Listen to it! Good-bye."

He long remembered the peculiar parting look she gave him: satiric, mischievous, yet charmingly provocative. She was keen of mind, she was brilliant of wit, but she was all woman—no doubt of that. He was suddenly sure that she had known well enough all day the effect that she had had upon him and that it had amused her. His cheek reddened at the thought. He wondered why on earth he should care to pursue an attempt at acquaintance with one whose manner with him was frequently so disturbing to his self-conceit. Well, at least he must forget her now and redeem himself with an hour's solid effort.

But, strange to say, although he had found it difficult to work in her presence, in her absence he found it impossible to work at all. He stuck doggedly to his desk for the appointed hour, then gave over the attempt and departed. The moral of all this, which he discovered he could not escape, was that though he had taken his university degree and had supplemented the academic education with the broader one of travel and observation, he had not at his command that first requisite for efficient labor: the power of sustained application. In a way he had been dimly suspicious of this since the day he had begun this pretense of work for his grandfather's old friend. Today, at sight of a girl's steady concentration upon a wearisome task in spite of his own supposedly diverting presence, it had been brought home to him with force that he was unquestionably reaping that inevitable product of protracted idleness: the loss of the power to work.

As he drove away, it suddenly occurred to him that on the morrow, instead of coming to the house in his car, he would leave it in the garage and walk. Between the discovery of his inefficiency and his resolution to dispense with a hitherto accustomed luxury, there may have been a subtler connection than appears to the eye.

Chapter 7

A TRAITOROUS PROCEEDING

"We shall have to make our work count this week, Mr. Kendrick. Next week I anticipate that there will be no chance whatever to do a stroke." So spoke Judge Gray to his assistant on one Monday morning as he shook hands with him in greeting.

"Very well, sir," replied the young man with, however, a sense of its not being at all well. It was to him a regrettable fact that he seldom saw much of the various members of the household, and of one particular member so little that he was tempted to wonder if she ever took the trouble to evade him. But, of course, there was always the chance of an encounter, and he never opened the house door without the feeling that just inside might be a certain figure on its way out.

"Next week is Christmas week," explained Judge Gray. He stood upon the hearth rug, his back to the open fire, warming his hands preparatory to taking up his pen. His fingers were apt to be a little stiff on these December mornings. "During Christmas week, this house is always given over to such holiday doings as I don't imagine another house in town ever knows. Christmas house parties are plenty, I believe, but not the sort of house party we indulge in. I am inclined to think ours beats the world."

He chuckled, running his hand through the thick white locks above his brow with a gesture that Richard had come to know meant special satisfaction.

"You have so many and such delightful people?" suggested his assistant.

The white head nodded. "The house could hardly hold more, nor could they be more delightful. You see, there are five brothers of us. I am the eldest, Robert the youngest. Rufus, Henry, and Philip come between. Henry and Philip live in small towns, Rufus in the country proper. Each

50

has a good-sized family, with several married sons and daughters who have children of their own. It has been my brother Robert's custom for twenty years to ask them all here for Christmas week." He began to laugh. "If the family keeps on growing much larger, I don't know that there will be room to accommodate them all, but so far my sister has always managed. Fortunately, this is an even more roomy old homestead than it looks. But you may easily imagine, Mr. Kendrick, that there is very little chance for solitude and quiet work during that week."

"I can fully imagine," agreed Richard. "And yet I can't imagine," he amended. "I never saw such a gathering in my life."

"Never did, eh? You must come in sometime during the week and get a glimpse of it. We have fine times, I can tell you. My old head sometimes whirls a bit," the judge admitted, "before the week is over, but it's worth it. Particularly on the night of the party. The children always have a party in the attic on Christmas Eve. It's a great affair. No dancing parties nor balls in other places can be mentioned in the same breath with it. You should see brother Rufus taking out my niece Roberta, and brother Henry dancing with Stephen's little wife. The girls accommodate themselves to the old-fashioned steps in great style."

"I certainly should like to see it," Richard said, wondering if there were any possible chance of his being invited.

But Judge Gray offered no suggestion of the sort, and Richard made up his mind that the Christmas Eve dance would be a strictly family affair. *Probably the country relatives are a strange lot,* he decided, *and the Grays don't care to show them off. Still, that's not like them, either. It's certainly like them to do such an eccentric thing as to get their cousins all here and try to give them a good time. I should like to see it. I should!*

He found his thoughts wandering many times during the morning's work to the image of Roberta dancing with the old uncle from the country. He had never met her at any of the society dances that were now and then honored by his presence. Unquestionably, the Grays moved in a circle with which he was not familiar—a circle made up of people distinguished rather for their good birth and the things that they had done than for their wealth. Nobody in the city stood upon a higher social level than the Grays, but they lived in a world in which the lively and fashionable set Richard knew were totally unknown and unhonored.

The more he thought about it the more he wished that, if only for a week, he were at least a sixteenth cousin of the Gray family, that he might be present at that Christmas party. But during the week, chance did not even throw him in the way of meeting the various members of the family proper, and when Saturday night came he had discovered no prospect of attaining his wish. He knew that the guests were to arrive on the following Monday. Christmas Day was on Saturday; the night of the party, then, would be Friday night. And the judge, in taking leave of him, did not even mention again his wish that Richard might see the guests together.

He was coming out of the library, on his way to the hall door, hope having died hard and his spirits being correspondingly depressed, when Fate at last intervened in his behalf. Fate took the form of young Mrs. Stephen Gray, descending the stairs with a two-year-old child in her arms, such a rosy, brown-eyed cherub of a child that an older and more hardened bachelor than Richard Kendrick need not have been suspected of dissimulation if he had stopped short in his course as Richard did, to admire and wonder.

"Is that a real, live boy?" cried the young man softly. "Or have you stolen him out of a frame somewhere?"

Mrs. Stephen stood still, smiling, on the bottom stair, and Richard approached with eager interest. He came close and stood looking into the small face, with eyes that took in every exquisite feature.

"Jove!" he said under his breath and looked up at the young mother. "I didn't know they made them like that."

She laughed softly with a mother's happy pride. "His little sister really ought to have had his looks," she said. "But we're hoping she'll develop them, and he'll grow plain in time to save him from being spoiled."

"Do you really hope that?" he laughed incredulously. "Don't hope it too fast. See here, boy, are you real? Come here and let me see." He held out his arms.

"He's very shy," began Mrs. Stephen in explanation of the situation she now expected to have develop. It did develop in so far that the child shyly buried his head in her shoulder. But in a moment he peeped out again. Richard continued to hold out his arms, smiling, and suddenly the little fellow leaned forward. Richard gently drew him away from his mother, and, though he looked back at her as if to make sure that she was there, he presently seemed to surrender himself with confidence into the stranger's care and gave him back smile for smile.

Richard sat down with little Gordon Gray on his knee, and there ensued such a conversation between the two, such a frolic of games and smiles, as his mother could only regard in wonder.

"He never makes friends easily," she said. "I can't understand it. You must have had plenty of experience with little children somehow, in spite of those statements about your never having seen a family like ours before."

"I never held a child like this one before in my life," said Richard Kendrick. He looked up at her as he spoke.

If Roberta could see him now, thought Mrs. Stephen, *she wouldn't be so hard on him. No man who isn't worth knowing can win a baby's confidence like that. I think he has one of the nicest faces I ever saw, even though it isn't lined with care.* Aloud she said, "It surprises me that you should care to begin now."

"It's one of those new experiences I'm getting from time to time under this roof; that's the only way I can account for it. I never even guessed at the pleasure of making the acquaintance of a small chap like this. But I've no right to keep you while I taste new experiences. Thank you for this one. I shan't forget it."

He surrendered the boy with evident reluctance. "I hear you are to have a houseful of guests next week," he ventured to add. "Do they include any first cousins of this little man?"

"Two of his own age and any number of older ones. I'll take you up to the playroom some afternoon next week and show you the babies together, if you're interested, and if Uncle Calvin will let me interrupt his work for a few minutes."

"Thank you; I'll gladly come to the house for that special purpose, if you'll let me know when. Judge Gray has decided not to try to work at all next week; he's giving me a holiday I really don't want."

"Are you so interested in your labors with him?"

Their eyes met. There was something very sweet and womanly in Mrs. Stephen's face and in the eyes that scanned his, or he would never have dared to say what he said next.

"Not in the work itself," he confessed frankly, "though I don't find it as hard as I did at first. But the association with Judge Gray, the—well, I suppose it's really having something definite to do with my time. Above all, just being in this house, though I don't belong to it, is getting to seem so interesting to me that I'm afraid I shall hardly know what to do with myself all next week."

She could not doubt the genuineness of his admission, strange as it sounded. So the young aristocrat was really dreading a week's vacation, he who had done nothing but idle away his time. She felt a touch of pity for him; yet how absurd it was!

"I wish you could meet some of the people who will be here next week," she said. "I wonder if you would care to?"

"If they're anything like those of the Gray family I already know, I should care immensely." He spoke with enthusiasm.

"I think some of them are the most interesting people I have ever met. My husband's Uncle Rufus, Judge Gray's brother—why, you must meet Uncle Rufus. I'll speak to Mrs. Robert Gray about it. I'm sure if she thought you cared she'd be delighted to have you know him. Then there's the Christmas Eve dance. I wonder if you would enjoy that? We don't usually have many people outside of the family, but there are always some of Rob's and Louis's special friends asked for the dance, and I'm sure I can arrange it. I'll mention it to Roberta."

"Must it . . . er . . . rest with Miss Roberta? I'm afraid she won't ask me," declared Richard anxiously.

"Won't she? Why? She will probably say that she doesn't believe you will enjoy it, but if I assure her that you want to come, I think she will trust me. She's very exacting as to the qualifications of the guests at this dance and will have nobody who isn't ready for a good time in every unconventional way. I warn you, Mr. Kendrick, who are used to leading cotillions, you may have to dance the Virginia reel with one of the dear little country cousins. I wonder if you will have the discernment to see that some of them are better worth meeting than a good many of the girls you probably know."

She gave him a keen, analyzing look. Small and sweet as she was, clearly she belonged to this singular Gray family as if she had been born into it. He met her look unflinchingly. Then his glance fell to little Gordon.

"You trusted me with the boy," said he. "I think you may trust me with the little country cousin—if she will do me the honor."

"I will see that you have the chance," she assured him, and he went away feeling like a boy who has been promised a long-desired and despaired-of treat.

But it was not of the Virginia reel he was thinking as he went swinging away down the wintry street.

They were sitting, most of them, before the living room fire, discussing the plans for the week of the house party, when Rosamond broke the news.

"I've taken a great liberty," said she serenely, "for which I hope you'll all forgive me. I've tentatively promised Mr. Kendrick an invitation to the Christmas dance."

There was a shout from Louis and Ted together. Ruth beamed with delight. Across the fireplace, Roberta shot at her sister-in-law one rebellious glance.

"I knew I had no right to do it," admitted Rosamond gaily. "But I knew we always asked a few young people to swell the company to the dancing size, and I was sure you couldn't ask anybody who would appreciate it more."

"Hasn't the poor fellow a chance at any other merrymaking?" mocked Louis. "Poor little millionaire! Won't anybody invite him to lead a Christmas Eve cotillion? I believe there's to be a most gorgeous affair of the sort at Mrs. Van Tassel Grieve's that night. Has he been inadvertently overlooked? Not with Miss Gladys Grieve to oversee the list of the lucky ones, I'll wager. It's a wonder he hadn't accepted that invitation before you got in yours."

"I didn't get mine in," was Rosamond's demure rejoinder. "I laid it in a humbly beseeching hand."

"How on earth did he know there was to be a dance here?" Stephen inquired.

"I mentioned it."

"I had already told him of it," put in Judge Gray from the background, where he was listening with interest. "I'm glad you asked him, Rosamond, and I'll answer for your forgiveness. While you are inviting, I should like to invite his grandfather also. Christmas Eve is a lonely time for him, I'll be bound, and it would do him good to meet Rufus and Phil and the rest again."

"I'll tell you what we're going to end by being," murmured Louis to Roberta. "A discontented millionaires' home."

On the stairs an hour afterward, a brief but significant colloquy took place between Rosamond Gray and her sister-in-law Roberta.

"Why do you mind having him come, Rob? Haven't you any charity for the poor at Christmas time?"

"Poor! He's poor enough, but he doesn't know it."

"Doesn't he? The night he was here at dinner, he told me he felt poor." Rosamond's look was triumphant. "He feels it very much; he's never known what family life meant."

"Do you imagine he can adapt himself to the conditions of the Christmas party? If I catch him laughing—ever so covertly—I'll send him home!"

"You savage person! You don't expect to catch him laughing! He's a gentleman. And I believe he's enough of a man to appreciate the aunts and uncles and cousins, even those of them who don't patronize city tailors and dressmakers. Why, they're perfectly delightful people, every one of them, and he will have the discernment to see it."

"I don't believe it. Where have you seen him that you have so much more confidence than I have?"

"I've had one or two little talks with him that have told me a good deal. And this afternoon he met me as I was coming downstairs with Gordon. Rob, what do you think? Gordon went to him exactly as he goes to Stephen; they had the greatest time. Gordon knows better than you do whom to trust."

"You and Gordon are very discerning. A handsome face and a wheedling manner and you think you have a fine, strong character. Handsome is as handsome does, Rosy Gray of the soft heart, and a wheedling manner is dust and ashes compared with the ability to accomplish something worth effort. But bring your nice young man to the party if you like; only take care of him. I shall be busy with the real men!"

Chapter 8

ROSES RED

It was certainly rather a curious coincidence that when Mr. Matthew Kendrick and his grandson Richard entered upon the scene of the Grays' Christmas Eve party, it should be at the moment when Mr. Rufus Gray and his niece Roberta were dancing a quadrille together. Richard had just been received by his hosts and had turned from them to look about him, when his searching eye caught sight of the pair. This was the precise moment—he always afterward recalled it—when his heart gave its first great, disconcerting leap at sight of her, such a leap as he had never known could shake a man to the foundations.

He had never seen precisely this Roberta before; he explained it to himself in that way. It was a good explanation. Any sane man who saw her for the first time that night must instantly have fallen under her spell.

The Christmas party was the event of the year dearest to Roberta's heart. The planning for it, since she had been old enough to take her part, had been in her hands; it was she who was responsible for every detail of decoration. The great attic room, which was a glorious playroom the rest of the year, was transformed on Christmas into a fairyland. The results were brought about in much the same way as in other places of revelry, with lighting and draping and the use of evergreens and flowers; but somehow one felt that no drawing room similarly treated could have been half so charming as the big attic spaces with their gables.

And the company! At first Richard saw only the pair who danced together in the quadrille. If he had glanced about him, he might have observed that the gaze of nearly all who were not dancing was centered upon those two.

Uncle Rufus was the plumpest, jolliest, most altogether delightful specimen of the country gentleman that Richard had ever seen. His ruddy face was clean-shaven, his heavy gray hair waved a little with a boyish effect about his ears. He was carefully dressed in a frock coat of a cut not so ancient as to be at all odd, and it fitted his broad shoulders with precision. He wore a white waistcoat and a flowing black tie, which helped to carry out the impression of his being a boy whose hair had accidentally turned gray. As he danced, he put every possible embellishment of posture and step into his task, and when he bowed to Roberta, his attitude expressed the deepest reverence, offset only by his laughing face as he advanced to take her hand.

But as for the girl herself—what was she? A beauty stepping out of a portrait by one of the masters? She wore her grandmother's ball gown of rose-colored brocade, and her hair was arranged in the fashion that went with it: small curls escaping from the knot at the back of her head, a style that set off her radiant face with peculiarly piquant effect. Her cheeks matched her frock, and her eyes—what were her eyes? Black stars or wells of darkness into which a man might fall and drown himself?

She seemed to draw to herself, as she danced, among the soberer colors of her elders and the white frocks of the country cousins, all the light in the room. *I would look at something else if I could,* thought Richard to himself, *but it would be only a blur to me after looking at her.*

When Roberta returned Uncle Rufus's bow, it was with a posturing such as Richard had seen only in plays; it struck him now that the graceful droop of her whole figure to the floor was the most perfect thing he had ever seen; and when her head came up and he saw her laughing face lift again to meet her partner's, he considered the boyish old gentleman who took her hand and led her on in the intricate figures of a dance a person to be envied.

"Aren't Rob and Uncle Rufus the greatest couple you ever laid eyes on?" exulted Louis Gray, coming up to greet him. "The next is going to be a waltz. Will you ask Mrs. Stephen? We'll let you begin easily, but shall expect you to end by dancing with Aunt Ruth, Uncle Rufus's wife, which will be no hardship when you really know her, I assure you. We indulge in no ultramodern dances on Christmas Eve, you see, and have no dance cards; it's always part of the fun to watch the scramble for partners when the number is announced."

So presently Richard found himself upon the floor with little Mrs. Stephen Gray, waltzing with her according to his own discretion, though all around them were dancers whose steps ranged from present-day methods to the ancient fashion of turning around and around without ever a reverse. He saw Roberta herself revolving in slow circles in an endless spiral, piloted by the proud arm of Mr. Philip Gray. She nodded at him past her uncle's shoulder, and he wondered seriously if she meant to dance with elderly uncles all the evening.

Before he could approach her, she was off in the next dance with a young cousin, a lad of seventeen. Richard himself took out one of the country cousins to whom Mrs. Stephen had presented him, a very pretty fair-haired girl in white muslin and blue ribbons; and he did his best to give her a good time. He found her pleasant company, as Mrs. Stephen had prophesied, and at another time, anytime, before he came into the attic room tonight, he might have found no little enjoyment in her bright society. But in his present condition, his one hope and endeavor was to get the queen of the revels, the rose of the garden, into his possession.

With this end in view, he faithfully devoted himself to whatever partner was given him by Louis, who had taken him in charge and was enjoying to the full the spectacle of Rich Kendrick exerting himself as he had probably never done before, to give pleasure to those with whom he was thrown. At last Fate and Roberta were kind to him. It was Louis, however, who manipulated Fate in his behalf.

Catching his sister as one of her cousins, a young son of Uncle Henry, released her, Louis drew her into a corner—as much of a corner as one could get into with a sister at whom, wherever she turned, half the company was looking.

"See here, Rob, you're not playing fair with the guest. Here's the evening half over and you haven't given him a solitary chance. What's the matter? You're not afraid of His Highness?"

"This is a dance for the uncles and cousins," retorted Roberta, "not for young society men."

"But he's done his duty like a man and a brother. He's danced with aunts and cousins, too, and has done it as if it were the joy of his life. But I know what he wants and I think he deserves a reward. The next waltz will be a peach, 'Roses Red.' Give it to the poor young millionaire, Robby; there's a good girl."

"Bring him here," said she with an air of resignation, and she turned to a group of young people who had followed her as bees follow their queen. "Not this time, dears," said she. "I'm engaged for this dance to a poor young man who has wandered in here and must be made to feel at home."

"Is that the one?" asked one of the pretty country cousins, indicating Richard, who, obeying Louis's beckoning hand, was crossing the floor in their direction. "Oh, you won't mind dancing with him. He's as nice as he is good-looking, too."

"I'm delighted to hear it," said Roberta.

The next minute "the poor young man" was before her. "Am I really to have it?" he asked her. "Will you give me the whole of it and not cut it in two, as I saw you do with the last one?"

"It would be rather a pity to cut 'Roses Red' in two, wouldn't it?" said she.

"The greatest pity in the world." He was looking at her cheek in the last instant before they were off. Talk of roses! Was there ever a rose like that cheek?

Then the music sent them away upon its wings, and for a space measured by the strains of "Roses Red," Richard Kendrick knew no more of earth. Not a word did he speak to her as they circled the great room again and again. He did not want to mar the beauty of it by speech— ordinary exchange of comment such as dancers feel that they must make. He wanted to dream instead.

"Look at Rob and Mr. Kendrick," said Ruth in Rosamond's ear. "Aren't they the most wonderful pair you ever saw? They look as if they were made for each other."

"Don't tell Rob that," Rosamond warned her enthusiastic sister-in-law. "She would never dance with him again."

"I can't think what makes her dislike him so. Look at her face turned just as far away as she can get it. And she never speaks to him at all. I've been watching them."

"It won't hurt him to be disliked a little," declared Mrs. Stephen wisely. "It's probably the first time in his life a girl has ever turned away her head, except to turn it back again instantly to see if he observed."

"What would Forbes Westcott say if he could see them? Do you know he's coming back soon? Then Rob will have her hands full! Do you suppose she will marry him?"

"Little matchmaker! I don't know. Nobody ever knows what Rob is going to do."

Nobody ever did, least of all her newest acquaintance. If he was to have a moment with her after the dance, he realized that he must be clever enough to manage it in spite of her. He laid his plans, and when the last strains of "Roses Red" were hastening to a delirious finish, he had Roberta at the far end of the room, at a point fairly deserted and close to one of the gable corners where rugs and chairs made a resting place half-hidden by a screen of holly.

"Please give me just a fraction of your time," he begged. "You've been dancing steadily all the evening; surely you're ready for a bit of quiet."

"I'm not as tired as I was before that dance," said she and let him seat her, though she still looked like some spirited creature poised for flight.

"Aren't you really?" His face lighted with pleasure. "I feel as if I had had a draught of . . . well, something both soothing and exhilarating, but I didn't dare to hope you enjoyed it, too."

"Oh, yes, you did," said she coolly, looking up at him for an instant. "You know perfectly well that you're one of the best dancers who ever made a girl feel as if she had wings. Of course I knew you would be. The leader of cotillions—"

"That's the second time I've had that accusation flung at me under this roof," said he, and his face clouded as quickly as it had lighted. "I am beginning to wonder what kind of a crime you people think it to be a leader of cotillions. As a matter of fact, I'm not one, for I never accept the part when I can by any chance get out of it."

"You have the enviable reputation of being the most accomplished person in that role the town can produce. You should be proud of it."

He pulled up a chair in front of her and sat down, looking, or trying to look, straight into her eyes.

"See here, Miss Gray," said he with sudden earnestness, "if that's the only thing you think I can do, you're certainly rating me pretty low."

"I'm not rating you at all. I don't know enough about you."

"That's a harder blow than the other one." He tried to speak lightly, but chagrin was in his face. "If you'd just added 'and don't want to know,' you'd have finished your work of making me feel about three feet high."

"Would you prefer to be made to feel eight feet? Plenty of people will do that for you. You see, I so often find a yardstick measures my own height, I know the humiliating sensation it is. And I'm never more convinced of my own smallness than when I see my uncles and their families at Christmas, especially Uncle Rufus. Do you know which one he is?"

"You were dancing with him when I came in."

"I didn't see you come in."

"I might have known that," he admitted with a rueful laugh. "Well, did you dance an old-fashioned square dance with him, and is he a delightful-looking elderly gentleman with a face like a jolly boy?"

"Exactly that. And he's a boy in heart, too, but a man in mind. I wonder if . . ."

"He'd care to meet me? I'm sure you weren't going to ask if I'd care to meet him. But I'd consider it an honor if he'd let me be presented to him."

"Now you're talking properly," said she. "It is an honor to be allowed to know Uncle Rufus, and I think you'll feel it so." She rose.

He got up reluctantly. "Thank you, I certainly shall," said he quite soberly. "But must we go this minute? Surely you can sit out one number, and I'll promise after that to stand on my head and dance with a broomstick if it will please your guests."

"I've a mind to hold you to that offer," said she with mischief in her eyes. "But the next number is the old-time Lancers, and I'm needed. Should you like to dance it?"

"With you? I—"

"Of course not. With . . . well, with Aunt Ruth, Uncle Rufus's wife. You ought to know her if you're to know him. She's just a bit lame, but we always get her to dance the Lancers once on Christmas Eve, and if you want the dearest partner in the room, you shall have her."

"I'll be delighted, if you'll tell me how it goes. If it's like the thing I saw you dancing, I can manage it, I'm sure."

"It's enough like it so you'll have no trouble. I'll dance opposite you and keep you straight. See here . . . " She gave him a hasty outline of the figures.

His eyes were sparkling as he followed her out of the alcove. To be allowed to dance opposite Roberta and be "kept straight" by her through the figures of an unfamiliar, old-fashioned affair like the Lancers was a privilege indeed. He laughed to himself to think what certain people he knew would say to his new idea of privilege.

He bent before Mrs. Rufus Gray, offered her his arm, and took her out upon the floor, accommodating his step to the little limp of his partner. As he stood waiting with her he was observing her as he had never before observed a woman of her years. Of all the sweet faces, of all the bright eyes, of all the pleasant voices, Aunt Ruth captured his interest and admiration from the moment when she first smiled at him.

He threw himself into the dance with the greatest heartiness. The music was played rather slowly, to give Aunt Ruth time to get about, and the result was almost the stately effect of a minuet. Never had he put more grace and finish into his steps, and when he bowed to Aunt Ruth it was as a courtier drops knee before a queen. His unfamiliarity with the figures gave him an excuse to keep his eyes upon Roberta, and she found him a pupil to whom she had only to nod or make the slightest gesture of the hand to show his part.

"Did you ever see anything so fascinating as Aunt Ruth and Mr. Kendrick?" asked Mrs. Stephen in her husband's ear as they stood looking on.

"There's certainly no criticism of his manner toward her," Stephen replied. "I'll say this for him: that he's a past master at adaptation. I'll wager he's enjoying himself, too. It's a new experience for the society youth."

"Stevie, why do you all insist on making a 'society youth' of him? It's his misfortune to have been born to that sort of thing, but I don't believe he cares half as much for it as he does for just this sort."

"This is a novelty to him, that's all. And he's clever enough to see that to please Rob, he must be polite to her family. Rob is the stake he's playing for—till some other pretty girl takes his fancy."

Rosamond shook her head. "You all do him injustice, I believe. Of course he admires Rob; men always do if they've any discrimination whatever. But there are other things that appeal to him. Stephen"—her appealing face flushed with interest—"when you have a chance, slip out with Mr. Kendrick and take him upstairs to see Gordon and Dorothy asleep. I just went up; they look too dear!"

"Why, Rosy, you don't imagine he'd care—"

"Try him. Just to please me. I could take him myself, but I'd rather you would. I want you to look at his face when he looks at them."

"He *has* got around you—" began her husband, but she made him promise.

When Stephen came upon Richard, the guest was with Uncle Rufus and Aunt Ruth. The young man was entering with great spirit into his conversation with the pair, and they were evidently enjoying him.

I'll have to give him credit for possessing genuine courtesy, thought Stephen.

At this moment a group of young people came up and demanded the presence of Mr. and Mrs. Rufus Gray in another part of the room, and Richard was set at liberty. Stephen took him by the arm.

"Before you engage again in the antic whirl, I have a special exhibit to show you outside the ballroom. Spare me five minutes?"

"Spare you anything," responded the guest, following Stephen out of the room as if he wanted nothing so much as to do whatever might be suggested to him.

In two minutes they were downstairs and at the far end of a long corridor that led to the rooms in a wing of the big house occupied by the Stephen Grays. Richard was led through a pleasant living room where a maid was reading a book under the droplight. She rose at their appearance, and Stephen nodded an *All right* to her. He conducted Richard to the door of an inner room, which, as he opened it, let a rush of cold air upon the two men entering.

"Turn up your collar; it's winter in here," said Stephen softly. He switched on a shaded light that revealed a nursery containing two small beds side by side. Two large windows at the farther end of the room were wide open, and all the breezes of the December night were playing about the sleepers.

The sleepers! Richard bent over them, one after the other, scanning each rosy face. The baby girl lay upon her side, a round little cheek, a fringe of dark eyelashes, and a tangle of fair curls showing against the pillow. The boy was stretched upon his back, his arms outflung, his head turned toward the light so that his face was fully visible. If he had been attractive with his wonderful eyes open, he was even more winsome with them closed. He looked the picture of the sleeping angel who has never known contact with earth.

"I thought he would never be done looking," Stephen acknowledged afterward when he told his exulting wife about the scene. "I was half-frozen, but he acted like a man hypnotized. Finally, he looked up at me. 'Gray, you're a rich man,' said he. 'I suppose you know it or you wouldn't have brought me up here to show me your wealth.' 'I believe I know it,' said I. 'What does it feel like,' he asked, 'to look at these and know they're yours?' I told him that that was a thing I couldn't express. 'Forgive me for asking,' said he. 'No man would want to try to express it to another.' I began to like him after that, Rosy. I really did. The fellow seems to have a heart that hasn't been altogether spoiled by the sort of life he's lived. On our way upstairs he said nothing until we were nearly back to the attic. Then he put his hand on my arm. 'Thank you for taking me, Gray,' he said. I told him you wanted me to do it. He only gave me a look in answer to that; but I fancy you would have liked the look, little susceptible girl."

It was Ted who got hold of the guest next. "I hope you're having a good time, Mr. Kendrick," said the young son of the house politely. "I've been so busy myself, dancing with all my girl cousins, I haven't had time to ask you."

"I've been having the time of my life, Ted. I can't remember when I've enjoyed anything so much."

"I saw you once with Rob. You're lucky to get her. She hasn't had time to dance once with me, and I'd rather have her than any girl here, she's so jolly. She always keeps me laughing. You and she didn't seem to be laughing at all, though."

"Did we look so serious? Perhaps she felt like laughing inside, though, at my awkward steps."

Ted stared. "Why, you're a bully dancer," he declared. "What girl are you going to have for the Virginia reel? We always end with that—at twelve o'clock, you know."

"I haven't a partner, Ted. I wish you'd get me the one I want."

"Tell me who it is and I'll try. We're going down to bring up supper now, we fellows. Want to help?"

"Of course I do. How is it done?"

"Everything's in the dining room and some of the younger ones go down. But we boys and men go and bring up everything for the older folks. Maybe I oughtn't to ask you, though," he hesitated. "You're company."

"Let me be one of the family tonight," urged Richard. "I'll bring up supper for Mr. and Mrs. Rufus Gray and pretend they're my aunt and uncle, too. I wish they were."

"I don't blame you; they *are* the jolliest ever, aren't they? Come on, then. Rosy's looking at us; maybe she'll tell you not to go."

They hurried away downstairs, racing with each other to the first floor.

"Hullo! You too?" Louis greeted the guest from the farther side of the table filled with all manner of toothsome viands, where he was piling up a tray to carry aloft. "Glad to see you're game for the whole show. Take one of those trays and load it with discretion—weight equally distributed, or you'll get into trouble on the stairs. You're new at this job, and it takes training."

"I'll manage it," and the young man fell to work, capably assisted by a maid, who showed him what to take first and how to ensure its safe delivery.

On his way up, walking cautiously on account of the cups of smoking bouillon that he was concerned he might spill, he encountered a rose-colored brocade frock on its way down.

"Good for you, Mr. Kendrick," hailed Roberta's voice, full and sweet.

He paused, balancing his tray. "Why are you going down? Won't you let me bring up yours when I've given this to Unc—... to Mr. and Mrs. Rufus Gray?"

"Are you enjoying your task so well? Look out! Keep your eyes on the tray! There's nothing so treacherous to carry as cups so full as those."

"Stop laughing at me and I'll get through all right. All I need is a little practice. Next time I come up, I'm going to try balancing the whole thing on my hand and carrying it shoulder-high."

"Please practice that sometime when you're all alone in your own house."

"I'll remember. And please remember I'm going to bring up your supper and my own. May we have it in the place where we were after the dance?"

"Yes, with six others who are waiting there already. That will be lovely, thank you. I'll be back by the time you have everything up."

Of all the hard creatures to corner, thought Richard, going on upward with his tray. *Anyhow, I can have the satisfaction of waiting on her, which is better than nothing.*

He found it so. The six people in the gable corner proved to be of the younger boys and girls, and though they were all eyes and ears for himself and Roberta, he had a sufficient sense of being paired off with the person he wanted to keep him contented. They ate and drank merrily enough, and the food upon his plate seemed to Richard the best he had ever tasted at an affair of the kind.

The evening was gone before he knew it. He could secure no more dances with Roberta, but he had one with Ruth, during which he made up for his silence with her sister by exchanging every comment possible during their exhilarating occupation. He began it himself:

"It's a real sorrow to me, Miss Ruth, to be warned that this party is nearly over."

"Is it, Mr. Kendrick? It would be to me if tomorrow weren't Christmas Day. It's worth having this stop to get to that. You see, tonight we hang up our stockings."

"Good heavens, Miss Ruth! Where? Not in front of any one chimney?"

"No, each in our own room, at the foot of the bed. The things that won't go into the stockings are on the breakfast table."

"I'll think of you when I'm waking to my solitary dressing. I never hung up my stocking in my life."

"You haven't!" Ruth's tone was all dismay. "But you must have had heaps of Christmas presents?"

"Oh, yes, I've a friend or two who present me with all sorts of interesting articles I seldom find a use for. And when I was a little chap I remember they always had a tree for me."

"I don't care much for trees," Ruth confided. "I like them better in shop windows than I do at home. But to hang up your stocking and then find it all stuffed and knobby in the morning, with always something perfectly delightful in the toe for the very last?! Oh, I love it!"

"I wish I were a cousin of yours, so I could look after that toe present myself," said Richard daringly.

"You do miss a lot of fun, not having a jolly family Christmas like ours."

"I'm convinced of it. See here, Miss Ruth, there's something I want you to do for me if you will. When you waken tomorrow morning send me a Christmas thought. Will you? I'll be looking for it."

Ruth drew back her head in order to look up into his face for an instant. "A Christmas thought?" she repeated, surprised.

He nodded. "As if I were a brother, you know, far away at the other side of the world and lonely. I'll really be as far away from all your merry-making as if I were at the other side of the world, you see—and I'm not sure but I'll be as lonely."

"Why, Mr. Kendrick! You—lonely! I can't believe it!" Ruth almost forgot to keep step in her surprise. "But of course, just you and your grandfather! Only, I've heard how popular . . . " She paused, not ventur-ing to tell him all she had heard of his vivacious and fashionable friends and how they were always inviting and pursuing him. "Are you always lonely at Christmas?" she ended.

"Always; though I've never realized what was the matter with me till this year. Do you care about finishing this dance? Let's stop in this nice corner and talk about it a minute."

It was the same corner, deserted now, where he had twice tried to keep her elusive sister. Ruth was easier to manage, for she was genuinely interested.

"Just this year," he explained, "I've found out why I've never cared for Christmas. It's a beastly day to me. I spend it as I should Sunday—get through it somehow. At last I go out to dinner somewhere in the evening and so end the day."

"We all go to church on Christmas morning," Ruth told him. "That's a lovely way to spend part of the morning, I think. It gives you the real Christmas feeling. Don't you ever do it?"

He shook his head. "Never have; but I will tomorrow if you'll tell me where to go."

"To St. Luke's. The service is so beautiful, and we all have been there since we were old enough to go. I'm sure you'll like it. Wouldn't your grandfather like to go with you?"

Richard stared at her. "Why, I shouldn't have thought of it. Possibly he would. We never go anywhere together, to tell the truth."

"That's odd, when you're both so lonely. He must be lonely, too, mustn't he?"

"I never thought about it," said the young man. "I suppose he is. He never says so."

"You never say so either, do you?" suggested the girl naïvely.

The two looked at each other for a minute without speaking.

"Miss Ruth," said her companion at length, lowering his eyes to the floor and speaking thoughtfully, "I believe, to tell the truth, I'm a selfish beast. You've put a totally new idea into my head—more shame to me that it should be new. It strikes me that I'll try a new way of spending Christmas; I'll see to it that whoever is lonely, Grandfather isn't,— if I can keep him from it."

"You can!" cried Ruth, beaming at him. "He thinks the world of you; anybody can see that. And you won't be lonely yourself!"

"Won't I? I'm not so sure of that after tonight. But I admit it's worth trying. May I report to you how it works?" he asked, smiling.

Ruth agreed delightedly, and when they separated, watched with interest to see that the new idea had already begun to work, as indicated by the way the younger Kendrick approached the elder, who was making his farewells.

"Going now, Grandfather?" said he with his hand on old Matthew Kendrick's arm. "We'll go together. I'll call James."

"You going too, Dick?" inquired his grandfather, evidently surprised. "That's good."

As he took leave of Roberta, Richard found opportunity to exchange with her an ever-so-brief conversation. "This has been quite a wonderful experience to me, Miss Gray," said he. "I shall not forget it."

Her eyes searched his for an instant, but found there only sincerity. "You have done your part better than could have been expected," she admitted.

"What grudging commendation! What should you have expected? That I should sulk in a corner because I couldn't have things all my own way?"

She colored richly, and he rejoiced at having put her in confusion for an instant. "Of course not. But everyone wouldn't have eyes to see the beauties of a family party where all the fun wasn't for the young people."

"There was only one dance I enjoyed better than the one with Mrs. Rufus Gray." He lowered his tone so that only she could hear. "Since you have commended me for doing as your brother bade me—be all things to all partners—will you give me my reward by letting me tell you that I shall never hear 'Roses Red' again without thinking of the most perfect dance I ever had?"

"That sounds like an appropriate farewell from the cotillion leader," said Roberta. Then instantly she knew that in her haste to cover a very girlish sense of pleasure in the thing he had said, she herself had said an unkind one. She knew it as a slow red came into her guest's handsome face and his eyes darkened. Before he could speak—though, indeed, he did not seem in haste to speak—she added, putting out her hand impulsively:

"Forgive me; I didn't mean it. You have been lovely to everyone tonight, and I have appreciated it. I am wrong; I think you are much more and have in you far more . . . than . . . as if you were only . . . the thing I said."

He made no immediate reply, though he took the hand she gave him. He continued to look at her for so long that her own eyes fell. When he did speak, it was in a low, odd tone that she could not quite understand.

"Miss Gray," said he, "if you want to cut a man to the quick, insist on thinking him that which he has never had any love for being, and which he has grown to detest the thought of. But perhaps it's a salutary sort of surgery, for—by the powers! If I can't make you think differently of me it won't be for lack of will. So thank you for being hard on me, thank you for everything. Good night!"

As she looked at him march away with his head up, her hand was aching with the force of the almost brutally hard grip he had given it with that last speech. Her final glimpse of him showed him with a tinge of the angry red still lingering on his cheek and a peculiar set to his finely cut mouth that she had never noticed there before. But, in spite of this, anything more courtly than his leave-taking of her mother and her Aunt Ruth she had never seen from one of the young men of the day.

Chapter 9

MR. KENDRICK ENTERTAINS

On their way downstairs, Matthew Kendrick and his grandson, escorted by Louis Gray, encountered a small company of people apparently just arrived from a train. Louis stopped for a moment to greet them, turned them over to his brother Stephen, whom he signaled from a stair landing above, and went on down to the entrance hall with the Kendricks.

"Too bad they're late for the party," he observed. "They had written they couldn't come, I believe. Mother will have to do a bit of figuring to dispose of them. But the more the merrier under this roof, every time."

"It's rather late to be putting people up for the night," Richard observed. "Your mother will be sending some of them to a hotel, I imagine. Couldn't we"—he glanced at his grandfather—"have the pleasure of taking them in our car? Or of sending it back for them, if there are too many?"

"Thank you, but I've no doubt Mother can arrange—" Louis Gray began when old Matthew Kendrick interrupted him.

"We can do better than that, Dick," said he. He turned to Louis. "We will wait," he said, "while you present my compliments to your mother and say that it will give me great satisfaction if she will allow me to entertain an overflow party of her guests."

Hardly able to believe his ears, Richard stared at his grandfather. What had come over him, who had lived in such seclusion for so many years, that he should be offering hospitality at midnight to total strangers? He smiled to himself. But the next moment a thought struck him.

"Grandfather," he said hurriedly, "why not specially invite that delightful couple: the one they call 'Uncle Rufus' and his wife?"

"An excellent idea," Mr. Kendrick agreed, "though they might not be willing to make the change at so late an hour."

"People who were dancing with spirit ten minutes ago will be ready to travel right now," prophesied Richard. He took flying leaps up the stairs in pursuit of Louis. Catching him on the next floor, he made his request known. Louis received it without sign of surprise, but inwardly, as he hurried away, he was speculating upon what agencies could be at work with the young man that he should be so eager to do this deed of extraordinary friendliness.

Mrs. Gray hesitated over Matthew Kendrick's invitation, although her hospitable home was already crowded to the rooftree.[1] But taking Judge Calvin Gray into her counsels, she was so strongly advised by him to accept the offer that she somewhat reluctantly consented to do so.

"It's great, Eleanor, simply great!" he urged. "It will do my friend Matthew more good than anything that has happened to him in a twelvemonth. As for young Richard—from what I've seen tonight, you've nothing to fear from his part in the affair. Let them have Rufus and Ruth—they'll enjoy it hugely. And give them as many more as will relieve the congestion. Matthew could take care of a regiment in that stone barracks of his."

"Sending Rufus and Ruth would give me quite space enough," she declared. "Rufus has the largest room in the house, and I could put this last party there. It is really very kind of Mr. Kendrick, and I shall be glad to solve my problem in that way, since you think it best."

Mr. and Mrs. Rufus Gray, having the question put to them, acceded to it with readiness. Both had been warmly drawn toward Richard, and though his grandfather had seemed to them a figure of somewhat unnecessarily dignified reserve, the mere fact of his extending the invitation at all was to them sufficient proof of his cordiality.

"It's nothing at all to pack up," Mrs. Rufus asserted. "I'll just take what I need for the night, and we'll be coming over for the tree in the morning, so I can get my other things then. I shall call it a real treat to be inside the home of such a wealthy man. How lonely he must be, living in such a great house, with only his grandson!"

So Aunt Ruth descended the stairs, wearing her little gray silk bonnet and a heavy cape of gray cloth, her hand on her husband's arm, her bright eyes shining with anticipation. Aunt Ruth dearly loved a bit of excitement and seldom found much in her quiet life upon the farm. As

---

[1] Roof ridgepole.

Matthew Kendrick looked up and saw her coming slowly down, her husband carefully adjusting himself to the dip and swing of her step as she put always the same foot foremost, he found himself distinctly glad of his grandson's suggestion, since it gave him so charming a guest to entertain as Mrs. Rufus Gray.

In the interval, Richard had retired to a telephone and had made the wires between his present location and the stone pile warm with his orders. In consequence, a certain gray-haired housekeeper, lately returned from some family festivities of her own and about to retire, found herself galvanized into activity by the sound of a well-known and slightly imperious voice issuing upsetting instructions to have the best suite of rooms in the house made ready for occupancy within half an hour and the house itself lighted for the reception of guests. Other commands to the butler and Mr. Richard's own manservant followed in quick succession, and when the young man turned away from the telephone he was again smiling to himself at the thought of the consternation he was causing in a household accustomed to be run upon such lines of conservatism and well-defined routine that any deviation therefrom was likely to prove most unacceptable. He himself was at home there such a small portion of his time, and during the periods he spent there, was so careful never to bring within its walls any festival-making of his own, he knew just how astonishing to the middle-aged housekeeper, the solemn-faced old butler, and the rest of them would be these midnight orders. He was enjoying the giving of such orders all the more for that!

Old Matthew Kendrick assisted Mrs. Rufus Gray into his luxuriously fitted, electric-lighted town car as if she had been a royal personage, wrapping soft, thick rugs about her until she was almost lost to view.

"Why, I couldn't be cold in this shut-in place," she protested. "Not a breath could touch anyone in here, I should say."

"I should call it pretty snug," Rufus Gray agreed with his wife, looking about him at the comfortable appointments of the car. "But there's just one thing a carriage like this wouldn't be good for, and that's taking a party of young folks on a sleigh ride on a snapping winter's night!" His bright brown eyes regarded those of Matthew Kendrick with some curiosity. "I reckon you never took that sort of a ride when you were a boy?" he queried.

"Yes, yes, I have—many a time," Mr. Kendrick insisted. "And great times we had. Boys and girls needed no electricity to keep them comfortable on the coldest of nights. It's my grandson Richard who feels this sort of thing a necessity. Until he came home, a carriage and pair of horses had been all the equipage I needed."

"Grandfather is getting to where a little extra warmth on a blustering winter's day is essential to his comfort," Richard declared, feeling a curious necessity, somehow, to justify the use of the expensive and commodious equipage in the eyes of the country gentleman who seemed to regard it so lightly.

"It's very nice," Mrs. Gray said quickly. "I should hardly know I was outdoors at all. And how smoothly it runs along over the streets. The young man out there in front must be a very good driver, I should think. He doesn't seem to mind the car-tracks at all."

"No, Rogers doesn't bother much about car-tracks," Richard agreed gravely. "His idea is to get home and to bed."

"It is pretty late, and I'm afraid waiting for us has made you a good deal later than you would have been," said Mrs. Gray regretfully.

"Not a bit—no, no."

"We'll go right to our room as soon as we get there," said she, "and you mustn't trouble to do a thing extra for us."

"It's going to be a great pleasure to have you under our roof," the young man assured her, smiling.

Arrived at the great stone mansion that was the well-known residence of Matthew Kendrick, as it had been of his family for several generations, Richard stared up at it with a sense of strangeness. Except for the halls and dining room, his grandfather's quarters and his own, he could not remember seeing it lighted as other homes were lighted, with rows of gleaming windows here and there, denoting occupancy by many people. Now, one whole wing, where lay the special suite of guest rooms used at long intervals for particularly distinguished persons, was brilliantly shining out upon the December night.

The car drew up beneath a massive covered entrance, and a great door swung back. A heavy-eyed, elderly butler admitted the party, which were ushered into an impressive but gloomy and inhospitable-looking reception room. Matthew Kendrick glanced somewhat uncertainly at his nephew, who promptly took things in charge.

"I thought perhaps Mr. and Mrs. Gray would have some sandwiches and . . . er . . . something more . . . with us before they go to their rooms," Richard suggested, nodding at Parks, the heavy-eyed butler.

"Yes, yes," agreed Mr. Kendrick, but Mrs. Rufus broke in upon him.

"Oh, no, Mr. Kendrick!" she cried softly, much distressed. "Please don't think of such a thing at this hour. And we've just had refreshments at

Eleanor's. Don't let us keep you up a minute. I'm sure you must be tired after this long evening."

"Not at all, madam. Nor do you yourself look so," responded Matthew Kendrick in his somewhat stately manner. "But you may be feeling like sleep, nonetheless. If you prefer, you shall go to your rest at once." He turned to his grandson again. "Dick—"

"I'll take them up," said that young man eagerly. He offered his arm to Aunt Ruth.

Uncle Rufus looked about him for the handbag that his wife had so hurriedly packed. "We had a little grip . . . ," said he uncertainly.

"We'll find it upstairs, I think," Richard assured him and led the way with Aunt Ruth. "I'm sorry we have no lift,"[2] he said to her, "but the stairs are rather easy, and we'll take them slowly."

Aunt Ruth puzzled a little over this speech, but made nothing of it and wisely let it go. The stairs were easy—extremely easy—and so heavily padded that she seemed to herself merely to be walking up a slight, velvet-floored incline. The whole house, it may be explained, was fitted and furnished after the style of that period in the latter half of the last century when heavily carpeted floors, heavily shrouded windows, heavily decorated walls, and heavily upholstered chairs were considered the essentials of luxury and comfort. Old Matthew Kendrick had never cared to make any changes, and his grandson had had too little interest in the place to recommend them. The younger man's own private rooms he had altered sufficiently to express his personal tastes, but the rest of the house was to him outside the range of his concern. The whole place, including his own quarters, was to him merely a sort of temporary habitation. He had no plans in relation to it, no sense of responsibility in regard to it. When he had ordered the finest suite of rooms in the house to be put in readiness for the guests, it was precisely as he would have requested the management of a great hotel to place at his disposal the best they had to offer. To tell the truth, he had no recollection at all of how the rooms looked or what their dimensions were.

Mr. and Mrs. Rufus Gray, entering the first room of the series, a large and elaborately furnished apartment with the effect of a drawing room, much gilt and brocade and many looking glasses[3] in evidence, looked at Richard in some surprise as he seated them. Richard then went to the door of a second room, glanced in, nodded, and returned to his guests.

"I hope you will find everything you want in there," he said. "If you

---

[2] Elevator.

[3] Mirrors.

don't, please ring. You will see your dressing room on the left, Mr. Gray. I will send you my man in the morning to see if he can do anything for you."

"I shan't need any man, thank you," protested Mr. Gray.

When, after lingering a minute or two, their young host had bade them good night and left them, the elderly pair looked at each other. Uncle Rufus's eyes were twinkling, but in his wife's showed a touch of soft indignation.

"It seems like making a joke of us," said she, "to put us in such a place as this, when he can guess what we're used to."

"He doesn't mean it as a joke," her husband protested good-humoredly. "He wants to give us the best he's got. I don't mind a mite. To be sure, I could get along with one looking glass to shave myself in, but it's kind of interesting to know how many some folks think necessary when they aren't limited. Let's go look in our sleeping room. Maybe that's a little less princely."

Aunt Ruth limped slowly across the Persian carpet and stood still in the doorway of the room Richard had designated as hers. Uncle Rufus stared in over her small shoulder.

"Well, well," he chuckled. "I reckon Napoleon Bonaparte wouldn't have thought this any too fine for him, but it sort of dazzles me. I'm glad somebody's got that bed ready to sleep in. I shouldn't have been sure 'twas meant for that if they hadn't. There seems to be another room on behind this one—what's that?"

He marched across and looked in. "Now, if I was rich, I wouldn't mind having one of these opening right out of my room. What there isn't in here for keeping yourself clean can't be thought of."

"Rufus," said his wife solemnly, following him into the white-tiled bathroom, "I want you should look at these bath towels. I never in my life set eyes on anything like them. They must have cost—I don't know what they cost—I didn't know there were such bath towels made!"

"I don't want to wrap myself in a blanket," asserted her husband. "I want to know I've got a towel in my hand that I can whisk around me and slap myself with. Look here, let's get to bed. We could sit up all night examining our accommodations. For my part, Eleanor's style of living suits me a good deal better than this kind of elegance. Her house is fine and comfortable but no foolishness. There's one thing I do like, though. This carpet feels mighty good to your bare feet, I'll make sure!"

He presently made sure, walking back and forth barefooted across the soft floor, chuckling like a boy, and making his toes sink into the heavy pile of the great rug. He surveyed his small wife in her dressing gown, sitting before the wide looking glasses of an elaborate dressing table, putting her white locks into crimping pins.

"Ruth," said he with sudden solemnity, "I forgot to undress in my dressing room. Had I better put my clothes on and go take 'em off again in there?"

He pointed across to an adjoining room, brilliant with lights and equipped with all manner of furnishings adapted to masculine uses.

His wife turned about, laughing like a girl. "Maybe in there," she suggested, "you could find a chair small enough to hang your coat across the back of. I'm afraid it'll get all wrinkled, folded like that."

Uncle Rufus explored. After a minute he came back. "There's a strange sort of bureau thing in there all filled with coat-and-pants hangers," he announced. "I'm going to put my things in it. It'll keep 'em from getting wrinkled, as you say."

When he returned: "There's another bed in there," he said. "I don't know what it's for. It's got the covers all turned back too, just like this one. Maybe we've made a mistake. Maybe there's somebody that has that room, and he hasn't come in yet. Do you suppose I'd better shut the door between?"

"Maybe you had," agreed his wife anxiously. "It would be dreadful if he should come in after a while. Still, young Mr. Kendrick called it your dressing room."

"And my clothes are in there," added Uncle Rufus. "It's all right. Probably the girl made a mistake when she fixed that bed—thought there was a child with us, maybe."

"You might just shut the door," Aunt Ruth suggested. "Then if anybody did come in . . . "

Uncle Rufus shook his head. "It's meant for us," he asserted with conviction as he climbed into bed. "He said 'dressing room' and pointed. The girl's made a mistake, that's all. It's a good place for my clothes, and I'm going to leave 'em there. Will you put out the lights?"

Aunt Ruth looked around the wall. "I can never get used to electric lights at Eleanor's," said she. "And I don't see the place here at all."

She searched for the switches some time in vain, but at length discovered them and succeeded in extinguishing the lights of the room the pair were in. But the lights of the adjoining rooms still burned with brilliancy.

"Oh, dear!" she sighed softly. Then she appealed to her husband.

Uncle Rufus, who had nearly fallen asleep while his wife had been searching, spoke without opening his eyes. "Shut all the doors and leave 'em going," he advised.

"Oh, no, I can't do that! Think of the cost, running all night so."

"I reckon they can afford it," he commented drowsily.

But Aunt Ruth continued to hunt, first in the large outer room that looked like a drawing room and possessed an elaborate central electrolier[4] whose control, even after she discovered the switch, caused the little lady considerable perplexity. When she had at length succeeded in extinguishing the illumination, she returned, guided by the lights in the other rooms. The bathroom keys[5] were soon found, and then she applied herself to discovering those in the dressing room. These eluded her for some minutes, but at length, all lights being turned off, Aunt Ruth found herself in total darkness. She groped about in it for some time without success, for the heavy curtains had been closely drawn, and not a ray of light penetrated the spacious rooms from any quarter. After having followed the wall for what seemed an interminable distance without reaching a recognizable position, she was forced to call to her husband. He was asleep and responded only after being many times addressed. Then he sat up in bed.

"Hey? What? What's the matter?" he inquired anxiously, peering into the darkness.

"Nothing, dear—only I couldn't find the bed after I turned the lights out. Keep on talking, and I'll work my way to you," answered his wife's voice from some distance.

Guided by his voice (he found plenty to say on the subject of putting people to bed in the midst of large, unfamiliar spaces), she groped her way to his side. He put out a gentle hand to welcome her, and as she took her place the two fell to laughing softly over the whole situation.

"Why," said Uncle Rufus, "for all I've slept for forty years in the same room—and a pretty sizable room I've always thought it—I've never got so I could plow a straight furrow through it in the dark. I reckon a lifetime would be too short to get to know my way around this plantation."

He could with difficulty be restrained from telling Richard about the incident next morning when that young man came to their rooms to escort them down to breakfast.

"I'm glad to have somebody pilot me," Uncle Rufus declared, his eyes twinkling as he followed after his wife, who leaned on Richard's arm. "A man must have a pretty good sense of direction to keep his bearings in a house as big as this."

Richard laughed. "It's rather a straight road to the dining room. I think

---

4 A chandelier for electric lights.

5 Small electric light switches.

I must have worn a path there since I came. Here we are—and here's Grandfather down before us. He's the first one in the house to be up, always."

Matthew Kendrick advanced to meet his guests, shaking hands with great cordiality.

"It seems very wonderful, Madam Gray," said he, "to have a lady in the house on Christmas morning. Will you do me the honor to take this seat?" He put her in a chair before a massive silver urn, under which burned a spirit lamp[6]. "And will you pour our coffee? It's many a year since we've had coffee served from the table, poured by a woman's hand."

"Why, I should be greatly pleased to pour the coffee," cried Aunt Ruth happily. Her bright glance was fastened upon a mass of scarlet flowers in the center of the table, for which Richard had sent between dark and daylight. He smiled across the table at her.

"Are they real?" she breathed.

"Absolutely! Splendid color, aren't they? I can't remember the name, but they look like Christmas."

Neither Mr. nor Mrs. Rufus Gray had ever in their lives eaten such a breakfast as was now served to them. Such extraordinary fruits, such perfectly cooked game, such delicious food of various sorts—they could only taste and wonder. Richard, with a young man's healthy appetite, kept them company, but his grandfather made a frugal meal of toast, coffee, and a single egg, quite as if he were more accustomed to such simple fare than to any other.

The breakfast over, Mr. Kendrick took them to his own private rooms to show them a painting of which he had been telling them. Richard accompanied them, having constituted himself chief assistant to Mrs. Gray, to whom he had taken a boyish liking that was steadily growing. Establishing her in a comfortable armchair, he sat down beside her.

"Now, Mr. Richard," said she presently while Mr. Matthew Kendrick and her husband were discussing an interesting question over their cigars in an adjoining room (Mr. Kendrick's adherence to the code of an earlier day making it impossible for him to think of smoking in the presence of a lady), "I wonder if there isn't something you would let me do for you. You and your grandfather live alone, so you must have things that need a woman's hand. While I sit here, I'd enjoy mending some socks or gloves for you."

Richard looked at her. The sincerity of her offer was so evident that he

---

[6] A lamp lit by petroleum.

could not turn it aside with an evasion or a refusal. But he had not an article in the world that needed mending. When things of his reached that stage they were invariably turned over to his man, Bliss. He considered.

"That's certainly awfully kind of you, Mrs. Gray," said he. "But . . . have you . . . ?"

She put her hand into a capacious pocket and produced therefrom a tiny housewife[7] stocked with thimble, needles, and all necessary implements.

"I never go without it," said she. "There's always somebody to be mended up when you least expect it. My niece Roberta tripped on one of her flounces last night, not being used to dancing in such full, old-fashioned skirts. Rosy was starting to pin it up, but I whipped out my kit, and how they laughed to see a pocket in a best dress!" She laughed herself, at the recollection. "But I had Robby sewed up in less time than it takes to tell it—much better than pinning!"

"How beautifully she danced those old-fashioned dances," Richard observed eagerly. "It was a great pleasure to see her."

"Yes, it's generally a pleasure to see Robby do things," Roberta's aunt agreed. "She goes into them with so much vim. When she comes out to visit us on the farm it's the same way. She must have a hand in the churning, or the sweeping, or something that'll keep her busy. Aren't you going to get me the things, Mr. Richard?"

The young man hastened away. Arrived before certain drawers and receptacles, he turned over piles of hosiery with a thoughtful air. Presently selecting a pair of black silk socks of particularly fine texture, he deliberately forced his thumb through either heel, taking care to make the edges rough as possible. Laughing to himself, he then selected a pair of gray street gloves, eyed them speculatively for a moment, then, taking out a penknife, cut the stitches in several places, making one particularly long rent down the side of the left thumb. He regarded these damages doubtfully, wondering if they looked entirely natural and accidental; then, shaking his head, he gathered up the socks and gloves and returned with them to Aunt Ruth.

She looked them over. "For pity's sake," said she, "you wear out your things in strange ways! How did you ever manage to get holes in your heels right on the bottom, like that? All the folks I ever knew wear out their heels on the back or side."

---

7 Pocketsize container for small articles such as thread.

Richard examined a sock. "That is rather odd," he admitted. "I must have done it dancing."

"I shall have to split my silk to darn these places," commented Aunt Ruth. "These must be summer socks, so thin as this." She glanced at the trimly shod foot of her companion and shook her head. "You young folks! In my day we never thought silk cobwebs warm enough for winter."

"Tell me about your day, won't you, please?" the young man urged. "Those must have been great days, to have produced such results."

The little lady found it impossible to resist such interest and was presently talking away as she mended, while her listener watched her flying fingers and enjoyed every word of her entertaining discourse. He artfully led her from the past to the present, brought out a tale or two of Roberta's visits at the farm, and learned with outward gravity but inward exultation that that young person had actually gone to the lengths of begging to be allowed to learn to milk a cow but had failed to achieve success.

"I can't imagine Miss Roberta's failing in anything she chose to attempt," was his joyous comment.

"She certainly failed in that." Aunt Ruth seemed rather pleased herself at the thought. "But then she didn't really go into it seriously. It was because Louis put her up to it, told her she couldn't do it. She only really tried once—and then spent the rest of the morning washing her hair. Such a task—it's so heavy and curly—" Aunt Ruth suddenly stopped talking about Roberta, as if it had occurred to her that this young man looked altogether too interested in such trifles as the dressing of certain thick, dark locks.

Presently, the mending over, the Grays were taken, according to promise, back to the Christmas celebration in the other house, and Richard, returning to his grandfather, proposed with some unwonted diffidence of manner that the two attend the service at St. Luke's together.

The old man looked up at his grandson, astonishment in his face.

"Church, Dick—with you?" he repeated. "Why, I . . ." He hesitated. "Did the little lady we entertained last night put that into your head?"

"She put several things into my head," Richard admitted, "but not that. Will you go, sir? It's fully time now, I believe."

Matthew Kendrick's keen eyes continued to search his grandson's face, to Richard's inner confusion. Outwardly, the younger man maintained an attitude of dignified questioning.

"I am willing to go," said Mr. Kendrick after a moment.

At St. Luke's that morning, from her place in the family pew, Ruth Gray, remembering a certain promise, looked about her as searchingly as was possible. Nowhere within her line of vision could she discern the figure of Richard Kendrick, but she was nonetheless confident that somewhere within the stately walls of the old church he was taking part in the impressive Christmas service. When it ended and she turned to make her way up the aisle, leading a bevy of young cousins, her eyes, beneath a sheltering hat brim, darted here and there until, unexpectedly nearby, they encountered the half-amused but wholly respectful recognition of those they sought. As Ruth made her slow progress toward the door, she was aware that the Kendricks, elder and younger, were close behind her, and just before the open air was reached she was able to exchange with Richard a low-spoken question and answer.

"Wasn't it beautiful? Aren't you glad you came?"

"It *was* beautiful, Miss Ruth, and I'm more than glad I came."

Several hours earlier on that same Christmas morning, Ruth had rushed into Roberta's room, crying out happily:

"Flowers! Flowers! Flowers! For you and Rosy and Mother and me! They just came. Mr. Richard Loring Kendrick's card is in ours; of course it's in yours. Here are yours; do open the box and let me see! Mother's are orchids, perfectly wonderful ones. Rosy's are mignonettes, great clusters, a whole armful—I didn't know florists grew such richness—they smell like the summer kind. She's so pleased. Mine are violets and lilies of the valley. I'm perfectly crazy over them. Yours—"

Roberta had the cover off. Roses! Somehow she had known they would be roses after last night. But such roses!

Ruth cried out in ecstasy, bending to bury her face in the glorious mass. "They're exactly the color of the old brocade frock, Robby," she exulted. She picked up the card in its envelope. "May I look at it?" she asked, with her fingers already in the flap. "Ours all have some Christmas wish, and Rosy's adds something about Gordon and Dorothy."

"You might just let me see first," said Roberta carelessly, stretching out her hand for the card. Ruth handed it over. Roberta turned her head. "Who's calling?" she murmured and ran to the door, card in hand.

"I didn't hear anyone," Ruth called after her.

But Roberta disappeared. Around the turn of the hall, she scanned her card.

"Thorns to the thorny," she read and stood staring at the unexpected words written in a firm, masculine hand. That was all. Did it sting? Yet, curiously enough, Roberta rather liked that odd message.

When she came back, Ruth, in the excitement of examining many other Christmas offerings, had rushed on, leaving the box of roses on Roberta's bed. The recipient took out a single rose and examined its stem. Thorns! She had never seen sharper ones, and not one had been removed. But the rose itself was perfection.

Chapter 10

OPINIONS AND THEORIES

Mr. and Mrs. Rufus Gray were the last to leave the city after the house party. They returned to their brother Robert's home for a day, when the other guests had gone, and it was on the evening before their departure that they related their experiences while at the house of Matthew Kendrick. With most of the members of the Gray household, they were sitting before the fire in the living room when Aunt Ruth suddenly spoke her mind.

"I don't know when I've felt so sorry for the too rich as I felt in that house," said she. She was knitting a gray silk mitten, and her needles were flying.

"Why, Aunt Ruth?" inquired her nephew Louis, who sat next to her, reveling in the comfort of home after a particularly harassing day at the office. "Did they seem to lack anything in particular?"

"I should say they did," she replied. "Nothing that money can buy, of course, but about everything that it can't."

"For instance?" he pursued, turning affectionate eyes upon his aunt's small figure in its gray gown as the firelight played upon it, touching her abundant silvering locks and making her eyes seem to sparkle almost as brilliantly as her swiftly moving needles!

Aunt Ruth put down her knitting for an instant and looked at her nephew. "Why, you know," said she, "you're sitting in the very middle of it this minute!"

Louis looked about him, smiling. He was, indeed, in the midst of an accustomed scene of both homelikeness and beauty. The living room was of such generous proportions that even when the entire family were gathered there, they could not crowd it. On a wide couch at one side of the fireplace sat his father and mother, talking in low tones concerning some matter of evident interest, to judge by their intent faces.

Rosamond, like the girl she resembled, sat girl fashion on a pile of cushions close by the fire; and Stephen, her husband, was not far away, by a table with a droplight, absorbed in a book. Uncle Rufus was examining a pile of photographs on the other side of the table. Ted sprawled on a couch at the far end of the room, deep in a boys' magazine, a reading light at his elbow. At the opposite end of the room, where the piano stood, Roberta, music rack before her, was drawing her bow across nearly noiseless strings while Ruth picked softly at her harp: indications of intention to burst forth into musical strains when a hush should chance to fall upon the company.

Judge Calvin Gray alone was absent from the gathering, and even as Louis's eyes wandered about the pleasant room, his uncle's figure appeared in the doorway. As if he were answering Aunt Ruth, Judge Gray spoke his thought.

"I wonder," said he, advancing toward the fireplace, "if anywhere in this wide world there is a happier family life than this!"

Louis sprang up to offer Judge Gray the chair he had been occupying: a favorite, luxuriously cushioned armchair with a reading light beside it ready to be switched on at will. This chair was Uncle Calvin's special treasure of an evening. Louis himself took up his position on the hearth rug, opposite Rosamond.

Aunt Ruth answered her brother energetically: "None happier, Calvin, I'll warrant, and few half as happy. I can't help wishing those two people Rufus and I've been visiting could look in here just now."

"Why make them envious?" suggested Louis, who loved to hear his Aunt Ruth's crisp speeches.

"The question is, would they be envious?" This came from Stephen, whose absorption in his book evidently admitted penetration from the outside.

"Why, of course they would!" declared Aunt Ruth. "You should have seen the way they had me pour the coffee and tea, all the while I was there. That young man Richard was always getting me to pour something—said he liked to see me do it. And he was always sending a servant off and doing things for me himself. If I'd been a young girl, he couldn't have hovered around any more devotedly."

A general laugh greeted this, for Aunt Ruth's expression of face as she told it was provocative.

"We can readily believe that, Ruth," declared Judge Gray, and his brother Robert nodded. The low-voiced talk between Mr. Robert Gray and his wife had ceased; Stephen had laid down his book; Ruth had stopped plucking at her harp strings; and only Roberta still seemed interested in anything but Aunt Ruth and her experiences and opinions.

"I mended his socks and gloves for him," announced Aunt Ruth contentedly. "You needn't tell me they don't miss a woman's hand about the house over there."

"She mended Rich Kendrick's socks and gloves!" murmured Louis with a laughing, incredulous glance at Rosamond, who lifted delighted eyes to him. "I can't believe it. He must have made holes in them on purpose."

"Why, not even a spendthrift would do that!" Aunt Ruth promptly denied the possibility of such folly. "I don't say but they are lavish with things there. Rufus and I were a good deal bothered by all their lights. We couldn't seem to get them all put out. And every time we put them out anywhere, somebody'd turn them on again for us."

Uncle Rufus broke in here, narrating their experience with the various switch buttons in the suite of rooms, and the company laughed until they wept over his comments.

"But all that's neither here nor there," said he finally. "Of course we weren't up to such elaborate arrangements, and it made us feel sort of rustic. But I can tell you they didn't spare any pains to make us comfortable and at home—if, as Ruth says, you can make anybody feel at home in a great place like that. I feel as she does, sorry for 'em both. They're pretty fine gentlemen, if I'm any judge, and I don't know which I like better, the older or the younger."

"There can be no question about the older," said his brother Robert Gray, joining in the talk with evident interest. "Mr. Matthew Kendrick made his place long ago in the business world as one of the great and just. He has taught that world many fine lessons of truth and honor, as well as of success."

Judge Gray nodded. "I'm glad to hear that you appreciate him, Robert," said he. "Few know better than I how deserved that is. And still fewer recognize the fine and sensitive nature behind the impression of power he has always given. He is the type of man, as sister Ruth here is quick to discern, who must be lonely in the midst of his great wealth for the lack of just such a privilege as this we have here tonight: the close association with people whom we love and with whom we sympathize in all that matters most. Matthew Kendrick was a devoted husband and father. In spite of his grandson's presence of late, he must sorely long for companionship."

"His grandson's going to give him more of that than he has," declared Aunt Ruth, smiling over her knitting as if recalling a pleasant memory.

"He and I had quite a bit of talk while I was there, and he's beginning to realize that he owes his grandfather more than he's given him. I had a good chance to see what was in that boy's heart, and I know there's plenty of warmth there. And there's real character in him, too. I've had enough sons of my own to know the signs, and the fact that they were poor in this world's goods and he is rich—too rich—doesn't make a mite of difference in the signs!"

Mrs. Robert Gray, who had been listening with an intent expression in eyes whose beauty was not more appealing than their power of observation was keen, now spoke, and all turned to her. She was a woman whose opinion on any subject of common interest was always waited for and attended upon. Her voice was rich and low—her family did not fully know how dear to their ears was the sound of that voice.

"Young Mr. Kendrick," said she, "couldn't wish, Ruth, for a more powerful advocate than you. To have you approve him, after seeing him under more intimate circumstances than we are likely to do, must commend him to our goodwill. To tell the frank truth, I have been rather afraid to admit him to my good graces, lest there be really no great force of character, or even promise of it, behind that handsome face and winning manner. But if you see the signs, as you say, we must look more hopefully upon him."

"She's not the only one who sees signs," asserted Judge Gray. "He's coming on—he's coming on well in his work with me. He's really learning to work. I admit he didn't know how when he came to me. Something has waked him up. I'm inclined to think," he went on, with a mischievous glance toward the end of the room where sat the noiseless musicians, "it might have been my niece Roberta's shining example of industry when she spent a day with us in my library, typing work for me back in October. Never was such a sight to serve as an inspiration for a laggardly young man!"

There was a general laugh, and all eyes were turned toward that end of the room devoted to the users of the musical instruments. In response came a deep, resonant note from Roberta's cello, over which the silent bow had been for some time suspended. There followed a minor scale, descending well into the depths and vibrating dismally as it went. Louis, a mocking light in his eye, strolled down the room to his sisters.

"That's the way you feel about it, eh?" he queried, regarding Roberta with brotherly interest. "Consigning the poor, innocent chap to the bottom of the ladder when he's doing his best to climb up to the sunshine of your smile. Have you no respect for the opinion of your betters?"

"Get out your fiddle and play the Grieg *Danse Caprice* with us," was her reply, and Louis obeyed, though not without a word or two more in her ear that made her lift her bow threateningly. Presently, the trio were off, playing with a spirit and dash that drew all ears, and at the close of the *Danse*, hearty applause called for more. After this diversion, naturally enough, new subjects came up for discussion.

Returning to the living room in search of a dropped letter, after the family had dispersed for the night, Roberta found her mother lingering there alone. She had drawn a low chair close to the fire, and having extinguished all other lights, was sitting quietly looking into the still-glowing embers. Roberta, forgetting her quest, came close and, flinging a cushion at her mother's knee, dropped down there. This was a frequent happening, and the most intimate hours the two spent together were after this fashion.

There was no speech for a little, though Mrs. Gray's hand wandered carelessly about her daughter's neck in a way Roberta dearly loved, drawing the loosened dark locks away from the small ears, or twisting a curly strand about her fingers. Suddenly, the girl burst out:

"Mother, what are you to do when you find all your theories upset?"

"*All* upset?" repeated Mrs. Gray in her rich and quiet voice. "That would be a calamity indeed. Surely there must be one or two of yours remaining stable?"

"It seems not, just now. One disproved overturns another. They all hinge on one another—at least mine do."

"Perhaps not as closely as you think. What is it, dear? Can you tell me anything about it?"

"Not much, I'm afraid. Oh, it's nothing very real, I suppose—just a sort of vague discomfort at feeling that certain ideals I thought were as fixed as the stars in the heavens seem to be wobbling as if they might shoot downward any minute, and . . . and leave only a trail of light behind!"

The last words came on a note of rather shaky laughter. Roberta's arm lay across her mother's knee, her head upon it. She turned her head downward for an instant, burying her face in the angle of her arm. Mrs. Gray regarded the mass of dark locks beneath her hand with a look amused yet sympathetic.

"That sort of discomfort attacks us all at times," she said. "Ideals change and develop with our growth. One would not want the same ones to serve her all her life."

"I know. But when it's not a new and better ideal that displaces the old one, but only an attraction . . . "

"An attraction not ideal?"

Roberta shook her head. "I'm afraid not. And I don't see why it should be an attraction at all. It ought not to be, if my ideals have been what they should have been. And they have. Why, you gave them to me, Mother, many of them—or at least helped me to work them out for myself. And I . . . I had confidence in them!"

"And they're shaken?"

"Not the ideals; they're all the same. Only they don't seem to be proof against assault. Oh, I'm talking in riddles, I know. I don't want to put any of it into words; it makes it seem more real. And it's only a shadowy sort of difficulty. Maybe that's all it will be."

Mothers are wonderful at divination; why should they not be, when all their task is a training in understanding young natures that do not understand themselves. From these halting phrases of mystery Mrs. Gray gathered much more than her daughter would have imagined. But she did not let that be seen.

"If it is only a shadowy difficulty, the rising of the sun will put it to flight," she predicted.

Roberta was silent for a space. Then suddenly she sat up.

"I had a long letter from Forbes Westcott today," she said in a tone that tried to be casual. "He's staying on in London, getting material for that difficult Letchworth case he's so anxious to win. It's a wonderfully interesting letter, though he doesn't say much about the case. He's one of the cleverest letter writers I ever knew in the flesh. It's really an art with him. If he hadn't made a lawyer of himself, he would have been a man of letters, his literary tastes are so fine. It's quite an education in the use of delightfully spirited English, a correspondence with him. I've appreciated that more with each letter."

She produced the letter. "Just listen to this account of an interview he had with a distinguished member of parliament, the one who has just made that daring speech in the House that set everybody on fire." And she read aloud from several closely written pages, holding the sheets toward the still-bright embers and giving the words the benefit of her own clear and understanding interpretation. Her mother listened with interest.

"That is, indeed, a fine description," she agreed. "There is no question that Forbes has a brilliant mind. The position he already occupies testifies to that, and the older men all acknowledge that he is rising more rapidly than could be expected of any ordinary man. He will be one of the great men of the legal profession, your father and uncle think, I know."

"One of the great men," repeated Roberta, her face still bent over her letter. "I suppose there's no doubt at all of that. And, Mother, you may imagine that when he sets himself to persuade . . . anyone to . . . any course, he knows how to put it as irresistibly as words can."

"Yes, I should imagine that, dear," said her mother, her eyes on the down-bent profile, whose outlines, against the background of the firelight, would have held a gaze less loving than her own.

"His age makes him interesting, you know," pursued Roberta. "He's just enough older and maturer than any of the men I know to make him seem immensely more worthwhile. His very looks—that thin, keen face of his, it's plain, yet attractive, and his eyes look as if they could see through stone walls. It flatters you to have him seem to find the things you say worth listening to. I just can't explain his peculiar fascination— I really think it is that, except that it's his splendid mind that grips yours, somehow. Oh, I sound like a schoolgirl," she burst out, "in spite of my twenty-four years. I wonder if you see what I mean."

"I think I do," said her mother, smiling a little. "You mean that your judgment approves him, but that your heart lags a little behind?"

"How did you know?" Roberta folded her arms upon her mother's lap and looked up eagerly into her face. "I didn't say anything about my heart."

"But you did, dear. The very fact that you can discuss him so coolly tells me that your heart isn't seriously involved as yet. Is it?"

"That's what I don't know," said the girl. "When he writes like this— the last two pages I can't read to you—I don't know what I think. And I'm not used to not knowing what I think! It's disconcerting. It's like being taken off your feet and not set down again. Yet, when I'm with him, I'm not at all sure I should ever want him nearer than—well, than three feet away. And he's so insistent, persistent. He wants an answer now, by mail."

"Are you ready to give it?"

"No. I'm afraid to give it at long distance."

"Then do not. You are under no obligation to do that. The test of actual presence is the only one to apply. Let him wait till he comes home. It will not hurt him."

She spoke with spirit, and her daughter responded to the tone.

"I know that's the best advice," Roberta said, getting to her feet. "Mother, do you like him?"

"Yes, I have always liked Forbes," said Mrs. Gray with cordiality. "Your father likes him and trusts him as a man of honor in his profession. That is much to say. Whether he is a man who would make you happy, that is a different question. No one can answer that but yourself."

"I haven't wanted anyone to make me happy." Roberta stood upon the hearth rug, a figure of charm among the lights and shadows. "I've been absorbed in my work and my play. I enjoy my men friends and am glad when they go away and leave me. Life is so full and rich, just of itself. There are so many wonderful people of all sorts. The world is so interesting, and home is so dear!" She lifted her arms, her head up. "Mother, let's play the Bach 'Air'," she said. "That always takes the fever out of me and makes me feel calm and rational. Is it very late? Are you too tired? Nobody will be disturbed at this distance."

"I should love to play it," said Mrs. Gray, and together the two went down the room to the great piano that stood there in the darkness. Roberta switched on one hooded light, produced the music for her mother, and tuned her cello, sitting at one side away from the light, with no notes before her. Presently, the slow, deep, and majestic notes of the "Air for the G String" were vibrating through the quiet room, the cello player drawing her bow across and across the one string with affection for each rich note in her very touch. The other string tones followed her with exquisite sympathy, for Mrs. Gray was a musician from whom three of her four children had inherited an intense love for harmonic values.

But only a few bars had sounded when a tall figure came noiselessly into the room, and Mr. Robert Gray dropped into the seat before the fire that his wife had lately occupied. With head thrown back he listened, and when silence fell at the close of the performance, his deep voice was the first to break it.

"To me," he said, "that is the slow flowing and receding of waves upon a smooth and rocky shore. The sky is gray, but the atmosphere is warm and friendly. It is all very restful after a day of perturbation."

"Oh, is it like that to you?" queried Roberta softly out of the darkness. "To me it's as if I were walking down the nave of a great cathedral—Westminster, perhaps—big and bare and wonderful, with the organ playing ever so far away. The sun is shining outside, so it's not gloomy, only very peaceful, and one can't imagine the world at the doors." She looked over at her mother, whose face was just visible in the shaded light. "What is it to you, lovely lady?"

"It is a prayer," said her mother slowly, "a prayer for peace and purity in a restless world, yet a prayer for service, too. The one who prays lies very low, with his face concealed, and his spirit is full of worship."

The light was put out; the three—father, mother, and daughter—came together in the fading fire-glow. Roberta laid a warm young hand upon the shoulder of each. "You dears," she said. "What fortunate and happy children your four are, to be the children of you!"

Her father placed his firm fingers under her chin, lifting her face. "Your mother and I," said he, "consider ourselves most fortunate and happy to be the parents of you. You are an interesting quartet. 'Age cannot wither nor custom stale' your 'infinite variety.' But age *will* wither you if you often sit up to play Bach at midnight when you must teach school next day. Therefore, good night, Namesake!"

Yet when she had gone, her father and mother lingered by the last embers of the fire.

"God give her wisdom!" said Roberta's mother.

"He will, with you to ask Him," replied Roberta's father with his arms about his wife. "I think He never refuses you anything! I don't see how He could!"

Chapter 11

THE TAMING OF
THE SHREW

"School again, Rob! Don't you hate it?"

"No, of course I don't hate it. I'm much, much happier when I'm teaching Ethel Revell to forget her important young self and remember the part she is supposed to play than I am when I am merely dusting my room or driving downtown on errands."

As she spoke, Roberta pushed into place the last hairpin in the close and trim arrangement of her dark hair, briefly surveyed the result with a hand-glass[1], and rose from her dressing table. Ruth, at a considerably earlier stage of her dressing, regarded her sister's head with interest.

"I can always tell the difference between a school day and another day just by looking at your hair," she observed sagely.

"How, Miss Big Eyes, if you please?"

"You never leave a curl sticking out on school days. They sometimes work out before night, but that's not your fault. You look like one of Jane Austen's heroines now."

Roberta laughed a laugh of derision. "Miss Austen's heroines undoubtedly had ringlets hanging in profusion on either side of their oval faces."

"Yes, but I mean every hair of theirs was in order, and so are yours."

"Thank you. Only so can I command respect when I lecture my girls on their frenzied coiffures. Oh, but I'm thankful I can live at home and don't have to spend the nights with them! Some of them are dears, but to be responsible for them day and night would harrow my soul. Hook me up, will you, Rufus, please?"

---

[1] Hand-held mirror.

"You look just like a smooth-feathered bluebird in this," commented Ruth as she obediently fastened the severely simple school dress of dark blue, relieved only by its daintily fresh collar and cuffs of embroidered white lawn.

"I mean to. Miss Copeland wouldn't have a fluffy, frilly teacher in her school—and I don't blame her. It's difficult enough to train fluffy, frilly girls to like simplicity, even if one's self is a model of plainness and repose."

"And you're truly glad to go back, after this lovely vacation? Shouldn't you sort of like to keep on typing for Uncle Calvin, with Mr. Richard Kendrick sitting close by, looking at you over the top of his book?"

Roberta wheeled, answering with vehemence: "I should say not, you romantic infant! When I work I want to work with workers, not with drones! A person who can only dawdle over his task is of no use at all. How Uncle Calvin gets on with a mere imitation of a secretary, I can't possibly see. Why, Ted himself could cover more ground in a morning!"

"I don't think you do him justice," Ruth objected, with all the dignity of her sixteen years in evidence. "Of course he couldn't work as well with you in the room—he isn't used to it. And you are—you certainly are—awfully nice to look at, Rob."

"Nonsense! It's lucky you're going back to school yourself, child, to get these sentimental notions out of your head. Come, vacation's over! Let's not sigh for more dances; let's go at our work with a will. I've plenty before me. The school play comes week after next, and I haven't as good material this year as last. How I'm ever going to get Olivia Cartwright to put sufficient backbone into her Petruchio, I don't know. I only wish I could play him myself!"

"Rob! Couldn't you?"

"It's never done. My part is just to coach and coach, to go over the lines a thousand times and the stage business ten thousand, and then to stay behind the scenes and hiss at them: 'More spirit! More life! Throw yourself into it!' and then to watch them walk it through like puppets! Well, *The Taming of the Shrew* is pretty stiff work for amateurs, no doubt of that, there's that much to be said. Breakfast time, childie! You must hurry, and I must be off."

Half an hour later, Ruth watched her sister walk away down the street with Louis, her step as lithe and vigorous as her brother's. Ruth herself was accustomed to drive with her father to the school which she attended—a rival school, as it happened, of the fashionable one at which Roberta taught. She was not so strong as her sister, and a two-mile walk to school was apt to overtire her. But Roberta chose to walk every day and all days, and the more stormy the weather the surer was she to scorn all offers of a place beside Ruth in the brougham.

Louis's comment on the return of his sister to her work at Miss Copeland's school was much like that of Ruth. "Sorry vacation's over, Rob? That's where I have the advantage of you. The office never closes for more than a day; therefore I'm always in training."

"That's an advantage, surely enough. But I'm ready to go back. As I was telling Ruth this morning, I'm anxious to know whether Olivia Cartwright has forgotten her lines, and whether she's going to be able to infuse a bit of life into her Petruchio. This trying to make a schoolgirl play a big man's part . . . "

"You could do it, yourself," observed Louis, even as Ruth had done.

"And shouldn't I love to! I'm just longing to stride about the stage in Petruchio's boots."

"I'll wager you are. I'd like to see you do it. But the part of Katherine would be the thing for you—fascinating shrew that you could be."

"This from a brother! Yes, I'd like to play Katherine, too. But give me the boots, if you please. Do you happen to remember Olivia Cartwright?"

"Of course I do. And a mighty pretty and interesting girl she is. I should think she might make a Petruchio for you."

"I thought she would. But the boots seem to have a devastating effect. The minute she gets them on—even in imagination, for we haven't had a dress rehearsal yet—her voice grows softer and her manner more lady-like. It's the funniest thing I ever knew, to hear her say the lines:

> What's this? mutton? . . .
> 'Tis burnt, and so is all the meat:
> What dogs are these! Where is the rascal cook?
> How durst you, villains, bring it from the dresser,
> And serve it thus to me that love it not?
> There, take it to you, trenchers, cups and all:
> You heedless joltheads, and unmannered slaves![2]

Passersby along the street beheld a young man consumed with mirth as Louis Gray heard these stirring words issuing from his sister's pretty mouth in a clever imitation of the schoolgirl Petruchio's ladylike tones.

"Now speak those lines as you would if you wore the boots," he urged, when he had recovered his gravity.

---

[2] *Complete Works of Shakespeare*: The Taming of the Shrew, Act 4, Scene 1.

Roberta waited till they were at a discreet distance from other pedestrians, then delivered the lines as she had already spoken them for her pupil twenty times or more, with a spirit and temper which gave them their character as the assumed bluster they were meant to picture.

"Good!" cried Louis. "Great! But you see, Sis, you have learned the absolute control of your voice, and that's a thing few schoolgirls have mastered. Besides, not every girl has a throat like yours."

"I mean to be patient," said Roberta soberly. "And Olivia really has a good speaking voice. It's the curious effect of the imaginary boots that stirs my wonder. She actually speaks in a higher key with them on than off. But we shall improve that in the fortnight before the play. They are really doing very well, and our Katherine—Ethel Revell—is going to forget herself completely in her part, if I can manage it. In spite of the hard work, I thoroughly enjoy the rehearsing of the yearly play; it's a relief from the routine work of the class. And the girls appreciate the best there is, in the great writers and dramatists, as you wouldn't imagine they could do."

"On the whole, would you rather be a teacher than an office stenographer?" suggested Louis, with a touch of mischief in his tone. "You know, I've always been a bit disappointed that you didn't come into our office, after working so hard to make an expert of yourself."

"That training wasn't wasted," defended Roberta. "I'm able to make friends with my working girls lots better on account of the stenography and typewriting I know. And I may need that resource yet. I'm not at all sure that I mean to be a teacher all my days."

"I'm very sure you'll not," said her brother, with a laughing glance, which Roberta ignored. It was a matter of considerable amusement to her brothers the serious way in which she had set about being independent. They fully approved of her decision to spend her time in a way worth the while, but when it came to planning for a lifetime—there were plenty of reasons for skepticism as to her needing to look far ahead. Indeed, it was well known that Roberta might have abandoned all effort long ago and have given any one of several extremely eligible young men the greatly desired opportunity of taking care of her in his own way.

The pair separated at a street corner, and as it happened, Louis heard little more about the progress of the school rehearsals for *The Taming of the Shrew* until the day before its public performance—if a performance could be called public that was to be given in so private a place as the ballroom in the home of one of the wealthiest patrons of the school, the audience composed wholly of invited guests, and admission to the affair for others extremely difficult to procure on any ground whatever.

Appearing at the close of the final rehearsal to escort his sister home—for the hour, like that of all final rehearsals, was late—Louis found a flushed and highly wrought Roberta delivering last instructions even as she put on her wraps.

"Remember, Olivia," he heard her say to a tall girl wrapped in a long cloak that evidently concealed male trappings, "I'm not going to tone down my part one bit to fit yours. If I'm stormy, you must be blustering; if I'm furious you must be fierce. You can do it, I know."

"I certainly hope so, Miss Gray," answered a none-too-confident voice. "But I'm simply frightened to death to play opposite you."

"Nonsense! I'll stick pins into you—metaphorically speaking," declared Roberta. "I'll keep you up to it. Now go straight to bed; no sitting up to talk it over with Ethel, poor child! Good night, dear, and don't you dare be afraid of me!"

"Are you going to play the boots, after all?" Louis queried as he and Roberta started toward home, walking at a rapid pace, as usual after rehearsals.

"I wish I were, if I must play some part. No, it's Katherine. Ethel Revell has come down with tonsillitis, just at the last minute. It was to be expected, of course—somebody always does it. But I did hope it wouldn't be one of the principals. Of course there's nobody who could possibly get up the part overnight except the coach, so I'm in for it. And the worst of it is that unless I'm very careful I shall over-Katherine my Petruchio! If Olivia will only keep her voice resonant! She can stride and gesture pretty well now, but highly dramatic moments always cause her to raise her key, and then the boots only serve to make the effect grotesque."

"Never mind; unconscious humor is always interesting to the audience. And we shall all be there to see your Katherine. I had thought of cutting the performance for a rather important address, but nothing would induce me to miss my sister as the Shrew."

Roberta laughed. "Nobody will question my fitness for the part, I fear. Well, if I teach expression in a girls' school, I must take the consequences and be willing to express anything that comes along."

If Roberta had expected any sympathy from her family in the exigency of the hour, she was disappointed. Instead of condoling with her the next morning, the breakfast table hearers of the news were able only to congratulate themselves upon the augmented interest the school play would now have for Roberta's friends, confident that the presence of one clever actress of maturer powers would compensate for much amateurishness in the others. Ruth, young devotee of her sister, was delighted beyond measure with the prospect. She joyfully spent the day taking necessary stitches in the apparel Roberta was to wear, considerable alteration being necessary to adapt the garments intended for the slim and girlish Katherine of Ethel Revell's proportions to the more perfectly rounded lines of her teacher.

Late in the afternoon, something was needed to complete Roberta's preparations that could be procured only in a downtown shop, and Ruth volunteered to order the brougham—now on runners—and go down for it. She left the house alone, but she did not complete her journey alone, for halfway down the two-mile boulevard she passed a figure she knew, and turned to bestow a girlish bow and smile. Richard Kendrick not only took off his hat but waved it with a gesture of entreaty as he quickened his steps, and Ruth, much excited by the encounter, bade Thomas stop the horses.

"Would you take a passenger?" he asked as he came up. "Unless, of course, you're going to stop for someone else?"

"Do get in," she urged shyly. "No, I'm all alone—going on an errand."

"I guessed it—not the errand, but the being alone. You looked so small, wrapped up in all these furs, I felt you needed company," explained Richard, smiling down into the animated young face, with its delicate color showing fresh and fair in the frosty air. There was something very attractive to the young man in this girl, who seemed to him the embodiment of sweetness and purity. He never saw her without feeling that he would have liked just such a little sister. He would have done much to please her, quite as he had followed her suggestion about the church-going on Christmas Day.

"I'm rushing down to find a scarf of a certain color for Rob," explained Ruth, too full of her commission to keep it to herself. "You see, she's playing Katherine tonight. The girl who was to have played it—Ethel Revel—is ill. Do you know any of Miss Copeland's girls? Olivia Cartwright plays Petruchio."

"Olivia Cartwright? Is she to be in some play? She's a distant cousin of mine."

"It's a school play—Miss Copeland's school, where Rob teaches, you know. The play is to be in the Stuart Hendersons' ballroom." And Ruth made known the situation to a listener who gave her his undivided attention.

"Well, well. Seems to me I should have had an invitation for that play," mused Richard, searching his memory. "I wish I'd had one. I should like to see your sister act Katherine. I suppose it's quite impossible to get one at this late hour?"

"I'm afraid so. It's really not at all strange that anyone is left out of the list of invitations," Ruth hastened to make clear. "You see, each girl is allowed only six, and that usually takes just her family or nearest friends. And if you are only a distant cousin of Olivia's . . . "

"It's not at all strange that she shouldn't ask me, for I'm afraid I've neglected to avail myself of former invitations of hers," admitted Richard, ruefully. "Too bad. Punishment for such neglect usually follows, and I certainly have it now. I know the Stuart Hendersons, though. I wonder . . . Never mind, Miss Ruth, don't look so sorry. You'll tell me about it afterward, won't you?"

"Indeed I will. Oh, it's been such an exciting day. Rob's been rehearsing her lines all day—when she wasn't trying on. She says she could have played Petruchio much better because she's had to coach Olivia Cartwright for that part so much more than she's had to coach Ethel for Katherine. But, then, she knows the whole play; she could take any part. She would have loved to play Petruchio though, on account of the boots and the slashing round the stage the way he does. But I think it's just as well, for Katherine certainly slashes, too, and Rob's not quite tall enough for Petruchio."

"I'm glad she plays Katherine," said Richard Kendrick decidedly. "I can't imagine your sister in boots! I've no doubt, though, she'd make them different from other boots if she wore them!"

"Of course she would," agreed Ruth. Then she began to talk about something else, for a bit of fear had come into her mind that Rob wouldn't enjoy all this discussion of herself, if she should know about it.

She was such an honest young person, however, that she had a good deal of difficulty, when she had done her errand and was at home again, in not telling Roberta of her meeting with Richard Kendrick. She did venture to ask a question.

"Is Mr. Kendrick invited for tonight, Rob?"

"Not by me," Roberta responded promptly.

"He might be by one of the girls, I suppose?"

"The girls invite whom they like. I haven't seen the list. I don't imagine he would be on it. I hope not, certainly."

"Why? Don't you think he would enjoy it?"

"No, I do not. Musical comedies are probably more to his taste than amateur productions of Shakespeare. But I'm not thinking about the audience; the players are enough for me." Then, suddenly, an idea that flashed into her mind caused her to turn and scan Ruth's ingenuous young face.

"You haven't been inviting Mr. Kendrick yourself, Rufus?"

"Why, how could I?" But the girl flushed rosily in a way which betrayed her interest. "I just wondered."

"How did you come to wonder? Have you seen him?"

Ruth being Ruth, there was nothing to do but to tell Roberta of the encounter with Richard. "He said he was glad you were to play Katherine, because he couldn't imagine you in boots," she added, hoping this news might appease her sister. But it did nothing of the sort.

"As if it made the slightest difference to him! But if he feels that way, I wish I were to wear the boots, and I wish he might be there to see me do it. As it is, I hope Mrs. Stuart Henderson will be deaf to his audacity, if he dares to ask an invitation. It would be quite like him!"

"I don't see why—" began Ruth.

But Roberta interrupted her. "There are lots of things you don't see, little sister," said she, with a swift and impetuous embrace of the slender form beside her. Then she turned, frowned, flung out her arm, and broke into one of Katherine's flaming speeches:

> Why, sir, I trust, I may have leave to speak;
> And speak I will; I am no child, no babe:
> Your betters have endured me say my mind,
> And if you cannot, best you stop your ears.[3]

"Oh, but you do have such a lovely voice!" cried Ruth. "You can't make even the Shrew sound shrewish—in her tone, I mean."

"Can't I, indeed? Wait till tonight! If your friend Mr. Kendrick is to be there I'll be more shrewish than you ever dreamed. It will be a real stimulus!"

Ruth shook her head in dumb wonder that anyone could be so impervious to the charms of the young man who so appealed to her youthful imagination. Three hours afterward, when she turned in her chair in the Stuart Henderson ballroom, at the summons of a low voice in her ear, to find Richard Kendrick in the row behind her, she wondered afresh what there could possibly be about him to rouse her sister's antagonism. His face was such an interesting one, his eyes so clear and their glance so straightforward, his fresh color so pleasant to note, his whole personality

---

3 *Complete Works of Shakespeare: The Taming of the Shrew,* Act 4, Scene 3.

so attractive, Ruth could only answer him in the happiest way at her command with a subdued but eager, "Oh, I'm so glad you came!"

"That's due to Mrs. Cartwright's wonderful kindness. She's the mother of Petruchio, you know," explained Richard, with a smiling glance at the gorgeously gowned woman beside him, who leaned forward also to say to Ruth:

"What is one to do with a sweetly apologetic young cousin who, at the last moment, begs to be allowed to come to view his cousin in doublet and hose? But I really didn't venture to tell Olivia. She would have fled from the stage if she had guessed that Cousin Richard, whom she greatly admires, was to be here. I can only hope she will not hear of it till the play is over."

If his being here is going to make Petruchio tremble more, and Katherine act naughtier, I shall feel dreadfully guilty, thought Ruth. But somehow when the curtain went up, she could not help being glad that he was there behind her.

Roberta had said much, in hours of relaxation after long and tense rehearsals, of the difficulty of making schoolgirls forget themselves in any part. It had been difficult, indeed, to train her pupils to speak and act with naturalness in roles so foreign to their experience. But she had been much more successful than she had dared to believe, and her own enthusiasm, her tireless drilling, above all her inspiring example as she spoke her girls' lines for them and demonstrated to them each telling detail of stage business, had done the work with astonishing effect. The hardest task of all had been to find and develop a satisfactory delineator of the difficult part of the Tamer of the Shrew, but Roberta had persevered, even taking a journey of some hours with Olivia Cartwright to have her see and study one of the greatest of Petruchios at two successive performances. She had succeeded in stimulating Olivia to a real determination to be worthy of her teacher's expressed belief in her, even to the mastering of her girlish tendency to let her voice revert to a high-keyed feminine quality just when it needed to be deepest and most stern.

The audience, as the play began, was in the customary benevolent mood of audiences beholding amateur productions, ready to see good if possible, anxious to show favor to all the young actors and to praise without discrimination, aware of the proximity of proud fathers and mothers. But this audience soon found itself genuinely interested and amused, and with the first advent of the enchanting Shrew herself became absorbed in her personality and her fortunes quite as it might have been in those of any talented actress of reputation.

To Ruth, sitting wide eyed and hot cheeked, her sister seemed the most spirited and bewitching Katherine ever played. Her shrewishness was that of the willful, madcap girl who has never been crossed, rather than that of the inherently ill-tempered woman, and her every word and gesture, her every expression of face and tone of voice, were worth noting and watching. By no means a finished work (as how should it be, in a young teacher but few years out of school herself), it yet had an originality and freshness of interpretation all its own, and the applause that praised it was very spontaneous and genuine. Roberta had been the joy of her class in college dramatics, and several of her former classmates in her audience tonight gleefully told one another that she was surpassing anything she had formerly done.

"It's simply superb, you know, don't you?—your sister's acting," said Richard Kendrick's voice in Ruth's ear again at the end of the first act, and she turned her burning cheek his way as she answered happily:

"It seems so to me, but then I'm prejudiced, you know."

"We're all prejudiced, when it comes to that—made so by this performance. I'm pretty proud of my cousin Petruchio, too," he went on, including Mrs. Cartwright at his side. "I'd no idea boots could be so becoming to any girl outside of a chorus. Olivia's splendid. Do you suppose"—he was addressing Ruth again—"you and I might go behind the scenes and tell them how we feel about it?"

"Oh, no, indeed, Mr. Kendrick," Ruth replied, much shocked. "It's lots different, a girls' play like this, from the regular theater. They'd be so astonished to see you. Rob's told me, heaps of times, how they go perfectly crazy after every act, and she has all she can do to keep them cool enough for the next. She'd never forgive us. And besides, Olivia Cartwright's not to know you're here, you know."

"That's true. I'd forgotten how disturbing my presence is supposed to be," and Richard leaned back again to laugh with Mrs. Cartwright.

But behind the scenes, the news had penetrated, nobody knew just how. Roberta learned, to her surprise and distraction, that Richard Kendrick was somehow a particularly interesting figure in the eyes of her young players, and she speedily discovered that they were all more or less excited at the knowledge that he was somewhere below the footlights. Olivia, indeed, was immediately in a flutter, quite as her mother had predicted, at the thought of Cousin Richard's eyes upon her in her masculine attire; and Roberta, in the brief interval she could spare for the purpose, had to take her sternly in hand. An autocratic Katherine might, then, have been overheard addressing a flurried Petruchio, in a corner:

"For pity's sake, child, who is he that you need to be afraid of him? He's no critic, I'll wager, and if he's your cousin he'll be sure to think you act like a veteran, anyhow. Forget him and go ahead. You're doing splendidly. Don't you dare slump just because you're remembering your audience!"

"Oh, of course I'll try, Miss Gray," replied an extremely feminine voice from beneath Petruchio's fierce mustachio. "But Richard Kendrick really is awfully sort of upsetting, don't you know?"

"Of course I don't know," denied Roberta promptly. "As long as Miss Copeland herself is pleased with us, nobody else matters. And Miss Copeland is delighted. She sent me special word just now. So stiffen your backbone, Petruchio, and make this next dialogue with me as rapid as you know. Come back at me like flash-fire—don't lag a breath. We'll stir the house to laughter or know the reason why. Ready?"

Her firm hand on Olivia's arm, her bracing words in Olivia's ear, put courage back into her temporarily stage-struck "leading man," and Olivia returned to the charge determined to play up to her teacher without lagging. In truth, Roberta's actual presence on the stage was proving a distinct advantage to those of the players who had parts with her. She warmed and held them to their tasks with the flash of her own eyes, not to mention an occasional almost imperceptible but pregnant gesture, and they found themselves somehow able to forget the audience, as she had so many times advised them to do, the better because she herself seemed so completely to have forgotten it.

The work of the young actors grew better with each act, and at the end of the fourth, when the curtain went down upon a scene that had been all storm on the part of the players and all laughter on the part of the audience, the applause was long and hearty. There were calls for the entire cast, and when they had several times responded, there was a special and persistent demand for Katherine herself, in the character of the producer of the play. She refused it until she could no longer do so without discourtesy; then she came before the curtain and said a few winsome words of gratitude on behalf of her company.

Ruth, staring up at her sister's face, brilliant with the mingled exertion and emotion of the hour, and thinking her the prettiest picture she had ever seen, there against the great dull-blue silk curtain of the stage, had no notion that just behind her somebody was thinking the same thing with a degree of fervor far beyond her own. Richard Kendrick's heart was thumping vigorously away in his breast as he looked his fill at the figure before the curtain, secure in the darkness of the house from observation at the moment.

When he had first met this girl he had told himself that he would soon know her well, would soon call her by her name. He wondered at himself that he could possibly have fancied conquest of her so easy. He was not a whit nearer knowing her, he was obliged to acknowledge, than on that first day, nor did he see any prospect of getting to know her beyond a certain point. Her chosen occupation seemed to place her beyond his reach; she was not to be got at by the ordinary methods of approach. Twice he had called and asked for her, to be told that she was busy with school papers and must be excused. Once he had ventured to invite her to go with Mrs. Stephen and himself to a carefully chosen play and a supper, but she had declined, gracefully enough, but she had declined, and Mrs. Stephen also. He could not make these people out, he told himself. Did they and he live in such different worlds that they could never meet on common ground?

The Taming of the Shrew came to a triumphant end. The curtain fell upon the effective closing scene in which the lovely Shrew, become a richly loving and tender wife without, somehow, surrendering a particle of her exquisite individuality, spoke her words of wisdom to other wives. Richard smiled to himself as he heard the lines fall from Roberta's lips. And beneath his breath he said:

"I don't see how you can bring yourself to say them, you modern girl. You'd never let a real husband feel his power that way, I'll wager. If you did, well, it would go to his head, I'm sure of that. What an idiot I am to think I could ever make you look at me the way you look even at that schoolgirl Petruchio—with a clever imitation of devotion. O Roberta Gray! But I'd rather worship you across the footlights than take any other girl in my arms. And somehow, somehow I've got to make you at least respect me. At least that, Roberta! Then, perhaps, more!"

At Ruth's side, when the play ended, Richard hoped to attain at least the chance to speak to Ruth's sister. The young players all appeared upon the stage, the curtain being raised for the rest of the evening, and the audience came up, group by group, to offer congratulations and pour into gratified ears the praise that was the reward of labor. Richard succeeded in getting by degrees into the immediate vicinity of Roberta, who was continuously surrounded by happy parents bent on presenting their felicitations. But just as he was about to make his way to her side, a diversion occurred that took her completely away from him. A girl nearby, who on account of physical frailty had had a minor part, grew suddenly faint, and in a trice Roberta had impressed into her service a strong pair of male arms, nearer at hand than Richard's, and had had the slim little figure carried behind the scenes, herself following.

Ten minutes later he learned from Ruth that Roberta had gone back to Miss Copeland's school with the girl, recovered but weak.

"Couldn't anybody else have gone?" he inquired, considerable impatience in his voice.

"Of course, lots of people could and would. Only it's just like Rob to seize the chance to get away from this and not come back. You'll see she won't. She hates being patted on the back, as she calls it. I never can see why, when people mean it, as I'm sure they do tonight. She's the strangest girl. She never wants what you'd think she would or wants it the way other people do. But she's awfully dear, just the same," Ruth hastened to add, fearful lest she seem to criticize the beloved sister. "And somehow you don't get tired of her, the way you do of some people. Perhaps that's just because she's different."

"I suspect it is," Richard agreed with conviction. Certainly, a girl who would run away from such adulation as she had been receiving must be, he considered, decidedly and interestingly "different." He only wished he might hit upon some "different" way to pique her interest.

Chapter 12

BLANKETS

There was destined to be a still longer break in the work which had been going on in Judge Calvin Gray's library than was intended. He and his assistant had barely resumed their labors after the Christmas house party when the judge was called out of town for a period whose limit, when he left, he was unable to fix. He could leave little for Richard to do, so that young man found his time again upon his hands and himself unable to dispose of it to advantage.

His mind at this period was in a curious state of dissatisfaction. Ever since the evening of the Christmas dance, when a girl's careless word had struck home with such unexpected force, he had been as restless and uneasy as a fish out of water. His condition bore as much resemblance to that of the gasping fish as this: in the old element of life about town, as he had been in the habit of living it, he now had the sensation of not being able to breathe freely.

It was with the intention of getting into the open, both mentally and physically, that on the second day following the judge's departure Richard started on a long drive in his car. Beyond a certain limit he knew that the roads were likely to prove none too good, though the winter had thus far been a light one and there was little chance of his encountering blocking snowdrifts upstate. He took no one with him. He could think of no one with whom he cared to go.

As he drove, his mind was busy with all sorts of speculations. In his hurt pride he had said to a girl: "If I can't make you think differently of me it won't be for lack of will." That meant—what did it mean? That he had recognized the fact that she despised idlers and that young rich men who spent a few hours, on an average of five days of the week, in assisting elderly gentlemen bereft of their eyesight in looking up old records, did not thereby in her estimation remove themselves from the class of those who do nothing in the world but attend to the spending of their incomes.

What should he do? How prove himself fit to deserve her approval? Unquestionably, he must devote himself seriously to some serious occupation. All sorts of ideas chased one another through his mind in response to this stimulus. What was he fitted to do? He had a certain facility in the use of the pen, as he had proved in the service of Judge Calvin Gray. Should he look for a job as reporter on one of the city dailies? He certainly could not offer himself for any post higher than that of the rawest scribe on the force; he had had no experience. The thought of seeking such a post made his lip curl with the absurdity of the notion. They would make a society reporter of him; it would be the first idea that would occur to them. It was the only thing for which they would think him fit!

The thing he should like to do would be to travel on some interesting commission for his grandfather. On what commission, for instance? The purchasing of rare works of art for the picture gallery of the great store? No mean exhibition it was that they had there. But he had not the training for such a commission; he would be cheated out of hand when it came to buying! They sent skilled buyers on such quests.

He thought of rushing off to the far West and buying a ranch. That was a fit and proper thing for a fellow like himself; plenty of rich men's sons had done it. If she could see him in cowboy garb, rough-clad, sunburnt, muscular, she would respect him then perhaps. There would be no more flinging at him that he was a cotillion leader! How he hated the term!

The day was fair and cold, the roads rather better than he had expected, and by lunchtime he had reached a large town, seventy miles away from his own city, where he knew of an exceptionally good place to obtain a refreshing meal. With this end in view, he was making more than ordinary village speed when disaster befell him in the shape of a break in his electric connections. Two blocks away from the hotel he sought, the car suddenly went dead.

While he was investigating, fingers blue with cold, a voice he knew hailed him. It came from a young man who advanced from the doorway of a store, in front of which the car had chanced to stop. "Something wrong, Rich?"

Richard stood up. He gripped his friend's hand cordially, glancing up at the sign above the store as he did so.

"Mighty glad to see you, Benson," he responded. "I didn't realize I'd stopped in front of your father's place of business."

Hugh Benson was a college classmate. In spite of the difference between their respective estates in the college world, the two had been rather good friends during the four years of their being thrown together. Since graduation, however, they had seldom met, and for the last two years Richard Kendrick had known no more of his former friend than that the good-sized dry goods store, standing on a prominent corner in the large town through which he often motored without stopping, still bore the name of Hugh Benson's father.

When the car was running again, Benson climbed in and showed Richard the way to his own home, where he prevailed on his friend to remain for lunch with himself and his mother. Richard learned for the first time that Benson's father had died within the last year.

"And you're going on with the business?" questioned Richard, as the two lingered alone together in Benson's hall before parting. The talk during the meal had been mostly of old college days, of former classmates, and of the recent history of nearly every mutual acquaintance except that of the speakers themselves.

"There was nothing else for me to do when Father left us," Benson responded in a low tone. "I'm not as well adapted to it as he was, but I expect to learn."

"I remember you thought of doing graduate work along scientific lines. Did you give that up?"

"Yes. I found Father needed me at home; his health must have been failing even then, though I didn't realize it. I've been in the store with him ever since. I'm glad I have, now."

"It's not been good for you," declared Richard, scrutinizing his friend's pale and rather worn face critically. It would have seemed to him still paler and more worn if he could have seen it in contrast with his own fresh-tinted features, ruddy with his morning's drive. "Better come with me for an afternoon spin farther upstate and a good dinner at a place I know. Get you back by bedtime."

"There's nothing I'd like better, Rich," said Benson longingly, "but I can't leave the store. I have rather a short force of clerks, and on a sunny day . . . "

"You'd sell more goods tomorrow," urged Richard, feeling increasingly anxious to do something that might bring light into a face he had not remembered as so somber.

But Benson shook his head again. Afterward, in front of the store to which the two had returned in the car, Richard could only give his friend a warm grip of the hand and an urgent invitation to visit him in the city.

"I suppose you come down often to buy goods," he suggested. "Or do you send buyers? I don't know much about the conduct of business in a town like this—or much about it at home, for that matter," he owned. "Though I'm not sure I'm proud of my ignorance."

"It doesn't matter whether you know anything about it or not, of course," said Benson, looking at him with a queer expression of wistfulness. "No, I'm my own buyer. And I don't buy of a great, high-grade firm like yours; I go to a different class of fellows for my stuff."

Richard drove on, thinking hard about Benson. What a pity for a fellow of twenty-six or twenty-seven to look like that, careworn and weary. He wondered whether it was the loss of his father and the probably sorrowful atmosphere at home that accounted for the look in Benson's eyes, or whether his business was not a particularly successful one. He recalled that the one careless glance he had given the windows of Benson's store had brought to his mind the fleeting impression that village shopkeepers had not much art in the dressing of their windows as a means of alluring the public.

As he drove on he felt in his pockets for a cigar and found his case unexpectedly empty. He turned back to a drugstore, went in, and supplied himself from the best in stock—none too good for his fastidious taste.

"What's your best dry goods shop here?" he inquired casually.

"Artwell & Chatford's the best—now," responded the druggist, glancing across the street, where a sign bearing those names met the eye. "Chaffee Brothers has run 'em a close second since Benson's dropped out of the competition. Benson's used to be the best, but it's fallen way behind. Look at Artwell's window display over there and see the reason," he added, pointing across the street with the citizen's pride in a successful enterprise in no way his own rival.

"Gorgeous!" responded Richard, eyeing an undoubtedly eye-catching arrangement of blankets of every hue and quality piled about a center figure consisting of a handsome brass bed made up as if for occupancy, the carefully folded-back covers revealing immaculate and downy blankets with pink borders, the whole suggestive of warmth and comfort throughout the most rigorous winter season.

"Catchy, on a day like this!" suggested the druggist, with a chuckle. "I'll admit they gave me the key[1] for my own windows."

Richard's gaze followed the other's glance and rested on piles of scarlet

---

[1] Idea or concept for.

flannel chest-protectors, flanked by small brass teakettles with alcohol lamps beneath.

"We carry a side line of spirit lamp stuff," explained the dealer. "It sells well this time of year. Got to keep track of the popular thing. Afternoon teas are all the go among the women of this town now. The hardware's the only other place they can get these, and they don't begin to keep the variety we do."

Richard congratulated the dealer on his window. Lingering by it, his hand on the door, he said:

"I noticed Benson's as I came by, and I see now the force of what you say about window display. I'm not sure I can tell what was in their windows."

"Nor anybody else," declared the druggist, chuckling, "unless he went with a notebook and made an inventory. Since the old man died last year the windows have been a hodgepodge of stuff that attracts nobody. It's merely an index to the way the place is running behind. Young Benson doesn't know how to buy nor how to sell; he'll never succeed. The store began to go down when the old man got too feeble to take the whole responsibility. Hugh began to overstock some departments and under-stock others. It's not so much lack of capital that'll be responsible for Hugh's failure when it comes—and I guess it's not far off—as it is lack of business experience. Why, he's got so little trade he's turned off [2] half his salespeople, and you know that talks!"

It did indeed. It talked louder now in light of the druggist's shrewd commentaries than it had when Benson had spoken of his "short force." Richard wondered just how short it was, that the proprietor could not venture to leave for even a few hours.

He drove on thoughtfully. He wanted to go back and look those windows over again, wanted to go through the whole store, but recognized that though he could have done this when he first arrived, he could not go back and do it now without exciting his friend's suspicion that sympathy was his motive.

He turned about at a point far short of the one he had intended to reach, and made record time back to the city, impelled by an odd wish he could hardly explain, to go by the windows of the great department stores of Kendrick & Company and examine their window displays. He was ordinarily accustomed to select any other streets than those upon which these magnificent places of custom were situated, merely because

---

[2] Laid off.

he not only had no interest in them but a positive distaste for seeing his own name emblazoned—though ever so chastely—above their princely portals. Therefore, it may be understood that an entirely new idea was working in his brain.

Speed as he would, however, running the risk as he approached the city streets of being stopped by some watchful authority for exceeding the limits, he could not get back to the broad avenue upon which the stores stood before six o'clock. There was all the better chance on that account, nevertheless, for examining the windows before which belated shoppers were still stopping to wonder and admire.

Well, looking at them with Benson's forlorn windows in his mind as a foil, he saw them as he never had before. What beauty, what originality, what art they showed! And at a time of year when, the holiday season past, it might seem as if there could be no real summons for anybody to go shopping. They were fairly dazzling, some of them, although many of them showed only white goods. His car came to a standstill before one great plate glass frame behind which was a representation of a sewing room with several people busily at work. So perfect were the figures that it hardly seemed as if they could be of wax. One pretty girl was sewing at a machine; another, on her knees, was fitting a frock to a little girl who laughed over her shoulder at a second child who was looking on. The mother of the family sewed by a droplight on a worktable. The whole scene was really charming, combining precisely the element of domesticity with that of accomplishment that strikes the eye of the average passer as looking like home, no matter what sort the home might be.

By heavens! If poor Ben had something like that, people wouldn't pass him by for the blanket store, he said to himself and drove on, still thinking.

The next day, at an hour before the morning tide of shopping at Kendrick & Company's had reached the flood, two pretty glove clerks were suddenly tempted into a furtive exchange of conversation at an unoccupied end of their counter.

"Look quick! See the young man coming this way? It's Rich Kendrick."

"It *is?* They told me he never came here. Say, but he's the real thing!"

"I should say. Never saw him so close myself. Wish he'd stop here."

"Bet you couldn't keep your head if he spoke to you!"

"Bet I could! Don't you worry; he don't buy his gloves in his own department store. He—"

"Shh! Granger's looking!"

There was really nothing about Richard Kendrick to attract attention except his wholesome good looks, for he dressed with exceptional quietness, and his manner matched his clothes. A floorwalker recognized him and bowed, but the elevator man did not know him, and on his way to the offices he passed only one clerk who could lay claim to a speaking acquaintance with the grandson of the owner.

But at the office of the general manager he was met by an office boy who knew and worshiped him from afar, and in five minutes he was closeted with the manager, who gave him his whole attention.

"Mr. Henderson, I wish you could give me," was the substance of Richard's remarks, "somebody who would go up to Eastman with me and tell me what's the matter with a dry goods store there that's on the verge of failure."

The general manager was, to put it mildly, astonished. He was a mighty man of valor himself, so mighty that his yearly salary would have seemed a small fortune to the average American citizen. The office he held was one so difficult to fill that similar houses had often scoured the country without avail. Other business owners had been forced to remain at the helm long after health and happiness demanded retirement. Among these, Henderson was held to be so competent a man that Matthew Kendrick was considered incredibly lucky to keep his hold upon him.

To Matthew Kendrick's grandson, Henderson put a number of pertinent inquiries concerning the store in question, which Richard found he could not intelligently answer. He flushed a little under the fire.

"I suppose you think I might have investigated a bit for myself," said he. "But that's just what I don't want to do. I want to send a man up there whom the owner doesn't know; then we can get at things without giving ourselves away."

The general manager inferred from this that philanthropy, not business interest, was at the bottom of young Kendrick's quest, and his surprise vanished. The young man was known to be kindhearted and generous; he was undoubtedly merely carrying out a careless impulse, though he certainly seemed much in earnest in the doing of it.

"You might take Carson, assistant buyer for the dress goods department, with you," suggested Henderson after a little consideration. "He could probably give you a day just now. Alger, his head, is back from London this week. Carson's a bright man—in line for promotion. He'll put his finger on the trouble without hesitation if it lies in the lack of business experience, buying and selling, as you say. I'll send for him."

In two minutes, Richard Kendrick and Alfred Carson were face to face, and an appointment had been made for the following day. Richard took a liking to the assistant buyer on the spot. He felt as if he were selecting a competent physician for his friend and was glad to send him a man whose personality was both prepossessing and inspiring of confidence.

As for Carson, it was an interesting experience for him, too. He thoroughly enjoyed the seventy-mile drive at the side of the young millionaire, who sent his powerful car flying over the frozen roads at a pace that made his passenger's face sting. Carson was more accustomed to travel in subways and sleeping cars than by long motor drives, and by the time Eastman was reached he was glad that the return drive would be preceded by a hot luncheon.

"We don't go past the store," Richard explained, making a detour from the main street of the town, regardless of the fact that he forsook a good road for a poor one. "I don't want him to see me today."

He pressed upon his guest the best that the hotel afforded, then sent him to the corner store with instructions to let nothing escape his attention. "Though I don't need to tell you that," he added with a laugh. "You'll see more in a minute than I should in a month."

Then he lit a cigar, from his own case this time, though he strolled in to see his friend the druggist when he had finished it, and bought of him various other sundries. He did not venture to mention Benson's name today, but the druggist did. Evidently Benson's imminent failure was the talk of the town and the regret, as well, of those who were not his rivals.

"Man can't succeed at a thing he picks up so late and when he'd rather do something else," volunteered the druggist. "Now I began in this shop by sweeping out, mornings, and running errands, delivering goods. Got interested, came to be a clerk after a while. Always saw myself making up medicines, compounding prescriptions. Went off to a school of pharmacy, came back, showed the old man I could look after the prescription business. Finally bought him out. Trained for the trade from the cradle, as you might say."

I wonder if I'm going to be useless, thought Richard, *because I'm not trained from the cradle. Carson says he began as a wrapper at fifteen. At my age—he looks my age—he's assistant buyer for one of Kendrick & Company's biggest departments and "in line for promotion," as Henderson says. Rich Kendrick, do you think you're in line for promotion —anywhere? I wonder!*

He had gone back to the hotel and was impatiently awaiting Carson for some time before the buyer appeared. Carson came in with a look of great interest and eagerness on his face. The assistant buyer had, Richard thought, one of the brightest faces he had ever seen. He was sure he had asked the right man to diagnose the case of the invalid business, even before

Carson began to talk. As the talk progressed, he was convinced of it.

Yet Carson began at the human, not the business, end of the matter. Richard Kendrick, himself full of concern for his friend Hugh Benson, liked that, too.

"I never felt sorrier for a man in my life," said Carson. "He shows a lot of pluck; he never once owned that the thing was too much for him. But I got him to talking a little. Didn't need to talk much; the whole place was shouting at me—every counter, every showcase. Thunder!"

"How did you get him to talking?" Richard asked eagerly.

"Represented myself as an ex-traveling man—the dry goods line. It's true enough, if not just the way he took it. Of course he didn't give me any facts about his business, but we discussed present conditions of the trade pretty well, and he owned that a good many things puzzled him just as much as when he was a little chap and used to listen to his father giving orders. What's going to be wanted and how much? When to load up and when to unload? How to catch the public fancy and not get caught yourself? In short, how to turn over the stock in season and out of season—turn it over and get out from under! He knows no more how to keep his head above water than a man who can't swim. Nice fellow, too; I could see it in every word he said. He'd be a success in, say, a professorship in a college—and not a business college, either."

"If the place were yours," Richard, alive with interest, put it to him, "now, this minute, what would be the first thing you would do?"

Carson laughed—not derisively, but like a boy who sees a chance at a game he likes to play. "Have a bonfire, I'd like to say," he vowed. "But that wouldn't be good business, and I wouldn't do it if I had the chance—unless there was insurance to cover! And there's money in the stock. Part of it could be got out[3]. But it ought to be got out before the moon is old. Then I'd like the fun of stocking up with new lines, new departments, things the town never heard of. I'd make that blankets window you told me about look sick. That is," he added modestly, "I think I could. Any good general buyer could. I'm a dress goods man myself, only I've grown up under Kendrick & Company's roof and I've been watching other lines than my own. It interests me, the possibilities of that store. Why, the man ought not to fail! He has the best location in town, the biggest windows, the best fixtures, judging by the outside of the places I saw as I came along. I looked at the blanket-window place. That's a dark store when you get back a dozen feet. Benson's, being on

---

3 Salvaged.

the corner, is fairly light to the back door. That counts more than any other thing about the building itself. And the fellow has his underwear in the brightest spot in the shop and the dress goods in the darkest! His heavy lines by the door, and his notions and fancy stuff way back where you've got to hunt for them! And his windows—oh, blazes! I wanted to climb up and jump on the mess and then throw it out!"

Richard drove Carson back to town, his heart afire with longing to do something, he did not yet know what. He could not consult Carson about the matter further than to find out from him what was wrong with the business from the standpoint of the customer; why the place did not attract the customer. Details of this phase of the question Carson had given him in plenty, all leading back to the one trouble: Benson had not understood how to appeal to the class of custom at his doors. He had not the right goods, nor the right means of display; he had not the rights sales-people; in brief, he had nothing, according to Carson, that he ought to have, and everything, poor fellow, that he ought not! It was a hard case.

As to actual business foundations and resources, neither of the young men could judge. They had no means of knowing how deeply Benson was in debt, nor what his assets were beyond the visible stock. Yet his fellow shopkeepers considered him on the verge of bankruptcy; they must know.

"I've enjoyed this trip, Mr. Kendrick," Carson said at parting, "in more ways than I can tell you. If I can be of use to you in any way, call on me, please. I'm honestly interested in your friend Mr. Benson. I'd like to see him win out."

"So should I." Richard shook hands heartily. "I've enjoyed the trip, too, Mr. Carson. I never had better company. Thank you for going and for teaching me a lot of things I wanted to know."

As he drove away he was thinking, *Carson's a success; I'm not. Odd thing, that I should find myself envying a chap whose place I couldn't be hired to take. I envy him —not exactly his knowledge and skill, but his being a definite factor, his being a man who carries responsibilities and makes good, so that —well, so that he's "in line for promotion." That phrase takes hold of me somehow; I wonder why? Well, the next thing is to see Grandfather.*

Old Matthew Kendrick was alone. His grandson had just left him. He was marching up and down his private library. His hands were clasped tightly behind his back; above his flushed brow his white hair stood erect from frequent thrustings of his agitated fingers; even his cravat, slightly awry, bore witness to his excitement.

Thank Heaven! he was saying to himself. *The boy's alive after all! The boy's waked up! He's taking notice! And the thing that's waked him up is a country store, by cricky! A country store! I believe I'm dreaming yet!*

If the citizens of the thriving town of Eastman, almost of a size to call itself a young city and boast of a mayor, could have heard him they might not have been flattered. Yet when they remembered that this was the owner of a business so colossal that its immense buildings and branches were to be found in three great cities, they might have understood that to him the corner store of Hugh Benson looked like a toy concern, indeed. But he liked the look of it, as it had been presented to his mind's eye that night; no doubt but he liked the look of it!

"Give him Carson to go up there and manage the business for those two infants-in-arms? But of course! Why, I'd go myself and make change at the desk for the new firm," he chuckled, "if that would keep Dick interested. But I guess he's interested enough or he wouldn't have agreed to my ruling that he must go into the thing himself, not stand off and throw out a rope to his drowning friend, Benson. If young Benson's the man Dick makes him out, it's as I told Dick: he wouldn't grasp the rope. But if Dick goes in after him, that's business. Bless the rascal! I wish his father could see him now. Sitting on the edge of my table and talking window-dressing to me as if he'd been born to it, which he was, only he wouldn't accept his birthright, the proud beggar! Talking about moving one of our show windows up there bodily for a white goods sale in February; date a trifle late for Kendrick & Company, but advance trade for Eastman, undoubtedly. Says he knows they can start every mother's daughter of 'em sewing for dear life, if they can get their eye on that sewing-room scene. Well"—he paused to chuckle again—"he says Carson says that window cost us five hundred dollars; but if it did it's cheap at the price, and I'll make the new firm a present of it. Benson & Company—and a grandson of Matthew Kendrick & Company!"

He laughed heartily, then paused to stand staring down into the jeweled shade of his electric droplight, as if in its softly blending colorings he saw the outlines of a new future for "the boy."

"I wonder what Cal will say to losing his literary assistant," he mused, smiling to himself. "I doubt if Dick's proved himself invaluable, and I presume the man he speaks of will give Cal much better service; but I shall be sorry not to have him going to the Grays' every day; it seemed like a safe harbor. Well, well, I never thought to find myself interested again in the fortunes of a country store. My goodness! I can't get over that. The fellow's been too proud to walk down the aisles of Kendrick &

Company to buy his silk socks at cost—preferred to pay two prices[4] at an exclusive haberdasher's instead! And now he's going to have a share in the sale of socks that retail for a quarter, five pairs for a dollar! Oh Dick, Dick, you rascal, your old grandfather hasn't been so happy since you were left to him to bring up. If only you'll stick! But you're your father's son, after all—and my grandson; I can't help believing you'll stick!"

---

[4] Pay double the regular price.

Chapter 13

LAVENDER LINEN

"I'm going to drive into town. Any of you girls want to go with me?" Mr. Rufus Gray addressed his wife and their two guests, his nieces Roberta and Ruth Gray. It was the midwinter vacation at the school where Roberta taught and at the equally desirable establishment where Ruth was taking a carefully selected course of study. Uncle Rufus and Aunt Ruth had invited them to spend the four days of this vacation at their country home, according to a custom they had of decoying one or another of the young people of Rufus's brothers' families to come and visit the aunt and uncle whose own children were all married and gone, sorely missed by the young-hearted pair. Roberta and Ruth had accepted eagerly, always delighted to spend a day or a month at the Gray farm, a most attractive place even in winter, and in summer a veritable pleasure-ground of enjoyment.

They all wanted to go to town, the three "girls" including the white-haired one whose face was almost as young as her nieces' as she looked out from the rear seat of the comfortable double sleigh driven by her husband and drawn by a pair of the handsomest horses the countryside could boast. It was only two miles from the fine old country homestead to the center of the neighboring village, and though the air was keen nobody was cold among the robes and rugs with which the sleigh overflowed.

"You folks want to do any shopping?" inquired Uncle Rufus, as he drove briskly along the lower end of Eastman's principal business street. "I suppose there's no need of asking that. When doesn't a woman want to go shopping?"

"Of course we do," Ruth responded, without so much as consulting the backseat.

"I meant to bring some lavender linen with me to work on," said Roberta to Aunt Ruth. "Where do you suppose I could find any here?"

"Why, I don't know, dearie," responded Aunt Ruth doubtfully. "White linen you ought to get anywhere, but lavender . . . you might try at Artwell & Chatford's. We'll go past Benson's, but it's no use looking there anymore. Everybody's expecting poor Hugh to fail any day."

"Oh, I'm sorry," said Roberta warmly. "I always liked Hugh Benson. Mr. Westcott told me some time ago that he was afraid Hugh wasn't succeeding."

"The store's been closed to the public a fortnight now," explained Uncle Rufus over his shoulder. "Hugh hasn't failed yet, and something's going on there; nobody seems to know just what. Inventory, maybe, or getting ready for a bankrupt sale. The Benson sign's still up just as it was before Hugh's father died. Windows covered with white soap or white-wash. Some say the store's going to open up under new parties. Guess nobody knows exactly. Hullo! Who's that making signs?"

He indicated a tall figure on the sidewalk coming toward them at a rapid rate, face alight, hat waving in air.

"It's Mr. Forbes Westcott," exulted Ruth, twisting around to look at her sister. "Funny how he always happens to be visiting his father and mother just as Rob is visiting you, isn't it, Aunt Ruth?"

Uncle Rufus drew up to the sidewalk, and the whole party shook hands with a tall man of dark, keen features, who bore an unmistakable air of having come from a larger world than that of the town of Eastman.

"Mrs. Gray—Miss Roberta—Miss Ruth—Mr. Gray. Why, this is delightful. When did you come? How long are you going to stay? It seems a thousand years since I saw you last!"

He was like an eager boy, though he was clearly no boy in years. He included them all in this greeting, but his eyes were ardently on Roberta as he ended. Ruth, turned around on the front seat and watching inter-estedly, could hardly blame him. Roberta, in her furry wrappings, was as vivid as a flower. Her eyes looked black beneath their dusky lashes, and her cheeks were brilliant with the touch of the winter wind.

"When did you come? How did you find your father and mother?" inquired Roberta demurely.

"Well and hearty as ever, and apparently glad to see their son, as he was to see them. I've been devoting myself to them for three days now and mean to give them the whole week. It's only fair, isn't it? After being away so long. How fortunate for me that I should meet you; I might not have found it out till I had missed much time."

"You've missed much time already," put in Uncle Rufus. "They came last night."

"Put your hat on, Forbes," was Aunt Ruth's admonition as Westcott continued to stand beside Roberta, exchanging question and answer concerning the long interval that had intervened since they last met. "Come over to supper tonight, and then you young people can talk without danger of catching your death of cold."

Westcott laughed and accepted, but the hat was not replaced upon his smooth, dark head until the sleigh had gone on.

"Subjects always keep uncovered before their queen," whispered Ruth in Uncle Rufus's ear, and he laughed and nodded.

"Times have changed since I was a young man," said he. "A fellow would have looked queer in my day unwinding his comforter and pulling off his coonskin cap and standing holding those things while he talked on a February morning. He'd have gone home and taken some pepper tea to ward off the effects of the chill!"

"There's 'Benson's,'" Roberta interrupted, "and it's open. Why, look at the people in front of the windows! Look at the windows themselves. There must be a new firm. Poor Hugh!"

"There's a new sign over the old one: a 'Successors to,' I think; but Benson's name is on it, 'Benson & Company,'" announced Ruth, straining her eyes to make it out.

"Somebody must have come to the rescue," said Uncle Rufus with joyous interest. "Well, well. The thing has been kept surprisingly still, and I can't think who it can be, but I'm certainly glad. I hated to see the boy fail. I suppose you all want to go in?"

They unquestionably did, but they wanted first to sit still and look at the windows from their vantage point above the passersby on foot, who were all stopping as they came along. It was small wonder that they should stop. The town of Eastman had never in its experience seen within its borders window displays like these.

Benson's possessed the advantage of having larger fronts of clear plate glass than any store in town. As it was a corner store, there were not only two big windows on the front but one equally large upon the side. Each of these showed an artful arrangement of fresh and alluring white goods, and in the center of each was a special scheme arranged with figures and furnishings to form a charming tableau. In one was the sewing room scene, adapted from that one that had first challenged Richard's interest in his grandfather's store; in a second, a children's tea party drew many admiring comments from the crowd; and in the side window, the figure of a pretty bride with veil and orange blossoms suggested that the surrounding draperies were fit for uses such as hers. The clever adaptability of Carson's art showed in the fact that the figure wore no longer the costly French robe with which she had been draped when she stood in a glass case at Kendrick & Company's, but a delicate frock of simpler materials, such as any village girl might afford, yet so cunningly fashioned that a princess might have worn it as well, and not have been ashamed.

Aunt Ruth and her nieces went enthusiastically in, and Uncle Rufus, declaring that he must go also and congratulate Hugh on this extraordinary transformation, tied his horses across the street where they could not interfere with the view of passing sleighs.

Entering, the visitors found inside the same atmosphere of successful, timely display of fresh and attractive goods as had been promised by the outside. The store did not look like a village store at all; its whole air was metropolitan. The smallest counter carried out this effect; on every hand were goods selected with rare skill, and this description held good of the cheaper articles as well as of those more expensive.

"Well, Hugh, we don't understand, but we are very glad," said Aunt Ruth heartily, shaking hands with the young man who advanced to meet them.

"That's kind of you. It goes without saying that I am very glad, too," responded the proprietor of the place. His thin face flushed a little as he greeted the others, and his eyes, like Westcott's, dwelt a trifle longer on the face of one of the party than on any of the others.

"Rob, I believe you'll find your lavender linen here," said Ruth in her sister's ear, as Uncle Rufus came in and Benson began to show them all about the store. "Look, there are all kinds of white linens; let's stop and ask."

With a word of explanation, Roberta delayed at the counter Ruth had indicated, making inquiry for the goods she sought. It chanced that this department was next to an enclosure which was partially of glass, the new office of the firm. The old firm had had no office, only a desk in a dark corner. In this place, two men were talking. One was facing the store, his glance even as he spoke upon the way things were going outside; the other's back was turned. But Ruth, gazing interestedly around as her sister examined linens, discovered something familiar about the set of one of the heads just beyond the glass partition, though she could not see the face. When this head was suddenly thrown back with a peculiar motion she had noted when its owner was particularly amused over something, Ruth said to herself: *Why, that's Mr. Richard Kendrick! What in the world is he doing out here at Eastman?*

As if she had called him, Richard turned about and his look encountered Ruth's. The next instant he was out of the glass enclosure and at her side. Roberta, hearing Ruth's low but eager, "Why, Mr. Kendrick, who ever expected to see you in Eastman!" turned about with an expression of astonishment, which was reflected in both the faces before her.

An interested village salesgirl now looked on at a little scene the likes of which had never come within the range of her experience. That three people, clearly so surprised to meet in this particular spot, should not proceed voluminously to explain to each other within her hearing the cause of their surprise, was to her an extraordinary thing. But after the first moment's expression of wonder the three seemed to accept the fact as a matter of course and began to exchange observations concerning the weather, the roads, and various other matters of comparatively small importance. It was not until Uncle Rufus, rounding a high-piled counter with his wife and Hugh Benson, came upon the group, that anything was said of which the curious young person behind the counter could make enough of to guess at the situation.

"Well, well, if it isn't Mr. Kendrick!" he exclaimed after one keen look and hastened forward, hand outstretched. So the group now became doubled in size, and Uncle Rufus expressed great pleasure at seeing again the young man whose hospitality he had enjoyed during the Christmas house party.

"But I didn't suppose we should ever see you up here in our town," said he, "especially in winter. Come by the morning train?"

"I've been here for a month, most of the time," Richard told him.

"You have? And didn't come to see us? Well, now . . . "

"I didn't know this was your home, Mr. Gray," admitted the young man frankly. "I don't remember your mentioning the name of Eastman while you and Mrs. Gray were with us. Probably you did, and if I had realized you were here . . . "

"You'd have come? Well, you know now, and I hope you'll waste no time in getting out to the Gray farm. Only two miles out, and the trolley runs by within a few rods of our turn of the road—conductor'll tell you. Better come tonight," he urged genially, "seeing my nieces are here and can help make you feel at home. They'll be going back in a day or two."

Richard, smiling, looked at Aunt Ruth, then at Roberta. "Do come," urged Aunt Ruth as cordially as her husband, and Roberta gave a little nod of acquiescence.

"I shall be delighted to come," he agreed.

"Putting up at the hotel?" inquired Uncle Rufus.

"I'm staying for the present with my friend Mr. Benson," Richard explained with a glance toward Benson himself, who had moved aside to speak to a clerk. "We were classmates at college. We have gone into business together here."

It was out. As he spoke the words his face changed color a little, but his eyes remained steadily fixed on Uncle Rufus.

"Well, well," exclaimed Mr. Rufus Gray. "So it's you who have come to the rescue of—"

But Richard interrupted him quickly. "I beg your pardon, not at all," said he. "It is my friend who has come to my rescue—given me the biggest interest I have yet discovered: the game of business. I'm having the time of my life. With the help of our mutual friend, Mr. Carson, who is to be the business manager of the new house, we hope to make a success."

Roberta was looking curiously at him, and his eyes suddenly met hers. For an instant the encounter lasted, and it ended by her glance dropping from his. There was something new to her in his face, something she could not understand. Instead of its former rather studiedly impassive expression, there was an awakened look, a determined look, as if he had something on hand he meant to do—and to do as soon as the present interview should be over. Strangely enough, it was the first time she had met him when he seemed not wholly occupied with herself, but rather on his way to some affair of strong interest in which she had no concern and from which she was detaining him. It was not that he was failing in the extreme courtesy she had learned to expect from him under all conditions. But, well, it struck her that he would return to his companion in the glass-screened office and immediately forget her. This was a change, indeed!

"However you choose to put it," declared Uncle Rufus kindly, "it's a mighty fine thing for Hugh, and we wish you both success."

"You will have it. I have found my lavender linen," said Roberta, turning back to the counter.

Richard came around to her side. "Didn't you expect to find it?" he inquired with interest.

"I really didn't at all. We seldom find summer goods shown in a town like this till spring is well along, least of all colored dress linens. But you have several shades, besides a beautiful lot of white."

"That's Carson's buying," said he, fingering a corner of the lilac-tinted goods she held up. "I shouldn't know it from gingham. I didn't know what gingham was till the other day, but I can recognize it now on sight and am no end proud of my knowledge."

"I suppose you are familiar with silk," said she with a quick glance.

He returned it. "Aren't you?"

"I'm not specially fond of it."

"What fabrics do you like best?"

"Thin, sheer things, fine but durable."

"Linens?"

"No, cottons, batistes, voiles—that sort of thing."

"I'm afraid you've got me now," he owned, looking puzzled. "Perhaps I'd know them if I saw them. If Benson has any—I mean, if we have any," he amended quickly, "I'd like to have you see them. Let me go and ask Carson."

He was off to consult the man in the office and was back in a minute. When Roberta had purchased the yard of lavender linen, he led her into another aisle and requested the clerk to show her his finest goods. Roberta looked on, much amused, while the display was made, and praised liberally. But suddenly she pounced upon a piece of white material with a tiny white flower embroidered upon its delicate surface.

"That's one of the prettiest pieces of Swiss muslin I ever saw," said she. "And at such a reasonable price. It looks like one of the finest imported Swisses. I'm going to have that pattern this minute."

She gave the order without hesitation.

"I didn't know women ever shopped like that," said Richard in her ear.

"Like what?"

"Why, bought the thing right off without asking to see everything in the store. That's what—I've been told they did."

"Not if they're wise, when they see a thing like that. There was only the one pattern. Why, another woman might have walked up and said right over my shoulder that she would take it."

"If she had I'd have seen that you got it," declared Richard.

He accompanied the party to the door when they went; he saw them to the sleigh and tucked them in.

"Bareheaded again," observed Uncle Rufus, regarding him with interest.

"Again?" queried Richard.

"All the young men we meet this morning insist on standing round outdoors with their hats off," explained the elder man. "It looks reckless to me."

"It would be more reckless not to, I imagine," returned Richard, laughing with Ruth and Roberta.

"We'll see you tonight," Uncle Rufus reminded him as he drove off. "Bring Hugh with you. I asked him in the store, but he seemed to hesitate. It will do him good to get out."

When the sleigh was a quarter of a mile up the road, Ruth turned to her uncle. "Do you imagine, Uncle Rufus," said she, "that all those men you've asked for tonight will be grateful when they see one another?"

Chapter 14

RAPID FIRE

"Well, now, we're glad to see you at our place, Mr. Kendrick," was Mr. Rufus Gray's hearty greeting. He had heard the sound of the motorcar as it came to a standstill just outside his window and was in the doorway to receive his guests. "As for Hugh, he knows he's always welcome, though it's a good while since he took advantage of it. Sit down here by the fire and warm up before we send you out again. You see," he explained cheerfully, "we have instructions what to do with you."

Richard Kendrick noted the pleasant room with its great fireplace roaring with logs ablaze; he noted also its absence of occupants. Only Aunt Ruth, coming forward with an expression of warm hospitality on her face, was to be discovered. "They're all down at the river, skating," she told the young men. "Forbes Westcott is just home again, and he and Robby had so much to talk over we asked him out to supper. He and the girls and Anna Drummond, one of our neighbors' daughters," she explained to Kendrick, "were taken with the idea of going skating. They didn't wait for you, because they wanted to get a fire built. When you're warmed up you can go down."

"There'll be a girl apiece for you," observed Uncle Rufus. "Hugh knows Anna—went to school with her. She's a fine girl, eh, Hugh?"

"She certainly is," agreed Benson heartily. "But I don't see how either of us is to skate with her or with anybody without—"

"Oh, that's all right. Look there," and Uncle Rufus pointed to a long row of skates lying on the floor in a corner. "All the nieces and nephews leave their skates here to have 'em handy when they come."

So presently the two young men were rushing down the winding, snowy road that led through pasture and meadow for a quarter of a mile toward a beckoning bonfire.

"I don't know when I've gone skating," said Hugh Benson.

"The last time I skated was two years ago on the Neva at St. Petersburg. And was it ever a carnival!" And Richard's thoughts went back for a minute to the face of the girl he had skated with. He had not cared much for skating since that night. All other opportunities had seemed tame after that.

"You've traveled a great deal—had a lot of experiences," Benson said, with a suppressed sigh.

"A few. But they don't prevent my looking forward to a new one tonight. I never went skating on a river in the country before. How far can you go?"

"Ten miles, if you like, down. Two miles up. There they are, coming round the bend four abreast. Westcott has more than his share of girls."

"More than he wants, probably. He'll cling to one and joyfully hand over the others."

"You'll like Anna Drummond; we're old school friends. Forbes and Miss Roberta naturally seem to get together wherever they are. And Miss Ruth is a mighty nice little girl."

Across the blazing bonfire two men scrutinized each other: Forbes Westcott, one of the cleverest attorneys of a large city, a man with a rising reputation, who held himself as a man does who knows that every day advances his success; Richard Kendrick, well-known young millionaire, hitherto a traveled idler and spender of his income, now a newly fledged businessman with all his honors yet to be won. They looked each other steadily in the eye as they grasped hands by the bonfire, and in his inmost heart each man recognized in the other an antagonist.

Richard skated away with Miss Drummond, a wholesomely gay and attractive girl who could skate as well as she could talk and laugh. He devoted himself to her for half an hour; then, with a skill of which he was master from long exercise, he brought about a change of partners. The next time he rounded the bend into a path that led straight down the moonlight it was in the company he longed for.

Richard's heart leaped exultantly as he skated around the river bend in the moonlight with Roberta. And when his hands gathered hers into his close grasp, it was somehow as if he had taken hold of an electric battery. He distinctly felt the difference between her hands and those of the other girl. It was very curious and he could not wholly understand it.

"What kind of gloves do you wear?" was his first inquiry. He held up the hand that was not in Roberta's muff and tried to see it in the dim light.

"You *are* deep in the new business, aren't you?" she mocked. "Whatever they are, will you put them into your stock?"

"Don't you dare make fun of my new business. I'm in it for scalps[1] and have no time for joking. Of course I want to put this make in stock. I never took hold of so warm a hand on so cold a night. The warmth comes right through your glove and mine to my hand, runs up my arm, and stirs up my circulation generally. It was running a little cold with some of the things Miss Drummond was telling me."

"What could they be?"

"About how all the rest of you know each other so well. She described all sorts of good times you have all had together on this river in the summer. It seems odd that Benson never told me about any of them while we were together at college."

"They have happened mostly in the last two summers, since Mr. Benson left college. We always spend at least part of our summers here, and we have had worlds of fun on the river and beside it and in it."

"I'm glad I'm a businessman in Eastman. I can imagine what this river is like in summer. It's wonderful tonight, isn't it? Let's skate on down to the mouth and out to sea. What do you say?"

"A beautiful plan. We have a good start; we must make time or it will be moonset before we come to the sea."

"This is a glorious stroke; let's hit it up a little, swing a little farther, and make for the mouth of the river. No talking till we come in sight. We're off!"

It was ten miles to the mouth of the river, as they both understood, so this was nonsense of the most obvious sort. But the imagination took hold of them and they swung away on over the smooth, shining floor with the long, vigorous strokes that are so exhilarating to the accomplished skater. In silence they flew, only the warm, clasped hands making a link between them, their faces turned straight toward the great golden disk in the eastern heavens. Richard was feeling that he could go on indefinitely and was exulting in his companion's untiring progress, when he felt her slowing pull upon his hands.

"Tired?" he asked, looking down at her.

"Not much, but we've all the way back to go—and we ought not to be away so long."

"Oughtn't we? I'd like to be away forever with you!"

She looked straight up at him. His eyes were like black coals in the dim

---

[1] With a serious, "take no prisoners" intent.

light. His hands would have tightened on hers, but she drew them away.

"Oh, no, you wouldn't, Mr. Richard Kendrick," said she, as quietly as one can whose breath comes with some difficulty after long-sustained exertion. "By the time we reached even the mouth of the river, you'd be tired of my company."

"Should I? I think not. I've thought of nothing but you since the day I saw you first."

"Really? That's how long? Was it November when you came to help Uncle Calvin? This is February. And you've never spent so much as a whole hour alone with me. You see, you don't even know me. What a foolish thing to say to a girl you barely know!"

"Foolish, is it?" He felt his heart racing now. What other girl he knew would have answered him like that? "Then you shall hear something that backs it up. I've loved you since that day I saw you first. What will you do with that?"

She was silent for a moment. Then she turned, striking out toward home. He was instantly after her, reached for her hand, and took her along with him. But he forced her to skate slowly.

"You'll trample on that, too, will you?" said he, growing wrathful under her silence.

But she answered, quite gently, now: "No, Mr. Kendrick, I don't trample on that. No girl would. I simply know you are mistaken."

"In what? My own feeling? Do you think I don't know—"

"I *know* you don't know. I'm not your kind of a girl, Mr. Kendrick. You think I am, because, well, perhaps because my eyes are blue and my eyelashes black; just such things as that do mislead people. I can dance fairly well—"

He smothered an angry exclamation.

"And skate well and play the cello a little, and that's nearly all you know about me. You don't even know whether I can teach well or talk well or what is stored away in my mind. And I know just as little about you."

"I've learned one thing about you in this last minute," he muttered. "You can keep your head."

"Why not?" There was a note of laughter in her voice. "There needs to be one who keeps her head when the other loses his—all because of a little winter moonlight. What would the summer moonlight do to you, I wonder?"

"Roberta Gray"—his voice was rough—"the moonlight does it no more than the sunlight. Whatever you think, I'm not that kind of fellow. The day I saw you first you had just come in out of the rain. You went back into it and I saw you go—and wanted to go with you. I've been wanting it ever since."

They moved on in silence that lasted until they were within a quarter mile of the bonfire, whose flashing light they could see above the banks that intervened. Then Roberta spoke:

"Mr. Kendrick"—her voice was low and rich with its kindest inflections—"I don't want you to think me careless or hard because I have treated what you have said tonight in a way that you don't like. I'm only trying to be honest with you. I'm quite sure you didn't mean to say it to me when you came tonight, and we all do and say things on a night like this that we should like to take back next day. It's quite true what I said, that you hardly know me, and whatever it is that takes your fancy, it can't be the real Roberta Gray, because you don't know her!"

"What you say is," he returned, staring straight ahead of him, "that I can't possibly know what you really are, at all; but you know so well what I am that you can tell me exactly what my own thoughts and feelings are."

"Oh, no, I didn't mean—"

"That's precisely what you do mean. I'm so plainly labeled 'worthless' that you don't have to stop to examine me. You—"

"I didn't—"

"I beg your pardon. I can tell you exactly what you think of me: a young fool who runs after the latest sensation, to drop it when he finds a newer one. His head turned by every pretty girl, to whom he says just the sort of thing he has said to you tonight. Superficial and ordinary, incapable of serious thought on any of the subjects that interest you. As for this business affair in Eastman—that's just a caprice, a game to be dropped when he tires of it. Everything in life will be like that to him, including his very friends. Come, now—isn't that what you've been thinking? There's no use denying it. Nearly every time I've seen you you've said some little thing that has shown me your opinion of me. I won't say there haven't been times in my life when I may have deserved it, but on my honor I don't think I deserve it now."

"Then I won't think it," said Roberta promptly, looking up. "I truly don't want to do you an injustice. But you are so different from the other men I have known—my brothers, my friends—that I can hardly imagine your seeing things from my point of view—"

"But you can see things from mine without any difficulty!"

"It isn't fair, is it?" Her tone was that of the comrade, now. "But you know women are credited with a sort of instinct—even intuition—that leads them safely where men's reasoning can't always follow."

"It never leads them astray, by any chance?"

"Yes, I think it does sometimes," she owned frankly. "But it's as well for the woman to be on her guard, isn't it? Because, sometimes, you know, she loses her head. And when that happens . . . "

"All is lost? Or does a man's reasoning, slower and not so infallible, but sometimes based on greater knowledge, step in and save the day?"

"It often does. But, in this case—well, it's not just a case of reasoning, is it?"

"The case of my falling in love with a girl I've only known—slightly— for four months? It has seemed to me all along it was just that. It's been a case of the head sanctioning the heart, and you probably know it's not always that way with a young man's experiences. Every ideal I've ever known—and I've had a few, though you might not think it—every good thought and purpose, have been stimulated by my contact with the people of your father's house. And since I have met you some new ideals have been born. They have become very dear to me, those new ideals, Miss Roberta, though they've had only a short time to grow. It hurts to have you treat me as if you thought me incapable of them."

"I'm sorry," she said simply, and her hands gave his a little quick pressure that meant apology and regret. His heart warmed a very little, for he had been sure she was capable of great generosity if appealed to in the right way. But justice and generosity were not all he craved, and he could see quite clearly that they were all he was likely to get from her as yet.

"You think," he said, pursuing his advantage, "we know too little of each other to be even friends. You are confident my tastes and pleasures are entirely different from yours, especially that my notions of real work are so different that we could never measure things with the same ruler."

He looked down at her searchingly.

She nodded. "Something like that," she admitted. "But that doesn't mean that either tastes or notions in either case are necessarily unworthy, only that they are different."

"I wonder if they are? What if we should try to find out? I'm going to stick pretty closely to Eastman this winter, but of course I shall be in town from time to time. May I come to see you now and then, if I promise not to become bothersome?"

It was her turn to look up searchingly at him. If he had expected the usual answer to such a request, he began, before she spoke, to realize that it was by no means a foregone conclusion that he should receive usual answers from her to any questioning whatsoever. But her reply surprised him more than he had ever been surprised by any girl in his life.

"Mr. Kendrick," said she slowly, "I wish that you need not see me again till . . . suppose we say Midsummer's Day, the twenty-fourth of June[2], you know."

He stared at her. "If you put it that way," he began stiffly, "you certainly need not—"

"But I didn't put it that way. I said I wished that you need not see me. That is quite different from wishing I need not see you. I don't mind seeing you in the least—"

"That's good of you!"

"Don't be angry. I'm going to be quite frank with you—"

"I'm prepared for that. I can't remember that you've ever been anything else."

"Please listen to me, Mr. Kendrick. When I say that I wish you would not see me—"

"You said 'need not.' "

"I shall have to put it 'would not' to make you understand. When I say I wish you would not see me until Midsummer I am saying the very kindest thing I can. Just now you are under the impression—hallucination—that you want to see much of me. To prove that you are mistaken I'm going to ask this of you: not to have anything whatever to do with me until at least Midsummer. If you carry out my wish, you will find out for yourself what I mean and will thank me for my wisdom."

"It's a wish, is it? It sounds to me more like a decree."

"It's not a decree. I'll not refuse to see you if you come. But if you will do as I ask I shall appreciate it more than I can tell you."

"It is certainly one of the cleverest schemes of getting rid of a fellow I ever heard. Hang it all! Do you expect me not to understand that you are simply letting me down easy? It's not in reason to suppose that you're forbidding all other men the house. I beg your pardon; I know that's none of my business; but it's not in human nature to keep from saying it, because of course that's bound to be the thing that cuts. If you were going into a convent, and all other fellows were cooling their heels outside with me, I could stand it."

"My dear Mr. Kendrick, you can stand it in any case. You're going to put all this out of mind and work at building up this business here in

---

[2] Midsummer comes at the time of the summer soltice, about June 21; but Midsummer's Day, the feast of St. John the Baptist, is June 24.

Eastman with Mr. Benson. You will find it a much more interesting game than the old one of . . . "

"Of what? Running after every pretty girl? For, of course, that's what you think I've done."

She did not answer that. He said something under his breath, and his hands tightened on hers savagely. They were rounding the next-to-last bend in the river, and the bonfire was close at hand.

"Can't you understand," he ground out, "that every other thought and feeling and experience I've ever had melts away before this? You can put me under ban for a year if you like; but if at the end of that time you're not married to another man you'll find me at your elbow. I told you I'd make you respect me; I'll do more, I'll make you listen to me. And if I promise not to come where you have to look at me till Midsummer, till the twenty-fourth of June—heaven knows why you pick out that day— I'll not promise not to make you think of me!"

"Oh, but that's part of what I mean. You mustn't send me letters and books and flowers—"

"Oh, thunder!"

"Because those things will help to keep this idea before your mind. I want you to forget me, Mr. Kendrick—do you realize that? Forget me absolutely all the rest of the winter and spring. By that time—"

"I'll wonder who you are when we do meet, I suppose?"

"Exactly. You—"

"All right. I agree to the terms. No letters, no books, no—ye birds and little fishies! If I could only send the flowers, now! Who would expect to win a girl without orchids? You do, you certainly do, rate me with the light-minded, don't you? Music also is proscribed, of course; that's the one other offering allowed me at the shrine of the fair one. All right, all right, I'll vanish, like a fairy prince in a child's story. But before I go I—"

With a dig of his steel-shod heel he brought himself and Roberta to a standstill. He bent over her till his face was rather close to hers. She looked back at him without fear, though she both saw and felt the tenseness with which he was making his farewell speech.

"Before I go, I say, I'm going to tell you that if you were any other girl on the old footstool I'd have one kiss from you before I let go of you if I knew it meant I'd never have another. I could take it—"

She did not shrink from him by a hair's breadth, but he felt her suddenly tremble as if with the cold.

"But I want you to know that I'm going to wait for it till Midsummer's

Day. Then"—he bent still closer—"you will give it to me yourself. I'm saying this foolhardy sort of thing to give you something to remember all these months. I've got to. You'll have so many other people saying things to you when I can't that I've got to startle you in order to make an impression that will stick. That one will, won't it?"

A reluctant smile touched her lips. "It's quite possible that it may," she conceded. "It probably would, whoever had the audacity to say it. But to know a fate that threatens is to be forewarned. And, fortunately, a girl can always run away."

"You can't run so far that I can't follow. Meanwhile, tell me just one thing—"

"I'll tell you nothing more. We've been gone for ages now. There come the others. Please start on."

"Good-bye, dear," said he under his breath. "Good-bye till Midsummer. But then——"

"No, no, you must *not* say it—or think it."

"I'm going to think it, and so are you. I defy you to forget it. You may see that lawyer Westcott every day, and no matter what you're saying to him, every once in a while will bob up the thought: Midsummer's Day!"

"Hush! I won't listen! Please skate faster!"

"You *shall* listen to just one thing more. Just halfway between now and Midsummer may I come to see you—just once?"

"No."

"Why?"

"Because I shall not want to see you."

"That's good," said he steadily. "Then let me tell you that I should not come even if you would let me. I wanted you to know that."

A little, half-smothered laugh came from her in spite of herself, in which he rather grimly joined. Then the others, calling questions and reproaches, bore down upon them, and the evening for Richard Kendrick was over. But the fight he meant to win was just begun.

Chapter 15

MAKING MEN

"Grandfather, have you a good courage for adventure?"

Matthew Kendrick looked up from his letters. His grandson Richard stood before him, his face lighted by that new look of expectancy and enthusiasm that the older man so often noted now. It was early in the day, Mr. Kendrick having but just partaken of his frugal breakfast. He had eaten alone this morning, having learned to his surprise that Richard was already off.

"Why, Dick? What do you want of me?" his grandfather asked, laying down his letters. They were important, but not so important, to his mind, as giving ear to his grandson. It was something about the business, he had no doubt. The boy was always talking about the business these days, and he found always a ready listener in the old man who was such a past master in the whole difficult subject.

"It's the mildest sort of weather—bright sun, good roads most of the way, and something worth seeing at the other end. Put on your fur-lined coat, sir, will you? And come with me up to Eastman. I want to show you the new shop."

Mr. Kendrick's eye brightened. So the boy wanted him, did he? Wanted to take him off for the day, the whole day, with himself. It was pleasant news. But he hesitated a little, looking toward the window, where the late March sun was, surely enough, streaming in warmly. The bare branches outside were motionless; there was no wind, such as had prevailed of late.

"I can keep you perfectly warm," Richard added, seeing the hesitation. "There's an electric foot-warmer in the car, and you shall have a heavy rug. I'll have you there in a couple of hours, and you'll not be even chilled. If the weather changes, you can come back by train. Please come. Will you?"

"I believe I will, Dick, if you'll not drive too fast. I should like to see this wonderful new store, to be sure."

"We'll go any pace you like, sir. I've been looking for a day when you could make the trip safely, and this is it." He glanced at the letters. "Could you be ready in half an hour?"

"As soon as I can dictate four short replies. Ring for Mr. Stanton, please, and I'll soon be with you."

Richard went out as his grandfather's private secretary came in. Although Matthew Kendrick no longer felt it necessary to go to his office in the great store every day, he was accustomed to attend to a certain amount of selected correspondence and ordinarily spent an hour after breakfast in dictation to a young stenographer who came to him for the purpose.

Within a half hour the two were off, Mr. Kendrick being quite as alert in the matter of dispatching business and getting under way toward fresh affairs as he had ever been. It was with an expression of interested antici- pation that the old man, wrapped from head to foot, took his place in the long, low-hung roadster, beneath the broad hood that Richard had raised, that his passenger might be as snug as possible.

For many miles the road was of macadam, and they bowled along at a rate that consumed the distance swiftly, though not too fast for Mr. Kendrick's comfort. Richard artfully increased his speed by fractional degrees, so that his grandfather, accustomed to being conveyed at a very moderate pace about the city in his closed car, should not be startled by the sense of flight that he might have had if the young man had started at his usual breakneck pace.

They did not talk much, for Matthew Kendrick was habitually cautious about using his voice in winter air, and Richard was too engaged with the car and with his own thoughts to attempt to keep up a one- sided conversation. More than once, however, a brief colloquy took place. One of the last of these, before approaching their destination, was as follows:

"Keeping warm, Grandfather?"

"Perfectly, Dick, thanks to your foot-warmer."

"Tired, at all?"

"Not a particle. On the contrary, I find the air very stimulating."

"I thought you would. Wonderful day for March, isn't it?"

"Unusually fine." .

"We'll be there before you know it. There's one bad stretch of a couple of miles, beyond the turn ahead, and another just this side of Eastman, but Old Faithful here will make light work of 'em. She could plough through quicksand if she had to, not to mention spring mud to the hubs."

"The car seems powerful," said the old man, smiling behind his upturned fur collar. "I suppose a young fellow like you wouldn't be content with anything that couldn't pull at least ten times as heavy a load as it needed to."

"I suppose not," laughed Richard. "Though it's not so much a question of a heavy load as of plenty of power when you want it and of speed all the time. Suppose we were being chased by wild Indians right now, Grandfather. Wouldn't it be a satisfaction to walk away from them like—this?"

The car shot ahead with a long, lithe spring, as if she had been using only a fraction of her power and had reserves greater than could be reckoned. Her gait increased as she flew down the long straightaway ahead until her speedometer on the dash recorded a pace with which the fastest locomotive on the track that ran parallel with the road would have had to race with wide-open throttle to keep neck to neck. Richard had not meant to treat his grandfather to an exhibition of this sort, being well aware of the older man's distaste for modern high speed, but the sight of the place where he was in the habit of racing with any passing train was too much for his young blood and love of swift flight, and he had covered the full two-mile stretch before he could bring himself to slow down to a more moderate gait.

Then he turned to look at as much of his grandfather's face as he could discern between cap brim and collar. The eagle eyes beneath their heavy brows were gazing straight ahead, the firmly molded lips were close-set, the whole profile, with its large but well-cut nose, suggested grim endurance. Matthew Kendrick had made no remonstrance, nor did he now complain, but Richard understood.

"You didn't like that, did you, Grandfather? I had no business to do it, when I said I wouldn't. Did I chill you, sir? I'm sorry," was his quick apology.

"You didn't chill my body, Dick," was the response. "You did make me realize the difference between youth and age."

"That's not what I ever want to do," declared the young man, with swift compunction. "Not when your age is worth a million times my youth, in knowledge and power. And of course I'm showing up a particularly unfortunate trait of youth: to lose its head! Somehow all the boy in me comes to the top when I see that track over there, even when there's no competing train. Did you ever know a boy who didn't want to be an engine driver?"

"I was a boy once," said Matthew Kendrick. "Trains in my day were doing well when they made twenty-five miles an hour. I shouldn't mind your racing with one of those."

"I'm racing with one of the fastest engines ever built when I set up a store in Eastman and try to appropriate some of your methods. I wonder what you'll think of it?" said Richard gaily. "Well, here's the bad stretch. Sit tight, Grandfather. I'll pick out the best footing there is, but we may jolt about a good bit. I'm going to try what can be done to get these fellows to put a bottom under their spring mud!"

When the town was reached Richard conveyed his companion straight to the best hotel, saw that he had a comfortable chair and as appetizing a meal as the house could afford, and let him rest for as long a time afterward as he himself could brook waiting. When Mr. Kendrick professed himself in trim for whatever might come next, Richard set out with him for the short walk to the store of Benson & Company.

The young man's heart was beating with surprising rapidity as the two approached the front of the brick building that represented his present venture into the business world. He knew just how keen an eye was to inspect the place and what thorough knowledge was to pass judgment upon it.

"Here we are," he said abruptly, with an effort to speak lightly. "These are our front windows. Carson dresses them himself. He seems a wonder to me—I can't get hold of it at all. Rather a good effect, don't you think?"

He was distinctly nervous, and he could not conceal it as Matthew Kendrick turned to look at the front of the building, taking it all in, it seemed, with one sweeping glance that dwelt only for a minute apiece on the two big windows, and then turned to the entrance, above which hung the signs, old and new. The visitor made no comment, only nodded and made straight for the door.

As it swung open under Richard's hand, the young man's first glance was for the general effect. He himself was looking at everything as if for the first time, intensely alive to the impression it was to make upon his judge. He found that the general effect was considerably obscured by the number of people at the counters and in the aisles; more, it seemed to him, than he had ever seen there before. His second observation was that the class of shoppers seemed particularly good, and he tried to recall the special feature of Carson's advertisement of the evening before. There were several different lines, he remembered, to which Carson had called special attention, with the assertion that the values were absolute and the quality guaranteed.

But his attention was very quickly diverted from any study of the store itself to the even more interesting and instructive study of the old man who accompanied him. He had invited an expert to look the situation over, there could be no possible doubt of that. And the expert was looking it over—there could be no doubt of that, either. As they passed down one aisle and up another, Richard could see how the eagle eyes noted one point after another, yet without any disturbing effect of searching scrutiny. Here and there Mr. Kendrick's gaze lingered a trifle longer, and more than once he came close to a counter and brought an eyeglass to bear on the goods there displayed, nodding pleasantly at the salespeople as he did so. And everywhere he went glances followed him.

It seemed to Richard that he had never realized before what a distinguished-looking old man his grandfather was. He was not of more than average height; he was dressed, though scrupulously, as unobtrusively as is any quiet gentleman of his years and position; but nonetheless there was something about him that spoke of the man of affairs, of the leader, the organizer, the general.

Alfred Carson came hurrying out of the little office as the two Kendricks came in sight. Matthew Kendrick greeted him with distinct evidence of pleasure.

"Ah, Mr. Carson," he said, "I am very glad to see you again. I have missed you from your department. How do you find the new business? More interesting than the old, eh?"

"It is always interesting, sir," responded Carson, "to enlarge one's field of operations."

Mr. Kendrick laughed heartily at this, turning to Richard as he did so. "That's a great compliment to you, Dick," he said, "that Mr. Carson feels he has enlarged his field by coming up here to you and leaving me."

"Don't you think it's true, Grandfather?" challenged Richard boldly.

"To be sure it's true," agreed Mr. Kendrick. "But it sometimes takes a wise man to see that a swing from the center of things to the rim is the way to swing back to the center, finally. Well, I've looked about quite a bit. What next, Dick?"

"Won't you come into the office, sir, and ask us any questions that you like? We want your criticism and your suggestions," declared Richard. "Where's Mr. Benson, Mr. Carson? I'd like him to meet my grandfather right away. I thought we'd find him somewhere about the place before now."

"He's just come into the office," said Carson, leading the way. "He'll be mightily pleased to see Mr. Kendrick."

This prophecy proved true. Hugh Benson, who had not known of his partner's intention to bring the senior Mr. Kendrick to visit the store, flushed with pleasure and a little nervousness when he saw him, and gave evidence of the latter as he cleared a chair for his guest and knocked down a pile of small pasteboard boxes as he did so.

"We don't usually keep such things in here," he apologized, and sent posthaste for a boy to take the offending objects away. Then the party settled down for a talk, Richard carefully closing the door, after notifying a clerk outside to prevent interruption for so long as it should remain closed.

"Now, Grandfather, talk business to us, will you?" he begged. "Tell us what you think of us, and don't spare us. That's what we want, isn't it?" And he appealed to his two associates with a look that bade them speak out.

"We certainly do, Mr. Kendrick," Hugh Benson assured the visitor eagerly. "It's our chance to have an expert opinion."

"It will be even more than that," said Alfred Carson. "It will be the opinion of the master of all experts in the business world."

"Fie, Mr. Carson," said the old man, with, however, a kind look at the young man, who he knew did not mean to flatter him but to speak the undeniable truth, "you must remember the old saying about praise to the face. Still, I must break that rule myself when I tell you all that I am greatly pleased with the appearance of the place, and with all that meets the eye in a brief visit."

Richard glowed with satisfaction at this, but both Benson and Carson appeared to be waiting for more. The old man looked at them and nodded.

"You have both had much more experience than this boy of mine," said he, "and you know that all has not been said when due acknowledgment has been made of the appearance of a place of business. What I want to know, gentlemen, is, does the appearance tell the absolute truth about the integrity of the business?"

Richard looked at him quickly, for with the last words his grandfather's tone had changed from mere suavity to a sudden suggestion of sternness. Instinctively he straightened in his chair, and his glance at the other two young men showed that they had quite as involuntarily straightened in theirs. As the head of the firm, Hugh Benson, after a moment's pause, answered, in a quietly firm tone that made Richard regard him with fresh respect:

"If it didn't, Mr. Kendrick, I shouldn't want to be my father's successor.

He may have been a failure in business, but it was not for want of absolute integrity."

The keen eyes softened as they rested on the young man's face, and Mr. Kendrick bent his head, as if he would do honor to the memory of a father who, however unsuccessful as the world judges success, could make a son speak as this son had spoken. "I am sure that is true, Mr. Benson," he said and paused for a moment before he went on:

"It is the foundation principle of business—that a reputation for trust-worthiness can be built only on the rock of real merit. The appearance of the store must not tell one lie—not one—from front door to back—not even the shadow of a lie. Nothing must be left to the customer's discretion. If he pays so much money he must get so much value, whether he knows it or not." He stopped abruptly, waited for a little, his eyes searching the faces before him. Then he said, with a change of tone:

"Do you want to tell me something about the management of the business, gentlemen?"

"We want to do just that, Mr. Kendrick," Benson answered.

So they set it before him, he and Alfred Carson, as they had worked it out, Richard remaining silent even when appealed to, merely saying quietly: "I'm only the crudest kind of a beginner. You fellows will have to do the talking," and so leaving it all to the others. They showed Mr. Kendrick the books of the firm, they explained to him their system of buying, of analyzing their sales that they might learn how to buy at best advantage and sell at greatest profit; of getting rid of goods quickly by attractive advertising; of all manner of details large and small, such as pertain to the conduct of a business of the character of theirs.

They grew eager, enthusiastic, as they talked, for they found their listener ready of understanding, quick of appreciation, kindly of criticism, yet so skillful at putting a finger on their weak places that they could only wonder and take earnest heed of every word he said. As Richard watched him, he found himself understanding a little Matthew Kendrick's extraordinary success. If his personality was still one to make a powerful impression on all who came in contact with him, what must it have been, Richard speculated, in his prime, in those wonderful years when he was building the great business, expanding it with a daring of conception and a rapidity of execution which had fairly taken away the breath of his contemporaries. He had introduced new methods, laid down new principles, defied old systems, and created better ones having no precedent anywhere but in his own productive brain. It might justly be said that he had virtually revolutionized the mercantile world, for when the bridges that he built were found to hold, in spite of all dire prophecy to the contrary, others had crossed them, too, and profited by his bridge building.

The three young men did their best to lead Mr. Kendrick to talk of himself, but of that he would do little. Constantly he spoke of the work of his associates, and when it became necessary to allude to himself it was always as if they had been identified with every move of his own. It was Alfred Carson who best recognized this trait of peculiar modesty in the old man, and who understood most fully how often the more impersonal "we" of his speech really stood for the "I" who had been the mainspring of all action in the growth of the great affairs he spoke of. Carson was the son of a man who had been one of the early heads of a newly created department in the days when departments were just being tried, and he had heard many a time of the way in which Matthew Kendrick had held to his course of introducing innovations, that had startled the men most closely associated with him and had made them wonder if he were not going too far for safety or success.

"Well, well, gentlemen," said Mr. Kendrick, rising abruptly at last, "you have beguiled me into long speech. It takes me back to old days to sit and discuss a young business like this one with young men like you. It has been very interesting, and it delights me to find you so ready to take counsel, while at the same time you show a healthy belief in your own judgment. You will come along, you will come along. You will make mistakes, but you will profit by them. And you will remember always, I hope, a motto I am going to give you."

He paused and looked searchingly into each face before him: Hugh Benson's, serious and sincere; Alfred Carson's, energy and purpose showing in every line; his own boy's, Richard's, keen interest and a certain proud wonder looking out of his fine eyes as he watched the old man who seemed to him today, somehow, almost a stranger in his unwontedly aroused speech.

"The most important thing a business can do," said Matthew Kendrick slowly, "is to make men of those who make the business."

He let the words sink in. He saw, after an instant, the response in each face, and he nodded, satisfied. He held out his hand to each in turn, including his grandson, and received three hearty grips of gratitude and understanding.

As he drove away with Richard, his eyes were bright under their heavy brows. It had done him good, this visit to the place where his thoughts had often been of late, and he was pleased with the way Richard had borne himself throughout the interview. He could not have asked better of the heir to the Kendrick millions than the unassuming and yet quietly assured manner Richard had shown. It had a certain quality, the old man proudly considered, which was lacking in that of both Benson and Carson, fine fellows though they were, and well-mannered in every way. It reminded Matthew Kendrick of the boy's own father, who had been a man among men and a gentleman besides.

"Grandfather, we shall pass Mr. Rufus Gray's farm in a minute. Don't you want to stop and see them?"

"Rufus Gray?" questioned Mr. Kendrick. "The people we entertained at Christmas? I should like to stop, if it will not delay us too long. It seems a colder air than it did this morning."

"There's a bit of wind, and it's usually colder, facing this way. If you prefer, after the call, I'll take you back to the station and run down alone."

"We'll see. Is this the place we're coming to? A pleasant old place enough, and it looks like the right home for such a pair," commented Mr. Kendrick, gazing interestedly ahead as the car swung in at a stone gateway and followed a winding roadway toward a low-lying, hospitable-looking white house with long porches beyond masses of bare shrubbery.

It seemed that the welcoming look of the house was justified in the attitude of its inmates, for the car had but stopped when the door flew open and Rufus Gray, his face beaming, bade them enter. Inside, his wife came forward with her well-remembered sunny smile, and in a trice Matthew Kendrick and his grandson found themselves sitting in front of a blazing fire upon a wide hearth, receiving every evidence that their presence brought delight.

Richard looked on with inward amusement and satisfaction at the unwonted sight of his grandfather partaking of a cup of steaming coffee rich with country cream, and eating with the appetite of a boy a huge, sugar-coated doughnut which his hostess assured him could not possibly hurt him.

"They're the real old-fashioned kind, Mr. Kendrick," said she. "Raised like bread, you know, and fried in lard we make ourselves in a way I have so that not a bit of grease gets inside. My husband thinks they're the only fit food to go with coffee."

"They are the most delicious food I ever ate, certainly, Madam Gray, and I find myself agreeing with him, now that I taste them," declared Mr. Kendrick, and Richard, disposing with zest of a particularly huge, light specimen of Mrs. Gray's art, seconded his grandfather's appreciation.

They made a long call, Mr. Kendrick appearing to enjoy himself as Richard could not remember seeing him do before. He and Mr. Gray found many subjects to discuss with mutual interest, and the nodding of the two heads in assent at frequent intervals proved how well they found themselves agreeing.

Richard, as at the time of the Grays' brief visit at his own home, devoted himself to the lady whom he always thought of as "Aunt Ruth," secretly dwelling on the hope that he might someday acquire the right to call her by that pleasant title. He led her, by artful circumlocutions, always tending toward one object, to speak of her nieces and nephews, and when he succeeded in drawing from her certain all-too-meager news of Roberta, he exulted in his ardent soul, though he did his best not to betray himself.

"Maybe," said she, quite suddenly, "you'd enjoy looking at the family album. Robby and Ruth always get it out when they come here. They like to see their father and mother the way they used to look. There's some of themselves, too, though the photographs folks have now are too big to go in an old-fashioned album like this, and the ones they've sent me lately aren't in here."

Never did a modern young man accept so eagerly the chance to scan the collection of curious old likenesses such as is found between the covers of the now despised "album" of the days of their grandfathers. Richard turned the pages eagerly, scanning them for faces he knew, and discovered much satisfaction in one charming picture of Roberta's mother at eighteen because of its suggestion of the daughter.

"Eleanor was the beauty of the family and is yet, I always say," asserted Aunt Ruth. "Robby's like her, they all think, but she can't hold a candle to her mother. She's got more spirit in her face, maybe, but her features aren't equal to Eleanor's."

Richard did not venture to disagree with this opinion, but he privately considered that, enchanting as was the face of Mrs. Robert Gray at eighteen, that of her daughter Roberta at twenty-four dangerously rivaled it.

"I could tell better about the likeness if I saw a late picture of Miss Roberta," he observed, his eyes and mouth grave but his voice expectant. Aunt Ruth promptly took the suggestion, and limping daintily away, returned after a minute with a framed photograph of Roberta and Ruth, taken by one of those masters of the art who understand how to bring out the values of the human face, yet to leave provocative shadows that make for mystery and charm. Richard received it with a respectful hand, and then had much ado to keep from showing how the sight of her pictured face made his heart throb.

When the two visitors rose to go, Aunt Ruth put in a plea for their remaining overnight.

"It's turned colder since you came up this morning, Mr. Kendrick," said she. "Why not stay with us and go back in the morning? We'd be so pleased to entertain you, and we've plenty of room—too much room for us two old folks, now the children are all married and gone."

To Richard's surprise his grandfather did not immediately decline. He looked at Aunt Ruth, her rosy, smiling face beaming with hospitality, then he glanced at Richard.

"Do stay," urged Uncle Rufus. "Remember how you took us in at midnight, and what a good time you gave us the two days we stayed? It would make us mighty happy to have you sleep under our roof, you and your grandson both, if he'll stay, too."

"I confess I should like to sleep under this roof," admitted Matthew Kendrick. "It reminds me of my father's old home. It's very good of you, Madam Gray, to ask us, and I believe I shall remain. As to Richard—"

"I'd like nothing better," declared that young man promptly.

So it was settled. Richard drove back to the store and gathered together various articles for his own and his grandfather's use and returned to the Gray fireside. The long and pleasant evening that followed the hearty country supper gave him one more new experience in the long list of them he was acquiring. Somehow he had seldom been happier than when he followed his hostess into the comfortable room upstairs she assigned him, opening from that she had given the elder man. Cheerful fires burned in old-fashioned, open-hearthed Franklin stoves in both rooms, and the atmosphere was fragrant with the mingled breath of crackling apple wood and lavender from the fine old linen with which both beds had been freshly made.

"Sleep well, my dear friends," said Aunt Ruth in her quaintly friendly way as she bade her guests goodnight and shook hands with them, receiving warm responses.

"One must find sweet repose under your roof," said Matthew Kendrick, and Richard, attending his hostess to the door, murmured, "You look as if you'd put two small boys to bed and tucked them in!" at which Aunt Ruth laughed with pleasure, nodding at him over her shoulder as she went away.

Presently, as Matthew Kendrick lay down in the soft bed, his face toward the glow of his fire that he might watch it, Richard knocked and came in from his own room and, crossing to the bed, stood leaning on the footboard.

"Too sleepy to talk, Grandfather?" he asked.

"Not at all, my boy," responded the old man, his heart stirring in his breast at this unwonted approach at an hour when the two were usually far apart. Never that he could remember had Richard come into his room after he had retired.

"I wanted to tell you," said the young man, speaking very gently, "that you've been awfully kind and have done us all a lot of good today. And you've done me the most of all."

"Why, that's pleasant news, Dick," answered old Matthew Kendrick, his eyes fixed on the shadowy outlines of the face at the foot of the bed. "Sit down and tell me about it."

So Richard sat down, and the two had such a talk as they had never had before in their lives: a long, intimate talk with the barriers down— barriers that both felt now never should have existed. Lying there in the soft bed of Aunt Ruth's best feathers, with the odor of her lavender in his nostrils, and the sound of the voice he loved in his ears, the old man drank in the delight of his grandson's confidence, and the wonder of something new: the consciousness of Richard's real affection. His heart beat with slow, heavy throbs of joy, such as he had never expected to feel again in this world.

"Altogether," said Richard, rising reluctantly at last as the tall, old clock on the landing nearby slowly boomed out the hour of midnight, "it's been a great day for me. I'd been looking forward with quite a bit of dread to bringing you up, I knew you'd see so plainly wherever we were lacking; but you were so splendidly kind about it—"

"And why shouldn't I be kind, Dick?" spoke his grandfather eagerly. "What have I in the world to interest me as you and your affairs interest me? Can any possible stroke of fortune seem so great to me as your development into a man of accomplishment? And when it is in the very world I know so well and have so near my heart—"

Richard interrupted him, not realizing that he was doing so, but full of longing to make all still further clear between them. "Grandfather, I want to make a confession. This world of yours—I didn't want to enter it."

"I know you didn't, Dick. And I know why. But you are getting over that, aren't you? You are beginning to realize that it isn't what a man does, but the way he does it, that matters."

"Yes," said Richard slowly. "Yes, I'm beginning to realize that. And do you want to know what made me realize it today, as never before?"

The old man waited.

"It was the sight of you, sir, and the recognition of the power you have been all your life . . . and the . . . sudden appreciation of the . . . " He stumbled a little, but he brought the words out forcefully at the end: "of the very great gentleman you are!"

He could not see the hot tears spring into the old eyes that had not known such a sign of emotion for many years. But he could feel the throb in the low voice that answered him after a moment.

"I may not deserve that, Dick, but . . . it touches me, coming from you."

When Richard had gone back to his own room, Matthew Kendrick lay for a long time, wide awake, too happy to sleep. In the next room his grandson, before he slept, had formulated one more new idea:

"There's something in the association with people like these that makes a fellow feel like being absolutely honest with them, with everybody— most of all with himself. What is it?"

And pondering this, he was lost in the world of dreams.

Chapter 16

ENCOUNTERS

"By the way, Rob, I saw Rich Kendrick today." Louis Gray detained his sister Roberta on the stairs as they stopped to exchange greetings on a certain evening in March. "It struck me suddenly that I hadn't seen him for a blue moon, and I asked him why he didn't come round when he was in town. He said he was sticking tight to that new business of his up in Eastman, but he admitted he was to be here in town over Sunday. I invited him round tonight, but to my surprise he wouldn't come. Said he had another engagement, of course—thanked me fervently and all that—but there was no getting him. It made me a bit suspicious of you, Robby."

"I can't imagine why." But, in spite of herself, Roberta colored. "He came here when he was helping Uncle Calvin. There's no reason for his coming now."

Her brother regarded her with the observing eye that sisters find difficult to evade. "He would have taken a job as nursemaid for Rosy, if it would have given him a chance to go in and out of this old house, I imagine. Rosy maintained it was his infatuation for the home and the members thereof, particularly Gordon and Dorothy. He undoubtedly was struck with them—it would have been a hard heart that wasn't touched by the sight of the boy—but if it was the kiddies he wanted, why didn't he keep coming? Steve and Rosy would have welcomed him."

"You had better ask him his reasons next time you see him," Roberta suggested, and escaped.

It was two months since she had seen Richard Kendrick. He seemed never so much as to pass the house, although it stood directly on his course when he drove back and forth from Eastman in his car. She wondered if he really did make a detour each time to avoid the very chance of meeting her. It was impossible not to think of him, rather disturbingly often, and to wonder how he was getting on.

147

The month of March in the year of this tale was on the whole an extraordinarily mild and springlike substitution for the rigorous, windswept season it should by all rights have been. On one of its most beguiling days, Roberta Gray was walking home from Miss Copeland's school. Usually she came by way of the broad avenue that led straight home. Today, out of sheer unwillingness to reach that home and end the walk, she took a quite different course. This led her up a somewhat similar street, parallel to her own but several blocks beyond, a street of more than ordinary attractiveness in that it was less of a thoroughfare than any other of equal beauty in the residential portion of the city.

She was walking slowly, drawing in the balmy air and noting with delight the beds of crocuses that were beginning to show here and there on lawns and beside paths, when a peculiar sound far up the avenue caught her ear. She recognized it instantly, for she had heard it often and she had never heard another quite like it. It was the warning song of a coming motorcar, and it was of unusual and striking musical quality. So Roberta knew, even before she caught sight of the long, low, powerful car that had stood many times before her own door during certain weeks of the last year, that she was about to meet for the first time in two months the person upon whom she had put a ban.

Would he see her? He could hardly help it, for there was not another pedestrian in sight upon the whole length of the block, and the March sunshine was full upon her. As the car came on, the girl who walked sedately to meet it found that her pulses had somehow curiously accelerated. So this was the route he took not to go by her home.

Did he see her? Evidently as far away as half a block, for at that distance his cap was suddenly pulled off, and it was with bared head that he passed her. At the moment the car was certainly not running as fast as it had been doing twenty rods back; it went by at a pace moderate enough to show the pair to each other with distinctness. Roberta saw clearly Richard Kendrick's intent eyes upon her, saw the flash of his smile and the grace of his bow, and saw—as if written upon the blue spring sky—the word he had left with her: "Midsummer." If he had shouted it at her as he passed, it could not have challenged her more defiantly.

He was obeying her literally—more literally than she could have demanded. Not to slow down, come to a standstill beside her, exchange at least a few words of greeting—this was indeed a strict interpretation of her edict. Evidently he meant to play the game rigorously. Still, he had been a compellingly attractive figure as he passed; that instant's glimpse of him was likely to remain with her quite as long as a more protracted interview. Did he guess that?

I wonder how I looked? was her first thought as she walked on—a purely feminine one, it must be admitted. When she reached home she glanced at herself in the hall looking glass on her way upstairs, a thing she seldom took the trouble to do.

A figure got hastily to its feet and came out into the hall to meet her as she passed the door of the reception room. "Miss Roberta!" said an eager voice.

"Why, Mr. Westcott! I didn't know you were in town!"

"I didn't intend to be until next month, as you knew. But this wonderful weather was too much for me."

He held her hand and looked down into her face from his tall height. He told her what he thought of her appearance—in detail with his eyes, in modified form with his lips.

"In my old school clothes?" laughed Roberta. "How draggy winter things seem the first warm days. This velvet hat weighs like lead on my head today." She took it off. "I'll run up and make myself presentable," said she.

"Please don't. You're exactly right as you are. And I want you to go for a walk if you're not too tired. The road that leads out by the West Wood marshes; it will be sheer spring out there today. I want to share it with you."

So Roberta put on her hat again and went to walk with Forbes Westcott out the road that led by the West Wood marshes. There was not a more romantic road to be found in a long way.

When they were well out into the country he began to press a question that she had heard before, and to which he had had as yet no answer.

"Still undecided?" said he, with a very sober face. "You can't make up your mind as to my qualifications?"

"Your qualifications are undoubted," said she, with a face as sober as his. "They are more than any girl could ask. But I . . . how can I know? I care so much for you, as a friend. Why can't we keep on being just good friends and let things develop naturally?"

"If I thought they would ever develop the way I want them," he said earnestly, "I would wait patiently a great while longer. But I don't seem to be making any progress. In fact, I seem to have gone backward a bit in your good graces. Since I saw that young prince of shopkeepers in your company over at Eastman, I've been wondering—"

"Prince of shopkeepers! What an extraordinary characterization! I thought he was a most amateurish shopkeeper. He didn't even know the name of his own batiste, much less where it was kept."

"He knew how to skate and to take you along with him. I beg your pardon! But ever since that night I've been experiencing a most disconcerting sense of jealousy whenever I think of that young man. He was such a magnificent figure there in the firelight; he made me feel as old as the Pyramids. And when you two were gone so long and came back with such an odd look, both of you—oh, I beg your pardon again! This is most unworthy of me, I know. But set me straight if you can! Have you seen much of him since that night?"

"Absolutely nothing," said Roberta quickly, with a sense of great relief. "Today he passed me in his car, on my way home from school, over on Egerton Avenue, and didn't even stop."

He scanned her face closely. "And you are not even interested in him?"

"Mr. Forbes Westcott," said Roberta desperately, "I have told you often and often that I'm not interested in any man except as one or two are my very good friends. Why can't all girls be allowed to live along in peace and comfort until they are at least thirty years old? You didn't have anybody besieging you to marry before you were thirty. If anybody had you'd have said no quickly enough. You had that much of your life comfortably to yourself."

He bit his lip, but he was obliged to laugh. His thin, keen face was more attractive when he laughed, but there was an odd, tense expression on it that did not leave it even then.

"I can see you are still hopeless," he owned. "But so long as you are hopeless for other men I can endure it, I suppose. I really meant not to speak again for a long time, as I promised you. But the thought of that embryo plutocrat making after you, as he has after so many girls—"

"How many girls, I wonder?" queried Roberta quite carelessly. "Do you happen to know? Has his fame spread so far?"

"I know nothing about him, of course, except that he's a merry young spendthrift. It goes without saying that he's flirted with every pretty face, for that kind invariably do."

"If it goes without saying, why say it? Particularly as you don't know it. I daresay he has. What serious harm? I presume it's quite as likely they've run after him. I'm sure it's a matter of no concern to me, for I know him very little and am likely to know him much less now that he doesn't come to work with Uncle Calvin any more. Let's go back, Mr. Westcott. I came out to look for pussy willows, not for Robby-will-you's!"

With which piece of audacity she dismissed the subject. It certainly was not a subject that harmonized well with that of Midsummer's Day, and the thought of Midsummer's Day, quickened into active life by the unexpected sight of the person who had made a certain preposterous prophecy concerning it, was a thought that was refusing to die down.

Chapter 17

INTRIGUE

"Hi! Mr. Kendrick! I say, Mr. Kendrick! Wait a minute!"

The car, about to leave the curb in front of one of Kendrick & Company's great city stores, halted. Its driver turned to see young Ted Gray tearing across the sidewalk in hot pursuit.

"Well, well. Glad to see you, Ted boy. Jump in and I'll take you along."

Ted jumped in. He gave Richard Kendrick's welcoming hand a hard squeeze. "I haven't seen you for an awful while," said he reproachfully. "Aren't you ever coming to our house anymore?"

"I hope so, Ted. But, you see," explained Richard carefully, "I'm a man of business now, and I can't have much time for calls. I'm in Eastman most of the time. How are you, Ted? Tell me all about it. Can you go for a spin with me? I had to come into town in a hurry, but there's no great hurry about getting back. I'll take you out into the country and show you the prettiest lot of apple trees in full bloom you ever saw in May."

"I'd like to first-rate, but could you take me home first? I have to let Mother know where I am after school."

"All right." And away they flew. But Richard turned off the avenue three blocks below the corner upon which stood Ted's home and ran up the street behind it. "Run in the back way, will you, Ted?" he requested. "I want to do a bit of work on the car while you're in."

So while Ted dashed up through the garden to the back of the house Richard got out and unscrewed a nut or two, which he screwed again into place without having accomplished anything visible to the eye, and was replacing his wrench when the boy returned.

"This is jolly," Ted declared. "I'll bet Rob envies me. This is her Wednesday off from teaching, and she was just going for a walk. She wanted me to go with her, but of course she let me go with you instead.

I . . . I suppose I could ride on the running board and let you take her if you want to," he proposed with some reluctance.

"I'd like nothing better, but she wouldn't go."

"Maybe not. Perhaps Mr. Westcott is coming for her. They walk a lot together."

"I thought Mr. Westcott practiced law with consuming zeal."

"With what? Anyhow, he's here a lot this spring. About every Wednesday, I think. I say, this is a bully car! If I were Rob I'd a lot rather ride with you than go walking with old Westcott, especially when it's so warm."

"I'm afraid," said Richard soberly, "that walking in the woods in May has its advantages over bowling along the main highway in any kind of a car."

Nevertheless he managed to make the drive a fascinating experience to Ted and a diverting one to himself. And on the way home they stopped at the West Wood marshes to gather a great bunch of trilliums as big as Ted's head.

"I'll take 'em to Rob," said her younger brother. "She likes 'em better than any spring flower."

"Take my bunch to Mrs. Stephen Gray then. And be sure you don't get them mixed."

"What if I did? They're exactly the same size." Ted held up the two nosegays side by side as the car sped on toward home.

"I know, but it's of the greatest importance that you keep them straight. That left-hand one is yours; be sure and remember that."

Ted looked piercingly at his friend, but Richard's face was perfectly grave.

"Must be you don't like Rob, if you're so afraid your flowers will get to her," he reflected. "Or else you think so much of Rosy you can't bear to let anybody else have the flowers you picked for her. I'll have to tell Steve that."

"Do, by all means. Mere words could never express my admiration for Mrs. Stephen."

"She is pretty nice," agreed Ted. "I like her myself. But she isn't in it with Rob. Why, Rosy's afraid of lots of things, regularly afraid, you know, so Steve has to laugh her out of them. But Rob—she isn't afraid of a thing in the world."

"Except one."

"One?" Ted pricked up his ears. "What's that? I'll bet she isn't really afraid of it—just shamming. She does that sometimes. What is it? Tell me, and I'll tell you if she's shamming."

"I'd give a good deal to know, but I'm afraid I can't tell you what it is."

"Why not? If she isn't really afraid of it she won't mind my knowing. And if she is maybe I can laugh her out of it, the way Steve does Rosy."

"I don't believe you're competent to treat the case, Ted. It's not a thing to be laughed out of, you see. The thing for you to remember is which bunch of trilliums you are to give Mrs. Stephen Gray from me."

"This one." Ted waved his left arm.

"Not a bit of it. The left one is yours."

"No, because mine was a little the biggest, and you see this right one is."

"You are mistaken," Richard assured him positively. "You give Mrs. Stephen the right one, and I'll take the consequences."

"Did yours have a red one in?"

"Has that right one?"

"No, the left one has. I remember seeing you pick it."

"But afterward I threw it out. You picked one and left it in. The right is mine."

"You've got me all mixed up," vowed Ted discontentedly, at which his companion laughed, delight in his eye. The left-hand bunch was unquestionably his own, but if he could only convince Ted of the contrary he should at least have the satisfaction of knowing that the flowers he had plucked had reached his lady, though they would have no significance to her. When the lad jumped out of the car at his own rear gate he had agreed that the bunch with the one deep-red trillium was to go to Roberta.

Ted turned to wave both white clusters at his friend'as the car went on, then he proceeded straight to his sister's room. Finding her absent, he laid one great white-and-green mass in a heap upon her bed and went his way with the other to Mrs. Stephen's room. Here he found both Roberta and Rosamond playing with little Gordon and Dorothy, whom their nurse had just brought in from an airing.

"Here's some trilliums for you, Rosy," announced Ted. "Mr. Kendrick sent 'em to you. I left yours on your bed, Rob. I picked yours; at least I think I did. He was awfully particular that his went to Rosy, but we got sort of mixed up about who picked which, so I can't be sure. I don't see any use of making such a fuss about a lot of trilliums, anyhow."

Roberta and Rosamond looked at each other. "I think you are decidedly mixed, Ted," said Rosamond. "It was Rob Mr. Kendrick meant to send his to."

Ted shook his head positively. "No, it wasn't. He said something about you that I told him I was going to tell Steve, only I don't know as I can remember it. Something about his admiring you a whole lot."

"Delightful! And he didn't say anything about Rob?"

"Not very much. Said she was afraid of something. I said she wasn't afraid of anything, and he said she was—of one thing. I tried to make him say what it was, because I knew he was all off about that, but he wouldn't tell."

"Evidently you and Mr. Kendrick talked a good deal of nonsense," was Roberta's comment, on her way from the room.

She found the mass of green and white upon her bed and stood contemplating it for a moment. The one deep-red trillium glowed richly against its snowy brethren, and she picked it out and examined it thoughtfully, as if she expected it to tell her of what Richard Kendrick thought she was afraid. But as it vouchsafed no information, she gathered up the whole mass and disposed it in a big crystal bowl that she set upon a small table by an open window.

"If I thought that really was the bunch he picked," said she to herself, "I should consider he had broken his promise, and I should feel obliged to throw it away. Perhaps I'd better do it anyhow. Yet, it seems a pity to throw away such a beautiful bowlful of white and green, and very likely they were of Ted's picking after all. But I don't like that one red one against all the white."

She laid fingers upon it to draw it out. But she did not draw it out. "I wonder if that represents the one thing I'm afraid of?" she considered whimsically. "What does his majesty mean—himself? Or myself? Or of . . . of . . . Yes, I suppose that's it! Am I afraid of it?"

She stood staring down at the one deep-red flower, the biggest, finest bloom of them all. It really did not belong there with the others in their cool, chaste whiteness. Quite suddenly she drew it out. She made the motion of throwing it out the window, but it seemed to cling to her fingers.

"Poor little flower," said she softly, "why should you have to go? Perhaps you're sorry because you're not white like the rest. But you can't help it; you were made that way."

If Richard Kendrick could have seen her standing there, staring down at the flower he had picked, he would have found it harder than ever to go on his appointed course. For this was what she was thinking:

I ought—I ought—to like best the white flowers of intellect and ability and training and every sort of fitness. I try and try to like them best. But, oh!—they are so white compared with this red, red one. I like the white ones;

they are pure and cool and beautiful. But the red one is warm, warm! Oh, I don't know. I don't know. And how am I going to know? Tell me that, red flower. Did he pick you? Shall I keep you on the doubt? Well . . . but not where you will show. Yes, I'll keep you, but away down in the middle, where no one will see you, and where you won't distract my attention from the beautiful white flowers that are so different from you.

She bent over the bowlful of snowy spring blossoms, drew them apart, and sank the red flower deep among them, drawing them together again so that not a hint of their alien brother should show against their whiteness.

"There," said she, turning away with a little laugh, but speaking over her shoulder, "you ought to be satisfied with that. That's certainly much better than being thrown out of the window to wilt in the sun!"

Chapter 18

THE NAILING OF A FLAG

"Well, well, well!" drawled a voice at Richard Kendrick's elbow. "How are you, old man? Haven't seen you since before the days of Noah! Off to that country shop of yours? I say, take me along, will you? Time hangs heavy on my hands just now, and I want to see you anyhow, about a plan of mine."

"Hop in, Lorimer. Mighty glad to see you. Want to go all the way to Eastman? That's fine! This is great weather, eh?"

Belden Lorimer hopped in, if that word may be used to express his eager acceptance rather than the alacrity of his movements, for he was accustomed to act with as much deliberation as he spoke. He was one of Richard's college friends, also one of his late intimate companions at clubs and in social affairs. Lorimer possessed as much money in his own right as Richard himself, though his expectations were hardly as great.

"To tell the truth," said Lorimer, when the car had left the city and was bowling along the main traveled highway upstate, "I wanted to see you as much as anything to get a good look at you. Fellows say you've changed. Say you have that 'captain of industry' expression now. Say you've acquired that broad brow, alert eye, stern mouth, dominant chin, and so forth, that goes with indomitable determination to 'get there.' To be sure, I'd have thought you'd arrived, or your family before you, but they say you've started out to arrive some more. It's a wonderful example for a chap like me, fellows say. Think so myself. Mind imparting—"

Richard broke in on Lorimer's drawl. It was rather an engaging drawl, by the way, and he had always enjoyed hearing it, but it struck upon his ears now with a certain futility. In a world of pressing affairs, why should a man cultivate a tone like that? But he liked Lorimer too much to mind how he talked.

"I'm delighted if I've acquired that expression," said he, letting out the car another notch, although it was already in swift flight. "It's been a lot of trouble. I've had to practice before a looking glass a good deal. It was the chin bothered me most. It sticks out pretty well, but not as far as my grandfather's. Could you advise any method of—"

"What I want to know is," proceeded Lorimer calmly, "how you came to go into it. Understand you wanted to help a fellow out of the ditch— good old Benson—most worthy. Couldn't help him out without getting in yourself? But going to get out soon as possible, of course? Unthinkable for Rich Kendrick to be a country shopkeeper!"

"Unthinkable, is it? Wait till you see the shop. It's the most fun I ever had. Get out? Not by a long shot. I'm in for keeps."

"Not you. With the Kendrick establishments waiting for you to come into your own? Which will mean, in your case, becoming the nominal head of a great system while it continues to be run for you, as now, by a lot of trained heads under salary—big salary."

"Great idea of my future you have, Lorry, haven't you? Well, I can't wonder. I've been doing my best for all the years of my life to implant that idea in your mind. But what about you? What are you at, yourself? You said you had a plan."

"He asks what I'm 'at,' " remarked Belden Lorimer to the rural land-scape through which the car was passing. "Ever know me to be 'at' anything? It's as much as I can do to support life until I can be off on my next little travel plan. It's me for a leisurely cruise around the world in the governor's little old boat—*The Ariel*—painted up within an inch of her life, brass all shining, lockers filled, a first-class cook engaged, and a brand-new skipper and crew—picked men. Sounds pretty good to me. How about you? Shopkeeping in it with that, me lord?"

His usually languid glance was sharp as he eyed his friend.

"Jove!" muttered Richard Kendrick, under his breath.

"I thought so. 'Jove!' it is, too—and also Jupiter! You've always said you'd be ready when I was. Well, I'm ready."

Richard was silent for a long minute while his friend waited confi-dently. Then, "Good luck to you, old Lorry," he said. "It's mighty fine of you to remember our ancient vow to do that trick some day. And I'd like to go—you know that. But I've a previous engagement."

"Not with that fool store up in the backwoods? Can't make me believe that, you know."

Richard's face was a study.

"Believe it or not, it's a fact. That store is the joint property of Benson

& Company. I'm the Company. I can't desert my partner just as we're getting the ground under our feet."

"Well—I'll—be—hanged," drawled Lorimer, more heavily than ever, as was his custom when opposed, "if I see it. You go and help a fellow out with capital and set him on his feet. You save his pride, I suppose, by making yourself a partner. Fine, sporting thing to do. But you've done it. You've contributed the capital. Can't reasonably suppose you contribute anything else. If you don't mind my saying it, your previous training—"

"Doesn't make me indispensable to the success of the business? Hardly, as yet. But for the very reason that I lack training, I've got to stay and get it."

"Take lessons in shopkeeping from Hugh Benson?"

"Exactly. And from Alf Carson. He's our manager."

"Don't know him. But from the way you allude to him, I judge he has the details at his finger-ends. That's all right. Leave him on the job."

"I will—and stay myself."

Richard's eyes were straight ahead, as the eyes of a man must be whose powerful car is running at high speed along a none too smoothly surfaced portion of state road. Therefore the glances of the two young men could not meet. But Lorimer's eyes could silently scan the well-cut profile presented to his view against the green of the fields beyond.

"Never observed," said he with a peculiar inflection, "just how rocklike that chin of yours is, Rich. Reminds me of your grandfather's, for fair."

"Glad to hear it."

"You know," pursued Lorimer presently, "you gave me your promise once, that you'd be with me on this cruise whenever it came off. That's where the chin ought to come in. Man of your word, you know, and all that."

"I'm mighty sorry, my dear fellow. Let's not talk about it."

And clearly he was sorry. It had been a pleasant plan, and he had not forgotten the circumstances of the laughing yet serious pledge the two had given each other one evening less than two years ago.

They kept on their way with a change of conversation, and at the rate of speed that Richard maintained, were running into Eastman before they were half done with asking each other questions concerning the months during which they had seldom met.

"This is the busy mart?" queried Lorimer, as the car came to a standstill before the corner store. "Well, beside Kendrick & Company's massive edifices of stone and marble—"

"Luckily, it's not beside them," retorted Richard, maintaining his good humor. "Will you come in?"

"Thanks, I will. That's what I came for. Curiosity leads me to want to view you behind the— No, no, of course it's behind the office glass partition that I'll view you, my boy. I want to hear Rich Kendrick talking business with a big B."

"I'll talk business to you, if you don't let up," declared his friend. "You've got to be cured of the idea that this is some kind of a joke, Lorry. Will you be kind enough to take me seriously?"

"Find—that—impossible," drawled Lorimer under his breath as he followed Richard into the store.

But once there, of course, his manner changed to the most courteous, of which he was master. He was taken to the office and there shook hands with Hugh Benson with cordiality, having known him at college as a man who commanded respect for high scholarship and modest but assured manners, though of a quite different class of comradeship from his own. He talked pleasantly with Alfred Carson and listened with evident interest to a business discussion between Richard and his associates, in the course of which he discovered that however much or little Richard had learned, he could speak intelligently concerning the matters then in hand. He went to lunch with Richard and Hugh Benson at a hotel and listened again, for a decision was to be made that called for haste, and no time could be lost in the consideration of it.

He spent the afternoon driving Richard's car on upstate, returning in time to pick up his friend at the appointed hour, late in the afternoon, at which they were to start back to the city. Up to the last moment of their departure, business still had the upper hand, and it was not until Benson and Kendrick parted at the curb that it ended for the day, as far as Richard's part in it was concerned.

"Six hours you've been at it," remarked Lorimer as the car swung away under Richard's hand. "It makes me fatigued all over to contemplate such zeal."

"Tell that to the men who really work. I'm getting off easy, to cut and run at the end of six hours."

"Rich. . . ," began his friend, then he paused. "By the Lord Harry, I'd like to know what's got you. I can't make you and the old Rich fit together at all. You and your books, you and your music, and your pictures, your polo, your 'wine, women, and song'—"

"Take that last back," commanded Richard Kendrick with sudden heat. "You know I've never gone in for that sort of thing, except as all our old crowd went in together. Personally, I haven't cared for it, and you know it. It's travel and adventure I've cared for—"

"And that you're throwing over now for a country shop."

"That I'm throwing over now to learn the ABC in the training school of responsibility for the big load that's to come on my shoulders. I've been asleep all these years. Thank heaven I've waked up in time. It's no merit of mine—"

"Mind telling me whose it is, then?"

"I should mind, very much, if you'll excuse me."

"Oh—beg pardon," drawled Lorimer.

Silence followed for a brief space, broken by Richard's voice in its old genial tone.

"Tell me more about the cruise. It's great that you can have your father's yacht. I thought he always used it through the summer."

"He's gone daffy on monoplanes—absolutely daffy. Can't see anything else."

"I don't blame him. I might have gone in for aviation myself if I hadn't got this bigger game on my hands."

"Bigger—there you go again! Well, every man to his taste. The governor's lost interest in the *Ariel*—let me have her without a reservation as to time limit. Don't care for flying myself. Necessary to sit up. Like to lie on my back too well for that."

"You do yourself injustice."

"Now, now—don't preach. I've been expecting it."

"You needn't. I'm too busy with my own case to attend to yours."

"Lucky for me. I feel you'd be a zealous preacher if you ever got started."

"What route do you expect to take?" pursued Richard, steering away from dangerous ground.

Lorimer outlined it in his most languid manner. One would have thought he had little real interest in his plan after all.

"It's great! You'll have the time of your life!"

"I might have had."

"You will have. You can't help it."

"Not without the man I want in the bunk next to mine," said Belden Lorimer, gazing through half-shut eyes at nothing in particular.

Richard experienced the severest pang of regret he had yet known. "If that's true, old Lorry," said he slowly, "I'm sorrier than I can tell you."

"Then *come along!*" Lorimer looked waked up at last. He laid a persuasive hand on Richard's arm.

There was a moment of tensity. Then:

"If I should do it," said Richard, regarding steadily a dog in the road some hundred yards ahead, "would you feel any respect whatever for me?"

"Dead loads of it, I assure you."

"Sure of that?"

"Why not?"

"Be honest. Would you?"

"You promised me first," said Lorimer.

"I know I did. Such idle promises to play don't count when real life asks for work. It's no good reminding me of that promise. Answer me straight, now, Lorry—on your honor. If I should give in and go with you, you'd rejoice for a little, perhaps. Then, someday when you and I were lying on deck, you'd look at me and think of me—against your will—I don't say it wouldn't be against your will—you'd think of me as a quitter. And you wouldn't like me quite as well as you do now. Eh? Be honest."

Lorimer was silent for a minute. Then, to Richard's surprise, he gave an assenting grunt, and followed it up with a reluctant, "Hang it all, I suppose you're right. But I'm badly disappointed, just the same. We'll let that go."

And let it go they did, parting, when they reached town, with the friendliest of grips, and a new, if not wholly comprehended, interest between them. As for Richard, he felt somehow as if he had nailed his flag to the mast![1]

---

[1] Made his commitment publicly, for all the world to see.

Chapter 19

IN THE MORNING

"By George, Carson, what do you think's happened now?"
Richard Kendrick had come into the store's little office like a
thunderbolt.

The manager looked up.

"Well, Mr. Kendrick?"

"Benson's down with typhoid. Came back with it from the trip to
Chicago. What do you think of that?"

"I thought he was looking a little seedy before he went. Well, well,
that's too bad. Right in the May trade, too. Is he pretty sick?"

"So the doctor says. He's been keeping up on that trip when he ought
to have been in bed. He's in bed now, all right. I took him in with a nurse
to City Hospital on the 10:40 limited; stretcher in the baggage car."

"Don't see where he got typhoid around here at this time of year,"
mused Carson.

"Nobody sees, but that doesn't matter. He has it, and it's up to us to
pull him through—and to get along without him."

They sat down to talk it over. While they were at it the telephone came
into the discussion with a summons of Richard to a long-distance
connection. To his amazement, when communication was established
between himself and his distant interlocutor, a voice he had dreamed of
but had not heard for four months came to him clear and vibrant over
the wire:

"Mr. Kendrick?"

"Yes. Is it—it isn't—"

"This is Miss Gray. Mr. Kendrick, your grandfather wants you very
much, at our home. He has had an accident."

"An accident? What sort of an accident? Is he much hurt, Miss Gray?"

"We can't tell yet. He fell down the porch steps; he had been calling on

163

Uncle Calvin. He is quite helpless, but the doctor thinks there are no bones broken. Doctor Thomas wouldn't allow Mr. Kendrick to be moved, so we have him here with a nurse. He is very anxious to see you."

"I'll be there as soon as I can get there in the car. I think I can make it quicker than by train at this hour. Thank you for calling me, Miss Gray. Please—give my love to Grandfather and tell him I'm coming."

"I will, Mr. Kendrick. I—we are all—so sorry. Good-bye."

Richard turned back to Carson with an anxious face. The manager was on his feet, concern in his manner.

"Something happened to old Mr. Kendrick, Mr. Richard?"

"A fall—can't move—wants me right away. It never rains but it pours, Carson—even in May. I thought Benson's illness was the worst thing that could happen to us, but this is worse yet. I'll have to leave everything to you to settle while I run down to the old gentleman. A fall, Carson—isn't that likely to be pretty serious at his age?"

"Depends on what caused it, I should say," Carson answered cautiously. "If it was any kind of shock—"

"Oh, it can't be that!" Richard Kendrick's voice showed his alarm at the thought. "Grandfather's been such an active old chap—no superfluous fat—he's not at all a high liver—takes his cold plunge just as he always has. It can't be that! But I'm off to see. Good-bye, Carson. I'll phone you when I know the situation. Meanwhile—wish Grandfather safely out of it, will you?"

"Of course I will; I think a great deal of Mr. Kendrick. Good-bye—and don't worry about things here." Carson wrung his employer's hand, then went out with him to the curb, where the car stood, and saw him off. *He really cares,* he was thinking. *Nobody could fake that anxiety. He doesn't want the old man to die—and he's his heir—to millions. Well, I like him better than ever for it. I believe if I got typhoid he'd personally carry me to the hospital or do any other thing that came into his head. Well, now it's for me to find a competent salesman for this May sale that's on with such a rush. It's going to be hard to manage without Benson.*

The long, low car had never made faster time to the city, and it was in the early dusk that it came to a standstill before the porch of the Gray home. Doors and windows were wide open, lights gleamed everywhere, but the house was very quiet. The car had stolen up as silently as a car of fine workmanship may in these days of motor perfection, but it had been heard, and Mrs. Robert Gray came out to meet Richard before he could ring.

"My dear Mr. Richard," she said, pressing his hand, her face very grave and sweet, "you have come quickly. I am glad, for we are anxious. Your grandfather has dropped into a strange, drowsy state, from which it seems impossible to rouse him. But I hope you may be able to do so. He has wanted you from the first moment."

"Tell me which way to go," cried Richard, under his breath. "Is he upstairs?"

She kept her hold upon his hand, and he gripped it tight as she led him up the stairs. It was as if he felt a mother's clasp for the first time since his babyhood and could not let it go.

"In here," she indicated softly, and the young man went in, his head bent, his lips set.

Two hours afterward he came out. She was waiting for him, though it was midnight. Louis and Stephen were waiting, too, and they in turn grasped his hand, their faces pitiful for the keen grief they saw in his. Then Mrs. Gray took him down to the porch, where the warm May night folded them softly about. She sat down beside him on a wide settle.

"He is all I have in the world!" cried Richard Kendrick. "If he goes . . . " He could not say more, and turning, he put his arms down upon the back of the seat and his head upon them. Great, tearless sobs shook him. Mrs. Gray laid her kind hand upon his shoulder, and spoke gentle, motherly words—a few words, not many—and kept her hand there until he had himself under control again.

By and by Mrs. Stephen Gray came out with a little tray upon which was set forth a simple meal, daintily served. The young man tried to eat, to show her how much this touched him, but succeeded in swallowing only a portion of the delicate food. Then he got up. "You are all so good," said he gratefully. "You have helped me more than I can tell you. I will go back now. I want to stay with him tonight, if you will allow me."

They gave him a room across the hall from that in which his grandfather lay, but he did not occupy it. All night he sat, a silent figure on the opposite side of the bed from that where the nurse was on guard. His grandfather's regular physician was in attendance the greater part of the night at his request, though there seemed nothing to do but await the issue. Another distinguished member of the profession had seen the case in consultation early in the evening, and the two had found themselves unable between them to discover a remote possibility of hope.

In the early morning, the watcher stole downstairs, feeling as if he must for at least a few moments get into the outer world. His eyes were heavy with his vigil, yet there was no sleep behind them, and he could not bear to be long away lest a change come suddenly. The old man had not roused when he had first spoken to him, and the nurse had said that his last conscious words had been a call for his grandson. Goaded by this thought, Richard turned back before he had so much as reached the foot of the garden, where he had thought he should spend at least a quarter of an hour.

As he came in at the door he was met by Roberta, cool and fresh in blue. It was but five in the morning; surely she did not commonly rise at this hour, even in May. The thought made his heart leap. She came straight to him and put both hands in his, saying in her friendly, low voice: "Mr. Kendrick, I'm sorry—sorry!"

He looked long and hungrily into her face, holding her hands with such a fierce grasp that he hurt her cruelly, though she made no sign. He did not even thank her—only held her until every detail of her face had been studied. She let him do it and only dropped her eyes and stood coloring warmly under the inquisition. It was as if she understood that the sight of her was a moment's sedative for an aching heart, and she must yield it or be more unkind than it was in the heart of woman to be. When he released her it was with a sigh that came up from the depths, and as she left him he stood and watched her until she was out of sight.

When Matthew Kendrick opened his eyes at ten o'clock on the morning after his fall, the first thing they rested upon was the face he loved best in the world. It came instantly nearer, the eyes meeting his imploringly, as if begging him to speak. So, with some little effort, he did speak. "Well, Dick," he said slowly, "I'm glad you came, boy. I wanted you; I didn't know but I was about getting through. But I believe I'm still here, after all."

Then he saw a strange sight. Great tears leaped into the eyes he was looking at, tears that rolled unheeded down the fresh-colored cheeks of his boy. Richard tried to speak, but could not. He could only gently grasp his grandfather's hand and press it tightly in both his own.

"I feel pretty well battered up," the old man continued, his voice growing stronger, "but I think I can move a little." He stirred slightly under his blanket, a fact the nurse noted with joyful intentness. "So, I think I'm all here. Are you so glad, Dick, that you can cry about it?"

The smile came then upon his grandson's lighting face. "Glad, Grandfather?" said he, with some difficulty. "Why, you're all I have in the world! I shouldn't know how to face it without you."

The old man dropped off to sleep again, his hand contentedly resting in his grandson's. Presently the doctor looked in, studied the situation in silence, held a minute's whispered colloquy with the nurse, then moved to Richard's side. The young man looked up at him and he nodded. He bent to Richard's ear.

"Things look different," he whispered succinctly. At the slight sibilance of the whisper the old man opened his eyes again. His glance traveled up the distinguished physician's body to his face. He smiled in quite his own whimsical way.

"Fooled even a noted person like you, did I, Winston?" he chuckled feebly. "Just because I chose to go to sleep and didn't fidget round much, you thought I'd got my quietus, did you?"

"I think you're a pretty vigorous personality," responded the physician, "and I'm quite willing to be fooled by you. Now I want you to take a little nourishment and go to sleep again. If you think so much of this young man of yours, you can have him again in an hour, but I'm going to send him away now. You see, he's been sitting right here all night."

Matthew Kendrick's eyes rested fondly again upon Richard's smiling face. "You rascal!" he sighed. "You always did give me trouble about being up o' nights!"

Richard Kendrick ran downstairs three steps at a bound. At the bottom he met Judge Calvin Gray. He seized the hand of his grandfather's old-time friend and wrung it. The expression of heavy sadness on the Judge's face changed to one of bewilderment, and as he scanned the radiant countenance of Matthew Kendrick's grandson he turned suddenly pale with joy.

"You don't mean . . . "

Then he comprehended that Richard was finding it as hard to speak good news as if it had been bad. But in an instant the young man was in command of himself again.

"It wasn't apoplexy—it wasn't paralysis—it was only the shock of the fall and the bruises. He's been talking to me; he's been twitting the doctor on having been fooled. Oh, he's as alive as possible, and I—Judge Gray, I never was so happy in my life!"

With congratulations in his heart for his old friend on the possession of this young love that was as genuine as it was strong, the judge said, "Well, my dear fellow, let us thank God and breathe again. This has been the darkest night I've spent in many a year—and this is the brightest morning."

Everybody in the house was presently rejoicing in the news. But if Richard expected Roberta to be as generous with him in his joy as she had been in his grief he found himself disappointed. She did not fail to express to him her sympathy with his relief, but she did it with reinforcements of her family at hand, and with Ruth's arm about her waist. She had trusted him when torn with anxiety; clearly she did not trust him now in the reaction from that anxiety. He was in wild spirits, no doubt of that; she could see it in his brilliant eyes.

It still lacked six weeks of Midsummer.

Chapter 20

SIDELIGHTS

Louis Gray sat in a capacious willow easy chair beside the high white iron hospital bed upon which lay Hugh Benson, convalescing from his attack of fever. "Pretty comfortable they make you here," Louis observed, glancing about. "I didn't know their private rooms were as big and airy as this one."

Benson smiled. "I don't imagine they all are. I didn't realize what sort of quarters I was in till I began to get better and Mother told me. According to her I have the best in the place. That's Rich. Whatever he looks after is sure to be gilt-edged. I wonder if you know what a prince of good fellows he is, anyway."

"I always knew he was a good fellow," Louis agreed. "He has that reputation, you know: kind-hearted and open-handed. I should know he would be a substantial friend to his college classmate and business partner."

"He's much more than that." Benson's slow and languid speech took on a more earnest tone. "Do you know, I think if any young man in this city has been misjudged and underrated, it's Rich. I know the reputation you speak of; it's another way of calling a man a spendthrift, to say he's free with his money among his friends. But I don't believe anybody knows how free Rich Kendrick is with it among people who have no claim on him. I never should have known if I hadn't come here. One of my nurses has told me a lot of things she wasn't supposed ever to tell; but once she had let a word drop, I got it out of her. Why, Louis, for three years Rich has paid the expenses of every sick child that came into this hospital, where the family was too poor to pay. He's paid for several big operations, too, on children that he wanted to see have the best. There are four special private rooms he keeps for those they call his patients, and he sees that whoever occupies them has everything they need—and

169

plenty of things they may not just need, but are bound to enjoy, including flowers like those."

He pointed to a splendid bowlful of blossoms on a stand behind Louis, such blossoms as even in June grow only in the choicest of gardens.

"All this is news to me," declared Louis. "Mighty good news, too. But how has he been able to keep it so quiet?"

"Hospital people all pledged not to tell; so of course you and I mustn't be responsible for letting it out, since he doesn't want it known. I'm glad I know it, though, and I felt somehow that you ought to know. I used to think a lot of Rich at college, but now that he's my partner I think so much more I can't be happy unless other people appreciate him. And in the business—I can't tell you what he is. He's more like a brother than a partner."

His thin cheeks flushed, and Louis suddenly bethought himself. "I'm letting you talk too much, Hugh," he said self-accusingly. "Convalescents mustn't overexert themselves. Suppose you lie still and let me read the morning paper to you."

"Thank you, my nurse has done it. Talking is really a great luxury and it does me good, a little of it. I want to tell you this about Rich—"

The door opened quietly as he spoke and Richard Kendrick himself came in. Quite as usual, he looked as if he had that moment left the hands of a most scrupulous valet. No wonder Louis's first thought was, as he looked at him, that people gave him credit for caring only for externals. One would not have said at first glance that he had ever soiled his hands with any labor more tiring than that of putting on his gloves. And yet, studying him more closely in the light of the revelations his friend had made, was there not in his attractive face more strength and force than Louis had ever observed before?

"How goes it this morning, Hugh?" was the newcomer's greeting. He grasped the thin hand of the convalescent, smiling down at him. Then he shook hands with Louis, saying, "It's good of such a busy man to come in and cheer up this idle one," and sat down as if he had come to stay. But he had no proprietary air, and when a nurse looked in he only bowed gravely, as if he had not often seen her before. If Louis had not known he would not have imagined that Richard's hand in the affair of Benson's illness had been other than that of a casual caller.

Louis Gray went away presently, thinking it over. He was thinking of it again that evening as he sat upon the big rear porch of the Gray home, which looked out upon the lawn and tennis court where he and Roberta had just been having a bout lasting into the twilight.

"I heard something today that surprised me more than anything for a long time," he began, and when his sister inquired what the strange news might be, he repeated to her as he could remember it Hugh Benson's outline of the extraordinary story about Richard Kendrick. When she had heard it she observed:

"I suppose there is much more of that sort of thing done by the very rich than we dream of."

"By old men, yes—and widows, and a few other classes of people. But I don't imagine it's so common as to be noticeable among the young men of his class, do you?"

"Perhaps not. Though you do hear of wonderful things the bachelors do at Christmas for the poor children."

"At Christmas—that's another story. Hearts get warmed up at Christmas, that, like old Scrooge's, are cold and careless the rest of the year. But for a fellow like Rich Kendrick to keep it up all the year round, you'll find that's not so commonplace a tale."

"I don't know much about rich young men."

"You've certainly kept this one at a distance," Louis observed, eying his sister curiously in the twilight. She was sitting in a boyish attitude, racket on lap, elbows on knees, chin on clasped hands, eyes on the shadowy garden. "He's been coming here evening after evening until now that his grandfather has gone home, and never once has anybody seen you so much as standing on the porch with him, to say nothing of strolling into the garden. What's the matter with you, Rob? Any other girl would be following him around and getting into his path. Not that you would need to, judging by the way I've seen him look at you once or twice. Have you drawn an imaginary circle around yourself and pointed out to him the danger of crossing it? I should take him for a fellow who would cross it then anyhow!"

"Imaginary circles are sometimes bigger barriers than stone walls," she admitted, smiling to herself. "Besides, Lou, I thought somebody else was the person you wanted to see walking in the garden with me."

"Forbes? The person I expected to see, you mean. Well, I don't know about Forbes Westcott. He's a mighty clever chap, but I sometimes think his blood is a little thin, like his body. I can't imagine his bothering about a sick child at a hospital, can you? I've never seen him take a minute's notice of Steve's pair; and they're little trumps, if ever children were. Corporations are more in his line than children."

One thing leads to another in this interesting world. It was not two days after this talk that Roberta herself had a private view of a little affair that proved more illuminating to her understanding of a certain fellow mortal than might have been all the evidence of other witnesses.

Returning from school on one of the last days of the term, weary of walls and longing for the soothing stillness and refreshment of outdoors, Roberta turned aside some distance from her regular course to pass through a large botanical park, originally part of a great estate and newly thrown open to the public. It was, as yet, less frequented than any other of the city parks. Much of it, according to the decree of its donor, a nature lover of discrimination, had been left in a state not far removed from wildness, and it was toward this portion than Roberta took her way. With each step along a winding, secluded path she had recently discovered, she experienced that sense of escape into luxurious freedom that comes only after enforced confinement when the world outside is at its most alluring.

At a point where the path swept high above a long, descending slope, at the foot of which lay a tiny pool surrounded by thick and beautifully kept turf, Roberta paused, and after looking about her for a minute to make sure that there was no one near, turned aside from the path and threw herself down beside a great clump of ferns, breathing a deep sigh of restful relief. She sat gazing dreamily down at the pool, in which was mirrored an exquisite reflection of tree and sky, the scene as silent and still as though drawn upon canvas. She had many things to think of, in these days, and a place like this was an ideal one in which to think.

Was it? Far below her she heard the low hum of a motor. None could come near her, but the road beneath wound near the pool, though out of sight except at one point. In spite of this, the girl drew back further into the shelter of the tall ferns, thinking as she did so that it was the first time she had seen this remoter part of the park invaded by either motorist or pedestrian. Watching the point at which the car must appear, she saw it come slowly into sight and stop. There were two occupants, a man and a boy, but at the distance she could not discern their faces. The man stepped out and, coming around to the other side of the car, put out his arms and lifted the boy. He did not set him down but carried him, seeming to hold him with peculiar care, and brought him through the surrounding trees and shrubbery to the pool itself, coming as he did so into full view of the unseen eyes above.

Roberta experienced a sudden strange leap of the heart as she saw that the supple figure of the man was Richard Kendrick's own, and that the slight frame he bore was that of a crippled child. She could see now the iron braces on the legs, like pipe stems, that stuck straight out from the embrace of the strong young arms that held them. She could discern clearly the pallor and emaciation of the small face, in pitiful contrast to the ruggedly healthy one of the child's bearer. Fascinated, she watched as Richard set his burden carefully down upon the grass, close to the edge of the pool, the boy's back against a big white birch trunk. The two were not so far below her but that she could see the expression on their faces, though she could not hear their words.

Richard ran back to the car, returning with a rug and something in a long and slender case. He arranged a cushion behind the little back. Roberta judged the boy to be about eight or nine years old, though small for his age, as such children are. Richard undid the case and produced a small fishing-rod, which he fell to preparing for use, talking gaily as he did so, watched eagerly by his youthful companion. Evidently the boy was to have a great and unaccustomed pleasure.

Well, it was certainly in line with that which Roberta had heard of this young man, but somehow to see something of it with her own eyes was singularly more convincing. She could not bring herself to get up and go away. Surely there could be no need to feel that she was spying if she stayed to watch the interesting scene. If Richard had chosen a spot that he fancied entirely secluded from observation, it was undoubtedly wholly on the boy's own account. She could easily imagine how such a child as this one would shrink from observation in a public place, particularly when he was to try the dearly imagined but wholly unknown delight of fishing. It was plain that he was very shy even with this kind friend, for it was only now and then that he replied in words to Richard's talk, though the response in the white face and big black eyes was eloquent enough.

It seemed in every way remarkable that a young man of Richard Kendrick's sort should devote himself to a poor and crippled child as he was doing now. Not a gesture or act of his was lost upon the girl who watched. Clearly he was taking all possible pains to please and interest his little protégé, and he was doing it in a way that showed much skill, suggesting previous practice in the art. This was no such interest as he had shown in Gordon and Dorothy Gray, whose beauty had been so powerful an appeal to his fancy. There was nothing about this child to take hold upon anyone except his helplessness and need. But Richard was as gentle with him, as patient with his awkward attempts at holding the light rod in the proper position for fishing, and as full of resources for entertaining him when the fish (if there were any) failed to bite, as he could have been with a small brother of his own.

There was another thing that it was impossible not to note: Never had Roberta seen this young man in circumstances so calculated to impress upon her the potency of his personality. Unconscious of the scrutiny of any other human being, wholly absorbed in the task of making a small boy happy, he was naturally showing her himself precisely as he was. In place of his usual careful manners when in her presence was entire freedom from restraint and therefore an effect uncolored by conventional environment. The tones of his voice, the frank smile upon his lips, the touch of his hand upon the little lad's—all these combined to set him before Roberta in a light so different from any she had seen him in before that she must needs admit she had been far from knowing him.

She stole away at length, feeling suddenly that she had seen enough and that her defenses against the siege being made upon her heart and judgment were weakening perilously. If she were to hold out before it, she must hear of no more affairs to Richard Kendrick's credit, especially such affairs as these. Not all his efforts at establishing a successful career in the world of achievement could touch her imagination as did the knowledge of his brotherly kindness toward the unfortunate. That was what meant most to Roberta, in a world which she had early discovered to be a hard place for the greater part of its inhabitants. Forgetfulness of self, devotion to the need of others—these were the qualities she most strove to cultivate in herself and most rejoiced at seeing developed in those for whom she cared.

Unluckily for his cause, if there had been a possible chance for its success, Forbes Westcott chose the evening of this same day to come again to Roberta Gray with his question burning on his lips. He arrived at a moment when, to his temporary satisfaction, Roberta was said to be playing a set of singles in the court with Ruth by the light of a fast-fading afterglow; and he took his way thither without delay. It was a simple matter, of course, to a man of his resource, to dispose of the young sister, in spite of the elder's attempt to foil him at his own game. So presently he had Roberta to himself, with every advantage of time and place and summer beauty all about.

Louis Gray, looking down the lawn from the rear porch steps upon which he sat with Rosamond and Stephen, descried the tall figure strolling by their sister's side along a stretch of closely shaven turf between rows of slim young birches.

"Forbes is persistent, eh?" he observed. "Think he has a fighting chance?"

"Oh, I hope not!" cried Rosamond impulsively.

Stephen's grave eyes followed the others to dwell upon the distant pair. "Forbes stands to win a big place among men," was his comment.

"Oh, really big?" Rosamond's tender eyes came to meet her husband's. "Stephen, do you think he is quite . . . scrupulous? Wholly honorable?"

"I have no reason to think otherwise, Rosy."

She shook her head. "Somehow I could never quite trust him. He would live strictly by the letter of the law, but the spirit . . . "

"Expect people to live by the spirit these days, little girl?" inquired Louis, with an affectionate glance at her.

She gazed straight back. "Yes. You do it, and so does Stephen and Father Gray and Uncle Calvin."

The eyes of the brothers met above her fair head, and they smiled.

"That's high distinction from you, dear," said her husband. "But you must not do Westcott injustice. He has the reputation of being sharp as a knife blade and of outwitting men in fair contest in court and out of it, but no shadow has ever touched his character."

Still she shook her head. "I can't help it. I don't want Rob to marry him."

The young men laughed together, and Rosamond smiled with them.

"There you have it," said Louis. "There's no going behind those returns. The county votes no, and the candidate is defeated. Let him console himself with the vote from other counties—if he can."

The three were still upon the porch half an hour later, with others of the family, when the two figures came again up the stretch of lawn between the slim white birches, showing ghostlike now in the June moonlight. They came in silence, as far as any sound of their voices reached the porch, and they disappeared like two shades toward the front of the house.

"He's not coming even to speak to us," whispered Rosamond to Stephen. "That's very unlike him. Do you suppose . . . "

"It may be a case of the voice sticking in the throat," returned her husband, under his breath. "I fancy he'll take it hard when Rob disposes of him—as she certainly ought to do by this time, if she's not going to take him. But she'd better think twice. He's a brilliant fellow, and he has no rivals within hailing distance, in his line."

But Rosamond shook her head again. "He would never make her happy," she breathed, with conviction. "Oh, I hope—I hope!"

Her hopes grew with Roberta's absence. Westcott had gone, for Ruth, appearing at Rosamond's side, announced that Roberta was in her own room and would not be down again tonight.

"I think she has a headache," said the little sister. "Queer, for I never knew Rob to have a headache before."

"The headache," murmured Louis in Rosamond's ear, "is the feminine defense against the world. A timely headache, now and then, is suffered by the best of men—and women. Well, let her rest, Rufus. She'll be all right in the morning."

Above them, by her open window, sat Roberta for a little while, elbows on sill, chin in hands. Then, presently, she stole downstairs again, out by a side entrance, and away from the shrubbery, to the furthest point of the grounds—not far in point of actual distance, but quite removed by its environment from contact with the world around. Here, stretched upon the warm turf, her arms outflung, her eyes gazing up at the star-set heavens above her, the girl rested from her encounter with a desperate besieging force.

For a time, the last words she had heard that evening were ringing in her ears—somber words, uttered in a deep tone of melancholy, by a voice that commanded cadences that had often reached the minds and hearts of men and swayed them. "Is that *all*, Roberta? Must I go away with *that?*"

She had sent him away, and her heart ached for him, for she could not doubt the depth and sincerity of his feeling for her. Being a woman with a warm and kindly nature, she was sad with the disquieting thought that anywhere under that starry sky was one whose spirit was heavy tonight because of her. But there had been no help for it. She knew now, beyond a doubt, that there had been no help, no other answer..

Chapter 21

PORTRAITS

Revelations were in order in these days. Another of a quite different sort came to Roberta within the week. On a morning when she knew Richard Kendrick to be in Eastman, she consented to drive with Mrs. Stephen to make a call upon Mr. Matthew Kendrick, now at home and recovering satisfactorily from his fall but still confined to his room. With a basketful of splendid garden roses upon her arm, she followed Rosamond into the great stone pile.

They seemed to have left the sunlight and the summer day itself outside as they sat waiting in the stiff and formal reception room, which looked as if no woman's hand or foot had touched it for a decade. As they were conducted to Mr. Kendrick's room upon the floor above, they noted with observant eyes the cheerless character of every foot of the way: lofty hall, somber staircase, gloomy corridor. Even Mr. Kendrick's own room, filled though it was with costly furniture, its walls hung with portraits and heavy oil paintings, after the fashion of the rich man who wants his home comfortable and attractive but does not know how to make it so, was by no means homelike.

"This is good of you—this is good of you," the old man said happily, as they approached his couch. He held out his hands to them, and when Roberta presented her roses, exclaimed over them like a pleased child, and sent his man hurrying about to find receptacles for them. He lay looking from the flowers to the faces while he talked, as if he did not know which were the more refreshing to his eyes, weary of the surroundings to which they had been so long accustomed.

"These will be the first thing Dick will spy when he comes tomorrow," he prophesied. "I never saw a fellow so fond of roses. The last time he was down he found time to tell me about somebody's old garden up there in Eastman, where they had some kind of wonderful, old-fashioned rose with the sweetest fragrance he ever knew. He had one in his coat; the sight of it took me back to my boyhood. But he wasn't all roses and gardens, not a bit of it! I never thought to see him so absorbed in such a subject as the management of a business. But he's full of it—he's full of it! You can't imagine how it delights me."

He was full of it himself. Though he more than once apologized for talking of his grandson and his pleasure in the way "the boy" was throwing himself into the real merits of the problems presented to the new firm in Eastman, he kept returning to this fascinating subject. It was not of interest to himself alone, and though Roberta only listened, Mrs. Stephen led him on, asking questions that he answered with eager readiness. But all at once he pulled himself up short.

"Dick would be the first person to hush my garrulous old tongue," said he. "But I feel like father and mother and grandfather all combined, in the matter of his success. I wouldn't have you think his making good— as they say these days—in the world I am used to is my only idea of success. No, no, he has a world of his own besides. I should like you to see—there are several things I should like you to see. Last winter Dick begged from me a portrait of his mother that I had done when he was a year old; she lived only six months after that. He has it now over his desk. His father's portrait is on the opposite wall. Should you care to step across the hall into my grandson's rooms? The portraits I speak of are in the second room of the suite. Stop and examine anything else that interests you. I am sure he would be proud. And he has brought back many interesting things, principally pictures, from his travels. I should like to go with you, but if you will be so kind—"

There was no refusing the enthusiastic old man. He sent his housekeeper to see that the rooms were open of window and ready for inspection, then waved his guests away. Mrs. Stephen went with alacrity; Roberta followed more slowly, as if she somehow feared to go. Of all the odd happenings! That she should be walking into Richard Kendrick's own habitation, with all the intimate revelations it was bound to make to her. She wondered what he would say if he knew.

The first room was precisely what she might have expected, quite obviously the apartment of a modern young man whose wishes lacked no opportunity to satisfy themselves. The room was not in bad taste; on the contrary, its somewhat heavy furnishings had an air of dignity in harmony with an earlier day rather than that more ostentatious period in which the rest of the house had been fitted. Upon its walls was a choice collection of pictures of various styles and schools of art, some of them unquestionably of much value. At one end of the room stood a closed grand piano. But, like the grandfather's room, the place could not by any stretch of the imagination be called homelike, and to this fact Rosamond called her companion's attention.

"It's really very interesting," said she, "and quite impressive, but I don't wonder in the least at his saying that he had no home. This might be a room in a fine hotel; there's nothing to make you feel as if anybody really lives here, in spite of the beautiful paintings. But Mr. Kendrick said the portraits were in the second room."

On her way into the second room, however, Rosamond's attention was attracted by a picture beside the door opening thereto, and with an exclamation, "Oh, this looks like Gordon! Where did he get it?" she paused. Roberta glanced that way, but a quite different object in the inner room had caught her eye, and leaving Rosamond to her wonder over a rather remarkable resemblance to her own little son in the exquisite color drawing of a child of similar age, she went on, to stand still in the doorway, surprised out of all restraint by what she beheld.

For this, contrary to all possible expectations, was either the room of a man of literary tastes, and of one who also preferred simplicity and utility to display of any sort, or it was an extremely clever imitation of such a room. And there were certain rather trustworthy evidences of the former.

The room, although smaller than the outer one, was a place of good size with several large windows. Its walls to a height of several feet were lined with bookshelves filled to overflowing, the whole representing no less than three or four thousand books; Roberta could hardly guess at their number. Several comfortable easy chairs and a massive desk were almost the only other furnishings, unless one included a few framed foreign photographs and the two portraits that hung on opposite walls. These presently called for study.

Rosamond came in and stood beside her sister, regarding the portraits with curiosity. "The father has a remarkably fine face, hasn't he?" she observed, turning from one to the other. "Unusually fine; and I think his son resembles him. But he is more like his mother. Isn't she beautiful? And he never knew her; she died when he was such a little fellow. Isn't it touching to see how he has her there above his desk as if he wanted to know her? How many books! I didn't know he cared for books, did you? Perhaps they were his father's; though his father was a businessman. Yet I don't know why we never credit businessmen with any interest in books. Perhaps they study them more than we imagine;

they must study something. Rob, did you see the picture in the other room that looks so like Gordon? It seems almost as if it must have been painted from him."

She flitted back into the outer room. Roberta stood still before the desk, above which hung the portrait of the lovely young woman who had been Richard's mother. Younger than Roberta herself she looked; such a girl to pass away and leave her baby, her firstborn! And he had her here in the place of honor above his desk, where he sat to write and read. For he did read, she grew sure of it as she looked about her. Though the room was obviously looked after by a servant, it was probable that there were orders not to touch the contents of the desktop itself, for this was as if it had been lately used. Books, a foreign review or two, a pile of letters, various desk furnishings in a curious design of wrought copper, and— what was this?—a little photograph in a frame! Horses, three of them, saddled and tied to a fence; at one side, in an attitude of arrested attention, a girl's figure in riding dress.

A wave of color surged over Roberta's face as she picked up the picture to examine it. She had never thought again of the shot he had snapped; he had never brought it to her. Instead he had put it into this frame—she noted the frame, of carved ivory and choice beyond question—and had placed it upon his desk. There were no other photographs of people in the room, not one. If she had found herself one among many she might have had more—or less—reason for displeasure; it was hard to say which. But to be the only one! Yet doubtless in his bedroom, the most intimate place of all, which she was not to see, would be found his real treasures: photographs of beauties he had known, married women, girls, actresses— She caught herself up!

Rosamond, eager over the color drawing, had taken it from its place on the wall and gone with it across the hall to discuss its extraordinary likeness with the old man, who had sent for little Gordon several times during his stay at the Gray home and would be sure to appreciate the resemblance. Roberta, again engaged with the portrait above the desk, had not noticed her sister's departure. There was something peculiarly fascinating about this pictured face of Richard Kendrick's mother. Whether it was the illusive likeness to the son, showing first in the eyes, then in the mouth, which was one of extraordinary sweetness, it was hard to tell. But the attempt to analyze it was absorbing.

The sound of a quick step in the outer room, as it struck a bit of bare floor between the costly rugs that lay thickly upon it, arrested her attention. That was not Rosy's step! Roberta turned, a sudden fear upon her, and saw the owner of the room standing, as if surprised out of power to proceed, in the doorway.

Now, it was manifestly impossible for Roberta to know just how she looked standing there as he had seen her for the instant before she turned. From her head to her feet she was dressed in white, therefore against the dull background of books and heavy, plain paneling above, her figure stood out with the effect of a cameo. Her dusky hair under her white hat-brim was the only shadowing in a picture that was to his gaze all light and radiance. He stood staring at it, his own face glowing. Then:

"Oh, *Roberta!*" he exclaimed under his breath. Then he came forward, both hands outstretched. She let him have one of hers for an instant, but drew it away again—with some difficulty.

"You must be surprised to find me here." Roberta strove for her usual cool control. "Rosy and I came to see your grandfather. He sent us in here to look at these portraits. Rosy has gone back to him with a picture she thought looked like Gordon. I was staying a minute to see this; it is very beautiful."

He laughed happily. "You have explained it all away. I wish you had let me go on thinking I was dreaming. To find you *here!*" He smothered an exultant breath and went on hastily: "I'm glad you find my mother beautiful. I never knew how beautiful she was till I brought her up here and put her where I could look at her. Such a little, girlish mother for such a strapping son! But she has the look—somehow she has the look! Don't you think she has? I was a year old when that was painted—just in time, for she died six months afterward. But she had had time to get the look, hadn't she?"

"Indeed she had. I can imagine her holding her little son. Is there no picture of her with you?"

"None at all that I can find. I don't know why. There's one of me on my father's knee, four years old—just before he went, too. I am lucky to have it. I can just remember him, but not my mother at all. Do you mind my telling you that it was after I saw your mother that I brought this portrait of mine up from the drawing room and put it here? It seemed to me I must have one somehow, if only the picture of one." His voice lowered. "I can't tell you what it has done for me, the having her here."

"I can guess," said Roberta softly, studying the young, gently smiling picture face. Somehow her former manner with this young man had temporarily deserted her. The appeal of the portrait seemed to have extended to its owner. "You don't want to disappoint her," she added thoughtfully.

"That's it—that's just it," he agreed eagerly. "How did you know?"

"Because that's the way I feel about mine. They care so much, you know." She moved slowly toward the door. "I must go back to your grandfather."

"Why? He has Mrs. Stephen, you say. And I like to see you here. There are a lot of things I want to show you." His eager gaze dropped to the desktop and fell upon the ivory-framed photograph. He looked quickly at her. Her cheeks were of a rich rose hue, her eyes—he could not tell what her eyes were like. But she moved on toward the door. He followed her into the other room.

"Won't you stay a minute here, then? I don't care for it as I do the other, but it's a place to talk in. And I haven't talked to you for four months. It's the middle of June. . . . Let me show you this picture over here."

He succeeded in detaining her for a few minutes, which raced by on wings for him. He did it only by keeping his speech strictly upon the subject of art, and presently, in spite of his endeavors, she was off across the room and out the door, through the hall and into the company of Mrs. Stephen and Mr. Matthew Kendrick. The pair, the old man and the girlish young mother, looked up from a collection of miniatures brought out in continuance of the discussion over child faces begun by Rosamond's interest in the color drawing found upon Richard's walls. They saw a flushed and heart-disturbing face under a drooping white hat-brim, and eyes that looked anywhere but at them, though Roberta's voice said quite steadily: "Rosy, do you know how long we are staying?"

In explanation of this sudden haste, another face appeared, seen over Roberta's shoulder. This face was also of a somewhat warm coloring, but these eyes did not hide; they looked as if they were seeing visions and noted nothing earthly.

"Why, Dick!" exclaimed Mr. Kendrick. "I didn't expect you till tomorrow." Gladness was in his voice. He held out welcoming hands, and his grandson came to him and took the hands and held them while he explained the errand that had brought him and upon which he must immediately depart. But he would come again upon the morrow, he promised. It was clear that the closest relations existed between the two; it was a pleasant thing to see. And when Richard turned about again toward the visitors he had his face in order.

Some imperceptible signaling had been exchanged between Roberta and Rosamond, and the call came shortly to an end, in spite of the old man's urgent invitation to them to remain.

"Do you see the roses they brought me, Dick?" He indicated the bowls and vases which stood about the room. "I told them you would notice them directly you came in. Where are your eyes, boy?"

"Do you really blame me for not seeing them, Grandfather?" retorted his grandson audaciously. "But I recognize them now; they are wonderful. I suppose they have thorns?" His eyes met Roberta's for one daring instant.

"You wouldn't like them if they didn't," said she.

"Shouldn't I? I'd like to find one with the thorns off; I'd wear it—if I might. May I have one, Grandfather?"

"Of course, Dick. They're mine now to give away, Miss Roberta? Perhaps you'll put it on for him?"

Since the suggestion was made by an old man, who might or might not have been wholly innocent of taking sides in a game in which his boy was playing for high stakes, Roberta could do no less than hurriedly to select a splendid crimson bud without regard to thorns (she was aware of more than one as she handled it) and fasten it upon a gray coat, intensely conscious of the momentary nearness of a personality whose influence upon her was the strangest, most perturbing thing she had ever experienced.

The flower in place, she could not get away too fast. Rosamond, understanding now that the air was electric and that her sister wanted nothing so much as to escape to a safe atmosphere, aided her by taking the lead and engaging Richard Kendrick in conversation all the way downstairs to the door and out to the waiting carriage. As they drove away Rosamond looked back at the figure leaping up the steps with the crimson rose showing brilliantly in the June sunshine.

"Rob, he's splendid, simply splendid," she whispered, so that the old family coachman in front, driving the old family horses, could not hear. "I don't wonder his grandfather is so proud of him. One can see that he's going to go right on now and make himself a man worth anybody's while. He's that now, but he's going to be more."

"I don't see how you can tell so much from hearing him make a few foolish remarks about some roses!" Roberta's face was carefully averted.

"Oh, it wasn't what he said, it's what he *is!* It shows in his face. I never saw purpose come out so in a face as it has in his in the time that we've known him. Besides, we began by taking him for nothing but a society man, and we were mistaken in that from the beginning. Stephen has been telling me some things Louis told him—"

"I know. About the hospital and the children."

"Yes. Isn't it interesting? And that's been going on for years; it's not a new pose for our benefit. I've no doubt there are lots of other things, if we knew them. But, oh, Rob, his grandfather says he bought the little head in color because he thought it looked like Gordon. I'm going to send him the last photograph right away. Rob, there's Forbes Westcott!"

"Where?"

"Right ahead. Shall we stop and take him in? Of course he's on his way to see you, as usual. How he does anything in his own office—"

"James!" Roberta leaned forward and spoke to the coachman. "Turn down this street—quickly, please. Don't look, Rosy—don't! Let's not go straight home; let's drive awhile. It . . . it's such a lovely day!"

"Why, Rob! I thought—"

"Please don't think anything. I'm trying not to."

Rosamond impulsively put her white-gloved hand on Roberta's. "I don't believe you are succeeding," she whispered daringly. "Particularly since . . . this morning!"

Chapter 22

ROBERTA WAKES EARLY

Midsummer's Day! Roberta woke with the thought in her mind, as it had been the last in her mind when she had gone to sleep. She had lain awake for a long time the night before, watching a strip of moonlight that lay like flickering silver across her wall. Who would have found it easy to sleep with the consciousness beating at her brain that on the morrow something momentous was as surely going to happen as that the sun would rise? Did she want it to happen? Would she rather not run away and prevent it happening? There was no doubt that, being a woman, she wanted to run away. At the same time, being a woman, she knew that she would not run. Something would stay her feet.

With wide-open eyes on this Midsummer morning she lay as she had lain the night before, regarding without attention the early sunlight flooding the room where moonlight had lain a few hours ago. Her bare, round arms, from which picturesque apologies for sleeves fell back, were thrown wide upon her pillows, her white throat and shoulders gleamed below the loose masses of her hair, her heart was beating a trifle more rapidly than was natural after a night of repose.

It was very early, as a little clock upon a desk announced: half after five. Yet someone in the house was up, for Roberta heard a light footfall outside her door. There followed a soft sound that drew her eyes that way; she saw something white appear beneath the door (in the old house, the sills were not tight). The white rectangle was obviously a letter.

Her curiosity alive, she lay looking at this apparition for some time, unwilling to be heard to move even by a maidservant. But at length she arose, stole across the floor, picked up the missive, and went back to her bed. She examined the envelope: It was of a heavy plain paper. The address was in a hand she had seen but once, on the day when she had

185

copied many pages of material upon the typewriter for her Uncle Calvin: a rather compact, very regular, and positive hand, unmistakably that of a person of education and character.

She opened the letter with fingers that hesitated. Midsummer's Day was at hand; it had begun early! Two closely written sheets appeared. Sitting among her pillows, her curly, dusky locks tumbling all about her face, her pulses beating now so fast that they shook the paper in her fingers, she read his letter:

MY ROBERTA:

I can't begin any other way, for even though you should never let me use the words again, you have become such a part of me, both of the man I am and of the man I want and mean to become, that in some degree you will always belong to me in spite of yourself.

Why do I write to you today? Because there are things I want to say to you that I could never wait to say when I see you, but that I want you to know before you answer me. I don't want to tell you the story of my life, but I do feel that you must understand a few of my thoughts, for only so can I be sure that you know me at all.

Before I came to your home, one night last October, I had unconsciously settled into a way of living that as a rule seemed to me all-sufficient. My friends, my clubs, my books—yes, I care for my books more than you have ever discovered—my plans for travel, made up a life that satisfied me—a part of the time. Deep down somewhere was a sense of unrest, a knowledge that I was neither getting nor giving all that I was meant to. But this I was accustomed to stifle—except at unhappy hours when stifling would not work, and then I was frankly miserable. Mostly, however, my time was so filled with diversion of one sort or another that I managed to keep such hours from overwhelming me; I worried through them somehow and forgot them as soon as I could.

From the first day that I came through your door my point of view was gradually and strangely altered. I saw for the first time in my life what a home might be. It attracted me; more, it showed me how empty my own life was, that I had thought so full. The sight of your mother, of your brothers, of your sisters, of your brother's little children—each of these had its effect on me. As for yourself—Roberta, I don't know how to tell you that; at least I don't know how to tell you on paper. I can imagine finding words to tell you, if you were very much nearer to me than you are now. I hardly dare think of that!

Yet I must try, for it's part of the story; it's all of it. With my first sight of you, I realized that here was what I had dreamed of but never hoped to find: beauty and charm and character. I had seen many women who possessed two of these attributes; it seemed impossible to discover one who had all three. Many women I had admired and despised; many I had respected and disliked. I am not good at analysis, but perhaps you can guess at what I mean. I may have been unfortunate; I don't know. There may be many women who are both beautiful and good. No, that is not what I mean! The combination I am trying to describe as impossibly desirable is that not only of beauty and goodness—I suppose there are really many who have those; but goodness and fascination! That's what a man wants. Can you possibly understand?

I wonder if I had better stop writing? I am showing myself up as hopelessly awkward at expression; probably because my heart is pounding so as I write that it is taking the blood from my brain. But I'll make one more try at it.

I had no special purpose in life last October. I meant to do a little good in the world if I could—without too much trouble. Sometime or other I supposed I should marry—intended to put it off as long as I could. I saw no reason why I shouldn't travel all I wanted to; it was the one thing I really cared for with enthusiasm. I didn't appreciate much what a selfish life I was leading, how I was neglecting the one person in the world who loved me and was anxious about me. Your little sister, Ruth, opened my eyes to that, by the way. I shall always thank her for it. I hadn't known what I was missing.

I don't know how the change came about. You

charmed me, yet you made me realize every time I was with you that I was not the sort of man you either admired or respected. I felt it whenever I looked at any of the people in your home. Every one of them was busy and happy; every one of them was leading a life worthwhile. Slowly I waked up. I believe I'm wide awake now. What's more, nothing could ever tempt me to go to sleep again. I've learned to *like* being awake!

You decreed that I should keep away from you all these months. I agreed, and I have kept my word. But all the while a fear has bothered me beyond endurance: that you did it to be rid of me. I said some bold words to you—to make you remember me. Roberta, I am humbler today than I was then. I shouldn't dare say them to you now. I was madly in love with you then; I dared say anything. I am not less in love now—great heavens! not less—but I have grown to worship you so that I have become afraid. When I saw you in my room before my mother's portrait I could have knelt at your feet. From the beginning I have felt that I was not worthy of you, but I feel it so much more deeply now that I don't know how to offer myself to you. I have written as if I wanted to persuade you that I am more of a man than when you knew me first, and therefore more worthy of you. I *am* more of a man, but by just so much more do I realize my own unworthiness.

And yet it is Midsummer's Day; this is the twenty-fourth of June—and I am on fire with love and longing for you, and I must know whether you care. If I were strong enough I would offer to wait longer before asking you to tell me—but I'm not strong enough for that.

I have a plan that I am hoping you will let me carry out, whatever answer you are going to give me. If you will allow it I will ask Mr. and Mrs. Stephen Gray to go with us on a long horseback ride this afternoon, to have supper at a place I know. I could take you all in my car if you prefer, but I hope you will not prefer it. You have never seemed like a motoring girl to me—every other one I know is—and ever since I saw you on Colonel last November I've been hoping to have a ride with you. If I can have it today—Midsummer—it will be a dream fulfilled. If only I dared hope my other and dearer dream were to come true!

Roberta, are we really so different? I have thought a thousand times of your "stout little cabin on the hilltop" where you would like to spend "the worst night of the winter." All alone? "Well, with a fire for company, and perhaps a dog." But not with a good comrade? "There are so few good comrades—people who can be tolerant of one's every mood." You were right; there are few. And this one might not be so clever as to understand every mood of yours, but—Roberta, Roberta—he would love you so much that you wouldn't mind if he didn't always understand. That is, you wouldn't mind if, in return, you— But I dare not say it. I can only hope—hope!

Unless you send me word to the contrary by ten o'clock, I will then ask Mr. and Mrs. Stephen and arrange to come for you at four this afternoon. You are committed to nothing by agreeing to this arrangement. But I am committed to everything for as long as I live.

RICHARD

It was well that it was not yet six o'clock in the morning and that Roberta had two long hours to herself before she need come forth from her room. She needed them, every minute of them, to get herself in hand.

It was a good letter, no doubt of that. It was neither clever nor eloquent, but it was better: it was manly and sincere. It showed self-respect; it showed also humility, a proud humility that rejoiced that it could feel its own unworthiness and know thereby that it would strive to be more fit. And it showed—oh, unquestionably it showed!—the depth of his feeling. Quite clearly he had restrained a pen that longed to pour forth his heart, yet there were phrases in which his tenderness had been more than he could hold back, and it was those phrases which made the recipient hold her breath a little as she read them, wondering how, if the written words were almost more than she could bear, she could face the spoken ones.

And now she really wanted to run away! If she could have had a week, a month, between the reading of this letter and the meeting of its writer, it seemed to her that it would have been the happiest month of her life. To take the letter with her into exile, to read it every day, but to wait—wait—for the real crisis till she could quiet her racing emotions. One sweet at a time, not an armful of them. But the man—true to his nature—the man wanted the armful, and at once. And she had made him wait all these months; she could not, knowing her own heart, put him off longer now. The cool composure with which, last winter, she had answered his first declaration that he loved her was all gone; the months of waiting had done more than show him whether his love was real: they had shown her that she wanted it to be real.

The day was a hard one to get through. The hours lagged—yet they flew. At eight o'clock she went down, feeling as if it were all in her face; but apparently nobody saw anything beyond the undoubted fact that in her white frock she looked as fresh and as vivid as a flower. At half after ten Rosamond came to her to know if she had received an invitation from Richard Kendrick to go for a horseback ride, adding that she herself was delighted at the thought and had telephoned Stephen, to find that he also was pleased and would be up in time.

"I wonder where he's going to take us," speculated Rosamond, in a flutter of anticipation. "Without doubt it will be somewhere that's perfectly charming; he knows how to do such things. Of course it's all for you, but I shall love to play chaperon, and Stevie and I shall have a lovely time out of it. I haven't been on a horse since Dorothy came; I hope I haven't grown too stout for my habit. What are you going to wear, Rob? The blue cloth? You are perfectly irresistible in that! Do wear that rakish-looking soft hat with the scarf; it's wonderfully becoming, if it isn't quite so correct; and I'm sure Richard Kendrick won't take us to any stupid fashionable hotel. He'll arrange an outdoor affair, I'm confident, with the Kendrick chef to prepare it and the Kendrick servants to see that it is served. Oh, it's such a glorious June day! Aren't you happy, Rob?"

"If I weren't, it would make me happy to look at you, you dear married child," and Roberta kissed her pretty sister-in-law, who could be as womanly as she was girlish, and whose companionship, with that of Stephen's, she felt to be the most discriminating choice of chaperonage Richard could have made. Stephen and Rosamond, off upon a holiday like this, would be celebrating a little honeymoon anniversary of their own, she knew, for they had been married in June and could never get over congratulating themselves on their own happiness.

Chapter 23

RICHARD HAS WAKED EARLIER

Twelve o'clock, one o'clock, two o'clock. Roberta wondered afterward what she had done with the hours! At three she had her bath; at half after she put up her hair, hardly venturing to look at her own face in her looking glass, so flushed and shy was it. Roberta shy?—she who, according to Ted, "wasn't afraid of anything in the world!" But she *had* been afraid of one thing, even as Richard Kendrick had averred. Was she not afraid of it now? She could not tell. But she knew that her hands shook as she put up her hair, and that it tumbled down twice and had to be done over again. Afraid! She was afraid, as every girl worth winning is, of the sight of her lover!

Yet when she heard hoofbeats on the driveway nothing could have kept her from peeking out. The rear porch, from which the riding party would start, was just below her window, the great pillars rising past her. She had closed one of her blinds an hour before; she now made use of its sheltering interstices. She saw Richard on a splendid black horse coming up the drive, looking, as she had foreseen he would look, at home in the saddle and at his best. She saw the color in his cheeks, the brightness in his eyes, caught his one quick glance upward. Did he know her window? He could not possibly see her, but she drew back, happiness and fear fighting within her for the ascendency. Could she ever go down and face him out there in the strong June light, where he could see every curving hair of eyelash? note the slightest ebb and flow of blood in cheek?

Rosamond was calling: "Come, Rob! Mr. Kendrick is here and Joe is bringing round the horses. Can I help you?"

Roberta opened her door. "I couldn't do my hair at all. Does it look a fright under this hat?"

Rosamond surveyed her. "Of course it doesn't. You're the most bewitching thing I ever saw, in that blue habit, and your hair is lovely, as it always is. Rob, I have grown stout; I had to let out two bands before I could get this on; it was made before I was married. Steve's been laughing at me. Here he is; now do let's hurry. I want every bit of this good time, don't you?"

There was no delaying longer. Rosamond, all eagerness, was leading the way downstairs, her little riding boots tapping her departure. Stephen was waiting for Roberta; she had to precede him. Next she knew, she was down and out upon the porch, and Richard Kendrick, hat and crop in hand, was meeting her halfway, his expectant eyes upon her face. One glance at him was all she was giving him, and he was mercifully making no sign that anyone looking on could have recognized beyond his eager scrutiny as his hand clasped hers. And then in two minutes they were off, and Roberta, feeling the saddle beneath her and Colonel's familiar tug on the bit at the start-off—he was always impatient to get away—was realizing that the worst, at least for the present, was over.

"Which way?" called Stephen, who was leading with Rosamond.

"Out the road past the West Wood marshes, please—straight out. Take it moderately; we're going about twelve miles and it's pretty warm yet."

There was not much talking while they were within the city limits— nor after they were past, for that matter. Rosamond, ahead with her husband, kept up a more or less fitful conversation with him, but the pair behind said little. Richard made no allusion to his letter of the morning beyond a declaration of his gratitude to the whole party for falling in with his plans. But the silence was somehow more suggestive of the great subject waiting for expression than any exchange of words could have been, out here in the open. Only once did the man's impatience to begin overcome his resolution to await the fitting hour.

Turning in his saddle as Colonel fell momentarily behind, passing the West Wood marshes, Richard allowed his eyes to rest upon horse and rider with full intent to take in the picture they made.

"I haven't ventured to let myself find out just how you look," he said. "The atmosphere seems to swim around you; I see you through a sort of haze. Do you suppose there can be anything the matter with my eyesight?"

"I should think there must be," she replied demurely. "It seems a serious symptom. Hadn't you better turn back?"

"While you go on? Not if I fall off my horse. I have a suspicion that it's made up of a curious compound of feelings that I don't dare to describe.

But—may I tell you? I *must* tell you! I never saw anything so beautiful in my life as yourself, today. I—" He broke off abruptly. "Do you see that old rosebush there by those burnt ruins of a house? Amber-white roses, and sweet as—I saw them there yesterday when I went by. Let me get them for you."

He rode away into the deserted yard and up to a tangle of neglected shrubbery. He had some difficulty in getting Thunderbolt, who was as restless a beast as his name implied, to stand still long enough to allow him to pick a bunch of the buds; he would have nothing but buds just breaking into bloom. These he presently brought back to Roberta. She fancied that he had planned to stop here for this very purpose. Clearly he had the artist's eye for finishing touches. He watched her fasten the roses upon the breast of the blue habit, then he turned determinedly away.

"If I don't look at you again," said he, his eyes straight before him, "it's because I can't do it and keep my head. You accused me once of losing it under a winter moon; this is a summer sun—more dangerous yet. . . . Shall we talk about the crops? This is fine weather for growing things, isn't it?"

"Wonderful. I haven't been out this road this season, as far as this. I'm beginning to wonder where you are taking us."

"To the hill where you and Miss Ruth and Ted and I toasted sandwiches last November. Could there be a better place for the end . . . of our ride? You haven't been out here this season? Are you sure?"

"No, indeed. I've been too busy with the close of school to ride anywhere, much less way out here."

"You like my choice, then? I hoped you would."

"Very much."

It was a queer, breathless sort of talking; Roberta hardly knew what she was saying. She much preferred to ride along in silence. The hour was at hand—so close at hand! And there was now no getting away. She knew perfectly well that her agreeing to come at all had told him his answer; none but the most cruel of women would allow a man to bring her upon such a ride, in the company of other interested people, only to refuse him at the end of it. But she had to admit to herself that if he were now exulting in the sure hope of possessing her he was keeping it well out of sight. There was now none of the arrogant self-confidence in his manner toward her that there had been on the February night when he had made a certain prophecy concerning Midsummer. Instead there was that in his every word and look which indicated a fine humility, almost a boyish sort of shyness, as if even while he knew the treasure to be within his grasp he could neither quite believe it nor feel himself fit to take it. From a young man of the world such as he had been it was the most exquisite tribute to her power to rouse the best in him that he could have given, and she felt it to the inmost soul of her.

"Here are the forks," said Richard suddenly, and Roberta recognized with a start that they were nearly at the end of their journey.

"Which way?" Stephen was shouting back, and Richard was waving toward the road at the left, which led up the steep hill.

"Here is where you dropped the bunch of rose haws," said he, with a quick glance as they began the ascent. "I have them yet—brown and dry. Did you know you dropped them?"

"I remember. But I didn't suppose anybody—"

"Found them? By the greatest luck—and stopped my car in a hurry. They were bright on my desk for a month after that; I cared more for them than for anything I owned. I had the greatest difficulty in keeping my man from throwing them away, though. You see, he hadn't my point of view! Roberta—here we are! Will you forgive what will seem like a piece of the most unwarrantable audacity?" He was speaking fast as they came up over the crown of the hill: "I didn't do it because I was sure of anything at all, but because it was something to make myself think I could carry out a wish of yours. Do you remember the 'stout little cabin on the hilltop,' Roberta? Could you—*could* you care for it, as I do?"

The last words were almost a whisper, but she heard them. Her eyes were riveted on the outlines, two hundred feet away through the trees, of a small brown building at the very crest of the hill overlooking the valley. Very small, very rough, with its unhewn logs, the "stout little cabin" stood there waiting.

Well! What was she to think? He *had* been sure, to build this and to bring her to it! And yet it was no house for a home, no expensive bungalow, not even a summer cottage. Only a "stout little cabin," such as might house a hunter on a winter's night; the only thing about it that looked like luxury was the chimney of cobblestones taken from the hillside below, which meant the possibility of the fire inside without which one could hardly spend an hour in the small shelter on any but a summer day. Suddenly she understood. It was the sheer romance of the thing that had appealed to him; there was no audacity about it.

He was watching her anxiously as she stared at the cabin; she came suddenly to the realization of that. Then he threw himself off his horse as they neared the rail fence, fastened him, and came back to Roberta. Nearby, Stephen was taking Rosamond down and she was exclaiming over the charm of the place.

Richard came close, looking straight up into Roberta's face, which was like a wild rose for coloring, but very sober. Her eyes would not meet his. His own face had paled a little, in spite of all its healthy, outdoor hues.

"Oh, don't misunderstand me," he whispered. "Wait till I can tell you all about it. I was wild to do something—anything—that would make you seem nearer. Don't misunderstand—*dear!*"

Stephen's voice, calling a question about the horses, brought him back to a realization of the fact that his time was not yet and that he must continue to act the part of the sane and responsible host. He turned, summoning all his social training, and replied to the question in his usual quiet tone. But as he took her from her horse, Roberta recognized the surge of his feeling, though he controlled his very touch of her and said not another word in her ear. She had all she could do, herself, to maintain an appearance of coolness under the shock of this extraordinary surprise. She had no doubt that Rosamond and Stephen comprehended the situation, more or less. Let them not be able to guess just how far things had developed, as yet.

Rosamond came to her aid with her own freely manifested pleasure in the place. Clever Rosy! Her sister-in-law was grateful to her for expressing that which Roberta could not trust herself to speak.

"What a dear little house, a real log cabin!" cried Rosamond, as the four drew near. "It's evidently just finished; see the chips. It opens the other way, doesn't it? Isn't that delightful! Not even a window on this side toward the road, though it's back so far. I suppose it looks toward the valley. A window on this end; see the solid shutters; it looks as if one could fortify one's self in it. Oh, and here's a porch! What a view—oh, what a view!"

They came around the end of the cabin together and stood at the front, surveying the wide porch, its thick pillars of untrimmed logs, its balustrade solid and sheltering, its roof low and overhanging. From the road everything was concealed; from this aspect it was open to the skies; its door and two front windows wide, yet showing—door as well as windows—the heavy shutters that would make the place a stronghold through what winter blasts might assault it. From the porch one could see for miles in every direction; at the sides, only the woods.

"It's an ideal spot for a camp," declared Stephen with enthusiasm. "Is it yours, Kendrick? I congratulate you. Invite me up here in the hunting season, will you? I can't imagine anything snugger. May we look inside?"

"By all means! It's barely finished—it's entirely rough inside—but I thought it would do for our supper tonight."

"*Do!*" Rosamond gave a little cry of delight as she looked in at the open door. "Rough! You don't want it smoother. Does he, Rob? Look at the rustic table and benches! And will you behold that splendid fireplace? Oh, all you want here is the right company!"

"And that I surely have." Richard made her a little bow, his face emphasizing his words. He went over to a cupboard in the wall, of which there were two, one on either side of the fireplace. He threw it open, disclosing hampers. "Here is our supper, I expect. Are you hungry? It's up to us to serve it. I didn't have the man stay; I thought it would be more fun to see to things ourselves."

"A thousand times more," Rosamond assured him, looking to Roberta for confirmation, who nodded, smiling.

They fell to work. Hats were removed, riding skirts were fastened out of the way, hampers were opened, and the contents set forth. Everything that could possibly be needed was found in the hampers, even to coffee, as steaming hot in the vacuum bottles as it had been poured into them.

"Some other time we'll come up and rough it," Richard explained, when Stephen told him he was no true camper to have everything prepared for him in detail like this. "But tonight I thought we'd spend as little time in preparations as possible and thus have more of the evening. It will be a 'Midsummer Night's Dream' on this hill tonight," said he, with a glance at Roberta that she would not acknowledge.

Presently they sat down, Roberta finding herself opposite their host, with the necessity upon her of eating and drinking like a common mortal, though she was dwelling in a world where it seemed as if she did not know how to do the everyday things and do them properly. It was a delicious meal, no doubt of that, and at least Stephen and Rosamond did justice to it.

"But you're not eating anything yourself, man," remonstrated Stephen, as Richard pressed upon him more cold fowl and delicate sandwiches, supplemented by a salad such as connoisseurs partake of with sighs of appreciation and with fruit that one must marvel to look upon.

"You haven't been watching me, that's evident," returned Richard, demonstrating his ability to consume food with relish by seizing upon a sandwich and making away with it in short order.

Roberta rose. "I can eat no more," she said, "with that wonderful sky before me out there." She escaped to the porch.

They all turned to exclaim at a gorgeous coloring beginning in the west, heralding the sunset which was coming. Rosamond ran out also, Stephen following.

"Stephen?" Rosamond stood at the edge of the hill below the porch. "Please come down here; it's simply perfect. You can lie on your side here among the pine needles and watch the sky."

They went around a clump of trees to a spot where the pine needles were thick, just out of sight of the cabin door. No doubt but Rosamond and Stephen liked to have things to themselves; there was no pretense about that. It was almost the anniversary of their marriage—their most happy marriage.

Roberta stood still upon the porch, looking, or appearing to look, off at the sunset. Once again she would have liked to run away. But where to go? Rosamond and Stephen did not want her; it would have been absurd to insist on following them. If she herself should stroll away among the pine trees, she would, of course, be instantly pursued. The porch was undoubtedly the most open and therefore the safest spot she could be in. So she leaned against the pillar and waited, her heart behaving disturbingly meanwhile. She could hear Richard within the cabin hurriedly clearing the table and stuffing everything away into the cupboards on either side of the fireplace. He was making short work of it. Before she could have much time to think, his step was upon the porch behind her; he was standing by her shoulder.

"It's a wonderful sight, isn't it? Must we talk about it?" he inquired softly.

"Don't you think it deserves to be talked about?" she answered, trying to speak naturally.

"No. There's only one thing in the world I want to talk about. I can't even see that sky, for looking at you. I've stood at the top of this slope more times than I can tell you, wondering if I should dare to build this little cabin. The idea possessed me: I couldn't get away from it. I bought the land—and still I was afraid. I gave the order to the builder—and all but took it back. I knew I ran every kind of risk that you wouldn't understand me—that you would think I still had that abominable confidence that I was fool enough to express to you last February. Does it look so?"

She nodded slowly without turning her head.

His voice grew even more solicitous; she could hear a little tremble in it, such as surely had not been there last February, such as she had never heard there before. "But it isn't so! With every log that's gone in, a fresh fear has gone in with it. Even on the way here today I had all I could do not to turn off some other way. The only thing that kept me coming on to meet my fate here and nowhere else, was the hope that you loved the spot itself so well that you . . . that your heart would be a bit softer here than . . . somewhere else. Oh Roberta—I'm not half good enough for you, but . . . I love you . . . love you . . . "

His voice broke on the words. It surely was a very far from confident suitor who pleaded his case in such phrases as these. He did not so much as take her hand, only waited there, a little behind her, his head bent so that he might see as much as he could of the face turned away from him.

She did not answer; something seemed to hold her from speech. One of her arms was twined about the rough, untrimmed pillar of the porch; her clasp tightened until she held it as if it were a bulwark against the human approach ready to take her from it at a word from her lips.

"I told you in my letter all I knew I couldn't say now. You know what you mean to me. I'm going to make all I can out of what there is in me whether you help me or not. But . . . if I could do it for you . . . "

Still she could not speak. She clung to the pillar, her breath quickening. He was silent until he could withstand it no longer, then he spoke so urgently in her ear that he broke in upon that strange choking reserve of hers that had kept her from yielding to him:

"Roberta—I *must* know—I can't bear it."

She turned, then, and put out her hand. He grasped it in both his own.

"What does that mean, dear? May I . . . may I have the rest of you?"

It was only a tiny nod she gave, this strange girl, Roberta, who had been so afraid of love and was so afraid of it yet. And as if he understood and appreciated her fear, he was very gentle with her. His arms came about her as they might have come about a frightened child, and drew her away from the pillar with a tender insistence that all at once produced an extraordinary effect. When she found that she was not to be seized with that devastating grasp of possession that she had dreaded, she was suddenly moved to desire it. His humbleness touched and melted her—his humbleness, in him who had been at first so arrogant—and with the first exquisite rush of response she was taken out of herself. She gave herself to his embrace . . . .

When this had happened, Roberta remembered, entirely too late, that it was this kiss that, whatever else she gave him, she had meant to refuse him—at least until tomorrow. Because today was undeniably the twenty-fourth of June: Midsummer's Day!

Chapter 24

THE PILLARS OF HOME

"Listen, Grandfather. They're playing! We'll catch them at it. Here's an open window."

Matthew Kendrick followed his grandson across the wide porch to a French window opening into the living room of the Gray home, at the opposite end from that where stood the piano, and from which the strains of cello and harp were proceeding. The two advanced cautiously to take up their position just within that far window, gazing down the room at the pair at the other end.

Roberta, in hot-weather white, with a bunch of blue cornflowers thrust into her girdle, sat with her cello at her knee, her dark head bent as she played. Ruth, a gay little figure in pink, was fingering her harp, and the poignantly rich harmonies of Saint-Säens's *Mon cœur s'ouvre à ta voix* were filling the room. Upon the great piano stood an enormous bowl of summer blooms; the air was fragrant with the breath of it. The room was as cool and fresh with its summer draperies and shaded windows as if it were not fervid July weather outside.

Richard flung one exulting glance at his grandfather, for the sight was one to please the eyes of any man even if he had no such interest in the performers as these two had. The elder man smiled, for he was very happy in these days, happier than he had been for a quarter of a century.

The music ceased with the last slow harp tones, the cello's earlier upflung bow waving in a gesture of triumph.

"Splendid, Rufus!" she commended. "You never did it half so well."

"She never did," agreed a familiar voice from the other end of the room, and the sisters turned with a start. Richard advanced down the room, Mr. Kendrick following more slowly.

"You look as cool as a pond lily, love," said Richard, "in spite of this July weather." His approving eyes regarded Roberta's cheek at close

199

range. "Is it as cool as it looks?" he inquired, and he placed his own cheek against it for an instant, regardless of the others present.

Roberta laid her hand in Mr. Kendrick's, and the old man raised it to his lips in a stately fashion he sometimes used.

"That was very beautiful music you were making," he said. "It seems a pity to bring it to an end. Richard and I want you for a little drive, to show you something that interests us very much. Will you go—and will Ruth go, too?"

"Oh, do you really want me?" cried Ruth eagerly.

"Of course we want you, little sister," Richard told her.

"I'll get our hats," offered Ruth and was off.

So presently, the four had taken their places in Mr. Kendrick's car, its windows open, its luxurious winter cushioning covered with dust-proof, cool-feeling materials. Richard sat opposite Roberta, and it was easy for her to see by the peculiar light in his eyes that there was something afoot that was giving him more than ordinary joy in her companionship. His lips could hardly keep themselves in order; the tones of his voice were vibrant; his glance would have met hers every other minute if she would have allowed it.

The car rolled along a certain aristocratic boulevard leading out of the city, past one stately residence after another. As the distance became greater from the center of affairs, the places took on a more and more comfortable aspect, with less majesty of outline and more homelikeness. Surrounding grounds grew more extensive, the houses themselves lower–spreading and more picturesque. It was a favorite drive, but there were comparatively few abroad on this July morning. Nearly every residence was closed and the inhabitants away, though the beauty of the environment was as carefully preserved as if the owners were there to observe and enjoy.

"We're the only people in the city this summer," observed Richard, "except ninety-nine-hundredths of the population, which fails to count, of course, in the eyes of these residents. Curious custom, isn't it? To close such homes as these just when they're at their most attractive, and go off to a country house. They'd be twice as comfortable at home, in this weather—just as we are. And this is the first summer I ever tried it! Robin, that's a pleasant place, isn't it?"

He indicated one of the houses they were passing, an unusually interesting combination of wood and stone, half hidden beneath spreading vines.

"Yes, that's charming," she agreed. "And I like the next even better, don't you?"

The next was of a different style entirely, less ambitious and more friendly of appearance, with long reaches of porch and pergola, and more than usually well-arranged masses of shrubbery enhancing the whole effect of withdrawal from the public gaze.

"I do, I think, for some reasons. You choose the least pretentious houses every time, don't you? Don't care a bit for showplaces?"

"Not a bit," owned the girl.

"Here's one, now," Richard pointed it out. "The owner spent a lot of money on that. Would you live in it?"

"Not willingly."

Richard glanced at his grandfather. "I wonder just how much she would suffer," he suggested, with sparkling eyes. "Suppose we should drive in there and tell her we'd bought it!"

Mr. Kendrick turned to the figure in white at his side. The eyes of the old man and the young woman met with understanding, and the two smiled affectionately before the meeting was over. Richard looked on approvingly. But he complained.

"I'd like one like that myself," said he. "Robin has looked at me only three times this morning, and once was when we met, for purposes of identification!"

He had a glance of his own, then, and apparently it went to his head, for he became more animated than ever in calling the party's attention to each piece of property passed by.

"These are all modern," he commented presently. "There's something about your really old house that can't be copied. Your own home, Robin—that's the type of antique beauty that's come to seem to me more desirable than any other. Isn't there one along here somewhere that reminds one of it?"

"There's the General Armitage place," Roberta said. "That must be close by, now. It used to be far out in the country. It was built by the same architect who built ours. General Armitage and my great-grandfather were intimate friends; they were in the Civil War together."

"Here it is." Ruth pointed it out eagerly. "I always like to go by it, because it looks quite a little like ours, only the grounds are much larger, and it has a wonderful old garden behind it. Mother has often said she wished she could transplant the Armitage garden bodily, now that the house has been closed so long. She says the old gardener is still here, and looks after the garden—or his grandsons do."

"Shall we drive in and see it?" proposed Richard. "A garden like that ought to have someone to admire it now and then."

He gave the order, and the car rolled in through the old stone gateway. The place, though of a noble old type, was far from a pretentious one, and there was no lodge at the gate, as with most of its neighbors. The house was no larger than the comfortable home of the Gray family, but its closed blinds and empty white-pillared portico gave it a deserted air. The grounds about it were not indicative of present-day, fastidious land-scape gardening, but suggested an old-time country gentleman's estate, sufficiently kept up to prevent wild and alien growth, though needing the supervision of an interested owner to suggest beneficial changes here and there.

"It's a beautiful old place, isn't it?" Richard looked to Roberta for confirmation, and saw it in her kindling eyes.

"It has always been our whole family's ideal of a home," she said. "Ours is so much nearer the center of things, we haven't the acres we should like, and whenever we have driven past this place we have looked longingly at it. Since General and Mrs. Armitage died, and their family became scattered, Father has often said that he was watching anxiously to see it come on the market, for there was no place he more coveted the right ownership for, even though he couldn't think of living here himself. It seems such a pity when homes like this go to people who don't appreciate them, and alter and spoil them."

"So it does," agreed Richard, and now he had much ado to keep his soaring spirits from betraying the happy secret that he saw his betrothed did not remotely suspect. He knew she expected to dwell hereafter in the "stone pile" that had been the home of the Kendricks for many years, and she had never by a word or look made him feel that such a prospect tried her spirit. That it was not to her a wholly happy prospect he had divined, as he might have divined that a wild bird would not be happy in a cage, nor a deer in a close corral.

"Oh, the garden!" breathed Roberta, and clasped her hands with an unconscious gesture of pleasure, as the car swept round the house and past the tall box borders of what was, indeed, such an old-time memo-rial, tended by faithful and loving hands, as must stir the interest of any admirer of the stately conceptions of an earlier day. A bowed figure, at work in a great bed of rosy phlox, straightened painfully as the car stopped, and the visitors looked into the seamed, tanned face of the presiding spirit of the place, the old gardener who had served General Armitage all his life.

All four alighted and walked through the winding paths, talked with old Symonds, and studied the charming spot with growing delight.

Richard, managing to get Roberta to himself for a brief space, eagerly questioned her.

"You find this prettier than any picture in any gallery, don't you?"

"Oh, it has great charm for me. I can hardly express the curious content it gives me to wander about such an old garden. The fragrance of the box is particularly pleasant to me, and I love the old-fashioned flowers better than any of the wonders the modern gardeners show. Just look at that mass of larkspur—did you ever see such a satisfying blue?"

"I have. The first time I came to your house to dinner you wore blue, the softest, richest blue imaginable, and you sat where the shaded light made a picture of you I shall never forget. I've never seen that peculiar blue since without thinking of you. It's one of the shades of that larkspur, isn't it?"

"I made fun of you, afterward, for telling Rosy you noticed the colors we wore," confessed Roberta, with a mischievous glance.

"You did, you rascal! Look up at me a minute—please. The blue of your eyes, with those black lashes, is another larkspur shade, in this light. I've called it sea-blue. Rob dearest, the nights I've dreamed about those eyes of yours!"

He got no further chance to observe them just then, as he might have expected, for Roberta immediately turned their light on the garden and away from his worshipful regard. She engaged the old gardener in conversation, and made his dull gaze brighten with her praise. Meanwhile Richard went off to the house, and presently returning, drew his party into a group and put a question, striving to maintain an appearance of indifference.

"It occurred to me you might care to look into the house itself. It's rather interesting inside, I believe. There seems to be a caretaker there, and she says we may come in. She'll meet us at the front. Shall we take a minute to do it?"

"I should like it very much," agreed Roberta promptly. "I've heard Mother speak of the fine old hall with its staircase—a different type from ours, and very interesting."

"There certainly is a remarkable attraction to me in this place," said Matthew Kendrick, walking beside Roberta with hands clasped behind his back and head well up. "It has a homelike look, in spite of its deserted state, that appeals to me. I wonder that the remnant of the family does not care to retain it."

"I hear the remnant is all but gone," his grandson informed him, with sober lips but dancing eyes. He was delighted with his grandfather for his assistance in playing the part of the casual observer. He led the way up the steps of the white-pillared portico and wheeled to see the others ascending. He watched Roberta as she preceded him over the threshold of the opened door.

Shall I see you coming in that door, you beautiful thing, years and years from now? he asked her in his heart and smiled happily to himself.

And now, indeed, old Matthew Kendrick played his part nobly and with skill. When the party had admired the distinction of the hall, and the stately sweep of its staircase, he led Ruth into a room on the left at the same moment that Richard summoned Roberta to look at something he had described in the room on the right. A question drew the caretaker after Mr. Kendrick, senior, and the younger man had the moment he was playing for.

"This fireplace, Robin—isn't it the very counterpart of the one in your own living room?" He asked it with his hand on the chimneypiece and his glowing eyes studying hers.

Roberta looked and nodded delightedly. "It certainly is, only still wider and higher. What a splendid one! And what a room! Oh, how could they leave it? Imagine it furnished and lived in."

"Imagine it! And a great fire on this hearth. It would take in an immense log, wouldn't it?"

"Poor hearth!" She turned again to it, and her glance sobered. "So cold now, even on a July day, after having been warmed with so many fires."

"Shall we warm it?" He took an eager step toward her. "Shall we build our own home fires upon it?"

Startled, she stared at him, the blue of her eyes growing deep. He smiled into them, his own gleaming with satisfaction.

"Richard! What do you mean?"

"What I say, darling. Could you be happy here? Should you like it better than the Kendrick house?—gloomy old place that that is!"

"But your grandfather! We . . . we couldn't possibly leave him lonely!"

"Bless your kind heart, dear—we couldn't. Shall we make a home for him here?"

"Would he be content?"

"So content that he's only waiting to know that you like it, and he'll tell you so. The plan is this, Robin, if you approve it. Three months of the year Grandfather will stay in the old home—the hard, winter months—and if you are willing, we'll stay with him. The rest of the year—here, in our own home. Eh? Do you like it?"

She stood a moment, staring into the empty fireplace, her eyes shining with a sudden hint of most unwonted tears. Then she turned to him.

"Oh, you dear!" she whispered and was swept into his arms.

"Then you do like it?" he insisted, presently.

"*Like* it! Oh, I can't tell you. To have such a home as this, so like the old one, yet so wonderful of itself. To make it ours—to put our own individuality into it, yet never hurt it. And that garden! What will Mother say? Oh, Richard—I was never so happy in my life!"

He knew that was true of himself, for his heart was full to bursting with the success of his scheming. They walked the length of the long room, looked out of each window, returned to the fireplace. He held her fast and whispered in her ear:

"Robin, I can see all sorts of things in this room. I saw them the minute I came into it first, a month ago. I've stood here dreaming more than once since then. I see ourselves, living here, and I see . . . Robin . . . I see . . . little figures!"

She nodded, with her face against his breast. He lifted her face, and his lips met hers in such a meeting as they had not yet known. Richard's heart beat hard with the sure knowledge of that which he had only dared before to believe would be true: that his wife would rejoice to be the mother of his children. Not in vain had this young man looked into child faces and brought joy to their eyes; he had learned that life would never be complete without children of his own. And now he knew, with certainty, that this woman whom he loved would gladly join her superb young life with his in the bringing of other lives into the world, with their full heritage and not a drop withheld. It was a wondrous moment.

They went out together in search of Mr. Kendrick and Ruth, and then the party proceeded over the house. With a word and a fee Richard dismissed the caretaker; now, at last, the four could speak freely of their affairs. Ruth was wild with delight at the news; Mr. Kendrick quietly happy at Roberta's words to him and her clasp of his hand.

"Richard was sure you would be pleased, my dear," he said, "and I myself could not doubt that, brought up in the atmosphere you have been, you must prefer such a home as this, so like your own. And if you would really care to have me here with you, a part of the year, I could but be gratified and contented."

They assured him of their joy at this: they mounted the stairs with him and searched for the apartments that should be his. In spite of his protests they insisted on his occupying those that were obviously the choicest of the house, declaring that nothing could be too good for him.

He was deeply touched at their devotion, and they were as glad as he.
The time passed rapidly in these momentous affairs.

"I suppose we must be off," admitted Richard reluctantly, discovering
the hour. "Robin, how can you bear to leave it so long untenanted?
From July to Christmas—what an interminable stretch of time!"

"Not with all you have planned to do," Roberta reminded him.
"Think what it will mean to get it all in order."

"I do think what it will mean. Don't I, though! It will mean shopping
with my love, choosing rugs and furniture, and plates and cups, Robin.
Plates and cups to eat and drink from. The fun of that! Will you help
us, Rufus?" He turned, laughing, to the young girl beside him. "Will
you come and eat and drink from our plates and cups? Ah, but this is
a great old world, yes? You three dear people! And I'm the happiest
fellow in it!"

There seemed small doubt that there could be few happier, just then,
as standing at the top of his own staircase and gazing down into the wide
and empty hall toward the open door that led out upon the white-
pillared portico of his home-that-was-to-be, Richard Kendrick flung up
one arm, lifting an imaginary cup high in the air, and calling joyously:

"Here's hoping!"

Chapter 25

A STOUT LITTLE CABIN

Christmas morning! And the bells in St. Luke's pealing the great old hymn, dear for scores of years to those who had heard it chiming from the ivy-grown towers—*Adeste, Fideles.*

"Oh, come, all ye faithful, joyful and triumphant!"

Joyful and triumphant, indeed, though yet subdued and humble (since this paradox may be at times in human hearts) was Richard Kendrick as he stood waiting in the vestibule of St. Luke's on Christmas morning, for a tryst he had made. Not with Roberta, for it was not possible for her to be present today, but with Ruth Gray, that young sister who had become so like a sister by blood to Richard that, at her suggestion, it had seemed to him the happiest thing in the world to go to church with her on Christmas morning—the morning of the day that was to see his marriage.

The Gray homestead was full of wedding guests, the usual family guests of the Christmas house party. On the evening before had occurred the Christmas dance, and Richard had led the festivities, with his bride-elect at his side. It had been a glorious merrymaking, and his pulses had thrilled wildly to the rapture of it. But today—today was another story.

A slender young figure, in brown velvet with a tiny twig of holly perched among the furry trimmings, hurried up the steps and into the vestibule. Richard met Ruth halfway, his face alight, his hand clasping hers eagerly.

"I'm so sorry I am late," she whispered. "Oh, it's so fine of you to come. Isn't it a lovely, lovely way to begin this day—your and Rob's day, too?"

He nodded, smiling down at her with eyes full of brotherly affection for a most lovable girl. He followed her into the church and took his place beside her, feeling that he would rather be here, just now, than anywhere in the world.

It must be admitted that he hardly heard the service, except for the music, which was of a sort to make its own way into the most abstracted consciousness. But the quiet spirit of the place had its effect upon him, and when he knelt beside Ruth, it seemed the most natural thing in the world to form a prayer in his heart that he might be a fit husband for the wife he was so soon to take to himself. Once, during a long period of kneeling, Ruth's hand slipped shyly into his, and he held it fast with a quickening perception of what it meant to have a pure young spirit like hers beside him in this sacred hour. His soul was full of high resolve to be a son and brother to this very special family into which he was entering, such as might do them honor. For it was a very significant fact that to him the people who stood nearest to Roberta were of great consequence. His association with this family was of great consequence; and that a source of extraordinary satisfaction to him, from the first, had been his connection with a family that seemed to him ideal, and association with which made up to him for much of which his life had been empty.

A proof of this had been his invitation through his grandfather, who had warmly seconded his wish, to Mr. and Mrs. Rufus Gray, to come and stay with the Kendricks throughout this Christmas party, precisely as they had done the year before. To have Aunt Ruth preside at breakfast on this auspicious morning had given Richard the greatest pleasure, and the kiss he had bestowed upon her had been one that she recognized as very like the tribute of a son. From her side he had gone to St. Luke's.

"Good-bye, dear, for a few hours," he whispered to Ruth as he put her into the brougham driven by the old family coachman, in which she had come alone to church. "When I see you next I'll be almost your brother. And in just a few minutes after that . . . "

"Oh, Richard—are you happy?" she whispered back, scanning his face with brimming eyes.

"So happy I can't tell even you. Give my love, my dearest love, to . . . "

"I will," as he paused on the name, as if he could not speak it just then. "She was so glad to have us go to church together. She wanted to come herself, so much."

He pressed the small gloved hand held out to him. He knew that Ruth idealized him far beyond his worth; he could read it in her gaze, which was all but reverential. He said to himself, as he turned away, that a man never had so many reasons to be true to the girl he was to marry. To bring the first shade of distrust into this little sister's tender eyes would be punishment enough for any disloyalty, no matter what the cause might be.

The wedding was to be at six o'clock. There was nothing about the whole affair, as it had been planned by Roberta with his full assent, to make it resemble any event of the sort in which he had ever taken part. Not one consideration of custom or of vogue had had weight with her, if it differed from her carefully wrought-out views of what should be. Her ruling idea had been to make it all as simple and sincere as possible, to invite no guests outside her large family and his small one except such personal friends as were peculiarly dear to both. When Richard had been asked to submit his list of these, he had been taken aback to find how pitifully few people he could put upon it. Half a dozen college classmates, a small number of fellow clubmen—these painstakingly considered from more than one standpoint—the Cartwrights, his cousins whom he really knew but indifferently well; two score easily covered the number of those whom by any stretch of the imagination he could call friends. The long roll of his fashionable acquaintances he dismissed as out of the question. If he had been married in church there would have been several hundreds of these who must unquestionably have been bidden; but since Roberta wanted, as she put it, "only those who truly care for us," he could but choose those who seemed to come somewhere near that ideal. To be quite honest, he was aware that his real friends were among those who could not be bidden to his marriage. The crippled children in the hospitals; the suffering poor who would send him their blessing when they read in tomorrow's paper that he was married; the shop people in Eastman who knew him for the kindest employer they had ever had. These were they who truly cared, and the knowledge was warm at his heart, as with a ruthless hand he crossed off names of the mighty in the world of society and finance.

"Dick, my boy, you've grown—you've grown!" was his grandfather's comment when Richard, with a rueful laugh, had shown the old man the finished list, upon which, well toward the top, had been the names of Mr. and Mrs. Alfred Carson. Of Hugh Benson, as best man, Matthew Kendrick heartily approved. "You've chosen the nugget of pure gold, Dick," he said, "where you might have been expected to take one with considerable alloy. He's worth all the others put together."

Richard had never realized this more thoroughly than when, on Christmas afternoon, he invited Benson to drive with him for a last inspection of a certain spot that had been prepared for the reception of the bridal pair at the first stage of their journey. He could not, as Hugh took his place beside him and the two whirled away down the frost-covered avenue, imagine asking any other man in the world to go with him on such a visit. There was no other man he knew who would not have made it the occasion for more or less distasteful raillery; but Hugh Benson was of the rare few, he felt, who would understand what that "stout little cabin" meant to him.

They came upon it presently, standing bleak and bare as to exterior upon its hilltop, with only a streaming pillar of smoke from its big chimney to suggest that it might be habitable within. But when the heavy door was thrown open, an interior of warmth and comfort presented itself such as brought an exclamation of wonder from the guest and made Richard's eyes shine with satisfaction.

The long, low room had been furnished simply but fittingly with such hangings, rugs, and few articles of furniture as should suggest homelikeness and service. Before the wide hearth stood two big winged chairs, and a set of bookshelves was filled with a carefully chosen collection of favorite books. The colorings were warm but harmonious, and upon a heavy table, now covered with a rich, dull-red cloth, stood a lamp of generous proportions and beauty of design.

"I've tried to steer a line between luxury and austerity," Richard explained, as Hugh looked about him with pleased observation. "We shall not be equipped for real roughing it—not this time, though sometimes we may like to come here dressed as hunters and try living on bare boards. I just wanted it to seem like a bit of home when she comes in tonight. There'll be some flowers here then, of course—lots of them, and that ought to give it the last touch. There are always flowers in her home, bowls of them, everywhere. It was one of the first things I noticed. Do you think she will like it here?" he ended, with a hint of almost boyish diffidence in his tone.

"Like it? It's wonderful. I never heard of anything so . . . so . . . all it should be for a girl like her," Hugh exclaimed lamely enough, yet with a certain eloquence of inflection that meant more than his choice of words. He turned to Richard. "I can't tell you," he went on, flushing with the effort to convey to his friend his deep feeling, "how fortunate I think you are, and how I hope—oh, I hope you and she will be the happiest people in the world!"

"I'm sure you hope that, old fellow," Richard answered, more touched by this difficult voicing of what he knew to be Hugh's genuine devotion than he should have been by the most felicitous phrasing of another's congratulations. "And I can tell you this. There's nobody else I know whom I would have brought here to see my preparations—nobody else who would have understood how I feel about what I'm doing today. I never should have believed it would have seemed so, well, so sacred a thing to take a girl away from all the people who love her, and bring her to a place like this. I wish—I wish I were a thousand times more fit for her."

"Rich Kendrick—" Benson was taken out of himself now. His voice was slightly tremulous, but he spoke with less difficulty than before. "You are fitter than you know. You've developed as I never thought any man could in so short a time. I've been watching you and I've seen it. There was always more in you than people gave you credit for—it was your inheritance from a father and grandfather who have meant a great deal in their world. You've found out what you were meant for, and you're coming up to new and finer standards every day. You *are* fit to take this girl. And that means much, because I know a little of what a . . . " Now he was floundering again, and his fine, thin face flamed more hotly than before. "Of what she is!" he ended, with a complete breakdown in the style of his phraseology, but with none at all in the conveyance of his meaning.

Richard flung out his hand, catching Hugh's and gripping it. "Bless you for a friend and a brother!" he cried, his eyes bright with sudden moisture. "You're another whom I mustn't disappoint. Disappoint? I ought to be flayed alive if I ever forget the people who believe in me— who are trusting me with Roberta!"

It was a pity she could not have heard him speak her name, have seen the way he looked at his friend as he spoke it, and have seen the way his friend looked back at him. There was a quality in their mentioning of her, here in this place where she was soon to be, that was its own tribute to the young womanhood she so radiantly imaged.

In spite of all these devices to make the hours pass rapidly, they seemed to Richard to crawl. That one came at last, however, that saw him knocking at the door of his grandfather's suite, dressed for his marriage and eager to depart. Bidden by Mr. Kendrick's man to enter, he presented himself in the old gentleman's dressing room, where its occupant, as scrupulously attired as himself, stood ready to descend to the waiting car. Richard closed the door behind him and stood looking at his grandfather with a smile.

"Well, Dick boy—ready? Ah, but you look fresh and fine! Clean in body and mind and heart for her, eh? That's how you look, sir—as a man should look and feel on his wedding day. Well, she's worth it, Dick—worth the best you can give."

"Worth far better than I can give, Grandfather," Richard responded, the glow in his smooth cheek deepening.

"Well, I don't mean to overrate you," said the old man, smiling, "but you seem to me pretty well worth any girl's taking. Not that you can't become more so—and will, I thoroughly believe. It's not so much what you've done this last year as what you show promise of doing—great promise. That's all one can ask at your age. Ten years later—but we won't go into that. Tonight's enough, eh, my dear boy! *My dear boy!*" he repeated, with a sudden access of tenderness in his voice. Then, as if afraid of emotion for them both, he pressed his grandson's hand and abruptly led the way into the outer room, where Thompson stood waiting with his fur-lined coat and muffler.

From this point on it seemed to Richard more or less like a rapidly shifting series of pictures, all wonderfully colored. The first was that of the electric light of the big car's interior shining on the faces of Uncle Rufus and Aunt Ruth, and on Mr. Kendrick and Hugh Benson—the latter a little pale but quite composed. Hugh had owned that he felt seriously inadequate for the role that was his tonight, being no society man and unaccustomed to taking conspicuous parts anywhere but in business. But Richard had assured him that it was all a very simple matter, since it was just a question of standing by a friend in the crisis of his life! And Hugh had responded that it would be a pity indeed if he were unwilling to do that.

The next picture was that of the wide hall at the Gray home. As he came into it, a vivid memory flashed over Richard of his first entrance there—less honored than tonight! Soft lights shone upon him; the spicy fragrance of the ropes and banks of Christmas "greens," bright with holly, saluted his nostrils; and the glimpse of a great fire burning, quite as usual, on the broad hearth of the living room—a place that had long since come to typify his ideal of a home—served to make him feel that there could be no spot more suitable for the beginning of a new home, there could be nothing in the world finer or more beautiful to model it upon.

Nothing seemed afterward clear in his memory until the moment when he came from his room upstairs, with Hugh close behind him, and met the rector of St. Luke's, who was to marry him. There followed a hazy impression of a descent of the staircase, of coming from a detour through the library out into the full light, and of standing interminably facing a large gathering of people, the only face at which he could venture to glance that of Judge Calvin Gray, standing dignified and stately beside another figure of equal dignity and stateliness—probably that of Mr. Matthew Kendrick. Then, at last, there was Roberta, coming toward him down a silken lane, her eyes fixed on his—such eyes, in such a face!

He fixed his own gaze upon it and held it—and forgot everything else, as he had hoped he would. Then there were the grave words of the clergyman, and his own voice responding—and sounding curiously unlike his own, of course, as the voice of the bridegroom has sounded in his own ears since time began. Then Roberta's—how clearly she spoke, bless her! Then, before he knew it, it was done, and he and she were rising from their knees, and there were smiles and pleasant murmurings all about them, and little Ruth was sobbing softly with her cheek against his!

It was here that he became conscious again of the family—Roberta's family, and of what it meant to have such people as these welcome him into their circle. When he looked into the face of Roberta's mother and felt her tender welcoming kiss upon his lips, his heart beat hard with joy. When Roberta's father, his voice deep with feeling, said to him, "Welcome to our hearts, my son," he could only grasp the firm hand with an answering, passionate pressure that meant that he had at last that which he had consciously or unconsciously longed for all his life. All down the line his overcharged spirit responded to the warmth of their reception of him: Stephen and Rosamond, Louis and Ruth and young Ted, smiling at him, saying the kindest things to him, making him one of them as only those can who are blessed with understanding natures. To be sure, it was all more or less confused in his memory, when he tried to recall it afterward, but enough of it remained vivid to assure him that it had been all he could have asked or hoped—and that it was far, far more than he deserved!

"The boy bears up pretty well, eh?" observed old Matthew Kendrick to his lifelong friend, Judge Calvin Gray, as the two stood aside, having gone through their own part in the greeting of the bridal pair. Mr. Kendrick's hand was still tingling with the wringing grip of his grandson's; his heart was warm with the remembrance of the way Richard's brilliant eyes had looked into his as he had said, low in the old man's ear, "I'm not less yours, Grandfather—and she's yours, too." Roberta had put both arms about his neck, whispering, "Indeed I am, dear Grandfather, if you'll have me." Well, it had been happiness enough, and it was good to watch them as they went on with their joyous task, knowing that he had a large share in their lives, and would continue to have it.

"Bears up? I should say he did. He looks as if he could assist in steadying the world upon the shoulders of old Atlas," answered Judge Gray happily. "It's a trying position for any man, and some of them only just escape looking craven."

"The man who could stand beside that young woman and look craven would deserve to be hamstrung," was the other's verdict. "Cal, she's enough to turn an old man's head; we can't wonder that a young one's is swimming. And the best of it is that it isn't all looks, it's real beauty to the core. She's rich in the qualities that stand wear in a wearing world—and her goodness isn't the sort that will ever pall on her husband. She'll keep him guessing to the end of time, but the answer will always give him fresh delight in her."

"You analyze her well," admitted Roberta's uncle. "But that's to be expected of a man who's been a past master all his life in understanding and dealing with human nature."

"When it was not too near me, Cal. When it came to the dearest thing I had in the world, I made a mistake with it. It was only when the boy came under this roof that he received the stimulus that has made him what he is. That was sure to tell in the end."

"Ah, but he had your blood in him," declared Calvin Gray heartily.

Thus, all about them, in many quarters, were the young pair affectionately discussed. Not the least eloquent in their praise were the youngest members of the company.

"I say, but I'm proud of my new brother," declared Ted Gray, the picture of youthful elegance, with every hair in place and a white rose on the lapel of his short evening jacket. He was playing escort to the prettiest of his girl cousins. "Isn't he a stunner tonight?"

"He always was—that is, since I've known him," responded Esther, Uncle Philip's daughter. "I can't help laughing when I think of the Christmas party last year, and how Rob made us all think he was a poor young man and she didn't like him at all. All of us girls thought she was so strange not to want to dance with him when he was so handsome and danced so beautifully. I suppose she was just pretending she didn't care for him."

"Nobody ever'll know when Rob did change her mind about him," Ted assured her. "She can make you think black's green when she wants to."

"Isn't she perfectly wonderful tonight?" sighed the pretty cousin, with a glance from her own homemade frock—in which, however, she looked like a freshly picked rose—to Roberta's bridal gown, shimmering through mistiness, simplicity itself, yet, as the little cousin well knew, the product of such art as she herself might never hope to command. "I always thought she was perfectly beautiful, but she's absolutely fascinating tonight."

"Tell that to Rich. I'm afraid he doesn't appreciate her," laughed Ted, indicating his new brother-in-law, who, at the moment being temporarily unemployed, was to be observed following his bride with his eyes with a wistful gaze indicating helplessness without her even for a fraction of time.

Roberta had been drawn a little away by her husband's best man, who had something to tell her that he had reserved for this hour.

"Mrs. Kendrick," he was beginning—at which he was bidden to remember that he had known the girl Roberta for many years; and so began again, smiling with gratitude:

"Roberta, have you any idea what is happening in Eastman tonight?"

"Indeed I haven't, Hugh. Anything I ought to know of?"

"I think it's time you did. Every employee in our store is sitting down to a great dinner, served by a caterer from this city, with a Christmas favor at every plate. The place cards have a K and G on them in monogram. There are such flowers for decorations as most of those people have never seen. I don't need to tell you whose doing this is."

He had the reward he had anticipated for the telling of this news: Roberta's cheek colored richly, and her eyes fell for a moment to hide the surprise and happiness in them.

"That may seem like enough," he went on gently, "but it wasn't enough for him. At every children's hospital in this city and in every children's ward, there is a Christmas tree tonight, loaded with gifts. And I want you to know that, busy as he has been until today, he picked out every gift himself and wrote the name on the card with his own hand."

It was too much to tell her all at once, and he knew it when he saw her eyes fill, though she smiled through the shining tears as she murmured:

"And he didn't tell me!"

"No, nor meant to. When I remonstrated with him he said you might think it a posing to impress you, whereas it simply meant the overflow of his own happiness. He said if he didn't have some such outlet he should burst with the pressure of it!"

Her moved laughter provided some sort of outlet for her own pressure of feeling about these tidings. When she had recovered control of herself she turned to glance toward her husband, and Hugh's heart stirred within him at the starry radiance of that look, which she could not veil successfully from him, who knew the cause of it.

It was the Alfred Carsons who came to her last; the young manager beaming with pleasure in the honor done him by his invitation to this family wedding, to which the great of the city were mostly intentionally unbidden; his pretty young wife, in effective modishness of attire by no means ill-chosen, glowing with pride and rosy with the effort to comport herself in keeping with the standards of these "democratically aristocratic" people, as her husband had shrewdly characterized them. As they stood talking with the bride, two of Richard's friends standing nearby, former close associates in the life of the clubs he was now too busy to pursue, exchanged a brief colloquy that would mightily have interested the subject of it if he could have heard it.

"Who are these?" demanded one of the other, gazing elsewhere as he spoke.

"Partner or manager or something, in that business of Rich's up in Eastman. So Belden Lorimer says."

"Bright looking chap—might be anybody, except for the wife. A bit too conscious, she."

"You might not notice that except in contrast with the new Mrs. Kendrick. There's the real thing, yes? Rich knew what he was doing when he picked her out."

"Undoubtedly he did. The whole family's pretty fine—not the usual sort. Watch Mrs. Clifford Cartwright. Even she's impressed. Odd, eh? With all the country cousins about, too."

"I know. It's in the air. And of course everybody knows the family blood is of the bluest. Unostentatious but sure of itself. The Cartwrights couldn't get that air, not in a thousand years."

"Rich himself has it, though—and the grandfather."

"True enough. I'm wondering which class we belong in!"

The two laughed and moved closer. Neither could afford to miss a chance of observing their old friend under these new conditions, for he had been a subject of their speculations ever since the change in him had begun. And though they had deplored the loss of him from their favorite haunts, they had been some time since forced to admit that he had never been so well worth knowing as now that he was virtually lost to them.

"Oh, Robby darling, I can never, never let you go!"

So softly wailed Ruth, her slim young form clinging to her sister's, regardless of her bridesmaid's crushed finery, daintily cherished till this moment. Over her head Roberta's eyes looked into her mother's. There were no tears in the fine eyes that met hers, but somehow Roberta knew that Ruth's heartache was a tiny pain beside that other's.

Richard, looking on, standing ready to take his bride way, wondered once more within himself how he could have the heart to do it. But it was done, and he and Roberta were off together down the steps; and he was putting her into Mr. Kendrick's closed car; and she was leaning past him to wave and wave again at the dear faces on the porch. Under the lights here and there one stood out more clearly than the rest: Louis's, flushed and virile; Rosamond's, lovely as a child's; old Mr. Kendrick's, intent and grave, forgetting to smile. The father and the mother were in the shadow, but little Gordon, Stephen's boy, made of himself a central figure by running forward at the last to fling up a sturdy arm and cry:

"Good-bye, Auntie Wob. Come back soon!"

It had been a white Christmas, and the snow had fallen lightly all day long. It was falling faster now, and the wind was rising, to Richard's intense satisfaction. He had been fairly praying for a gale, improbable though that seemed. There was a considerable semblance of a storm, however, through which to drive the twelve miles to the waiting cabin on the hilltop, and when the car stopped and the door was opened, a heavy gust came swirling in. The absence of lights everywhere made the darkness seem blacker out here in the country, and the general effect of utter desolation was as near this strange young man's desire as could have been hoped.

"Good driving, Rogers. It was a quick trip, in spite of the heavy roads at the last. Thank you and good night."

"Thank you, sir. Good night, Mr. Kendrick—and Mrs. Kendrick, if I may."

"Good night, Rogers," called the voice Rogers had learned greatly to admire, and he saw her face smiling at him as the lights of the car streamed out upon it.

Then the great car was gone, and Richard was throwing open the door of the cabin, letting all the warmth and glow and fragrance of the snug interior greet his bride as he led her in and shut the door with a resounding force against the winter night and storm.

It had been a dream of his that he should put her into one of the big, cushioned, winged chairs, and take his own place on the hearth rug at her feet. Together they should sit and look into the fire, and be as silent or as full of happy speech as might seem to befit the hour. Now, when he had bereft her of her furry wraps and welcomed her as he saw fit, he made his dream come true. He told her of it as he put her in her chair and saw her lean back against the comfortable cushioning with a long breath of inevitable weariness after many hours of tension.

"And you wondered which it would be, speech or silence?" queried Roberta, as he took that place he had meant to take, at her knee, and looked up, smiling, into her downbent face.

"I did wonder, but I don't wonder now. I know. There aren't any words, are there?"

"No," she answered, looking now into the fire, yet seeing, as clearly as before, his fine and ardent, yet reverent face, "I think there are no words."

THE END

Afterword
DISCUSSION WITH PROFESSOR WHEELER
(For Formal School, Home School, and Book Club Discussions)

First of all, permit me to define my perception of the role of the teacher. I believe that the ideal teaching relationship involves the teacher and the student, both looking in the same direction, and both with a sense of wonder. A teacher is not an important person dishing out rote learning to an unimportant person. I furthermore do not believe that a Ph.D. automatically brings with it omniscience, despite the way some of us act. In discussions, I tell my students beforehand that my opinions and conclusions are no more valid than theirs, for each of us sees reality from a different perspective.

Now that my role is clear, let's continue. The purpose of the discussion section of the series is to encourage debate, to dig deeper into the book than would be true without it, and to spawn other questions that may build on the ones I begin with here. If you take advantage of this section, you will be gaining just as good an understanding of the book as you would were you actually sitting in one of my classroom circles.

As you read this book, record your thoughts and reactions each day in a journal. Also, an unabridged dictionary is almost essential in completely understanding the text. If your vocabulary is to grow, something else is needed besides the dictionary: vocabulary cards. Take a stack of three-by-five-inch index cards, and write the words you don't know on one side and their definitions on the other, with each word used in a sentence. Every time you stumble upon words you are unsure of (I found quite a number myself!), make a card for it. Continually go over these cards; and keep all, except those you never miss, in a card file. You will be amazed at how fast your vocabulary will grow!

The Introduction Must Be Read Before Beginning the Next Section.

219

Questions to Deepen Your Understanding

Chapter 1. The Curtain Rises on a Home

1. *If* is one of the most potent two-letter words in the English language. It is a lever with the power to move worlds. Coupled with *only*, it becomes the most tragic two words we know: *If only*.

    Discuss the significance of the word *if* and how we should relate to it in our lives. Then discuss it in terms of this book, keeping it as a reference as you read the text. What role does "if" play throughout the story? An interesting word to compare is *chance*. How much of our destinies depends on these two swinging doors: *if* and *chance!*

    For an entirely different concept of *if*, let's turn to Rudyard Kipling's famous poem:

IF...

If you can keep your head when all about you
Are losing theirs and blaming it on you;
If you can trust yourself when all men doubt you,
But make allowance for their doubting too;
If you can wait and not be tired by waiting,
Or being lied about, don't deal in lies,
Or being hated, don't give way to hating,
And yet don't look too good, nor talk too wise;

If you can dream—and not make dreams your master;
If you can think—and not make thoughts your aim;
If you can meet with Triumph and Disaster
And treat those two impostors just the same;
If you can bear to hear the truth you've spoken
Twisted by knaves to make a trap for fools,
Or watch the things you gave your life to, broken,
And stoop and build 'em up with worn-out tools;

If you can make one heap of all your winnings
And risk it on one turn of pitch-and-toss,
And lose, and start again at your beginnings
And never breathe a word about your loss;
If you can force your heart and nerve and sinew

To serve your turn long after they are gone,
And so hold on when there is nothing in you
Except the Will which says to them: "Hold on!"

If you can talk with crowds and keep your virtue,
Or walk with Kings—nor lose the common touch,
If neither foes nor loving friends can hurt you,
If all men count with you, but none too much;
If you can fill the unforgiving minute
With sixty seconds' worth of distance run—
Yours is the Earth and everything that's in it,
And—which is more—you'll be a Man, my son!
In Kipling's 1910 collection *Rewards and Fairies*

I shall never forget one day, after my freshman English composition class was done, when a coed came up to me, close to tears. "Oh, Dr. Wheeler," she said, "what a poem! But why did Kipling leave women out?" I went home and tinkered with the poem and came up with the following. (Mr. Kipling, please forgive me for tinkering with your immortal words.)

And will He not say: "Well done, My daughter!
Well done, My son!"

The poem is nothing less than an entire philosophy of life, a deep well one could continuously draw from yet never plumb the depths. In your own words, write down the essence of each "if" sequence, in terms of relevance to *your* life.

2. Note Richmond's description of the *atmosphere* of the house. What does she do to create that image in your mind? How much by description? How much by dialogue? Which has the greater impact?

3. There is much in this chapter, and in later ones as well, that has to do with the difference between a *house* and a *home*. Starting with this chapter, keep a running commentary in your daily journal entries dealing with these two synonyms. Close in meaning, yet miles apart! After finishing the book, read back through all these "house" and "home" entries and arrive at a synthesis of what you think the word *home* meant to Richmond. What would be the key qualities to be expected in such a place?

4. Richmond also feels that one's voice should never be taken lightly. After all, Richard first falls in love with a voice. Note the repeated references to Roberta's voice in the book; also her mother's when you get to Chapter 10. Discuss the voice in terms of people you know and your own voice. What conclusions do you reach?

5. In literary terminology are two related terms: *metonymy* and *synecdoche*, both referring to parts standing for a whole. In some respects, Roberta's vivid scarf symbolizes the vividness of her entire personality. Watch to see if there are other examples in the book of equating a part to the whole.

6. What is it about a fireplace that calls to us? Note the wonderful metaphor Richmond uses: "a great wide-throated fireplace." To me, a home without a fireplace is not quite complete. As you journey through the book, pay particular attention to the role fireplaces play in the narrative.

7. Note the similarities to an impressionistic painting or piece of music in this first chapter. One might liken the snatches of conversation, sounds on the stairs, strains of music from distant instruments, blurs made by people hurrying past, and so on, to splashes of pigment on canvas or Debussy-like mood music. Watch for other impressionistic splashes as the story progresses.

8. Richmond felt that the home environment made a seismic impact for good or evil on children and adolescents. Pay particular attention, throughout the book, to how she develops this concept.

9. Although Richmond believed in democracy, like many if not most of her contemporaries, she also believed in class, in the impact generations of culture have on descendants—hence the tinge of noblesse oblige that tints her stories. Birth and breeding were important to her. What impact do *you* feel they have?

10. Pay particular attention throughout the book to the dialogue, to how character is revealed in conversation (as opposed to being incorporated into description). How effective is this?

11. Always look for those serendipities, metaphors and similes, in your reading. Note the extra dimension, the extra pleasure, they give. Keep lists, and every time you discover one, *write it down* in your

journal (usually at the back). In this book you will find metaphors such as

- " . . . her laugh a song to listen to."
- " . . . never know happiness until he shook hands with labor."
- "Her cheeks had been stung into a brilliant rose color."
- "Louis . . . cherished a violin under his chin."
- " . . . who could stand the sunlight on her clear cheek and the sunlight on her soul."
- "That's somebody's heart there on that sheet of old paper."
- "What was she? A beauty stepping out of a portrait by one of the masters?"
- "What were her eyes? Black stars, or wells of darkness into which a man might fall and drown himself."
  and similes such as
- " . . . eyes eager as a collie's."
- " . . . like a sick schoolboy shut up in the nursery enviously watching his playmates go forth to valiant games."
- "You throw back your head just like Sheik when he's going to bolt."
- "She turned to a group of young people who had followed her as bees follow their queen."
- " . . . watching a strip of moonlight that lay like flickering silver across her wall."

Chapter 2. Richard Changes His Plans

12. Note how much more formal this age was than today's. The family was the inviolate core of societal life, and a young man could not even talk with a young woman until he had been officially introduced to her. Furthermore, unless a young man's suit had the blessing of the family (immediate and extended), the relationship was unlikely to go anywhere.

Note too that even after people *were* officially introduced, they still tended to call the other "Mr.," "Mrs.," and "Miss." Even when addressing their parents or grandparents, "sir" or "ma'am" was an integral part of filial respect.

Compare that world's formality with today's easy familiarity when even people who have never met you call you by your first name. Which is better? What are the advantages and disadvantages of both?

13. There is much in the book about the role of work in our lives and, by contrast, the impact idleness makes on those who either do not, or do not choose to, work. Keep track of Richmond's arguments (either stated overtly or through dialogue), and by the end of the book, arrive at conclusions of your own.

14. Note something else: This is the pre-electronic age. Telephones are used only in an emergency, no TV, no movies, no radio, no videos, no computers, no Faxes, no E-mail. Letters carry one's thoughts, and people entertain themselves. And they *read* and develop their talents. Compare with today, the pluses and minuses of each, and arrive at conclusions. Perhaps even come up with a compromise that would work today.

15. Also compare courtship then with that of today. Today our media programs us to accept instant gratification as the norm. For many, sex often comes within minutes of meeting someone for the first time, and a lasting relationship is merely an option. Tabloids and magazines screech out the news that sex is a sport, like tennis. Not so then. Then, what counted was love, deep-seated love based on shared values, goals, and dreams, on a shared perception of the roles of family and God in life. Because sex was usually saved until after marriage, courtship represented a dreaming time, an opportunity to idealize the other, to search for a meeting-ground of souls. All this is denied today when sexuality is the stated all-in-all. Compare attitudes then with ones held today, as the book progresses, and arrive at conclusions.

16. What is the comparative value of character versus wealth? Might character itself be a form of wealth? Study this aspect through the rest of the chapters.

17. Today the average father spends 44 seconds a day communicating with each child; contrast that with the amount of time Roberta's mother, Eleanor, has for those seeking her counsel. Discuss.

Chapter 3. While It Rains
18. Should even children of the rich have to *earn* their way to success? Or should executive positions be handed to them just because of who they are? What is the impact on the person involved of either option?

19.   We have already discussed the impact of life without work; now we tackle the impact of pleasure unrelieved by work. What are the results of never being able to take a vacation from a life that is all vacation?

20.   Love. If we don't have to work for it, do we value it? If love does not make us better, ennoble us, is it the right love for us? Pay particular attention to Richard in the opening chapters, then chronicle the changes in his life as a result of his respect, admiration, and love for the girl with the flaming scarf. Do you feel the changes he makes as a result will be lasting ones? Why or why not?

21.   Just what is it that Richard most admires about Roberta's love of life? What are the things she does and participates in that seem unorthodox? What makes her different from the other girls and women Richard has known? How does all this change *him*?

Isn't the book really about what the Bible calls "the abundant life"? What does it mean to live life to its fullest?

22.   What does Richard learn about work from Roberta?

Chapter 4. Pictures

23.   Note how the Gray sisters play instruments well. In previous generations to ours, it was expected that each child would develop talents, especially musical. When family reunions, school programs, or church functions took place, children and youth were expected to perform. In real life, Richmond's own children developed into accomplished musicians, so this expectation was no mere rhetoric to her. What is lost by failing to develop one's talents?

What attitude is projected as the family performs? Is there any grandstanding or self-awareness?

24.   Compare the kind of conversation Richard was used to, with what he experiences around the Gray family table. How is it different? How does it compare with similar conversations at your home or in homes you know? How about the intergenerational involvement? Respect for elders? Discuss at length.

25.   What is the perception of the role of a mother in this book? Continue to gather data as you read.

26. What is the picture you get of a happy, fulfilling marriage (gained by observing the interaction of the Gray family)? How does it compare with marriage as portrayed by today's media? What are the implications?

27. Regarding Richard's rather flippant "I've been wondering if the motto of the Gray family might be 'Let us, then, be up and doing,'" it is instructive to note the source: Longfellow's "Psalm of Life" (last stanza), the most famous and most-oft-recited poem of the nineteenth century. The poem was anything but mere rhetoric to Longfellow, for he wrote it in the midst of searing pain and trauma: First came the untimely death of his sister Elizabeth; then in Holland, during his second study trip abroad, the only child he and his young wife Mary ever had, died. In her terrible grief, Mary soon followed her baby to the grave.

The catalyst for the poem occurred upon Longfellow's return to Harvard when he was preparing for a new course, "Literature and the Literary Life." What then was life all about? Calvinistic fatalism certainly didn't hold the answer; neither did dreamy romanticism. Studying Goethe, Longfellow found comfort and inspiration, and out of this crucible of pain he forged "Psalm of Life." Nothing like it had ever been written, and the English-speaking world found in it a philosophy to live by in their world of continual suffering, illness, and early death. It was more than mere philosophy: It was a clarion call to rise above that suffering and, with God's help, *THIS DO*—as that riveting last stanza urges:

A PSALM OF LIFE

Tell me not, in mournful numbers,
    Life is but an empty dream!
For the soul is dead that slumbers,
    And things are not what they seem.

Life is real! Life is earnest!
    And the grave is not its goal;
Dust thou art, to dust returnest,
    Was not spoken of the soul.

Not enjoyment, and not sorrow,
    Is our destined end or way;
But to act, that each to-morrow
    Find us farther than to-day.

Art is long, and Time is fleeting,
    And our hearts, though stout and brave,
Still, like muffled drums, are beating,
    Funeral marches to the grave.

In the world's broad field of battle,
    In the bivouac of Life,
Be not like dumb, driven cattle!
    Be a hero in the strife!

Trust no Future, howe'er pleasant!
    Let the dead Past bury its dead!
Act—act in the living Present!
    Heart within, and God o'erhead!

Lives of great men all remind us
    We can make our lives sublime,
And, departing, leave behind us
    Footprints on the sands of time—

Footprints, that perhaps another,
    Sailing o'er life's solemn main,
A forlorn and shipwrecked brother,
    Seeing, shall take heart again.

Let us, then, be up and doing,
    With a heart for any fate;
Still achieving, still pursuing,
    Learn to labor and to wait.
      Henry Wadsworth Longfellow (1838)

(*The Literature of the United States*, ed. Walter Blair, Theodore Hornberger, and Randall Stewart [Chicago: Scott, Foresman and Company, 1949], pp. 374–75; *American Authors*, ed. Leslie Lee Culpepper and Mildred McClary Tymeson [Washington, D.C..: Review and Herald Publishing, 1942, p. 69.)

Now study the poem, holding it in mind as a constant as you read through this book. At the end, reread it and decide just how closely the message of "Psalm of Life" equates with Richmond's book and Roberta's philosophy of life.

28. Do families have mottoes they live by today, as did the Grays? Would it be a good idea to live by one? Discuss.

29. Watch for words that jump out at you. Words such as *blush, demure, madcap,* and *bewitching* generally reflect a simpler and less sophisticated, brash, and jaded age than the one we know.

30. It is interesting to observe the closeness of the young-marrieds to the rest of the family. This living together under one roof used to be fairly common in America. While it certainly had its downside, it did serve as a major marriage stabilizer. Ought we to return to it?

31. There is nothing that can possibly equate with the radiant, all-encompassing love on a mother's face as she looks down at the baby she risked her life to bring into the world. Might it not be this very agony that makes mother-love the deepest (short of God's) we know? Discuss.

32. What does Roberta *really* mean by her statement (at the chapter's end) about colors that will wash and not fade?

Chapter 5. Richard Pricks His Fingers

33. Health. Without it, money is of little value; with it, virtually anything is possible. Given this great truth, how passing strange that millions today deliberately destroy that health through substance abuse, deviant or sedentary lifestyles, and other methods of smashing the body's defense system. Your thoughts on this?

34. Indian summer, the pause before winter, is a most special time of year. How effectively does Richmond capture it in this chapter?

35. What is there in us that loves a view? I was amused when first moving to Maryland to discover that, on the Chesapeake, one would pay dearly for a frontal water view, pay almost as much for a partial water view, and pay less yet for a "winter water view" (one could see the water only when the trees shed all their leaves!). The same principle is generally true in the mountains of Colorado: the more dramatic the view, the higher the asking price. What is the role of "view" in this chapter, this book?

36. One would grow weary of a Shangri-la. We complain about storms, yet there is something about their elemental fury that appeals to us, just as there is in all intense living. Be thinking, as the story progresses, about the role of a dream cabin built for storms.

37. Roberta represents the exception rather than the norm in turn-of-the-century literature for her self-reliance, strength of will, and no-nonsense attitude toward love—a feminine portrayal far ahead of her time. Does she seem contemporary to you? How so?

38. How true it is that while many people will share conversation with us, only a blessed few have the sensitivity to nuances that enable them to share silence with us. Discuss this aspect of our human relationships.

39. Richard discovers that there are two kinds of women, two kinds of allure: one that embodies every type of feminine wile and artifice known to the species; the other that is built on the rock of honesty, of the real. Discuss the two types of women as they exist today.

Chapter 6. Unsustained Application
40. Men were deferential to women then in ways not true today. In some ways women have gained by their new freedoms today, in some ways they have lost. Discuss.

41. How quickly technology changes our lives! The typewriter used by Roberta was an old-fashioned manual—slow and incapable of correcting errors. Today my students find it exceedingly difficult to create except on a computer screen. How will the youth of tomorrow communicate?

42. One of the key issues brought up in this book has to do with a great truth that Hollywood appears to have forgotten: Any romantic relationship not constructed on the bedrock of respect is foredoomed. Love as a feeling is ephemeral and quickly passes, whereas love as a principle endures for all time, reaching its greatest power and beauty when intertwined with feelings, emotions, and divine love. Compare all this and the respect element in the book with what Hollywood brings to us in its place. Which do you feel is likely to endure longer? Why?

43. Robert Browning used "Such a Starved Bank of Moss" as the prologue to *The Two Poets of Croisic*, first published in 1878. In your journal, discuss the reasons why you think Richmond interwove it into this chapter. What is the significance in terms of Richard's life, for instance? In Roberta's?

Note the powerful star metaphor in the second stanza. It might be apropos here to step backward in time to an earlier manifestation of that same metaphor in Browning's work. Browning had been captivated by the mind, heart, and soul of a young recluse poetess, Elizabeth Barrett, and wrote her for the first time on January 10, 1845; during the correspondence that followed, each fell in love with the other before they had even seen each other. Since Elizabeth's domineering father refused to let her marry, they eloped on September 12, 1846. They would experience 15 years of blissful marriage before her untimely death in Florence, Italy, June 29, 1861. In the annals of literary history, few more idyllic marriages have ever been known.

Nine years into that marriage of souls, minds, and bodies, Browning penned his counterpart to his wife's immortal tribute to him, *Sonnets from the Portuguese* (the most famous of which was her "How Do I Love Thee?") first published in 1850. Note the star motif:

MY STAR

All that I know
    Of a certain star
Is, it can throw
    (Like the angled spar)
Now a dart of red,
    Now a dart of blue;
Till my friends have said
    They would fain see, too,
My star that dartles the red and the blue!
Then it stops like a bird; like a flower, hangs furled:
They must solace themselves with the Saturn above it.
What matter to me if their star is a world?
Mine has opened its soul to me; therefore I love it.

When Elizabeth died, for her widowed husband, it was as if her passing "tore a great rent across" his life (*Victorian and Later English Poets*, ed. James Stephen, Edwin L. Beck, and Royall H. Snow [New York: American Book Company, 1934], p. 225). With that in mind, let us now turn to Browning's "Such a Starved Bank of Moss," penned 17 years after his wife's passing. Note the vivid metaphoric imagery: "Starved bank of moss," "blue flash" "violets," and "scowling shroud-like cloud" that is pierced by jagged rents, in the process revealing, high up in the heavens, his splendid star (her face: "God's own smile"). Clearly, this poem can be fully understood and appreciated only by first reading the older poem.

With this background, now layer in the additional dimensions: the unknown justice's writing out the poem in longhand years before, Judge Gray's keeping it all through the years, and Richard's seeing himself and Roberta in those same lines.

What is the impact of tying all of these dimensions into this one chapter? Discuss.

44. To Roberta, there is music everywhere: "Music in the hammer on the anvil, in the throb of the engine, in the hum of the dynamo." Discuss the significance of this statement within the framework of Richmond's/Roberta's philosophy of work.

45. Richard discovers a truth Roberta already knows: Idleness results in loss of concentration power. Indolence is deadly because *all* unused talents atrophy. My brother Romayne (pianist, composer, and poet) has practiced since childhood a minimum of eight hours a day. Skilled musicians know full well that failing to continually practice blunts their future performance edge. The same is true of every other talent God has entrusted to us—including reading, thinking, conceptualizing, and writing. One never arrives, one is never home free: Always it is a struggle to stay competitive. Discuss this reality in terms of your own allocation of time.

Chapter 7. A Traitorous Proceeding

46. Richard stumbles into a new world when he is permitted to join the Gray family Christmas celebration. It is a world built upon the multigenerational family: each person valued and respected, regardless of age or stature in the world outside the family. The family traditions provide continuity in a world where continual change shakes foundations everywhere. In this family, what matters is what you are inside, how well you have developed your God-entrusted talents, how genuine and caring you are. There could be worse schools! What is the role of family in *your* life?

47. Babies and children—without them, how much poorer we would all be! Study Richard's response to the holding of little Gordon Gray in terms of your perception of Richard's development and growth.

48. What does Roberta mean by her "Handsome is as handsome does" speech to her sister-in-law?

Chapter 8. Roses Red

49. There are moments that define our lives, moments that act like train track switches—one minute we are mindlessly barreling along a major travel route, our minds in overdrive; suddenly, we see a flashing light ahead: The train slows to a crawl, then veers onto a side track that takes us to places we have never been before. In the first paragraph of "Roses Red," Richard experiences such a life-changing epiphany. After that moment of revelation, his life cannot possibly ever be the same again. Have you experienced such a defining moment in your life? Discuss.

50. Each of us does indeed have within us ideals we yearn toward. And each man harbors an ideal image of his dream woman—for men pay more attention to externals than do women. That ideal usually changes as the boy matures into a man, but always it is there far off in the mists. It is just such an ideal that Richard conceptualizes. What is the role of such ideals in our lives?

51. What is it about eyes that captivate us so? Perhaps it is because all the rest of the body is but a wall, revealing almost nothing of what is behind that façade. But the eyes, while they can be and often are veiled, when the owner behind the wall opens up all the inner doors of those two deep wells, reveal the very soul in all its radiance. What is the role of eyes in this book?

52. "For a space measured by the strains of 'Roses Red,' Richard Kendrick knew no more of earth." Why do certain periods of time—defined by certain pieces of music—seem to cause normal time to cease? Music does have that time-stopping power. In fact, it's almost as if one were temporarily outside of time. What power does music have over you Discuss.

53. An old saying puts it this way: "Faint heart never won fair lady." At least it *used* to be generally true in generations past, for it wasn't considered ladylike for a woman to make the first move. Notice that Richard early on realizes he has the steepest of uphill struggles to ever break through Roberta's self-imposed walls. Had he given up, that would have been the end of it. But he persevered; he followed a certain course of action. Discuss.

54. Can there possibly be anything in life comparable to watching a sleeping child? What is the impact on Richard?

55. An example of personification (attributing human characteristics to inanimate objects) is the following line: "On his way up. . . , he encountered a rose brocade frock on its way down." How effective is it compared with merely describing her coming down the stairs?

56. Today, sadly, all too often the aged among us are virtually forgotten. Not so in the Gray family. What can we learn from them in this respect?

57. A provocative question is this: Had Roberta capitulated quickly to Richard's siege of her heart, would he have reformed? How much? Would he have appreciated her as much? Give reasons.

Chapter 9. Mr. Kendrick Entertains

58. Oftentimes we fail to act because we mistakenly assume we are powerless to accomplish much on our own. Certainly, Ruth's suggestion to Richard that he bridge to his lonely grandfather and invite him to attend Christmas services with him, we would consider to be a small thing, a casual thing. Who could have imagined the domino effect that would cascade on into infinity as a result!

In this respect, the most powerful poem I know was written well over a hundred years ago. In ancient times, only one person could, with impunity, tell the truth to a monarch: the court jester, or fool. He alone was considered to have no agenda, no ax to grind, no favors to urge. On this particular day, the bored king who reverences no one, not even God, commands his fool to kneel and pray, then he and the court can be counted on to make of it a travesty, a sacrilege. Instead, the fool preaches a sermon about life:

THE FOOL'S PRAYER

The royal feast was done; the King
Sought some new sport to banish care,
And to his jester cried: "Sir Fool,
Kneel now, and make for us a prayer!"

The jester doffed his cap and bells,
And stood the mocking court before;
They could not see the bitter smile
Behind the painted grin he wore.

He bowed his head, and bent his knee
Upon the monarch's silken stool;
His pleading voice arose: "O Lord,
Be merciful to me, a fool!

"No pity, Lord, could change the heart
From red with wrong to white as wool:
The rod must heal the sin; but, Lord,
Be merciful to me, a fool!

"'Tis not by guilt the onward sweep
Of truth and right, O Lord, we stay
'Tis by our follies that so long

We hold the earth from heaven away.
"These clumsy feet, still in the mire,
Go crushing blossoms without end;
These hard, well-meaning hands we thrust
Among the heart-strings of a friend.

"The ill-timed truth we might have kept—
Who knows how sharp it pierced and stung!
The word we had not sense to say—
Who knows how grandly it had rung!

"Earth bears no balsam for mistakes;
Men crown the knave, and scourge the tool
That did his will; but Thou, O Lord,
Be merciful to me, a fool!"

The room was hushed; in silence rose
The King, and sought his gardens cool,
And walked apart, and murmured low,
"Be merciful to me, a fool!"

Edward Rowland Sill (1841–1887)

I have always felt that the sixth and seventh stanzas are among the most sublime in all literature, especially apropos in terms of Ruth's daring to make such a suggestion to a man she barely knew. I italicize them for emphasis:

"*These clumsy feet, still in the mire,*
Go crushing blossoms without end;
These hard, well-meaning hands we thrust
Among the heart-strings of a friend.

"The ill-timed truth we might have kept—
Who knows how sharp it pierced and stung!
The word we had not sense to say—
Who knows how grandly it had rung!"

Ruth had the sense to say it, and how grandly it rang! How about us? Do our words wound our friends? Or do they ring grandly (blessing instead of blistering)?

59. Another thing that struck me about the book is the fact that houses then tended to be built to last. When a house was lived in by generations of a family, that continuity contributed to a sense of connectedness, of family pride, of responsibility. Today when one out of every two marriages ends in divorce, when one-third of all children are born out of wedlock, there is not likely to be a house that is *home* for life: rather, a succession of houses that seem more like motels than homes. What can we do to change this sad picture?

60. How times have changed! In the days of which Richmond wrote, gentlemen of the old school did not smoke in the presence of ladies. For a woman to smoke was to give a clear signal to all who knew her that she had lost her femininity and with it, community respect. Today, women not only smoke cigarettes, but they have also taken up cigars, and their death rate from tobacco-related diseases is rapidly catching up with that of men. It is indeed a different world than Richmond knew. Reactions?

61. Flowers have always been able to speak in every language. They speak when the sender's tongue is speechless. What is the impact in this chapter of Richard's flower gifts? What role do flowers have in *your* life?

Chapter 10. Opinions and Theories

62. Quite a statement by Aunt Ruth: The Kendricks lacked "nothing that money can buy . . . but about everything that it can't." On a recent TV talk show, the host interviewed a number of people who had won big lotteries or sweepstakes. Surprisingly, they were a remarkably unhappy group. Apparently, just deciding what to do with all that money and the rest of their lives proved to be a major problem. Divorce was often the result. The level of greed manifested among children, friends, relatives, and neighbors who didn't even

know them was almost unbelievable. Subsequently, as I was talking with an executive of one of Colorado's most posh resort hotels (where rooms started at $800 a night), I asked him about the super-rich who came there; what were they like to deal with? I shall never forget his response: "Sir, a more miserable bunch of people you will never see!" Apparently, they are grouchy, bored, unhappy, grasping, and suspicious. The only exceptions to this norm are wealthy people who don't act wealthy, who have busy careers, philanthropic involvements, causes they enthusiastically support. Only they appear to be happy.

So, given this state of affairs, why *do* we envy the rich? Why do we feel that if we'd only win Publishers Clearinghouse Sweepstakes, we'd be happy? Since this perception is obviously a fallacy, might it not then be wise for us to reorder our priorities where money is concerned? What lessons can we learn from all this?

63. In the discussion Judge Gray has with his brother about Matthew Kendrick, it is said that the millionaire appears to be a most lonely man. Could that be one reason why all those wealthy hotel guests are so miserable—because they are *lonely?* If most of your life's energy is used defensively, to keep others from getting their hands on your money, then wouldn't loneliness be a natural result? Discuss.

64. Note the serenity of the Gray home, how Mrs. Gray and her family often sit around the fire . . . just dreaming, reminiscing, discussing the day's events, and posing deep questions about life. Is such a thing possible when electronic noise is on?

Case in point is Roberta's question: "Mother, what are you to do when you find all your theories upset? . . . . just a sort of vague discomfort at feeling that certain ideals I thought were as fixed as the stars in the heavens seem to be wobbling as if they might shoot downward any minute and leave only a trail of light behind."

It isn't Mrs. Gray's specific response that is important; rather, it is the fact that she and her husband provide a climate and a quietness conducive to reflection and questions about life. Well we know, if such a climate is not provided at home, the child or youth will seek the answers elsewhere—and there, the answers will most likely be quite different! What are the implications?

65. Forbes Westcott is the other force Roberta must deal with. It is safe to say that no decision we ever make in life is more far-reaching in its results than is our choice of a life-partner (other than one's decision whether or not to serve God). From the moment such a decision has been made, nothing will ever be the same again.

In the time period Richmond wrote, marriage was not merely an option: It was for life. To live together outside the bonds of matrimony was to become, in most of America, pariahs, outcasts, outside the civilized pale. Interestingly enough, in that time period, Westcott would have been the norm rather than Kendrick, for he would have dominated their marriage rather than welcoming Roberta as an equal partner as did Kendrick.

Studies show that women tend to be three years more mature than men up until the late twenties, when men catch up. Men, up until their mid-twenties, tend to choose on the basis of externals rather than what is within; belatedly, they begin looking for more lasting qualities. This is a process that women share. Note that Roberta's choice at the end of the book is not the choice she would have made nine months before. For her, too, maturity comes with time. What are the factors that cause this change in her? Pay particular attention to what Richmond has to say, in the book, about love and lasting marriage.

66. Interesting, isn't it, that even though it's the same piece of music, the three different people listening to it experience it in three different ways. Each of us perceives life through different eyes, different ears. What kind of imagery comes to mind when *you* listen to classical music? When you listen to Bach's "Air for the G String"?

67. At the end of this chapter, Robert Gray, after observing Eleanor and Roberta perform Bach's "Air for the G String" expresses his conviction that in these two, plus Roberta's siblings, there is such vitality and individuality that they merit inclusion in Enobarbus's tribute to Cleopatra:

> Age cannot wither her, nor custom stale
> Her infinite variety. Other women cloy
> The appetites they feed, but she makes hungry
> Where most she satisfies.
>> William Shakespeare,
>> *Antony and Cleopatra*, Act 2, Scene 2 (1606)

How apt a description of Roberta is this? Substantiate.

Chapter 11. *The Taming of the Shrew*

68. Louis obviously has doubts that Roberta will ever hold down a job for long. In that society, when a woman married she was expected to make that relationship, and the children later on, the number one priority of her lifetime. Once she married, her husband was expected to "take care of her." On the plus side, this resulted in a strong family-oriented society; on the minus side, women were given little opportunity to grow or flower in careers of their own. Compare, in this respect, the two time periods: then and now.

69. Richard longs for a sister like Ruth, an embodiment of sweetness and purity, two attributes almost totally absent in movies produced today. If what is seen on the cinema today is perceived to be the norm, what do you think is likely to be the philosophy of life and marriage of the viewers?

70. What insights into drama training have you gained in the book so far? What methods would you like to try?

71. Note that in the first part of the book Richard determines that he will *conquer* Roberta (a typical male attitude of the time). Pay particular attention to Richard's attitude, in this respect, as the book draws to a close.

72. As we have noted before in this series, the opposite of love is not hate, it is indifference. One is far more likely to flip-flop from a strong antipathy to love than one is from indifference to love. In this respect, pay particular attention to Roberta as the book progresses.

73. I have already called attention to the formality of the period. As a case in point, note that Richard cannot even yet call Roberta by her first name. Reactions?

Chapter 12. Blankets

74. Thanks to his interaction with the Grays, Richard belatedly realizes that he has nothing but money: He has money, but he is nothing without it. He has no marketable skills. Does all this give you a new perspective on the role of work in our lives? Why?

75. What causes Richard to seek out a career? What are the developments that lead up to the choice he makes? If you are interested at all in marketing, you will find this book a treasure-house of information about turn-of-the-century marketing practices. What lessons does Richard learn? What about street-side windows? What does he learn about them?

    I find this aspect of the book intriguing: Where did Richmond gain her business expertise (considering the fact that business then was considered a male enclave)?

Chapter 13. Lavender Linen
76. What changes does Roberta notice in Richard's face? What has caused these changes?

77. What is your reaction to the men's taking off their hats in the presence of ladies? Compare then with now in this respect. Discuss.

Chapter 14. Rapid Fire
78. How does Richmond handle the first face-to-face meeting of the rivals Westcott and Kendrick? How does each respond to the other?

79. What are your reactions to Roberta's quenching Richard's professions of love? Her request that he not communicate with her in any way until June 24? The way he responds to the terms? Is she fair with him? Elaborate.

Chapter 15. Making Men
80. Compare Richard's attitude toward automobile speed with his grandfather's. Do such differences between the generations still exist today? Explain your position.

81. At Eastman, what does Matthew Kendrick learn about his grandson? What does Richard learn about his grandfather?

82. What does Mr. Kendrick mean by this statement: "But it sometimes takes a wise man to see that a swing from the center of things to the rim is the way to swing back to the center, finally"? Do you agree?

83. What does Mr. Kendrick mean by his question: "Does the appearance

tell the absolute truth about the integrity of the business?" What businesses are you familiar with, and how do you feel their CEOs would answer such a question?

And what about Mr. Kendrick's startling statement: "The most important thing a business can do is to make men of those who make the business." How do you think he would have gone about accomplishing such an ambitious goal? Do you think that is likely to be a key goal of most CEOs today? Should it be? Elaborate and arrive at conclusions.

84. What about Mr. Kendrick's response to Hugh Benson's statement: "My father . . . may have been a failure in business, but it was not for want of absolute integrity"? Do you feel that even today a father ought to leave such a legacy to his son or daughter? Is such absolute integrity common today? Why or why not? Is integrity a trait the media appears to value in TV and cinema portrayals? Discuss the implications.

85. What about the warm-hearted hospitality of Uncle Rufus and Aunt Ruth? What lessons can we learn from them in this respect? What does it mean to be a good host, a good hostess?

86. Old photograph albums: people frozen in time. When you think of such a book, what thoughts go through your mind? What kind of a record does your family make of your lives together in this respect?

87. In that old farmhouse, a new closeness comes to Richard and his grandfather. What is there about this place, these people, this day, that accomplishes what had not been in other places and days? What is the significance?

Chapter 16. Encounters
88. One of the cardinal rules of success in business is this: Never run down your competition. Yet this is what Westcott does during a visit to Roberta. What are the results?

89. What about the line "It goes without saying." Can it be dangerous to use? Discuss.

90. Richard had made much of what he might do on June 24. What

is the result of this (where Roberta was concerned)? Does it help Westcott's suit, or hinder it? Why?

Chapter 17. Intrigue

91. In this chapter, what is the significance of Richard's act of making sure Roberta receives both a mass of white trilliums and one red trillium? How does she respond to the white ones? The red one? But what is she *really* thinking about as she does so? What are the qualities she associates with each color?

Chapter 18. The Nailing of a Flag

92. Why is this chapter important? What does Lorimer find difficult to accept? What changes have taken place since Richard promised to accompany him on his cruise around the world? As a result of this chapter, construct a paragraph or two that portrays, in detail, the old Richard; then construct a second that does the same with the new Richard.

93. Had Richard gone, do you agree with his contention that even Lorimer would have thought less of him? Explain.

94. Today the extremely wealthy have found ways to make sure their wealth stays with the family after their deaths, rather than getting swallowed up by the IRS or given away to deserving causes. These legacies often skip generations that are already well taken care of financially. We call these recipients "trust kids" because these trusts keep them financially independent for life whether they work or not. Is it good not to have to work? What are the dangers? You might use Lorimer as a case in point, and Richard as another.

Supposedly, one contemporary billionaire has stated that he plans to give all his money away rather than have it destroy his children. Do you agree that unearned wealth tends to destroy? Explain.

95. What does it mean to nail one's flag to the mast? What does it mean to Richard?

Chapter 19. In the Morning

96. What is it about money that causes it to loom larger than the people who are dearest to us? The news headlines are full of stories about family warfare over money and assets. Carson had wondered

if this human frailty was present in his friend Richard; what does he now discover? What about us? What amount of money would it take to cause us to turn on a member of our family who stands in the way of our getting it? Since so many families are destroyed over this issue, it is well worth our time to think seriously about it in advance.

97. What is the greatest fear Richard's grandfather has as he returns to awareness?

Chapter 20. Sidelights

98. This chapter is significant because Richmond introduces into the narrative acts from Richard's past that muddy the waters considerably. Clearly, he has not experienced a behavior transplant just because he fell in love with Roberta. Rather, these acts go quite a ways back. Had Richard told Roberta about them they would most likely have been viewed as self-serving—but he did not. She hears of them second-, third-, or fourth-hand. Is the discovery of such acts enhanced when they are received in this way? What is the impact of these discoveries on the family? On Roberta? What aspects impress or move her most?

99. How easy it is to misjudge people! Discuss this truism within the framework of this revelatory chapter.

100. Why is it, do you think, that such acts as those done by Richard are done so rarely by the wealthy young, as opposed to the wealthy old?

101. Do acts of charity count as much at Christmas? Explain.

102. What is meant by this line: "Imaginary circles are sometimes bigger barriers than stone walls"?

103. What does Louis mean by his use of the metaphor "thin blood"?

104. After all these reported stories, what is the impact on Roberta of experiencing one *firsthand*? What impresses her most? Elaborate on the following line within the context of the story: "Forgetfulness of self, devotion to the need of others . . ."

105. Why is this an inauspicious evening for Westcott to press his suit?

106. What does Richmond mean by, "He would live strictly by the letter of the law, but the spirit . . . "?

Chapter 21. Portraits
107. Contrast the Kendrick home with the Gray home.

108. What are the most significant things to look for when studying someone's living quarters? What impresses Roberta most?

109. What is the significance of the painting of Richard's mother in the story? In his life? What about Roberta's line: "You don't want to disappoint her"? How powerful a factor is this, in terms of our behavior in life?

110. There is an old saying that is apropos here: "What you *are* roars so loudly in my ears that I can't hear what you *say.*" In light of this chapter especially, discuss this aspect of life. Does our rhetoric mean nothing if our day-to-day behavior and life fail to mesh? What about parenting: Is that true, too, when a father or mother tells a child to behave in a certain way, but the parent does not behave in the way advised? Might not this be another scary truth? How should we deal with it?

Chapter 22. Roberta Wakes Early
111. How effective is it to tie the denouement to the summer solstice (longest day of the year)? What is its significance? How would Midsummer's Day compare with August 13 or September 27? Give reasons. How does Richmond use it to heighten the suspense?

112. Compare the impact of a letter versus a telephone call or direct conversation. Which approach would *you* have used if you were in Richard's place? Explain why.

113. What do you think one's handwriting reveals about that person? Be specific.

114. Beauty, charm, character, and fascination—why is it so difficult to find all four in the same person?

115. Analyze Richard's letter (as a persuasive piece of rhetoric). How effective is it? In a paragraph or two, sketch out just what he accomplishes by it. What is the *tone* of the letter? How is the letter

different from what he might have written her the day after his promise to accept her ban?

116. Meanwhile, how has Roberta changed from what she had been, her attitudes toward life, love, and marriage, the previous October? Be specific.

117. In those days, chaperons always accompanied couples on dates. And chaperons were a fact of life clear through the 1950s for many Americans. What do you think of the institution of chaperonage? A good thing? A bad thing? Explain why. Do you think chaperonage would work today? Why or why not?

Chapter 23. Richard Has Waked Earlier

118. Do you think horseback riding represents the perfect option for the evening—or ought the journey to have been in an automobile? Give reasons.

119. Roberta notes that Richard clearly has "the artistic eye for finishing touches." In a paragraph or two, sketch out in detail specifics that either substantiate this assumption or disprove it.

120. I find Richmond's choice of words intriguing. For instance: "if he were now exulting in the sure hope of possessing her. . . ." If the same scene were conceptualized today I would think that "dream of possession" would not be as likely as "dreams of mutual love and belonging." The modern woman, after all, much prefers "mutual belonging" to "being possessed by." Having said that, perhaps I am making too much out of the word, for Richard certainly doesn't project possessiveness—not in the negative sense of the word. But reinforcing this perception is another line: "while he knew the treasure to be within his grasp . . . " Perhaps I view these lines in a different way because I believe strongly that no human being should ever possess another because that is a violation of the *will*—and even God refuses to do that! The battered spouse syndrome we hear so much about is graphic proof that possessiveness (in the negative sense of the word) is very much with us: one partner continually violating the will and inner space of the other. What are your thoughts on this issue?

121. Certainly, Richard's buying the property and building the "stout

little cabin on the hilltop" was an act of audacity. Or was it only an act of romance? Or was it something more than either? Put yourself in Roberta's place. How would you have felt if you had been she? How, if you had been *you?* Elaborate.

122. It is only now that Richmond adds another dimension to the story: "It will be a 'Midsummer Night's Dream' on this hill tonight." Roberta, a connoisseur of Shakespeare, must have really wondered, because that play *(A Midsummer Night's Dream),* from start to finish, is one incredible farce. But, taken another way, during medieval times, Midsummer's Day and Night were given an emphasis unknown today. That eve, a master of revels might choreograph entertainment not soon forgotten. Richard here assumes that time-honored role of master of revels—only his tone is 180 degrees away from Shakespeare's. But, in the sense of its being a magical evening, there could hardly be one more so.

Discuss the Shakespeare tie-in and the magical aspect of Midsummer Night. Note that, to Roberta, the evening appears to be so magical that she feels herself to be nonmortal.

123. At the end, what finally decides Roberta? After all, she *had* been afraid of love, of being possessed. Reactions?

Note that a kiss was taken far more seriously then than is true today; it was considered a symbol of commitment—a stepping stone to marriage. Compare that attitude with today's . Which do you like best? Why?

Chapter 24. The Pillars of Home

124. It is difficult for us to transport ourselves to a time when there were no air-conditioned offices, stores, schools, or churches; no air-conditioned automobiles, streetcars, buses, or trains; and no air-conditioned houses. To make life survivable, ceilings were higher than they are in contemporary houses; windows were either shaded with curtains or draperies or left open for cross-drafts (when possible; often *not* possible in urban areas); and shade from nearby trees was coveted. But, especially in more urban areas, the rich, near-rich, and upper middle class all fled to the mountains or to the sea during the hottest summer months, for only there could they find respite from the blasting heat. The rest of society stayed home and

endured as best they could. Would you have liked to live back then? Why or why not?

125. What is it Roberta and Richard desire in a house and grounds? Be specific. How does that compare with *your* dream home?

126. A place for Grandfather, too. And note which rooms are given to him. As one grows older, loneliness is what is dreaded most. How do Richard and Roberta address this?

127. Children—what would life be like without them? What kind of parents do you imagine Richard and Roberta will make? Give reasons.

Chapter 25. A Stout Little Cabin

128. Compare this Christmas wedding with other Christmas weddings you have known. Which do you prefer, and why? If you have never attended a Christmas wedding, compare the Kendricks' wedding with ones you have attended at other times of the year.

129. What do you think about Roberta's invitation criterion (wanting "only those who truly care for us")?

130. The honeymoon—what power it has to make or break a marriage! And there are so many ingredients, so many things to go right or wrong. Clearly, to Richard, marrying Roberta is a sacred trust, as is the honeymoon. What do you think of the honeymoon Richard prepares for Roberta?

131. Compare home weddings with church weddings. Which do you prefer? Why? What do you think of *this* one?

132. The entire book could be summed up in one word: *family*. What are the most significant insights, in that respect, that you have gained from reading this book?

133. What a powerful analysis is Grandfather Kendrick's:

> "The man who could stand beside that young woman
> and look craven would deserve to be hamstrung. . . .
> Cal, she's enough to turn an old man's head; we can't
> wonder that a young one's swimming. And the best of

it is that it isn't all looks, it's real beauty to the core. She's rich in the qualities that stand wearing in a wearing world—and her goodness isn't the sort that will ever pall on her husband. She'll keep him guessing to the end of time, but the answer will always give him fresh delight in her."

What are your responses?

134. Can you even imagine a greater bridal gift than the one Hugh gives Roberta? What impact do you feel it has on her? What impact would such a gift have on *you?*

135. Beginnings and endings are absolutely essential if one would write books worth remembering. What about this ending? How does it compare with other favorite endings of yours? Would you have wanted it to end any other way? If so, how?

Now go back to the beginning of the story. How effective was it in pulling you in? What was there about the beginning that hooked you? Or did it? What was your overall response to the story?

CODA

Reactions, responses, and suggestions are very important to us. Also, if a particular book—especially an older one—has been loved by you or your family, and you would like to see us incorporate it into this series, drop us a line, with details you know about its earliest publisher, printing date, and so on, and send it to

Joe Wheeler, Ph.D.
c/o Focus on the Family
Colorado Springs, CO 80920

ABOUT THE EDITOR

Joseph Leininger Wheeler's earliest memories have to do with books and stories—more specifically, of listening to his mother read aloud both in public and to him at home. Wheeler recalls that, as soon as he was able to read, he followed his mother around the house, relentlessly reading his storybooks to her.

Shortly after Wheeler turned eight, his parents moved from California to Latin America as missionaries. From the third through the tenth grade, he was home-schooled by his mother. Of those years, he says today, "I was incredibly lucky and blessed. My mother, a trained teacher and elocutionist, was a voracious reader of books worth reading and had memorized thousands of pages of readings, poetry, and stories. All of that she poured into me. Wherever we went, she encouraged me to devour entire libraries."

At 16, Wheeler returned to California to complete his high school years at Monterey Bay Academy near Santa Cruz. Because of his inherited love of the printed word, Wheeler majored in history at Pacific Union College in the Napa Valley, completing both bachelor's and master's degrees there. After completing a master's in English at California State University in Sacramento, Wheeler attended Vanderbilt University, where he obtained a Ph.D. in English.

Today, after 34 years of teaching at the adult education, college, high school, and junior high levels, Wheeler is Professor Emeritus at Columbia Union College in Takoma Park, Maryland. The world's foremost authority on frontier writer Zane Grey, Wheeler is also the founder and executive director of Zane Grey's West Society and Senior Fellow for Cultural Studies at the Center for the New West in Denver, Colorado. He is editor/compiler of the popular *Christmas in My Heart* series (Review & Herald; Doubleday, Dell, Bantam); editor/compiler of the story anthologies *Dad in My Heart* and *Mom in My Heart* (Tyndale House); and editor/compiler of Focus on the Family's *Great Stories Remembered* and *Great Stories* Collection series (Tyndale House). Along the way, Wheeler has established nine libraries in schools and colleges, as well as building up his own collection (as large as some college libraries).

Joe Wheeler and his wife, Connie, are the parents of two grown children, Greg and Michelle, and now make their home in Conifer, Colorado.

IF YOU LIKED *THE TWENTY-FOURTH OF JUNE*, YOU'LL LOVE THE OTHER BOOKS FROM FOCUS ON THE FAMILY'S® "GREAT STORIES" COLLECTION!

Ben-Hur
In an unforgettable account of betrayal, revenge, and rebellion,
a nobleman learns the grace of God when he falls from
Roman favor and is sentenced to life as a slave.

Anne of Green Gables
When Matthew goes to the train station to pick up a boy sent from an orphanage, he discovers a *girl* has been sent instead! Not having the heart to disappoint her, he agrees to take her home and their lives are changed forever.

Little Women
Despite the Civil War, four sisters discover the importance of family
and manage to keep laughter and love in their hearts—even through
illness and poverty, disappointment, and sacrifice.

Little Men
In this exciting sequel to *Little Women,* Jo and her husband open
their hearts and home to school a handful of rowdy boys—
then the fun, adventures, and lessons begin!

A Christmas Carol
When the miserly Scrooge retires for the day on Christmas Eve, he is
visited by the ghost of his long-dead partner who warns him
of what surely will be if he doesn't change his stingy ways.

Robinson Crusoe
A shipwreck's sole survivor struggles to triumph over crippling fear,
doubt, and isolation as a castaway on a lonely island—and learns
the amazing revelation that God is always with us.

The Farther Adventures of Robinson Crusoe
Daniel Defoe's faith-filled *The Farther Adventures of Robinson Crusoe* finds Crusoe
back on the high seas, returning to the island he left years before. Readers will be
captivated by this sequel which is every bit as engaging as the original.

• • •

Call 1-800-A-FAMILY or write to us at Focus on the Family, Colorado Springs,
CO 80995. In Canada, call 1-800-661-9800 or write to Focus on the Family,
P.O. Box 9800, Stn. Terminal, Vancouver, B.C. V6B 4G3.
Or, visit your local Christian bookstore!

Focus on the Family®

Welcome to the Family!

Whether you received this book as a gift, borrowed it from
a friend, or purchased it yourself, we're glad you read it! It's just
one of the many helpful, insightful, and encouraging
resources produced by Focus on the Family.

In fact, that's what Focus on the Family is all about—providing inspiration, information, and biblically based advice to people in all stages of life.

It began in 1977 with the vision of one man, Dr. James Dobson, a licensed
psychologist and author of 16 best-selling books on marriage, parenting,
and family. Alarmed by the societal, political, and economic pressures
that were threatening the existence of the American family, Dr. Dobson
founded Focus on the Family with one employee—an assistant—
and a once-a-week radio broadcast aired on only 36 stations.

Now an international organization, Focus on the Family is dedicated
to preserving Judeo-Christian values and strengthening the family
through more than 70 different ministries, including eight separate
daily radio broadcasts; television public service announcements;
11 publications; and a steady series of award-winning books,
films, and videos for people of all ages and interests.

Recognizing the needs of, as well as the sacrifices and important
contributions made by, such diverse groups as educators, physicians,
attorneys, crisis pregnancy center staff, and single parents,
Focus on the Family offers specific outreaches to uphold and
minister to these individuals, too. And it's all done for one purpose,
and one purpose only: to encourage and strengthen individuals
and families through the life-changing message of Jesus Christ.

• • •

For more information about the ministry, or if we can be of help to your
family, simply write to Focus on the Family, Colorado Springs, CO 80995
or call 1-800-A-FAMILY (1-800-232-6459). Friends in Canada may write to
Focus on the Family, P.O. Box 9800, Stn. Terminal, Vancouver, B.C. V6B 4G3
or call 1-800-661-9800. Visit our Web site—www.family.org—
to learn more about the ministry or to find out if there is a
Focus on the Family office in your country.

We'd love to hear from you!